The Timberton Trail

Book # 3 of the series: Trails

Sally Demaray Hull

The Timberton Trail
Book #3 of the Series: Trails
By Sally Demaray Hull
ISBN-13: 978-1514780985 for CreateSpace Published print book
ISBN-10: 1514780984
Copyright 2010, 2015 by Sally Hull All Rights Reserved
Seventh Edition
Originally published by Lulu Press Inc. 2010

All Scripture is quoted from the King James Version of the Bible

Website: sallydemarayhullbooks.vpweb.com

The Trails Series:
1. The Trail Beyond-Book #1
2. Beyond the Trail-Book #2
3. The Timberton Trail-Book #3
4. War Trails-Book #4

Companion Books of the Series: Trails
The Shepherd's Trail
Carolyn's Story-companion book of the series: Trails

Dedicated to my nephew Shannon

How the years have slipped by!
It doesn't seem so very long ago that you were just a boy—
And here you are a man.
You've done well!
God bless you.
With love from the author,
Aunt Sally

Prologue

Rachel smiled at the young man who sat in her living room with her, quietly reading her diary aloud to her, clearly caught up in the story that she had penned over the years of her life's trails. He seemed oblivious of her as he read, so absorbed in the words. As he read, her mind shifted from him to the words he was reading to her, swept up in a barrage of memories.

"'I had not been certain,'" he read aloud, just as if he had not taken a break, "'if Mitch and the children celebrated Christmas, still not really understanding what they believed. But I had invited them for Christmas dinner anyway. And I could tell by the sparkle in their eyes that they were going to accept even before they said the words. Young Jen and Arthur Corin matched their older brother Mitch in being excited over the invitation.

"'Patrick had also carried invitations to Sam Jarnick and Matthew Bon-Hemmer. I had not wanted them to be spending Christmas alone. And, as it appeared, they had felt the same way. Before I knew it, I had also invited Sarah and Phil Morrison as well. Patrick had laughed at the time, asking me how I was planning on fitting everyone around the table. But I had only shrugged and said that I would think of something. But even as my guests arrived on our first Christmas Day in Timberton, I still had not decided where everyone would sit. And Patrick somehow guessed it. Although he carefully avoided smiling whenever he looked at the table, he could not keep the laughter out of his eyes.

"'Watching him, I had to admit that there was a funny side to the problem, and I started laughing. He turned and stared at me and he could not refrain from joining me in my laughter. After all, what was one crowded meal in comparison to the joy that friends and family brought? Why not laugh? My own family grew often since we regularly adopted a new member, the young woman Angela Stone being our newest member. Our children, ranging from three to fourteen, were all adopted into the family as well. Jed was everyone's grandfather, though technically only Georgy's and Elizabeth's by birth. And then there was Patrick and me, bringing a total of nine to our family alone to crowd around our table.

"'And then Georgy and Ion entered the cabin, coming in backwards, carrying what looked remarkably like one end of our old table. And then, one by one Mitch, Johnny, and Jed entered, likewise holding onto the table. I had thought that it had been chopped and burned up after Patrick had made the new one...'"

Patrick and Rachel O'Riley

Chapter 1

After the men and boys eased the heavy old table down onto the floor near the new one, Georgy looked up and grinned at Rachel. Shrugging, he explained, "Well, I just couldn't make myself chop it up."

Johnny cut in, adding, "We hid it in the woods. We've been using it—sort of."

Rachel turned to Ion and waited. He locked into her gaze steadily, taking his time to reply to her silent question, in quite the same way as Patrick was accustomed to doing, taking his time to decide on exactly what he wanted to say. Finally he simply said, "Some of us boys meet together after school. We use the table for our meetings. Things like that."

Rachel smiled, deciding to refrain from pressing the issue any further, choosing to allow the boys to have their secrets. After they made a quick exit from the cabin, she thought about the sacrifice they had made in admitting to the existence of their secret boys' club, as well as letting Mitch and Jed in on the location of their hideout. Without the other members of their club to help them carry the heavy table, they had been left with no choice but to reveal the place that had likely been guarded with great care until then.

"But it doesn't help all that much," Elizabeth sighed, shaking her head as she stared at the old table that was jammed in the remaining space in the kitchen. "Where will the folks sit?"

Rachel smiled at her deaf daughter, replying slowly enough for her to read her lips, "If the boys saved the table from the chopping block, I'm certain that they also saved the benches."

Elizabeth chewed on the corner of her mouth in thought, clearly not as convinced as Rachel was as to the presence of such practical wisdom residing in her brothers. She rolled her eyes at Rachel when the boys returned, carrying the benches between them. "Thank you, boys," Rachel called out as they set them around the table. "Johnny take Charles outside."

"But Rachel," Johnny began in shock.

"Dogs don't belong in the house."

"He's not a dog. He's a puppy. Besides, lots of families have dogs in their houses."

"We aren't one of them," Rachel insisted.

"Come on, John," Georgy called out heartily, "we'll find a cozy little spot in the barn for ol' Chucky-boy."

"That's Charles!" Johnny cried out. "He's named after my papa!"

Georgy grinned good-naturedly, insisting, "I know that. Don't you like nicknames?"

"His name's not Chucky-boy," Johnny insisted darkly.

"Boys," Rachel sighed, before the argument could become unfriendly. "Georgy's right—about the barn," she added quickly, seeing a look of shock dash into Johnny's eyes. "Puppies belong in a barn."

"Cats belong in a barn," Georgy corrected in a long drawn out manner of speech.

Rachel rolled her eyes at the boy. "Out—now!" she called out.

Georgy grinned and nudged Johnny's shoulder. "Get your ol' Chucky-boy and we'll go out and build him a doghouse."

Ion snorted at that but made no other comment and simply followed Georgy and Johnny outside, while the younger boy carried his squirming puppy. Arthur trailed along behind them. As the door shut, Rachel sighed out over the sudden quiet. Jennifer began giggling then. As Rachel turned to eye the two girls who were watching her in clear amusement, she shook her head and smiled. "Those boys," she murmured. "Well, let's finish getting everything ready. The Morrisons, Sam, and Matthew should be here any minute.

Georgy allowed his eyes to roam around the crowded table. His stomach felt uncomfortably full. All he really wanted to do was to get up and run around the cabin until he was hungry again and then return to Rachel's table and gorge himself some more. He chewed on the corner of his mouth, wondering if she would allow him to return once he left. He found himself suddenly locked into Ion's gaze. A perturbed expression rested there. Clearly he too had grown weary of the adult conversation which continued on and on even after everyone had finished eating. Georgy began wondering if having company was worth it after all. Without company, they were all allowed to chat freely while eating, as long as they had already swallowed their food. But once company came to the table, Rachel expected them to mind their Ps. and Qs. and be silent while the adults talked about boring things.

"All right, children," Rachel called out quietly. "You're excused."

Georgy grinned and lunged to his feet, not waiting for a second invitation to be set free. It took all of his restraint to hold back the whoop that screamed to be let out. He made no attempt to remain in the cabin a moment longer, but burst outside ahead of all the rest. They quickly followed him, kicking at the newly fallen snow. "Let's play dead chicken!" Georgy called out.

"No," Johnny replied, "not in the snow."

"But that's when it's the most fun, flopping around in the snow like a chicken with its head cut off."

"What are you saying?" Elizabeth cut in.

Johnny turned to her, replying slowly, "Dead chicken."

"No," Elizabeth replied scornfully, "not on Christmas!"

"Never bothered you before," Georgy snorted. "You're just getting finicky like a old woman—"

"You take that back Georgy Northwood!"

Georgy laughed and slowly began circling his sister, calling out, "Old woman! Old woman!"

Johnny began laughing and joined Georgy in his teasing, circling Elizabeth. "It's that brush and comb set she got today that's making her all fussy."

Georgy turned surprised eyes on the boy, chuckling out, "You didn't want to play dead chicken neither! You're just as fussy as an old woman too—"

"Am not!" Johnny cried out.

It was then that Ion stepped up between the two boys. "They'll take your presents back if you start fighting today!"

Georgy and Johnny both turned and stared at Ion in surprise. "No they won't," Georgy replied, unable to hold the shock from his voice. He wondered over the odd ideas Ion had from time to time.

"Yes they will!" Ion insisted, his eyes narrowing as he glared at Georgy for daring to disagree with him.

"Uh-uh," Georgy replied firmly. "They love us."

"That's not what you said yesterday. You said that if Pat really loved us, he'd let us start running our own trap lines."

"I didn't say that."

"Yes you did, Georgy Northwood!"

Georgy frowned slightly, vaguely recalling the words he had spoken in the heat of the moment. "Yeah, well," he muttered, "maybe I did. And maybe it's true!" he added more firmly, beginning to warm up to the conversation. "Maybe he doesn't really love us as much as he says!" The words sounded wrong even to his own ears, but the shame of taking them back was too much to contemplate.

Suddenly Elizabeth nudged Georgy's shoulder uncomfortably hard. Apparently she had been able to follow enough of the conversation to get its basic gist. "That's not true and you know it! Now take it back!"

Georgy sighed, wondering how he could get out of this one. His tongue had rattled on ahead of his brain and now he was in a fix. Suddenly he grinned. "We'll put it to a test. I'll go and ask Pat if I can borrow his guitar so we can have us a singing time in the barn. However he answers, we'll know if he really loves us or not. If he says yes, we'll know for all time certain that he loves us. And if he says no—well, we'll know what that means too." He could not hold back his grin, knowing full well that Patrick would lend him the guitar. He never withheld the instrument from him since he had taught Georgy how to play it. Georgy could keep his pride and the others could be reassured of Patrick's love. No one would lose.

Ion stared hard at Georgy, clearly displeased with the whole thing. Nodding sidewise toward the barn, he murmured, "Everyone go to the barn while Georgy and I get the guitar."

Without another word Johnny and Art hurried ahead of Elizabeth and Jennifer toward the barn. Once they were out of earshot, Ion glared at Georgy. Georgy lifted his shoulders innocently, but the boy was not buying it. "You're wrong," he murmured to Georgy. Georgy swallowed over the quiet tone, guilt sweeping over him. "It ain't fair to Pat. And you know it!"

"I don't know anything of the sort," Georgy replied lightly, though his heart told him that Ion was right and he was wrong.

"Just tell them you was wrong and you won't have to do this."

"I'm not wrong!" Georgy shot back, suddenly not quite so pleased with himself.

"This ain't no kind of test of love, and you know it! Now just admit that you was wrong, Georgy!"

Georgy set his jaw and shook his head. "I'm not wrong!" he insisted stubbornly. "Love means giving, doesn't it?"

Ion continued glaring at Georgy. "Sometimes it means saying no. And you know it! Why won't you admit it?"

"Just go to the barn and keep everybody happy 'til I get back—with the guitar!"

Ion eyed him for another moment before finally turning and heading toward the barn without another word. His silence was worse than his words. Georgy found himself wishing that Ion had voiced his last argument in order that Georgy could have defended himself. "How did I get into this?" he murmured to himself.

Shrugging, he stepped back into the house. No one noticed. They were all still sitting at the table, enjoying their coffee and boring conversation. Quietly stepping up to the table, just behind where Patrick and Rachel were sitting, he waited for the conversation to come to a momentary lull. Finally he got his chance and asked, "Pat? Can I borrow your guitar? Everybody's in the barn waiting for me. We're going to sing us some Christmas carols."

Patrick turned and eyed him, smiling and shaking his head. "No, lad, not this time." Georgy blinked in shock. "One o'the strings is viry thin, almost ready to break. And Matthew 'as none left at the store." When Georgy made no reply but simply stared in mounting horror at him, Patrick added quietly, "It'll last me until I can buy another. Bit ye are a little more rambunctious and pluck the strings a little 'arder than I do. It'd break on ye," he added quietly enough that the others around the table, except for Rachel, who had continued with their conversation likely did not even hear.

Across Georgy's mind swept the image of the reception he would receive if he went to the barn without the guitar. He would either have to make good on his words and convince everyone that Patrick did not really love them, or he would have to admit that he had been wrong about making such an assumption in the first place. Ion would not help matters. He would hold Georgy accountable for his words. "If you really loved me," Georgy muttered, "you wouldn't say no. You'd trust me not to break your ol' string if you really loved me."

Patrick flinched back at the unexpected words. Georgy frowned and lowered his eyes to the floor. He was uncertain if anyone else had heard his words, but Patrick and Rachel both had. And he had. He sighed out deeply. Things were simply getting worse and worse. Turning, he stepped over to the door and reached for the knob. But the thought of the reception he would receive in the barn made him pause and stand there for a few moments. Finally he turned toward Rachel's rocking chair and stepped over to it and sat down in it, trying to decide on the best course of action now.

As he slowly rocked, he overheard Rachel saying quietly, "He didn't mean it."

"I think 'e did," Patrick replied just as quietly. "'E 'as bin dropping hints about thit viry thing lately, trying to convince me to let 'im and Ion run a trap line. Bit," he added, a smile returning to his lips, "I'll hiv a talk with 'im."

Georgy wondered over the fact that they had spoken in front of him that way. Clearly they did not realize that he had remained inside. They must have turned back around when he had stepped away, thinking that he had returned outside. Quietly he eased up from the chair and silently moved across the floor, slipping into Patrick and Rachel's bedroom, where Patrick kept his guitar. As he eyed the guitar that was carefully leaning against the wall, he hesitated, knowing that he was crossing a line. But the thought of everyone's expectant faces as they waited for him in the barn crashed into his mind. Squaring his shoulders in resolve, he stepped across the room and picked up the guitar. Once it was in his hand he turned and eyed the bedroom doorway, inching back over to it. Peering out, he stared at the backs of Patrick and Rachel, who had resumed their conversation with their guests. Suddenly Jed began speaking and everyone's eyes were drawn to him. Georgy took his chance then and casually strolled out of the bedroom, guitar in hand and stepped over to the door, quietly opening it. He knew his gramps well enough to know that when he was in the middle of telling one of his stories, he paid no attention to the world around him. And no one else was looking in Georgy's direction.

The next moment Georgy was outside and scurrying over the snow to the barn. An unexpected wild feeling of adventure coursed through him then, making him feel free from the constraints of rules. He chuckled over his daring action of actually taking the guitar. He would sneak it back in the cabin after he was finished using it and no one would be the wiser to it.

Bursting into the barn, he laughed as every set of eyes fastened themselves upon him. "He loves us," he insisted merrily. "Here's proof!" he added, holding up the guitar as a trophy. He wondered at the sudden hollow feeling that came to him. The feeling of adventure was not as strong now. Across his mind crept a picture of Patrick's face, a look of disappointment in his eyes. He blinked and shook his head. "Let's get to singing!" he called out louder than was absolutely necessary.

Everyone, except for Ion, laughed merrily and called out names of songs to sing. As Georgy crossed the barn and eased down onto the floor, he felt Ion's eyes upon him. Finally, positioning the guitar on his lap he met the boy's eyes that seemed to bore into him. "You got a problem?" he asked, wondering over the harshness in his own voice.

Ion slowly shook his head. "Not me," he murmured. But his eyes warned Georgy that he had guessed that something was not quite right. "You?"

"Not me," Georgy chuckled back, but there was only a hollow ring in his voice. No one but Ion seemed to notice and continued calling out the songs they wanted to sing. Georgy began strumming the guitar and fell into song.

The children's voices rang out in the age-old Christmas carols. Even Ion relaxed after a time and joined in on the singing. Georgy soon put the matter of disobeying Patrick behind him and sang heartier than anyone.

Twang! Georgy's hands immediately stilled themselves at the sound of the breaking string. At first he was the only one to stop singing. It was not the first string he had broken, after all. It never stopped them from singing in times past. As the others continued singing, Georgy's gaze shot over to Ion, who was eying him carefully. Georgy swallowed. Even in the coldness of the barn he began feeling beads of sweat forming on his forehead and upper lip. Ion simply stared at him for several moments and then asked, "What did you do?"

Georgy eased out his breath and shook his head. By now the others had stopped singing and were eying him with questions in their eyes. "Pat told me the string was getting ready to break," he admitted.

Ion frowned, his eyes narrowing accusingly. "He told you you couldn't borrow it, didn't he?" When Georgy nodded miserably, Ion added, "You better go tell him now, or it'll only be worse if you wait."

"But," Johnny cut in quietly, "does that mean he doesn't really love us? He said no."

Georgy continued meeting Ion's accusing eyes. Now he would have to admit to all of it. "No," he sighed out, "it doesn't mean that at all." He shifted his gaze from one face to another as he continued speaking. "I made that up. Pat loves us. I just—I was just—"

"Telling a fib," Ion muttered darkly. "Some Christmas you made this turn out to be!"

"It's not my fault!" Georgy grumbled. "You're the one who made me say all that stuff!" Suddenly Ion began laughing, causing Georgy to squirm uncomfortably. "Well you did!" But when Ion continued to refuse to grace his accusation with a reply, Georgy frowned and muttered, "Well you did."

Johnny was quietly repeating all the words to Elizabeth. It was suddenly too quiet in the barn. Finally Elizabeth turned to face Georgy and shook her head. "You're in trouble now, Georgy," she sighed.

"Maybe not," he murmured. Shifting his gaze back to Ion, he simply eyed him, feeling miserable.

Ion suddenly managed a small smile that held a look of compassion in it. "Maybe not," he agreed. "I mean, you didn't hurt anybody. You just gave us a fun time. And it's Christmas. Maybe he'll overlook it this once."

Georgy knew that Ion was actually trying to encourage him. But his words had the opposite effect. Even his best arguments for Georgy not being punished had holes in them. Georgy sighed long and loud and finally admitted, "I'm in a peck of trouble."

"Well," Ion murmured, "you'll be in less trouble if you go now and tell him what you did. If he finds out on his own, it'll be all the worse for you."

"I expects so."

"You want me to come with you?" Ion asked.

Georgy stared in surprise. Easing one side of his mouth up, he finally shook his head. "Naw, I'm man enough to go alone." But in spite of his words, his heart felt strangely warmed by Ion's offer. He struggled up to his feet, still grasping the guitar. "I best get it over with." Ion nodded in agreement and Georgy turned and quietly stepped out of the barn.

After finishing their coffee, the men seemed to grow a little restless and soon left to check on Patrick's trap lines. Rachel suspected that they were not as interested in checking the traps as much as in simply walking off their healthy lunch they had indulged in. Rachel chatted with Sarah and Angela after the men had left, finding the female conversation more satisfying than that of the mixed group had been. Angela's tongue was noticeably less barbed and had been since opening up her Christmas present that morning. In addition to this fact and that Sarah was always pleasant to talk with, the time slipped away enjoyably.

The door opened and in stepped a somber looking Georgy, guitar in hand. Rachel's mouth fell open in surprise. "Georgy?" she murmured, too stunned to say more at the moment. Across her mind swept the countless times that Georgy had broken rules, but never had he seemed to do so this blatantly. She met his remorseful eyes and simply said, "You know that you'll be punished."

He nodded and sighed. "It's worse than you think."

Staring hard at him, she demanded, "Worse than disobedience?"

"I busted a string," he admitted in a low voice.

Rachel eased her eyes shut for one awful moment as she thought about Patrick's guitar being the only one in the settlement. It was the sole musical accompaniment for church services. Opening her eyes again, she replied crisply, "We'll talk about it later, after Patrick returns. Go and take care of it."

"I'm sorry," he said in a voice that began trembling.

Rachel was torn between the forlorn figure he made at the moment and the knowledge that he had defied Patrick on purpose and had also robbed the entire community of its sole musical instrument. "I'm not the one you ought to be telling it to. It's Patrick's guitar. And it was Patrick you disobeyed. You need to tell him you're sorry. Now go and put it back in our room."

"Georgy get 'panked?" Anna Marie asked from her perch on Rachel's rocking chair, where she sat rocking her Christmas doll. She had just awakened from her nap and was getting ready to release her energy for the afternoon.

"Maybe," Rachel replied, nodding. The little girl seemed satisfied with the answer and promptly returned her attention to the doll in her arms. Georgy looked even more miserable after that and turned to carry the guitar into the bedroom "Dear oh dear," Rachel sighed.

Ion glanced up from where he sat at the table. He and the others had finally returned to the cabin, only to learn that Georgy had not yet had the opportunity to tell Patrick what he had done. He was waiting for Patrick to return with the other men. The rest of the afternoon stretched on endlessly.

"Well, can't we finish building Charles' doghouse?" Johnny finally asked.

Ion shifted his gaze to where Georgy sat on the floor just inside the boys' bedroom doorway, leaning against the doorjamb. The boy slowly shook his head. "Don't much feel like it, John," he mumbled.

"Yeah, but Charles needs it."

Ion stood up from where he sat at the table where the women chatted. "I'll help you, Johnny," he said quietly. Rachel glanced over at him and nodded appreciatively at him. A troubled sparkle rested in her eyes. Ion shifted his eyes to Georgy, knowing who had put that look in her face. As he and Johnny stepped outside and headed for the barn they simply walked quietly along. Johnny kept taking in a breath as if getting ready to say something and then at the last moment decided to say nothing. Ion did not press him but walked silently beside him, knowing the boy would speak his mind soon enough, not being one to keep anything to himself for very long.

As they stepped into the barn, they were greeted by the wriggling puppy who excitedly yapped and wagged his tail so hard it looked like it might fall off any moment and fly in the air. Johnny stooped and pick up the little dog, a grin slipping to his face in spite of his somber mood. Ion continued onward to the doghouse they had begun building before lunch. He eyed it critically, noting that it was not such a bad effort. In fact, they had done a remarkably superb job. He rolled his eyes over his choice of words. It was all Rachel's fault for including the word superb on the spelling list. Now he was unable to get it out of his head.

"Ion," Johnny sighed out, finally stepping up to him. Ion waited for the inevitable, only wishing that the question would have been asked to someone else instead of to him. "Do you think Pat really loves us?"

Ion shifted his gaze to the younger boy who was looking up at him with trusting eyes. He wondered over that look of trust. It made him feel a little taller than he had felt all day. "What do you think?" he replied quietly.

"I always thought he did."

"And now?"

"Well," Johnny sighed and shrugged, "Georgy said that if he said no to us, then that means he doesn't love us."

Ion looked steadily at the sincere face and simply asked, "Do believe everything Georgy tells you?"

Johnny blinked in surprise. "No," he snorted.

"Do you believe anything he tells you?"

Johnny suddenly began giggling. Even Ion smiled, thinking about Georgy's reaction if he had heard the question. "Yeah, I believe some of the things."

"How do you decide?" Ion asked in his normal straightforward manner.

Again Johnny shrugged. "When he's telling me the truth, I believe him."

"So you tell me," Ion said simply. "Was Georgy telling us the truth or not?"

"I don't know!" Johnny cried out in frustration. "That's why I'm asking you!"

"If you don't know the truth about this, then no matter what I say, you're not going to believe me anyway."

Johnny's shoulders dropped then. His lower lip began trembling. And Ion found himself suddenly wanting to give the boy some sort of comfort, though he could not figure out why. "I don't want it to be true. But if it isn't true, then that meant that Georgy lied to us—not just a sudden kind of lie that sort of pops out of our mouth sometimes, but the kind that took some planning—the kind that was done on purpose! I don't want that to be true either."

Ion motioned toward the stumps they had dragged into the barn to sit on that morning. "Sit down, John," he murmured, using the name that so far Georgy alone had used. It suddenly made Ion feel like he really was the boy's big brother. As they sat down on the stumps, Ion studied Johnny closely. "It doesn't matter what you want to be true. What matters is what is true. My pa was a brute. I didn't want it to be true, so I pretended it wasn't. But that didn't change the fact that he really was a brute. And on the inside, I knew it. You've got to go by the facts, John," he sighed out. "First off, did Pat ever love us?"

"Sure he did!"

"Are you positive-certain? Or are you just hoping-certain?"

"Positive-certain."

"Then what makes you think he stopped?"

Johnny drew in his breath sharply, a smile blossoming on his lips. And Ion knew then and there that he had made the point Johnny needed him to make. They sat there silently playing with the puppy as each was lost in his own thoughts. "Ion?" Johnny finally asked.

"Yeah?"

"Why did Georgy lie?"

One side of Ion's mouth crept up as he replied. "He dug himself in a hole and couldn't figure a way out except for lying. And that just made it worse. If he'd just said straight out that he'd been wrong about Pat not loving us when he told us we weren't ready to have our own trap lines, everything would've turned out all right. But he didn't want to admit it. And by then, the hole he dug was just too deep to crawl out of."

"Do you think Pat's going to give him a whipping for taking his guitar and breaking the string?"

"Not for breaking the string, but for stealing the guitar, yeah, I think so."

"He didn't really steal it," Johnny sighed. But the uncertain look on his face did nothing to promote his words. "I mean, he only brought it out here to the barn. That's not really stealing."

"I'm not the one you've got to convince."

"Would you punish him?" Johnny asked suddenly.

Ion flinched at the thought. Jerking his head sidewise, he muttered, "No. Now let's get to building that house for your pup. Enough talking."

Half an hour slipped away as the two worked side by side. The sound of voices brought a cessation to their labor as the men at last returned from checking over the trap lines. A few minutes after they stepped into the cabin, the Morrisons returned outside and walked down the path toward their home, apparently not staying for supper. Ion suddenly no longer had the heart to work on the doghouse any longer and suggested that they return to the cabin. Johnny made no argument, simply fixing up a snug place for the puppy to spend the night in and followed Ion outside. By the time they stepped into the cabin, Rachel and Angela were busy setting food on the table while Elizabeth and Jenny arranged the plates. Georgy was nowhere in sight. Ion figured he was probably in their bedroom, warding off the time he would have to confess his crime to Patrick.

Within minutes everyone was gathered around the table, enjoying Christmas leftovers. "And how is that pup of yours, Johnny?" Sam asked as the conversation came to a lull.

"He's fine. Ion and me—"

"Ion and I," Rachel corrected.

"Ion and I got his doghouse almost finished. If we hadn't taken time out to sing with the guitar after lunch, we'd have it already done now." Suddenly he stopped talking and glanced over at Patrick. Ion could not refrain from also looking at the man. Patrick shifted a surprised gaze over to Georgy who sat with downcast eyes. He made no attempt to speak to the boy or even address the issue in general. Ion drew in a deep breath, knowing that the inevitable was about to happen. And because Georgy had not been the one to tell Patrick himself, the inevitable would be worse than usual.

The meal continued, though except for Mitch, Matthew, and Sam, no one's mind was entirely on the meal. Though these three knew nothing about the incident, Ion wondered if the men realized that something was wrong. He himself could feel the tension, but then, he reminded himself, he already knew it existed. The three men seemed to be enjoying their meal. He decided that they were concentrating on the food so much that they were not paying attention to the lack of conversation around the normally noisy dinner table.

Finally Patrick lowered his coffee cup to the table and turned his attention to Georgy. "Bring me yeer razor strap lad," he said simply.

No one spoke as Georgy rose to his feet and disappeared into the boys' bedroom. He did not linger, but quickly returned with his brand new, Christmas present razor strap in his hand. Across Ion's mind raced the picture of that morning when Georgy had unwrapped his package and had been so excited over being given a man's gift. Together Patrick and Georgy stepped outside and headed toward the barn.

No one said anything. No one even moved. Finally Ion turned to Rachel and asked firmly, "Why does he have to be punished?"

Rachel shifted her gaze and studied Ion for a moment before answering. Her eyes softened. "Well, Ion, do you remember what the Lord said that children are supposed to do?" he stared at her, frowning slightly, choosing not to reply, though he knew exactly what she getting at. She paused only long enough to determine that he was not about to answer and then added, "They're supposed to obey their parents. And when they don't, they're also disobeying God's command. And when we disobey God, that's called sin. Sin has to be punished—all sin, no matter how small we think it is. All sin keeps us from God. That's why the Lord Jesus came to earth. He took our sin and was punished in our place. You see, even if we went to Hell and were punished forever, we could never completely pay for our sins. Only God could completely pay for them. And that's why He took our punishment, so that we could be right with God."

Ion's frown deepened. She had given too big of an answer to be satisfying. Shifting his gaze, he flinched back slightly at the look on Mitch's face. He seemed to be wanting to hear more. "I've never heard that before," Mitch murmured.

"Never?" Johnny asked in surprise.

"Never," Mitch sighed.

"You want to hear more?" Johnny asked, causing Ion to sigh. It was bad enough that they had to sit through a sermon every Sunday, and family devotions every morning. And here Johnny was encouraging more of the same.

"Yeah," Mitch murmured. "I want to hear more.

As Johnny swung into his own version of the Bible story about Jesus, Mitch seemed to be captivated by it. Rachel knew that Patrick could be of tremendous use just then, being able to answer Mitch's questions better than she and the children could. Rising to her feet, she headed for the door, turning toward the barn. It would not take too long to give Georgy his necessary punishment and the talk that would follow. She would wait just outside the door and then usher Patrick back into the cabin to help Mitch understand the gospel as soon as the two of them were finished.

Georgy held onto his razor strap, watching as Patrick slowly removed his own coat. He had not yet instructed Georgy to do the same. But when the man began unbuttoning his shirt and removed it, Georgy scrunched up his brow in puzzlement. "What are you doing, Pat?" he asked in a dumbfounded tone.

Patrick turned to face him and smiled fondly at him. "I'm proving m'love to ye, lad. Now, I'm thinking thit ye and Ion are getting too old for mere spankings. Ye've reached the age for the razor strap, which hurts a lot more. And I'd never use it on yeer bare skin. Normally I'll hiv ye lean over and touch yeer toes and I'll use the strap on ye a dozen times or so. Does that sound fair to ye?"

Georgy nodded reluctantly. "That's how you prove your love to me? By hitting me with the razor strap?"

Patrick nodded. "Aye, it is. Except this time I'm going to prove it another way." When Georgy lifted his shoulders slightly, wondering what Patrick was talking about, Patrick added, "This time I'm going to prove m'love for ye by taking yeer punishment m'self." Georgy stared at him in horror. "On m'back, lad," he added, turning away from Georgy and reaching his hands to grasp the beam in front of him.

"No!" Georgy cried out indignantly. "I'm not going to whip you Pat!"

"Aye, laddie," Patrick replied with authority in his voice. "Thit is exactly what ye are going to do. Ye've broken m'law. I've judged ye, found ye guilty and sentenced ye. Bit, to prove m'love for ye I'm going to bear yeer punishment m'self. This way both justice and mercy will be shone. Now do it!"

Georgy half heartedly raised the strap and brought it down on Patrick's back. "Harder, lad. That one doesn't count. Ivery time ye don't hit me hard enough, ye'll hiv to do it over. Now lay it on me good and hard!" he ordered sternly.

Georgy swallowed and did as ordered. As the strap cracked against Patrick's unprotected skin, the man flinched. An ugly red stripe crossed his back. "Again lad. Eleven more!"

"Please Pat," Georgy moaned, a tear slipping down his cheek, "don't make me do this."

"Eleven more!" Patrick growled back.

Again Georgy raised the strap and landed it hard on the man's back. Again he flinched. And a second thin stripe rested there. "Ten more!" Patrick ordered. "Sin mist be punished! Why do ye care that someone else bears thit punishment for ye? Ye got yeer way, after all! Ye played the guitar and 'ad yeer fun. Now it's time to pay for yeer crime. And ye get off scot-free. The crime is paid for and ye are forgiven. What more could ye ask for?"

"Please Pat, I'm so sorry! Please forgive me!"

"I've forgiven, ye laddie. Bit sin must still be paid for by semone. I'm taking yeer punishment this time."

"But I don't want you to."

"Ten more! Now!"

A sob tore from Georgy's throat as he landed a third stripe on Patrick's back. An unexpected sound made Georgy turn around and stare straight into the eyes of Rachel who was pressing her hand against her mouth. She made no comment, but simply turned around and stepped back outside, closing the barn door. Again Georgy raised the strap and hit Patrick with it again and again, until finally twelve, angry red stripes crisscrossed the man's back. Only then did Patrick turn around and look at Georgy. Opening up his arms, he drew the boy to himself and held him close. Georgy shivered. Unable to hug him back, fearing lest he bring even more pain to the man, Georgy simply stood there, leaning his head against Patrick's shoulder. "I'm so sorry," he half wept. "I'm so sorry Pat."

"I know, laddie," the man murmured, softly patting his head as he held him close. "D'ye believe now thit I love ye?"

Georgy nodded. "I always knew," he sobbed.

"Did ye, lad? I don't know for sure. Ye see, if there hadn't been a question, I don't think ye would even hiv come up with thit line of argument. Ye know, Jesus proved 'Is love for us by taking our punishment 'Imself. Do ye know thit Jesus loves ye, Georgy? Do ye really know it?"

Georgy nodded. "I know it."

"And what hiv ye done with thit love? Hiv ye thrown it away or hiv ye done what 'E says to do?"

"What does He want me to do, Pat?" Georgy asked, suddenly for the first time in His life understanding that Jesus' love for him was real.

"'E wants ye to repent of yeer sin, lad. Are ye sorry ye've sinned against 'Im? I know ye're sorry ye've sinned against me. Bit are ye sorry ye've sinned against Jesus who took all of yeer punishment and paid for all of yeer sin?"

"I'm sorry to Him too," Georgy wept.

"Then tell 'Im, laddie. Do ye believe thit 'E is the Christ, the Son of God?"

"Yes."

"Then tell 'Im, Georgy. Tell 'Im what's in yeer heart. And ask 'Im to save ye and be yeer Lord—yeer boss."

Georgy sniffed and steadied his voice, still resting against Patrick. "Jesus," he murmured, "I'm sorry. I'm sorry I've sinned against you. Won't you forgive me? Thank you for being punished instead of me. Won't you save me and make me a Christian? I know that you're God's Son—His only Son. I know that You're the Savior. I want to live for You, Jesus. I'll do what You say. You're my boss now." He fell silent then, suddenly engulfed in the most peaceful feeling he had ever known. He was not quite sure how to put it into words, but he suddenly felt clean—sparkling clean like the way Rachel washed her white linens. Something felt so different—so untried and not yet ruined—so new and beautiful.

"Aye laddie," Patrick sighed holding him close. "I know."

Georgy lifted his head from Patrick's shoulder and stared in shock at the tears slipping down the face of the strongest man he knew. And they had not come from the whipping. They had not come to his eyes until Georgy had prayed. Georgy eased into a smile and laid his head back down against Patrick's shoulder. "Thank you for loving me Pat," he murmured. "I love you too."

Rachel returned to the cabin, trying to hold down her emotions at the sight she had seen in the barn of Patrick taking Georgy's punishment, receiving it on his unprotected back instead of on his cloth-protected seat. "Help me, Jesus," she prayed as she reached for the door. "Hold for me what I saw just now, and help me to focus on Mitch's need right now." As she stepped into the cabin and crossed the floor to the table, she saw that most of the children had deserted Mitch. Only Ion and Johnny remained at the table. She could hear Jennifer and Elizabeth in the bedroom entertaining Anna Marie. Art was camped in Rachel's rocking chair. Even Jed had retired to his room for the night. Sam and Matthew had taken their leave while she had been at the barn—whether because of the long day or the turn of the conversation around the table—Rachel was uncertain.

Mitch glanced up at Rachel, a light in his eyes as he smiled at her. "Rachel," he murmured, "I've never heard this before. Can it be true? I mean—did Jesus die for me?"

"Yes, Mitch. You see, 'God so loved the world that he gave his only begotten son, that whosoever believeth in him should not perish, but have everlasting life. For God sent not his son into the world to condemn the world, but that the world through him might be saved.'"[i]

"Well, how do I get saved?" he asked excitedly.

"'Believe on the Lord Jesus Christ, and thou shalt be saved, and thy house.'[ii] Do you know what that means?" When he lifted his shoulders hesitantly, she added, "It means believe He is who He says He is. He says He is the Son of God, our Savior. Do you believe that He died for you, taking your punishment Himself so that you could be clean? Clean enough to have a right relationship with God Himself?"

Mitch nodded. "Yeah, I do. I'm not sure why I believe it—but I do."

Ion stared hard at the young man, growing pale. Clearly he had never seen anything like this before. He turned and eyed Rachel. She smiled at him. "Do you believe, Ion?"

He shrugged slightly. "I don't know," he grumbled.

"Johnny? Do you believe?"

Little-boy shoulders curled up. "Sometimes."

Rachel smiled, seeing that neither of them were quite ready. Turning back to Mitch, she asked, "Would you like to get saved now?"

"Yeah," he replied suddenly.

"Are you sure? It's a life-long commitment. It means that you're giving God charge of your life. And it means that when you die, you'll go to Heaven and spend eternity with Him."

Mitch grinned and then squeezed his eyes shut, needing no more prompting. "God? Jesus? I know who You are now! I believe You're God! I believe You're the Son of God—the Savior—my Savior! Please save me! Please forgive me of my sins. I'm sorry I've sinned. I want to live for You forever! Won't You take charge of my life? It's Yours, God. I give it to You. I'll do whatever You say. You're my boss now. And I'll teach Jen and Art about You too." He paused and added in a delighted tone. "Thank you Jesus!"

Chapter 2

Georgy let out his breath in a sigh, only half listening as Angela spoke to his class assembled on the recitation bench in front of the teacher's desk. When Rachel had been the teacher, lessons had been fun—at least most of the time. He did not regret that her baby was so near to being born, but he just wished there had been a way that she could have continued teaching right up until the end of the school year. Ion nudged him with his elbow. Everyone was looking at him. Angela's eyes bore down upon him in a glare as she pursed her lips.

"Georgy Northwood!" Angela called out sternly.

"Yes ma'am," Georgy replied meekly.

"Why are you daydreaming?"

Georgy swallowed, trying to decide whether or not to tell the truth. When Ion quietly began clearing his throat, Georgy decided that he would neither lie, nor tell the entire truth. He could hardly tell the woman that his mind wandered because she was boring.

"I'm waiting for your answer!"

"Yes ma'am," he sighed. "Well, I was thinking about Rachel and the baby," he began and then simply allowed his voice to fall away with his thought unfinished.

"And what has that accomplished?" she demanded in her tone of voice that was in its usual too-high-of-pitch to be restful to the ears.

Georgy lifted his shoulders slightly, admitting, "It's got me in a peck of trouble?"

Angela did not look amused. But he was not trying to be amusing, only answer her question. She rolled her eyes, murmuring to herself, only just loud enough for those gathered around her desk to hear. "I can't wait for her to return to her duties of teaching either! Such children!" Lifting the delicate pendant watch that was suspended on the chain that hung around her neck, she studied it for a moment. Sighing, she rose to her feet and called out for the entire class to hear, "You are dismissed for lunch. Go out into the sunshine!"

A mad scramble followed her words as the children hurried to obey, looks of relief painted on each face over being released. Georgy rose to his feet and headed for the coat pegs at the back of the school. Above the pegs rested the shelf where each student had placed his lunch. It took a few moments to reach the crowded wall, but finally he grabbed the former coffee tin that had been converted into his lunchbox. The next moment he was hurling himself out through the open door, dashing across the playground.

Plopping himself onto the split log bench where he and Ion normally sat to eat lunch, he tore open the top of the tin and thrust his hand inside, withdrawing the cloth-enwrapped sandwich. A moment later he opened his mouth as wide as he could and shoved in a third or more of the sandwich and tore it off with his teeth. As he chewed, he eased his eyes shut and lowered his sandwich back to the tin, savoring every morsel.

"Rachel's gonna give you extra chores," Johnny chuckled as he sat down beside Georgy, "if she finds out you're bolting your food again."

Opening one eye, Georgy studied the boy. "Haw see fon ot?"

Johnny chuckled over the garbled words. "How? I'll tell her. That's how she'll find out. And you're talking with your mouth full too."

"Um not," Georgy grumbled, unable to form his words more correctly with the huge chunk of sandwich in his mouth. Opening up his other eye, he frowned and glanced around. "Wear Een?" he asked.

Again Johnny giggled and pointed across the schoolyard. "Where else? He's sitting with Mary O'Brin."

As Georgy followed the direction in which Johnny was pointing, his eyes landed on Ion. Just as Johnny had said, he was indeed sitting beside Mary. He grew thoughtful as he continued chewing, wondering over Ion's growing infatuation. Finally he swallowed and turned back to Johnny, "You aren't going to be teasing him, are you?"

Johnny's eyes sparkled. "What do you think?"

"I think if you do, the three of us are going to end up having to do kitchen chores again."

"Rachel doesn't give us chores for teasing."

"Yeah but," Georgy murmured, shaking his head, "every time you tease Ion, he gives it right back to you, and you get mad and take a swing at him. And I try to stop the two of you from killing each other. And that's when Rachel walks in and sees us. And then she makes us do Bet's kitchen chores that night. I don't want to wash dishes tonight! So don't tease Ion!"

Johnny simply laughed and took a bite of his sandwich. Georgy rolled his eyes, knowing that Johnny would do what he wanted to do, regardless of what Georgy might say. A sudden scream silenced everyone in the yard. From the corner of his eye, Georgy saw something falling from one of the trees. The next moment he realized that it was one of the younger boys. Jumping to his feet, Georgy tore across the yard, yelling, "Don't touch him!"

Already a crowd was gathering around the crumpled form of the sobbing

Joshua O'Brin. Georgy pushed through the other students and knelt down beside Joshua. The boy was cradling his left arm and crying. "Let me look, Joshua," Georgy said soothingly. Across his mind swept the images he had seen while helping Doc Morrison treat injured lumbermen during the forest fire. It seemed only natural that he would be the one to help Joshua. "Johnny, run and fetch Miss Stone," he said quietly, easing his hand around Joshua's left arm. "No, don't be moving it," he said soothingly to Joshua. "I need to see how it is. You trust me?"

The boy met Georgy's gaze with tear-filled eyes. "I don't know," he admitted.

Georgy grinned. "You're a smart boy, Joshua O'Brin," he chuckled. That seemed to soothe the boy's fears more than anything else. He relaxed his grip around his arm and allowed Georgy to touch it. "That hurts!" he cried out.

"I know," Georgy murmured, sympathy ringing out in his voice. "Ion, fetch me a couple of sticks—good and stout. And does anybody have any string?"

A small ball of string was thrust in front of him then. And Ion handed him the sticks he had asked for. As Georgy laid one stick on one side of the boy's arm, which was bent at the elbow, and the other on the other side, he said with a note of authority in his voice, "Ion, hold these sticks in place while I tie them on."

Ion made no attempt at protesting. As the two worked in securing the splint, Angela stepped up to the crowd. "What in the world happened?" she demanded.

Instantly Joshua began whimpering. Georgy glanced up at the woman for a moment before turning back to his work, replying, "Well, I suspect that Joshua broke his arm. So Ion and I are splinting it. I think we should send for the doc."

"No," Joshua moaned.

"Oh," Georgy chuckled, "Doc Morrison isn't somebody to be scared of. He'll fix you up dandy."

As Angela sent a messenger for the doctor, Georgy finished wrapping the splinted arm with the string. Finally Angela pushed out her breath in indignation, demanding, "How did this happen?"

Georgy met the little boy's frightened eyes and winked at him. Turning to face Angela, Georgy replied in a long, drawn out sigh, "I suspect that it had something to do with falling out of the tree."

"Tree?" Angela cried out. Glaring down at Joshua, she demanded, "I have told you children there will be no tree-climbing at this school!"

"Yes ma'am," Joshua replied in a trembling voice.

"Well," Georgy cut in, hoping to take the uncomfortable attention away from Joshua, "I think we could use a scarf. Bet? You have one?"

After the words were slowly repeated to her, Elizabeth thrust her scarf into Georgy's hand. Even Angela fell silent as Georgy slipped one hand beneath Joshua's back, while the other supported the broken arm and eased the boy into a sitting position. Joshua moaned but did not struggle against him. As the boy sat there, Georgy quickly tied the scarf into a sling and slipped it over Joshua's head, easing the injured arm into the soft cradle. "There, that'll help some."

"Thank you Georgy," Joshua said, looking at Georgy with such trust in his eyes that Georgy blinked in surprise.

"You're welcome," he replied quietly. Turning to look at Angela, Georgy suggested, "Maybe until the doc comes, we best get him back inside and sitting at his desk."

Angela nodded and turned around, heading back to the schoolhouse. Together Georgy and Ion lifted the boy and carried him across the yard. "Did you eat yet, Josh?" Georgy asked. But when the boy made no reply, Georgy stared at him.

It was Ion who spoke up. "The O'Brins didn't bring any lunch today. I gave most of mine to Mary. She gave part of it to Sam, but we couldn't find Josh. Now I know why," he added dryly. "He was up in the tree."

Georgy let his breath out long and hard, knowing the right thing to do, but not enjoying it. "Well, Josh, you can have what's left of my lunch. I'll go and fetch it after we get you settled at your desk." No one spoke another word until they had the boy sitting at his desk, cradling his arm. Ion and Georgy stepped away from the boy then and Georgy lowered his voice, saying, "I'm going to stay with Josh, just to make sure he's all right. Will you go fetch my lunch? It's where we usually sit." Again he sighed, adding, "I sure am glad that that was a big mouthful I took. It's going to have to last all afternoon."

Ion grinned, but said nothing. Turning to the door, he stepped outside. Georgy returned to Joshua and eased down on the desk bench in front of the boy, his legs in the aisle as he turned to face him. "Does it hurt real bad?" he asked quietly.

The small boy nodded. The movement was enough to dislodge the tears that had filled his eyes. As they coursed down his cheeks, he looked so pitiful that Georgy no longer resented sharing his lunch with him. "Why didn't you bring anything to eat today?" he finally asked.

Joshua lowered his eyes to the desktop, murmuring, "Ma is sick. Pa said he wasn't wasting time and effort to pack a lunch for us. Mary said she'd do it. But Pa said no. Ma didn't know he wouldn't give us any lunch. But Mary told me that tonight she'll make us some sandwiches and hide them in the old stump down the path. It's out of sight of the cabin. So when we get them tomorrow, Pa won't know."

Georgy sat stunned as he listened. Glancing up, he suddenly realized that Ion was standing there listening. "Even my pa never made me go hungry—not without a reason anyway." He sighed and handed the remainder of Georgy's sandwich to Joshua.

When Joshua eyed it, he stared in shock, his eyes suddenly darting up to Georgy. "That looks like just one bite you took! You bit off half of the sandwich in just one bite?"

"Third," Georgy corrected.

"Half," Ion cut in. "He always bites off half for the first mouthful."

Joshua's eyes shone with a bit of awe mingled with amusement. Turning his attention back to the sandwich, he took a bite and sighed. Ion and Georgy exchanged glances, only then guessing that the boy had been denied breakfast as well as lunch. "Don't you worry," Georgy sighed out to Joshua. "Me and Ion—"

"Ion and I," Ion corrected.

Georgy rolled his eyes. "Ion and I," he sighed, "will bring extra for you and your brother and sister. You won't go hungry any more. A broken arm and still hungry—that's hungrier than I've ever been," he added quietly, returning his gaze to a troubled looking Ion.

"Yeah, me too," Ion sighed.

Rachel sat at the table and peered across it and out the window, wondering how she could wait another whole month for the baby to arrive. It had seemed to take almost forever for even May to arrive. June still seemed so incredibly far away. She eased out her breath in a sigh, thinking about how the upcoming birth had changed so many things. It had been hard turning the school over to Angela. The men who had agreed to serve as the school board had not been in favor of it, knowing that Angela had had no formal training in being a teacher. Patrick had convinced them, however, insisting that his wife was no longer available to teach and they would simply have to find another teacher. He had made it clear that if they made it too hard on Rachel to take this time off, he would simply refuse to consider the possibility of her returning to the classroom once the baby got a little older. Rachel smiled at the memory of how the men had immediately backed down from their position and had quickly agreed to the idea of Angela filling in for the teacher for as long as necessary.

Glancing to her left, Rachel studied the three-year-old Anna Marie who was quietly playing with the wooden blocks Patrick, Jed and the boys had carved for her, thinking of the rambunctious afternoon she had spent outside after waking up from her nap. Rachel had been hard-pressed to keep up with her and had finally lured her back into the cabin to play with her blocks, promising her a cookie. Rachel sighed and turned back to the sewing project she was working on. The little quilt was taking shape nicely, but Rachel wondered over the wisdom of sewing a quilt for a child who would be born in June. She sighed, reminding herself that winter would come quickly on the heals of summer and she would be glad then that she had used this time to sew the quilt. After all, with a newborn baby soon in the household, she would likely not be having any time at all for such sewing projects.

Suddenly Georgy burst in through the door, testifying that school was out for another day. He grinned, something undefined sparkling in his eyes, and asked, "How was your day?"

"Fine," she replied slowly, wondering. His expression warned her that he had some news but was doing his best to show proper manners first. "How was school?"

His eyes began dancing then. Apparently he felt he had been patient enough and plunged into the topic on his mind. "Doc Morrison came!"

"What? Was someone ill?"

"Not exactly," he replied, excitement coloring his tone. "Josh O'Brin fell out of a tree while we were eating."

"Did he get hurt?"

Suddenly the excitement slipped away from the boy's face, being replaced with a look of surprise mingled with scoffing. "Of course he got hurt," he replied, actual bewilderment rested in his face over Rachel's apparently silly question. "But I took care of him 'til Doc got there. And Doc said I did just the right thing. And guess what?"

Rachel stared hard at him. "There's more?" she demanded, feeling like shaking the boy to get out all of the information at once.

"Doc says I can come over and help him when I'm not in school. I'm going to be a doctor when I grow up." With that he hurried into his room to change out of his good school clothes."

"You must have run all the way," Rachel finally said, finding her voice again as she peered out through the window. "I don't even see the others coming yet."

"I did run," Georgy called out from the bedroom. A few minutes later he was out again, dressed in his work and romping clothes. "Doc's waiting for me!" he called out as he hurried back to the cabin door. "I might be late for supper if we have to go and take care of somebody." And with that he was gone, running down the trail, heading for the Morrison cabin.

Rachel stared after him in shock. "A doctor? Georgy?" She let her breath slip slowly from her lungs as she thought about the new idea. Georgy would be fifteen in only two months. Already he was nearly as tall as Patrick. She shook her head, thinking of the young boy he had been when she had first met him on the Oregon Trail. She could not deny the fact that he was nearly grown up already. "But a doctor?" she murmured. "Can we afford to send him back East to medical school?" Again she sighed, finding herself wishing that she could have had a few more years with the boy before he grew up and became a man.

As she continued looking out the window from where she sat at the table, the other children came into view, walking, not running. Ion's face was drawn up into a perturbed sort of frown as he eyed a laughing Johnny. "Oh Ion," she murmured. "You're nearly as old as Georgy. You'll be fifteen in October. Are you too thinking about spreading your wings?" She thought about the boy who had been part of their family for nearly ten months now. Already it was clear that he was taking after his father, Colon MacAlister, in height, though not yet in bulk. Colon had been a big man, but Ion looked to be leaner than he.

Elizabeth came into view then. Having turned twelve in March, she was already showing signs of growing into the woman she would soon be. "Don't be thinking that Patrick and I will let you begin courting anytime soon." Across her mind swept the question of whether or not the young men might begin approaching Patrick in four or five years, asking for permission to marry her. Certainly back in Boston that would be far too young. "But out here?" she murmured. "They marry early, don't they?"

Pushing out her breath, she eyed the approaching Johnny who had just passed his eleventh birthday in April. By all rights he should have been able to assume the Nathan family business. But it no longer existed. And the shame of it was that already Johnny was showing interest in the business field, just as his father before him. "You aren't cut out to be a farmer, Johnny Nathan," she sighed. But neither was he a candidate for a lumberman. "I don't know of any other jobs out here. Well, of course, there's preaching and teaching. But you definitely aren't preacher material. A teacher perhaps—but not likely." A smile crept to her lips as she thought of her little brother who was turning into quite a little gentleman, in spite of his surroundings—the kind he had been born to become in Boston.

Suddenly the door burst open and the three tumbled inside, all talking at once. Rachel worked on sorting out each conversation, hoping she was doing justice to each, responding adequately.

"Ion's going to marry Mary O'Brin!" Johnny called out.

"I told you to be quiet Johnny!" Ion shot back. "Rachel, can Georgy and I take a little extra lunch from now on to share with the O'Brins?"

"Everybody thinks Georgy's special now," Elizabeth called out, a grin on her face. "But we know who he really is."

"Why do the O'Brins need some of your lunch?" Rachel asked Ion. "And that'll be enough out of you, Johnny," she added, glancing over at the giggling boy.

"But I ain't fibbing," Johnny laughed.

"I'm not lying," Rachel corrected.

"Their pa wouldn't let them have any breakfast or lunch today—probably not any dinner either, unless their ma can get out of bed to fix it. But she's sick. Mary can cook, but unless her pa wants something to eat, he won't let her fix anything for her and the boys."

"Annie, did you have a good day?" Elizabeth called out, hurrying over to the little girl, plunking down beside her."

"Good day Lizzy!" the little girl giggled.

"So I can say it, because it's true," Johnny persisted.

"Does it pass the kindness test?" Rachel asked. Turning back to Ion, she asked, just to make certain she had heard right, "They were given nothing to eat all day?"

"Yeah, except for what Georgy and I shared with them."

"I imagine you're hungry then," Rachel added.

"I am too," Johnny called out. "It takes a lot out of a fellow to hold back news like Ion marrying Mary O'Brin."

"You didn't hold it back!" Ion growled, turning to the boy. "You yelled it all the way from school!"

Johnny laughed and darted into the boys' bedroom to change his clothes.

"Yes, I'll add a little extra to Georgy's and your lunches tomorrow. But, suppose they bring their own lunches tomorrow?"

Ion's eyes suddenly began sparkling. He shrugged in feigned indifference. "Well, I guess we'll have to eat it ourselves. It doesn't seem quite right to let it go to waste."

"Was this Georgy's idea?"

"Yes ma'am," he replied solemnly, though the corners of his mouth rose slightly.

"Can I take Annie outside for awhile?" Elizabeth asked.

"Yes you may, after you change out of your school clothes," Rachel replied, just as Ion stepped past her and headed for the bedroom. The two girls wasted no time, but ran into their bedroom to comply with Rachel's order. All at once the room was silent. Rachel had the uncanny feeling that it would happen like that—One day her children would still be children under her roof. And the next moment they'd be grown and off to their own homes, leaving Patrick and herself, Jed, and Angela alone in a quiet, empty house. Just then the tiny life inside of her stirred. Her hand crept protectively over her stomach, caressing her unborn child. "Well, at least we'll get to keep you for awhile yet," she murmured. The sudden breeze that blew in caught Rachel's attention. Turning, she eyed the door that had gotten left open. "Johnny," she called out. "Take Charles outside!" The puppy, now nearly grown, had pushed his way into the cabin, though he knew he was not to enter. "You know the dogs aren't allowed inside. Leprechaun is sure to follow Charles!"

"I didn't let him in," Johnny called back.

"You didn't close the door either."

"Lizzy was the last one inside."

"And gentlemen are supposed to close doors for ladies."

"Lizzy's no lady."

"Johnny Nathan!" Rachel ordered sternly.

"Sorry Rachel." The next moment the boy dashed back out of the bedroom, buttoning his everyday shirt as he hurried along. "Come on Charles," he called out. "Let's go outside!"

As boy and dog reached the door, they nearly collided with Angela as she entered. Her face was not a happy face. "Sorry Miss Stone," Johnny called out, clearly not a bit sorry, and pushed past her, his dog at his heals.

"Did you have a good day?" Rachel asked, already knowing the answer to her question, by the tired look in her eyes. Already knowing about Joshua falling out of a tree while under her care, Rachel could only guess at the turmoil that was going on inside of the woman. She made no pretense at enjoying teaching. And Rachel could not help but feel a little sorry for her just then. "I made some tea," she said softly.

A look of relief flooded over Angela's face. For a moment she almost looked friendly. "No, sit down," Angela said in her normal snippety tone as Rachel moved to stand up. "I'll pour it myself." Rachel smiled in spite of herself, having come to realize some time ago that even Angela, in her own unfriendly way, tried to relieve Rachel of any sort of manual labor she could. Rachel had simply decided to accept the help and ignore the woman's uppity mannerisms and her often wrinkled up nose, deciding that these unpleasant traits were simply an inseparable part of the woman.

Just then Patrick walked through the doorway. Rachel's smile died on her lips as she studied her husband's sober-looking face. "What's wrong, Patrick?" she asked.

He met her gaze and seemed as if he were trying to decide how to break the news to her. Finally he sighed and simply said, "A stranger came to Matthew's store today—a wegon mister. 'E is looking for folk who want to return East."

Rachel stared hard at him. The sound of tinkling china brought her attention over to Angela who stood in front of the fireplace, teacup in hand. The hand that held the cup and saucer was shaking too much to hold it still. Her face had grown pale.

Patrick crossed the floor and eased down onto the bench. "Ladies," he sighed, "this may be the end o'Timberton."

"I don't understand," Rachel shot back, stunned.

Patrick stretched out his arm and laid his hand over Rachel's. "Most o'the people here were planning on returning East. The only reason they didn't wis thit Colon died, and so they 'ad no one to guide thim back." The sound of footsteps made him pause. Ion stepped out of the bedroom and eyed Patrick, a sober look on his face. "Well," Patrick continued, "now they hiv another wegon mister to lead thim back East. The problem is, if too miny of thim leave, there won't be a way for the rist of us to survive 'ere—not alone in this wilderness."

"But do you think they still want to leave?" Rachel asked, stunned. "They've made Timberton their home. It may not be fancy, but it's a good place to live."

Patrick smiled and squeezed her hand. "Ye're right, Mrs. O'Riley. 'Tis a viry good place to live. We'll pray for guidance. And we'll ask our Lord to 'elp iveryone follow 'Is guidance. And we'll ask for the grace we need to accept 'Is answer."

Rachel nodded, suddenly feeling more peaceful again. "Mary said," Ion sighed, "that her pa wants to leave Timberton. The only thing that's been keeping them here is that her ma is so sick all the time. But if Mr. O'Brin hears about a wagon master being here, I bet he'll move the family back East—or at least part way."

"Why would ye say thit, lad?" Patrick asked slowly. "Part way?"

Ion's eyes grew dark. "If it was—were up to him, he'd settle in Indian territory."

Rachel and Patrick exchanged troubled glances. Patrick nodded. "Aye," he sighed, "I think 'e would indeed. And Mrs. O'Brin wouldn't survive."

"We'll just have to pray especially hard then for the O'Brins," Rachel said quietly. When Ion nodded, Rachel smiled at him. His eyes looked a mixture of trouble and relief at the same time. And all at once Rachel understood what Johnny had been saying earlier. Ion really did have plans for marrying Mary O'Brin.

Ion had been trudging along aimlessly, not paying any attention as to where he was going, nor caring until all at once he found himself at the Morrison's cabin and temporary doctor's office. He stopped in his tracks, certain that Georgy was inside. He eased his hands into his pockets and simply stood there, trying to decide what to do. A few minutes had already passed when the door opened. Mrs. Morrison stepped outside and called out quietly, "Good afternoon Ion. Would you like to come inside?"

"No ma'am," he sighed. "I'm just walking." He hesitated and nearly turned around altogether when suddenly he asked, "Is Georgy inside?"

The woman smiled. "Yes he is. As a matter of fact he was just getting ready to leave when my husband stopped him for a moment to show him something in one of his medical books. Would you like to come in and wait for him?"

"No ma'am," he sighed. "I'll just be going. It's getting near suppertime." Even he could hear the disappointment in his voice, though he was not certain where it had come from. Certainly he could not be even remotely disappointed that Georgy was unavailable for him to talk to. He had not even come to talk with Georgy. He turned around and began slowly retracing his steps. He had not been walking for many minutes when he heard his name being called. He glanced over his shoulder and saw Georgy running toward him.

"Wait for me, Ion!"

Ion paused in his step and did as Georgy asked. When Georgy caught up to him, he eyed Ion curiously, studying him hard. Ion frowned and muttered the first thing that came to his mind. "You're going to be late for supper—dinner—whatever you want to call it."

Georgy smiled with curiosity shining in his eyes. "Why would you care if I miss supper? There'd be more for you if I did. You eat like a horse."

"No I don't," Ion muttered.

It was then that Georgy caught hold of Ion's shoulder and brought him to a halt. "Ion, what's wrong?" he asked.

Something in the boy's quiet tone made Ion look him full in the eyes and admit, "I think Mary's going to be moving away."

He waited for the scoffing look to dash to Georgy's face. But it did not come. Instead a look of genuine compassion rested there. Ion's throat suddenly felt uncomfortably tight and he knew beyond doubt that if he tried to say even one word, he would give way to emotions in a way that he was certain was unmanly. It was then that he noticed that Georgy's hand was still on his shoulder in a most comforting way. "What makes you think that?" Georgy finally asked. "I've seen the way she looks at you," he added with a slow grin. "It'd take a team of horses to drag her away—I'm thinking," he added.

Ion blinked and thought over the words, hope rising in him. "Even if her pa moves the family away?"

Georgy nodded confidently. "Even then."

Ion drew in a deep breath. He knew it was unlikely, but it still felt a lot better thinking about it that way than the other. He dipped his head in a nod and glanced at the ground, mumbling, "Thanks Georgy."

Georgy clapped him on the back "That's what big brothers are for!" he replied heartily.

Ion tore his eyes from the ground and stared in shock at the boy. "You're not my big brother!"

Georgy's grin grew and his eyes danced merrily, much to Ion's annoyance. "Sure I am! I'm older than you are."

"Less than four months," Ion grumbled. "That doesn't count."

"Sure it does little brother."

Ion stared at Georgy as the words sank in. Little brother. He had never been anyone's brother before becoming part of the O'Riley family. For the first time in his life, the term little brother had been applied to him and it suddenly felt like a comforting arm slipping around him.

Without another word the two began walking again, heading for home and supper. "So, tell me what's put a bur under Mr. O'Brin's saddle to make him want to move?"

Rachel glanced up from her place beside Patrick at the supper table. Everyone was nearly finished eating when Ion and Georgy stepped through the doorway. The two were never late for a meal. She wondered if punishment was necessary, knowing that it likely was not merely the neglect of good manners that had prompted them to be late. They probably had a good reason—at least she hoped so.

"Sorry Rachel," Georgy called out. "I got to talking with Doc and lost track of the time. But Ion came and got me."

"Oh," Rachel replied in surprise. "I didn't know you'd gone after him, Ion."

As the boys slipped into their places at the table, Ion shrugged. "I didn't set out to. But once I got all the way there I told Mrs. Morrison it was our suppertime."

"Thank you Ion, but I was getting a little worried about you. I knew where Georgy was, but I didn't know where you were. Next time you plan to be gone that long, it'd be considerate on your part if you let one of us know. All right?" Ion dipped his head in a nod, but he seemed to have his mind on other things. "Well," Rachel added, "we would've waited longer, but with the town meeting being called tonight, I wanted to make sure we get there early."

"Rachel, ye aren't planning on coming to the meeting, are ye lassie?" Patrick asked in a surprised tone.

It was her turn to be surprised. Turning to him, she replied in a shocked voice, "Of course!"

He shook his head. "I don't think thit's a wise idea—not with the baby so near."

"Patrick," she replied, unable to keep the shock out of her voice. "Of course I'm coming!"

"'Tis an unnecessary risk to the wee one—and maybe to yeerself as well."

"Not unnecessary," she said firmly. "Why, the future of this town will be settled tonight. I want to be there when it's decided if we're going to continue being a town or if the majority decides to return East. And what will we do then? Continue on west to the coast like how you'd originally planned?"

Patrick sighed and shook his head. "I don't know where we'll go. Bit, whether ye're there or not, it won't affect the people's decisions."

"Oh I know that," she murmured, wondering how she could make him understand her need to be there. "But I want to be part of it."

All at once his look of love for her shone out so deeply, she could not help but smile. Shaking her head she whispered, "That isn't fair, Patrick O'Riley."

He grinned. "Then ye'll stay home?" A hopeful note slipped into his voice.

Pushing out her breath, the corners of her mouth twitching upward in spite of her best effort to look as exasperated as she felt, she murmured, "I'll stay. But you better pay especial close attention to everything that goes on and give me a detailed account!"

"Agreed. And one o'the lads will stay with ye."

"No, let Elizabeth," she said firmly. "You know how she hates meetings—not being able to hear what's being said. No one speaks slowly enough for even Johnny to translate for her. And he does it better than anyone in the family."

A proud sort of chuckle sounded out from Johnny's end of the table. "I don't know," Patrick sighed out. "If ye need inything, ye'll be needing one of the lads—Georgy or Ion."

"If I need anything, I'll send Elizabeth to come and get you or one of the boys. Agreed?"

Patrick scanned the occupants at the table and fell silent, thinking the matter over. By the looks on both Georgy's and Ion's faces, she knew beyond doubt that both boys wanted to attend the meeting. It went without saying that Angela needed to attend. She had been noticeably silent since hearing the news of the possibility of returning East. Jed too would attend the meeting, without question. If the older boys went, it hardly seemed fair to Johnny to insist that he remain behind. Anna Marie would stay at home with Rachel, but would not be of any help if there was a need. Elizabeth met her gaze, having followed enough of the conversation to understand what was being discussed. Clearly, by the look in her eyes, she wanted to stay home rather than be bored to tears at what could prove to be an endless meeting.

"All right," Patrick finally said, nodding. "All the ladies except for Miss Stone will stay home." Suddenly shaking himself as in afterthought, he turned to Angela, adding, "Thit is, if ye want to attend the meeting."

She dipped her head in a nod. Her coloring was still off. And a dent rested between her brows where normally there was none. "I'll go to the meeting," she replied crisply. Something in her tone made everyone stare at her. Was it a sob that had escaped her? Suddenly she looked far too vulnerable for having everyone staring at her.

"Children," Rachel called out quickly. "Finish eating and clear the table. The meeting will start soon. I don't want you being late."

"Yeah, we want good seats," Georgy chuckled and returned his attention to the food on his plate.

"Georgy, you and Ion will stand along the wall with the men and leave the seats for the women and children," Rachel replied firmly.

Lifting his eyes to Rachel, a slow grin spread across Georgy's face. She smiled back, acknowledging the truth behind her words. Georgy and Ion would soon be men and needed to start acting like it. The two older boys exchanged glances then. Young shoulders shifted back slightly. Even the troubled look on Ion's face relaxed a bit then. Rachel could not help but wish, however, that they were not in such a mad rush to grow up.

Patrick stood beside Sam as they surveyed the crowd gathered in the schoolhouse. The meeting had progressed fairly well so far. Wagon Master Emilio Johnston was answering most of the questions, Sam and Patrick replying to some of them. The hand of a young man went up, from the back of the crowded room. Beside him stood an equally young woman who apparently had been unable to find a place to sit. Patrick was glad that at least he could report that not only had Ion and Georgy willingly stood at the back in order to make room for the women and children, Johnny also had chosen to stand up. He wore a rather smug smile as he stood with the men.

"Toby," Emilio called out, acknowledging the young man who had come with the group of wagons that had just arrived in Timberton with him.

"For those of you who haven't met us, I'm Toby Shaleman and this is my wife Annette. We traveled on a little further west than Timberton, but just couldn't make a go of it and decided to give up and return East with Mr. Johnston here. But when we got here—well you people have a settlement here. And we can't help but wonder why you want to leave. Now, my question is this: is there a place here for my wife and me to start over again?"

Emilio turned and eyed Sam and Patrick questioningly. Sam in turn eyed

Patrick. Clearing his throat, Patrick nodded, calling out, "Aye, there's lot's o'land and perhaps ye might even make a deal with semeone who's planning to return East and simply take over their cabin for thim in exchange for what they might need for traveling along the trail."

"That would be me!" called out a deep voice in the crowd. Every set of eyes shifted over to Roger Baker. "I'm fixin' to go back home. If you want the land I've staked out and the cabin I built in exchange for your wagon and team, then it's a deal. My wagon is just about ready to fall apart. It'll serve you here in Timberton. But it wouldn't make it along the trail back to the East. I'm figuring that your team of horses is likely in better shape than mine is, or else you wouldn't be in this here wagon train to begin with. Is it a deal?"

Toby grinned and glanced down at Annette who smiled back and nodded. Turning back to Roger, he called out excitedly, "It's a deal, sir!"

It was then that eyes began shifting from face to face, a low murmur of voices rumbling out. It had finally begun. People were taking sides and either pulling up stakes, or deciding to stay permanently. Finally the wagon master held up his hands to silence the crowd. "Now, it doesn't make much difference to me if you go or stay. Mostly I'm just heading back in order to lead another wagon train out here. You can come with me or not. But I'm leaving in two days whether any or all of you come with me. But I would like a tentative headcount as to who plans to come with me. Now if you're thinking of coming, lift up your hand now—just the head of each household."

Again a low murmur sounded out as family members conferred with one another and neighbor with neighbor. The first hand that went in the air seemed almost timid. But the second one was more forceful. Patrick blinked and then stared hard as Angela Stone lifted her hand. Her face was as pale as he had ever seen it. She was all the way across the room from him, so he could not speak with her concerning her decision. Her jaws appeared to be gripped tightly together, pursing her lips even beyond what was normal for her in one of her fits of annoyance. He cocked his head as he shifted his gaze, a slow grin growing on his lips as he studied Matthew Bon-Hemmer, who stood a few feet from where Angela was sitting. Utter shock was painted on his normally slightly amused, slightly smug face as he stared openly at the woman.

Sam leaned over, murmuring in Patrick's ear, "Looks like Matthew is in a—what's that word he likes to use—quandary."

Patrick did his best not to grin, but was finding it too difficult after all. "Aye, 'e is in a quandary all right."

"Any one else planning to come with me?" Emilio called out. "Thank you. You may lower your hands. Well folks, by my count there's only half a dozen of you who plan to pull up stakes." Turning to face Sam, he added in a chuckle, "Well Sheriff, it looks like you've got a town full of people who plan to stay."

Sam grinned and nodded. "Looks that that way, Emilio." As his eyes drifted back over the crowd, he suddenly called out, "I'd say that Timberton is here to stay!"

Instantly a cheer sounded out, laughter and smiles replacing frowns and muttering. As Patrick studied face after face, it seemed to him that there were really only two people in the entire schoolhouse who did not look relieved: Angela Stone and Matthew Bon-Hemmer.

Rachel struggled to her feet from where she was sitting in her rocking chair at the sound of her approaching family. She swallowed, waiting for them to enter the cabin and tell her the news if they would be staying or moving on. They began hurrying inside, their eyes sparkling. Rachel found herself wanting to hope, but not knowing if she dared. "Well?" she asked the moment Patrick stepped inside.

"Only a few families—"

"Want to stay?" she cut in, unable to hold it back even for a moment. Clear disappointment rang in her tone, though she had tried to keep it out of her voice.

His eyes twinkled. "Want to go," he added softly.

"What?" The question tore from her. "Oh, truly Patrick?"

He nodded and stepped over to her, slipping his arms around her. She squeezed him with all of her might. "We're home?" she asked, barely able to get the words out. "We're really home Patrick? Home to stay?"

"Home to stay," he murmured. He held her for some moments before easing back and gently guiding her back to her rocking chair. "I think ye need to be sitting down," he added.

"Oh Patrick, I've been sitting down all evening." She paused then, studying his face closely. "There's more," she murmured. "What is it you aren't telling me?"

It was Johnny who piped up them, saying in a surprised sort of tone, "Miss Stone is going back East."

"What? Why?" Rachel asked, allowing Patrick to help ease her back down onto her rocking chair.

"I don't know," Johnny admitted. "I thought she was starting to like us—a little anyway."

Shifting her gaze over to Ion, Rachel asked, "What about the O'Brins? Are they leaving?"

Ion lifted his shoulders slightly. "Mr. O'Brin didn't raise his hand with the rest who are leaving," he replied quietly."

"Well that's a good sign," Rachel replied. When Ion nodded, Rachel asked, "What about the others? Who else is leaving?"

"Ol' man Baker," Georgy called out. Jed immediately slapped the boy's arm with his hat. "Well," Georgy defended himself, "his name is Baker, and he's old."

"He ain't neither. Why he's only in his sixties if he's a day."

"That's old!"

Rachel was eying Georgy critically, waiting for the two to silence themselves. When they did, Rachel reproved him, insisting, "Whatever Mr. Baker's age is, you've been rude, Georgy. You don't call anyone old man or old woman for that matter. You show respect to your elders!"

"Yes ma'am," Georgy sighed. "Well anyway," he added, again warming up to his news, "he traded his homestead to a couple for their wagon and team. I guess he'd had enough of living in the same town as his grandson Keith and decided to leave!"

Rachel glanced at Patrick, waiting for an explanation. "A young couple by the name of Shaleman will be taking over Mr. Baker's farm—Toby and Annette. I didn't get to talk to thim for viry long, bit long enough to know thit they'll be joining us for church ivery Sunday."

Rachel smiled at the good news. When she would have questioned her family further, Angela stepped into the cabin. Suddenly everyone fell silent, each set of eyes turning to her. Her eyes were red and she had made no attempt to disguise the fact that she had been crying. "Angela?" Rachel said softly. "Are you leaving us?" When the woman nodded, Rachel asked, "But why? I thought you liked it here with us. I thought—" She paused, stunned over the emotion that swept over her at the thought of the woman leaving. "I thought we were your family."

For once the uppity woman did not try to convince everyone that she was far superior to all of them put together and had no desire to be part of such a low class family. For once she had no comment at all. A tear slipped down her cheek. Rachel reached out her hand to the woman. And for the first time, Angela actually accepted it, slipping her hand into Rachel's.

"I'm not who I pretend to be," she finally said, still holding Rachel's hand, almost as if a life preserver. Before I came out West, I was nothing but a servant—a maid. Miss Sharon—Miss Sharon Joon—yes the Boston Joons— was my employer." Rachel flinched over that piece of information. She knew Sharon Joon personally, though the woman was her mother's age, rather than Rachel's. In all likelihood, Rachel had even met Angela before in the Joon mansion, though clearly neither had made any connection with whatever random memory they might have over the chance meeting.

Angela sighed, continuing quietly with her account. "If you had known Miss Sharon, you'd understand what I mean when I say that I learned to speak and conduct myself with the finery of the epitome of genteelness. Miss Sharon would allow nothing less. I had her mannerisms down so well, in fact, I convinced myself that I could pass myself off as a lady of high birth, rather than as a foundling snatched from the orphanage and trained as a maid to such a lady. I saved my money. And whenever Miss Sharon chose to donate her gowns and other finery to charity, I chose myself as the recipient, since she gave the decision entirely over to me. Was I not a charity case after all? Once I finally owned enough possessions to pass myself off as a lady born to means, I purchased my passage on a wagon train, hoping to pass myself off as the lady I appeared to be. I planned to catch the eye of a rich gentleman out West and marry him. So far from civilization, who would ever know, after all, that I was a mere maid—a servant?"

The room was so silent now Rachel hardly dared to breath. "I soon learned," Angela continued, rolling her eyes and shaking her head slightly, "that it was not the wealthy who made their way out West, but the hardy. The hardy had no interest in my fine manners. And I had no interest in their lack of manners. The rare wealthy travelers I met were all married or promised. This was my last hope—this vulgar Timberton. And now," she added, returning her gaze to Rachel, the light having gone completely out of her eyes, "I shall return to Miss Sharon and beg her for a position. Likely she has no opening for a lady in waiting. But her kitchen staff is constantly changing. No one enjoys working for her cook, nor for her housekeeper. I can almost certainly obtain a job as a kitchen maid. And I can make it work. Back in the orphanage I was in charge of the kitchen during my teen years, just before Miss Sharon rescued me."

Rachel squeezed her hand. "If there were a way for you to stay in Timberton, would you?" Suddenly across her mind swept images she had paid little attention to. But now they screamed out to be noticed. It had been no coincidence that whenever Matthew Bon-Hemmer visited, Angela was dressed in one of her loveliest dresses. Nor had it been mere chance that it was Angela who always placed the cup of coffee in front of the man. Rachel eyed her closely, knowingly.

Angela's stare was just as knowing. Silent communication passed between the two. "There is only one way I know," she murmured firmly. "And nothing has come of it, nor likely shall. Two days remain for something to open up. And then if all remains unchanged, I will leave."

"But you'd stay if the circumstances changed?" Rachel persisted, firmness in her own tone.

Angela looked hard at Rachel, strength that Rachel had been unaware existed boring near holes into Rachel from that look. "I would stay."

Rachel smiled then and reached her other hand out, patting the hand she held as if in a pact. "Then circumstances will change, madam. Circumstances will change."

"Ah Rachel," Patrick sighed, holding her close after blowing out the flame from the kerosene lamp beside the bed. As she snuggled into his arms, he chuckled quietly. "Ye kinnot be thinking o' match-making."

"And why not? You yourself said that Matthew looked miserable when he learned that Angela was leaving."

"And ye think 'e would be less miserable if 'e married the woman? Lassie! Think what ye're saying. Ye know better than most 'ow difficult she kin be."

"But apparently the other women he's met haven't made much of an impression on him. It's only Angela's leaving that seems to have upset him."

Patrick sighed a long sigh, causing Rachel to giggle. He simply turned his head and kissed her forehead. "Well, we'll know in two days time," he murmured. "Now, lassie, where's m'kiss?"

"Where it always is, sir, just waiting for you."

All thoughts of Angela and Matthew drifted from his mind as Patrick pressed his lips against Rachel's. And by her eager response, he was certain that he alone was filling her thoughts.

The next day began as every day normally did, even though these were suddenly not normal days at all. Everyone had decided that Angela would open school as usual, though with the thought of sending her students home early after bidding them farewell. Patrick had planned to go over to Matthew's store to have a talk with him, but the man showed up at the O'Riley door unannounced shortly after Angela had left for school. Patrick could see no alternative but to include Jed and Rachel in on the talk he had planned to have in private with the man. By the look in the Matthew's eyes, Patrick guessed that he was just as miserable as he had appeared to be the evening before. It was no coincidence that he had showed up at the home where Angela lived.

As the four sat around the table, Matthew toyed with his coffee cup. "I didn't know there'd be school today," he murmured.

Patrick glanced over at Rachel, who was smiling primly. "Yes," she replied, in an especially proper tone. "We all thought it best to let Angela have one last day with the children."

Matthew tore his eyes from his cup and stared painfully at Rachel. "So it's certain? She really is leaving?"

Rachel slid her eyes over to Patrick and waited for him to reply. Rolling his eyes at her, he allowed one side of his mouth to inch upward. "Well," he said simply, "not too much is certain in this life, beyond God's Word, thit is."

Matthew swung a surprised look over at him. "Meaning?"

Clearing his throat, he decided that there was not enough time left to be gentle. "What is it thit's stopping ye frim marrying the lassie?" Matthew's eyes opened wide. "'Tis clear to all of us—except to Angela 'erself—thit ye don't want 'er to leave. Hiv ye considered asking 'er to stay?"

He shook his head slowly. "No. I never thought of that. Do you think it'd make a difference in her decision?"

Jed chuckled then, drawing everyone's attention to himself. "Well son," he said in a grandfatherly tone of voice, "there's only one way to find out. You're just gonna have to ask her yourself. What do you have to lose? Either it makes a difference and she stays or else it doesn't make a difference and she leaves. What do you have to lose?"

"But," Rachel cut in, "not in front of anyone."

Matthew turned amused eyes upon her. "That much I know," he murmured. "I see it now," he chuckled. "A conspiracy. Just what has Miss Stone said?" No one attempted to answer him. But he no longer looked miserable. "What time is school dismissed?"

Georgy slapped himself in the forehead as he and the other O'Riley children walked home from school. Ion chuckled in the dark manner he often used when making sport of Georgy, and simply said, "You'll get used to it."

Georgy turned puzzled eyes upon the boy, asking, "Get used to what?"

"Having a thought."

Punching Ion in the shoulder, Georgy pushed out his breath in irritation. "I've had thoughts before," he muttered. Shaking himself, he added, "We forgot to bring Rachel's books with us. The last thing she said this morning was, 'Don't forget to bring my books home. I don't want them sitting in an empty schoolhouse all summer.'"

Ion frowned and paused in his step, causing the other three to also stop walking. "Here," he said to Johnny, thrusting his lunch tin, tablet and poetry book into Johnny's arms. "You and Lizzy go on home. Georgy and I'll go after Rachel's books."

Georgy handed his tin and tablet over to Elizabeth and turned back to the schoolhouse with Ion, leaving the other two to continue on to the O'Riley cabin without them. "Miss Stone sure looked sad when she told us all goodbye," Georgy murmured.

Ion nodded. "Yeah she did. I wonder why. I mean, she hasn't tried to keep it a secret that she hates being a teacher."

Georgy nodded in thought. "You think she might be thinking that she's going to miss our family when she goes back East?"

Ion rolled his eyes. "Is that what you think?"

Georgy chewed on the corner of his mouth, wondering whether or not to admit the truth. "Well, I think it's possible. I mean," he added with a sudden grin, "we're a great family! Why wouldn't she miss us?"

"She hates us," Ion grumbled. "That's why."

"Naw—I mean no she don't—doesn't hate us. She just wants us to think it."

Ion turned a thoughtful expression on Georgy. Georgy grinned, relishing the moment. He rarely made the boy think hard about anything except how to win an argument. Ion's expression softened as he nodded. "I think you're right. It doesn't hurt as much to be thrown away if nobody knows you care one way or the other."

Georgy blinked. He had not actually gone that deep into his idea, having only just thought of it. But it sounded right. And he found himself feeling a little sorry for the irritable woman. "You think that's why she's—uh—disagreeable?"

Ion chuckled quietly. "Partly. But, nobody can be that disagreeable without meaning at least some of it."

Georgy grinned. Glancing at the schoolhouse as they topped the hill, he stared in surprise at the buggy in front of it. "Ain't—Isn't that Matthew's buggy?"

Ion snorted. "Nobody else in Timberton has a buggy, Georgy. You know that."

"Well, what's he doing at the schoolhouse?"

"You think I know?"

"Well," Georgy grumbled, "you want everybody to think you know everything."

Ion slid his gaze over to Georgy, eying him in silence long enough for Georgy to grow nervous enough to turn and eye him. A smug expression rested on the boy's face as he studied Georgy. "That's only because I usually do."

Georgy rolled his eyes and fell silent. In his private imagination, he often saw scene after scene of these sorts of arguments. But always, it was Georgy himself who got in the last word. He sighed, wishing that reality could be a little more like the world he imagined. But he was finding it steadily more difficult to win arguments of logic with Ion. Even Johnny was getting better at it, learning a lot from Ion's victories over Georgy in their verbal jousting. He grinned, assured that whether he won or lost, he still had more fun in the process than the other two put together. He chuckled over the idea, which brought a sudden puzzled expression to Ion's face.

They fell silent as they neared the schoolhouse. No one was in sight, all of the children having hurried home after Angela had dismissed them for the summer. Just as they were about to enter, Ion's arm shot out, blocking the way. Georgy turned to him in surprise. Ion lifted his finger to his lips and jerked his head in a sideways nod, indicating inside the schoolhouse. It was only then that Georgy began paying attention to the conversation going on. Peering inside, he and Ion both studied the two occupants. Georgy wondered over the look on Matthew's face. It seemed almost one of pain. The two were studying each other too intently to notice Georgy and Ion.

"But why won't you consider staying in Timberton?" Matthew asked, a note of frustration in his voice. His normal self-assurance stance was not as visible as usual. Obviously this was not the first time he had asked her this question.

Angela studied him with clenched jaws. The coolness of her expression should have sent him away. Georgy wondered why the man lingered when she clearly wanted him to leave. Something in her eyes, however seemed to deny her otherwise disdainful expression. Georgy was not certain what label to give it. Certainly it could not be what it appeared to him, knowing Angela the way he did. However, if he had not known her for being a woman who wanted and needed no one, he would have called it longing that sparkled from her eyes.

"Boston is my home," she said in a clipped tone of dismissal.

"This is your home now!" Matthew shot back, not making any attempt whatsoever in disguising his frustration. Georgy almost expected him to reach out and pull out his hair or hit his head against one of the logs in the wall. The look on his face made it only too clear that he was at the end of his rope.

Angela, except for the look in her eyes, appeared the epitome of control as she pursed her lips and shook her head. She attempted to roll her eyes, but the look fell short of its usual affect because of the unshielded look of pain in her eyes. "This stagnant, backwater town is hardly my home!"

"But the O'Rileys—they're your family! You can't just run out on them!"

"They are most certainly not my family!" she cried out.

Georgy and Ion glanced at each other. If Georgy's expression matched that of Ion's, then he bore a more shocked look on his face than he ever had before. If Ion had not reacted as he had, Georgy could have perhaps convinced himself that he had not heard an actual sob in the woman's voice. But Ion had clearly heard it too. As if on cue, they both turned back to the couple. A tear was slipping down Angela's cheek.

"But they are," Matthew replied in a soften tone. Clearly he too had heard that sob that denied her words. "Miss Stone, they love you. Don't you know it's breaking their hearts to see you leave, knowing that they can't stop you?" He swallowed and glanced down at the floor.

The woman's stare softened as she studied the man's bowed head. "And if they could stop me from leaving," she murmured, "what would their intentions be?"

Matthew swallowed and slowly raised his head, meeting her gaze. "Well," he began, but fell silent. Again he swallowed, looking so nervous that Georgy wondered how he was managing to remain standing. Again Georgy slid his eyes over to Ion who was likewise looking at him, a knowing look in his eyes. One side of Georgy's mouth crept upward, suddenly glad that they had forgotten Rachel's books until then. He and Ion would not have missed seeing this for all the treats in Rachel's kitchen. Even if Johnny ate up all of their portion, he would not trade places with the boy.

"Miss Stone," Matthew murmured, "I'm sure—I know—that your family wants you to stay. Give them time to work out a solution. They need time."

The cold look was nowhere to be seen on the woman's face, however she did not appear completely at ease either. Wariness mingled with knowing in a way that made Georgy wonder just what the woman was thinking. It was only too clear what Matthew was thinking. But for the life of him, he could not tell what she was. He wondered if Matthew was just as uncertain. He also wondered if Georgy himself would be so uncertain when it came time for him to start courting. Would it be just as puzzling to him what the girl was thinking?

"They have until tomorrow," she said simply.

"Then, you won't even consider staying?" he said quietly, the rest of hope draining from his face.

"If I had a reason to consider staying, certainly I would. But you've given me none. What else am I to do, sir?"

As if sudden understanding coursed through him, he smiled. This time it was his normal self-assured look that crept into his eyes. "Perhaps you could marry and set up your own home."

She met his gaze with such boldness, Georgy wondered. He was certain that women were not supposed to be bold. He slowly shook his head, recalling that Rachel was bold with Patrick. "Perhaps," Angela replied. "But then again, there are far more such proposals to choose from back in civilization. You've given me no reason to change my mind."

Matthew was smiling in earnest now. Suddenly he lowered himself to one knee and gently took hold of Angela's hand. "If you would do me the honor of becoming my wife, Miss Stone, I would be the happiest man in Timberton."

Georgy blinked in surprise when the woman did not immediately agree. She drew in a deep breath and seemed to ponder his words. Finally she said in a tone that was not drenched in the expected love-smitten kind of voice, "Well, that is certainly true. I would make you the happiest man in Timberton. But that isn't saying much."

Matthew chuckled, clearly captivated by the woman's self-assurance. "True. Let me put it another way. If you were to become my wife, I'd be the happiest man in all of Boston and New York City put together. And you and I both know how happy Bostonians and New Yorkers are."

The corner of her mouth twitched upward, amusement sparkling in her eyes. "Indeed," she said in her normal clipped tone.

Matthew leaned down and softly kissed her fingers he was still grasping. When he lifted his head, he met her gaze once again. In that moment of time, the merriment had left both of their faces, being replaced with such serious expressions Georgy could hardly attach a name to the emotions that prompted such looks. Angela gently tugged her hand from his and turned, stepping over to the window near her desk. The look of pain that shot across Matthew's face even tore into Georgy as he studied the crestfallen man rising to his feet. "Mr. Bon-hemmer," Angela said in a tone that lacked it's normal biting quality. "Now that I've actually received a proposal for marriage, I am only just now realizing that I can't go through with such deception. I came out West for the sole purpose of finding a rich young gentleman to marry me. Had it been some cad who offered to marry me, perhaps I could have continued on with the lie. But you are unworthy of living the lie I would bring with me into marriage. I'm not a lady of high birth. I have no idea who my family is. I was left at an orphanage when I was only two. I grew up there. And when I left, it was to be in the employ of a Miss Sharon Joon. I was her servant, sir."

"I already know that," Matthew replied softly, stepping over to her, though her back still faced him. "Tony and Eleanor Thomas told me your story months ago. I've always known who you are." It was then that Angela turned back around, her mouth hanging slightly open in wonder as she searched his face. He smiled softly at her. "They don't go around telling your business to everyone. But the fact that you've been with them since leaving Boston, until moving in with the O'Rileys—well, did you forget that they know who you are?"

"Does everyone know?" she whispered.

He grinned and gently slipped his hands to her upper arms. "Does it matter?"

She drew in her breath. "Well, if you want the truth—yes, it does matter to me."

He suddenly began laughing. She studied him, curiosity sparkling from her eyes. "You're perfect," he finally said. "Miss Stone—Angela—don't you know that you've made me fall in love with you—for who you are. I turned my back on my birthright and my culture, only to find it all rolled up in you in this uncivilized piece of earth called Timberton. And that's when I realized that it wasn't what I was born to that I was turning my back on. It's just that until I met you, it never meant anything to me. But now it all means something to me, because it's who you are. You might not have been born to it, but it's still who you are. And I love you Angela. Will you marry me?"

Nodding, she finally murmured, "Yes."

Lowering his head, he laid his lips on hers. Ion punched Georgy in the arm and jerked his head back slightly. Georgy frowned in disappointment, but did as Ion silently ordered anyway. Together they stepped away from the doorway and headed across the schoolyard and up the hill toward home. "I guess we'll have to come back later for Rachel's books."

Ion chuckled. "Miss Stone would've killed us if she'd found us listening."

Georgy began laughing as well as he thought about her rage if she had known. "So, who's going to tell Rachel that they're getting married?"

Ion shrugged. "We better let Miss Stone do the telling. Otherwise we'll have to admit that we were eavesdropping. And then both Rachel and Miss Stone would be mad at us."

Georgy nodded over the logic. "You're right. Ion?" he asked, glancing over at the boy, "I don't think I could ever ask a woman to marry me."

"I could," Ion sighed back. Georgy grinned, knowing that images of Mary O'Brin were now coursing through Ion's mind.

Taking off running, Georgy called back over his shoulder, "I forgot! Rachel said she'd have a cinnamon roll waiting for us after school! Let's get home before Johnny and Gramps eats it all up!"

Chapter 3

As Rachel reclined in bed, holding her newborn daughter, Patrick stepped into the bedroom. The rest of the household had been strictly forbidden from entering. Doctor Morrison had insisted that they needed to remain outside until invited back into the cabin. Rachel lifted her eyes and studied Patrick's face. He simply stood there, staring at the two of them, a look of wonder on his face.

"Well come on, Papa." she murmured, "Come meet Patricia O'Riley." Hearing the tiny girl's name spoken out loud brought a smile to both of them.

Stepping over to the bed, Patrick lowered himself down onto the edge and reached over to pull back the light blanket from the baby's face. Rachel was torn between gazing down at the sleeping babe and memorizing Patrick's face as he studied his little girl. He had seen her only moments after she was born, but this was the first time seeing her since Sarah had cleaned her up. Shifting her arms, Rachel asked gently, "Do you want to hold her?"

Patrick's eyes darted to Rachel's face. Something akin to fear rested there. "Oh—I—I've never 'eld a newborn in m'life, Rachel."

She smiled, thinking about the tremendous amount of courage that rested in this man, and yet now he sat there, nervous about holding his own daughter. "Don't you think it's time you did?" she asked gently, trying to keep the amusement out of her voice. By the knowing look in his eyes, she realized that she had not fooled him.

Chuckling then, he leaned down and kissed her cheek. Leaning back up, his hand began caressing that cheek. "Aye," he murmured back. "'Tis time."

Together they managed to position the babe into his arms. She looked all the tinier. The man's face grew tender as he concentrated all of his attention on her. "Good morning Pattie, m'lass. I'm yeer Papa."

Rachel bit down on her trembling lower lip as she studied the big man and the tiny girl. Without consciously thinking to do so, she lifted her hand to cradle Patrick's arm that held Pattie. He had always looked kingly to her, the way he held himself and walked with his head up, unashamed of being the man he was. He was not prideful in his carriage, simply content in being who he was, no matter what anyone else might think. But as she studied him now, she saw something new. Pattie was not their first child, but she was the first one they got to hold from birth. Even Christine had not been held. She had been born too soon and Patrick had insisted that Rachel not even see her. But here was Pattie, fully developed into a tiny baby girl, being held by her parents for the first time ever, peacefully sleeping in her daddy's arms.

Patrick's eyes slid over to meet Rachel's. Loosening one arm from around the baby, Patrick lifted his hand to Rachel's face and gently brushed at her falling tears. "Ah Lassie," he said in a tone filled with emotions of his own, "I've never felt quite like this b'fore."

Rachel nodded, unable to get words past her throat. She noticed that Patrick's eyes were sparkling with joyful tears themselves. It was then that she suddenly recalled the first time she had looked at this face that had grown so dear to her. Try as she might, she simply could not bring even the memory of the horror she had felt on that day when she had learned that he—an Irishman—and a preacher at that—was now her father's partner and would spend the entire trip to Oregon with her family.

"And what's bringing that far off look, Rachel?" he asked softly.

Slipping her hand over his that was still resting alongside her cheek, she admitted, "I was thinking about how you and I met."

He chuckled. "Aye," he sighed. "What do ye suppose thit either of us would've thought if we could've looked into the future only two short years later to see us 'olding our viry own daughter."

She giggled and slowly shook her head. "Dear oh dear," she sighed. "I think I would've found a stout tree with a high branch."

Cocking his head, he asked in merry bewilderment. "What would ye hiv done with this tree?"

Meeting his gaze steadily, she replied in a firm tone, "Why, I would've hanged myself."

Throwing his head back, Patrick laughed until he shook all over. The babe in his arms stirred then, bringing both of their attentions back to her. In wonder they watched as the tiny eyelids opened and dark eyes looked up at her father. "Ah Pattie m'love," Patrick said softly, "do ye know thit Jesus loves ye so mich 'E died for ye and came back to life because 'Is sacrifice was acceptable? 'E paid for yeer sins, lassie. And yeer mamma and I are going to tell ye about 'Im ivery day for the rist of yeer life. We want to spend eternity with ye, lassie. And we're on our way to Heaven. We want ye to come too."

Rachel sobbed quietly then and squeezed Patrick's hand. Gently he lowered the baby back into Rachel's arms and then gently gathered up the two of them into his. As he held them, he softly prayed. "Lord, Rachel and I thank ye so mich for giving Pattie to us to raise for yeer honor and glory. We commit to teaching her about ye. We will do all in our power to get 'er ready for Heaven. We ask thit ye do what we kinnot, even if we went to Hell itself for 'er: Please give 'er new birth, bringing 'er into yeer own family as a child o'God.

May she b'come a Christian as a young child, thit 'er walk with ye may be all the sweeter for not hiving walked in the path o'sin. May she b'come what ye gave 'er life to b'come. Accomplish yeer purpose in 'er, we ask. And Lord, we thank ye for our older children too and continue to ask ye to save thim thit aren't yet saved. Thank ye for showing the truth of the gospel to Georgy. Oh thit Ion and Lizzie, Johnny and Annie will come to know the truth also. And Jed too. And also Angela. Ye hiv truly blessed this family, especially so today. Thank ye for our dear Pattie. Lord," he added almost hesitantly. "Please continue to watch over our wee Christine. We love 'er so! And we're looking forward to being with 'er in Heaven and holding 'er. Thank ye for Rachel, the love of m'life, second only to ye yeerself, Lord. And now Lord, 'elp the children as they come in to meet their new sister—'elp thim not to get overly rambunctious." When Rachel giggled over that request, Patrick cleared his throat and then continued. "Lord, 'elp me not to be too mich in the way o'being overly protective over this wee one." Amusement colored his voice as he spoke these last words. "In Jesus name, amen."

Johnny pushed through the crowd of O'Riley's gathered around Rachel and the baby. Smiles were on every face. Patrick hovered in a way he had never seen him do before, keeping first one hand on Georgy's shoulder, and then one on Ion's. The next moment, he was clapping Jed on the back in camaraderie. Gently patting Lizzie on the back, Patrick then caught Annie in his arms just as she was making a beeline to the bed.

Georgy was the first to step close enough to the bed to examine Pattie. He reached over a tentative hand and in a surprisingly soft manner traced the baby's cheek with his finger. "Hi Pattie. This is your big brother talking to you. Now you got another big brother, Ion, but he's younger than me—than I am," he hastily corrected, darting his glance over to Rachel. When she smiled and nodded over his corrected grammar, he turned back and continued talking to the baby. The rest of his words were lost on Johnnie as he pondered the idea that it was only Georgy and Ion who were Pattie's big brothers. He had not really considered the matter before, but as Rachel's brother that made him Pattie's uncle, not brother. Until that moment, it had been a matter of fact, but nothing more.

"Now," Georgy was continuing speaking, "I'm going to be a famous doctor someday. You can grow up and be my nurse—"

"She's going to grow up to be my secretary," Ion cut in. "I'll write books that make it on the best seller list and she'll copy my manuscripts for me in fine print so I can give them to the editor—"

"You hear that, Pattie?" Georgy chuckled. "You just got Mary's job!"

"Georgy!" Ion grumbled.

"All right," Patrick called out before anything more could come of the exchange. "It's Lizzy's turn." As Georgy stepped away from the side of the bed, Patrick nudged Elizabeth's shoulder, directing her to the bed.

Easing down on the edge of the bed, Elizabeth met Rachel's gaze and smiled. "She's beautiful, Rachel! I never seen a baby with red hair before!" Returning her attention to Pattie, she gently tickled her under the chin. The baby squirmed and seemed to enjoy the attention. Her eyes were open, as if trying to take everything in. "You're just perfect," Elizabeth murmured. "Someday I'm going to grow up and have perfect babies just like you. And I'll name them all Georgy-don't." Her giggle ended in Georgy cuffing her on the shoulder.

Instantly Patrick's hand latched onto Georgy's shoulder, drawing him back away from the bed. "Laddie," he murmured, "ye mist be careful around the wee one—" Georgy grinned good-naturedly, but broke out into laughter as Patrick, with dancing eyes, added, "and around Pattie too."

Elizabeth, happily unaware of the fact that Patrick was teasing her, returned her attention to the baby. "Well, Pattie, at least Georgy's older now. When I got borned, he was still little—only two and a half. He won't pull your hair like he did mine. He knows better than that now. Besides, he knows if he ever did that, he'd have the whole family to answer to."

Johnny grinned over her words. They were certainly true. He himself would challenge Georgy for doing such a thing, even if Georgy did tower over him.

Without having to be told that her time was over, Elizabeth stood up and made room for the next family member to meet Pattie. This time it was Jed who stepped up and leaned down to study the faces of mother and daughter. Finally he straightened back up and said, "She's a keeper." Everyone laughed at that. Johnny met Jed's sparkling eyes as he stepped away from the bed and stood beside Johnny, allowing Ion to meet the baby. Johnny rolled his eyes at the older man, knowing that already Jed would lay down his life for his newest granddaughter. Jed clapped Johnny on the back and seemed to be enjoying himself more than ever.

Ion crouched down beside the bed and got his face on the same level as Pattie's. A softened sparkle shone from his eyes. "I never saw a baby this little before," he murmured. Hesitantly he lifted his hand. Glancing over at Rachel, he paused. When she nodded, smiling gently at him, he softly ran his fingers over the red hair that covered the tiny head. He said nothing more, but simply studied her for several moments. Rising to his feet, he stepped back to make room for the next in line. Angela nudged Johnny, but he nodded to her, saying quietly, "You can go first."

Her eyes narrowed slightly, as if she could see through him, but then she turned and stepped up to the bed. Easing herself down onto the bed, she gazed down at the baby, her face suddenly softening. It did that often any more, ever since Matthew Bon-Hemmer had asked her to marry him. But it never lasted for long, Johnny reminded himself, one side of his mouth creeping up wryly.

"Would you like to hold her?" Rachel asked.

Georgy piped up then, complaining, "But you didn't let me hold her!"

"Laddie," Patrick murmured, his hand still resting on the boy's shoulder. "This is a time of celebration. Don't ruin it."

Georgy grinned and shrugged. "All right, Pat. Besides, I don't know how to hold a baby."

"This we know," Patrick chuckled. "Ye'll each get yeer lessons in holding 'er, bit not today. All right laddie?"

Georgy nodded. Suddenly he grew serious and whispered so loudly everyone could hear him as clearly as if he had spoken in a normal tone of voice, "Do you think Miss Stone knows how to hold a baby?"

Angela turned and eyed Georgy, giving him the look that all of her students knew only too well. It silenced Georgy completely. Turning back to Rachel and the baby, she replied to Georgy in a snippety sort of tone, "I'll have you know that I've held every one of the Joon children only moments after they were born."

"Miss Sharon?" Georgy asked. "But Patrick," he murmured, "don't Miss mean not married?"

"Miss Sharon is Mrs. Tobias Joon, wife of the most notable Tobias Joon, and mother of five equally notably distinguished children. Is that sufficient information, Mr. Northwood?" she asked sarcastically.

Georgy lifted his shoulders and met Patrick's amused gaze. "Yes ma'am," he replied, unable to keep a slow grin from rising to his lips. "I s'pect—expect it's fine for you to hold Pattie."

"Thank you!" Angela called out in a mocking form of grandeur. Reaching over, she expertly lifted Pattie from Rachel's arms. As Johnny watched, he could find no fault in her mannerism. Even Angela held Pattie as if she were a rare treasure. "Now," she said simply, firmly but not gruffly, "I am your Aunt Angela—Aunt Angie to you."

"Are you our aunt too?" Georgy called out. Johnny swallowed quickly at the look of horror that sprang to Angela's face.

Clearing her throat and lifting her chin slightly, as if she had been a queen and chose to rise to the occasion, detestable as it was, she met Georgy's gaze. "You are Pattie's brother, are you not?"

"Yes ma'am," Georgy replied directly, eying her with his clear gaze, never one to put on airs.

"Then I must be your aunt too."

"Aunt Angie?" he cried out with a grin.

The room went instantly silent. Johnny eyed Elizabeth, who had followed little of the conversation. She turned to him, questions in her eyes. He was usually the only one of the children who thought to repeat conversations for her slowly enough for her to understand. He mouthed the word, "later," as he nodded in promise. She nodded back, knowing his word was good.

"Of course," Angela replied, eying Georgy with such strength that most would have cringed, though Georgy did not. He simply stood there, waiting for her to finish, as her words sounded unfinished.

"But?" Georgy prompted.

Angela simply shrugged indifferently and turned her attention back to Pattie, replying as if in mere afterthought, "Oh, it's simply only a nickname small children use. But I suspect that backward, pioneer sort, don't know that, so no one would know if you used the name."

Johnny frowned in thought, allowing his eyes to drift from face to face, puzzling over the words. Was Angela honestly trying to keep them from embarrassing themselves? But then, he had heard adults use the nickname of Angie. And they were not backward pioneers, as Angela put it. He puzzled over the laughter dancing from Patrick's eyes. Even Rachel seemed highly amused. Ion wore a perturbed expression and rolled his eyes at Georgy. Only then did Georgy seem to understand. His jaw dropped as he and Ion exchanged stares. Johnny was still uncertain just what was going on. Likely he was not going to figure it out on his own. And it was never certain if Georgy and Ion would explain when he missed the meaning of a joke.

"Well," Georgy finally sighed out, sounding serious, though his eyes were dancing. "I guess we grown children could just call you Aunt Anj." Angela's head whirled around again to stare in renewed horror at Georgy. "But," he sighed out, "how about if we just call you Auntie Angela—" At the relieved look that dashed to Angela's face, Georgy added, "And Uncle Matt."

"Matt?" Angela cried out in shock.

Patrick could apparently not hold back his laughter for another minute. Nudging Georgy again, he chuckled, "Matthew, lad. Uncle Matthew."

Georgy shrugged good-naturedly, his eyes still sparkling. "If you say so, Pat," he replied in an innocent sounding tone.

As Johnny puzzled over it, waiting for his turn to go up to meet Pattie, Angela expertly patted the baby, even getting a gurgled cooing to come from her. "Honestly Rachel," she began in her normal uppity tone, "you really should have made the children wash their hands before coming in here. But, this being your first baby, no one can expect you to know such things."

Rachel met Johnny's eyes, rolling her own. Johnny grinned and shrugged. Finally Angela returned the baby to Rachel's arms, making room for Johnny to go to her. As he neared her, he was surprised by the amount of feelings that were suddenly coursing through him. He sat down beside Rachel and gently touched Pattie's tiny hand. "She's got four fingers and a thumb!" Everyone burst out laughing, startling the baby. "Don't scare her!" Johnny called out the moment she flinched at the sound.

"Don't worry, Pattie," Georgy called out, though quietly, "your Uncle Johnny will protect you." Johnny grinned and studied the little face in front of him. "She looks a lot like Pat," he said. "But Rachel, part of her looks like Cousin Courtney, doesn't she?"

Rachel lowered her eyes to Pattie and nodded in thought. "Why, she does, doesn't she? I hadn't noticed before, but she does take after Courtney some." Johnny grinned at the look that came to Rachel's eyes. He alone could share this with Rachel, seeing family resemblances.

"Hey, if Miss Stone is now Auntie Angela, and Johnny is Pattie's uncle, does that make Auntie Angela and John brother and sister?"

Johnny found himself looking into the eyes of Angela. He was uncertain which of the two was the most offended by the remark. It was then that Patrick called out quietly, though with a suspicious sound of laughter in his voice, "'Tis time to give Rachel and Pattie some rist. Now, off with ye. And ye'll be giving Miss Stone—Auntie Angela 'elp in fixing lunch. Lads, the wood box is nearly empty. And so is the water bucket. I've told ye b'fore, when ye're not in school, 'tis yeer job to see thit the wood and water don't run out."

"Well," Georgy sighed in thought as he and the others stepped out of the bedroom, "I know that the widow's oil and flour didn't run out because she obeyed the prophet of God and gave him something to eat before she and her son got to eat, but I don't recall any Bible story that talked about wood and water not running out."

"Off with ye, lad," Patrick called back, amusement in his voice.

Johnny stepped out of the bedroom, the last to leave and glanced over his shoulder at his sister and niece. Georgy's teasing words still swarmed around in his mind. He really was only the baby's uncle, not her brother after all. He drew in a deep breath. Just then Elizabeth tugged at his arm. He followed her outside, prepared to tell her the entire conversation that had gone on concerning baby Pattie.

Patrick leaned back into his pillow, stretched out in bed, and watched as Rachel leaned down over the crib and kissed their two-week old sleeping daughter goodnight. Her hair hung down loosened from its usual braid, flowing over her shoulders and down her back. When she turned around and stepped over to the bed, he smiled up at her, stretching his arm out for her to come into. She stole into his arms and held him close.

"Patrick, tomorrow I plan to take over my work," she said simply.

He pulled back enough to study her face, stunned that she was even thinking of returning to her normal work only two weeks after having the baby. "Bit Rachel, ye needn't so soon. Angela is taking care o'things. She doesn't mind. I want ye to get yeer strength back."

"Oh Patrick," she pouted, though Patrick clearly saw through it for what it was: a mere ruse to get him to agree with her. "Don't you miss me when I'm not out at the table?"

He chuckled quietly. "Ah lassie, thit isn't going to work. I already know yeer game."

Rachel smiled good-naturedly. "Well, it was worth a try. All right, I'll come to the point. I'm fine. And you know it. It isn't like the last time. Something was wrong then, but not this time. And besides, I'll get back my strength faster if you let me do my work. I can't stay in bed or in the rocking chair for the rest of my life. It'll make me into an invalid."

"The rist o'yeer life, no. Bit another couple o'weeks isn't going to make an invalid out o'ye." As he studied her face, he saw that there was still something more she was not saying. "What is it, lassie? Tell me."

She met his gaze and smiled her smile of love. "I can't hide anything from you," she sighed.

"Why do ye want to?"

She chuckled quietly. "Well, isn't it fun not knowing everything?"

"No," he murmured, "actually it isn't." But he could not hold back the chuckle that wanted to burst forth. "Well, a little maybe. Bit mostly 'tis the not knowing thit makes me nervous."

She giggled and held him close for some moments before continuing. He breathed in deeply, savoring her nearness. There was precious little time for the two of them being alone in a household of ten. He had learned to take the time that was given to him and enjoy it for as long as it lasted. He now realized that he and Rachel had been especially blessed in the early days of their marriage, spending almost every waking moment together on the wagon seat, traveling to Oregon. Now such privacy was a distant memory.

"October will be here before you know it," Rachel murmured.

"'Tis four months away," Patrick sighed in a calming tone. "What's worrying ye about semthing so far away as thit?"

"I'm not worried," she replied quietly. "But that's when Angela and Matthew are getting married."

"Aye, and what of it?"

Rachel laughed quietly and sighed as if wondering over his inability to understand the point she was trying to make. But for the life of him, he could see no connection with Rachel's need to return to her housework duties and Angela's wedding, which was four months away. "Patrick, Angela has no dowry."[iii]

Patrick sighed in relief. "Oh, only thit. Ye 'ad me worried for a minute, lassie. I thought it wis semthing serious."

"It is serious, Patrick." Patrick blinked and met her gaze. Something in her eyes assured him that he still did not understand. "She has no dowry. She doesn't even have a trousseaux.[iv] Why, it isn't done, Patrick, entering marriage without bringing something with her. We're her family. It's up to us to provide a dowry for her. If the only dowry we can provide is a trousseaux, then at least we can do that!"

"Bit Rachel, m'love," he replied softly, trying to understand what was bothering her so. "Ye yeerself 'ad no dowry, nor a trousseaux whin we got married."

She said nothing for several moments. Finally she whispered, "I know."

Patrick studied her face in the light of the kerosene lamp. She was even more beautiful than the first time he had met her. But something in her expression warned him that she was hurting inside. "Did it bother ye, Rachel, not hiving a dowry?" he asked, stunned over the thought. After all, theirs had been a marriage of convenience in the beginning. He had not expected her to bring anything into the marriage except herself and Johnny. "Did it bother ye?" he persisted. When she nodded, not even able to meet his eyes, he found himself unable to think of even one word to say. Her expression of shame tore into his heart. All at once he realized that she had been carrying this pain for two years, and he had not once guessed it was even there. Finally he said the one thing that was in his heart. "I love ye, Rachel."

A smile crept to her lips. As she lifted her eyes back to his, he knew that that had been just the right thing to say. "I love you too, Patrick," she sighed, lifting her hand to caress his cheek. "I just don't want Angela to go to Matthew empty-handed. She's had to make-do all of her life. I don't want her to go empty-handed. I want her to have a dowry. Patrick, she needs curtains, and doilies—sheets and quilts—"

"Bit Matthew 'as all of thit."

"So did you—well except for the doilies, and curtains, and sheets," she murmured. Suddenly she saw the humor of her words and laughed quietly. He loved her all the more. And he knew then and there that he would give in to her desire to get back to her homemaking duties. It meant too much to her to refuse her to free up Angela so she could work on her trousseaux. "Patrick, please, let me do this one thing. I know that Matthew has no need of Angela bringing anything into their marriage. He has enough money to buy everything they'll ever need. But Angela needs to know that this time, it's not just another handout. This time she has a family who's taking care of her and giving her the dignity of bringing a trousseaux on her wedding day. It matters so much to me, Patrick. It matters to Angela too, though she'd never admit it. Please, Patrick—I don't want her to go through what I went through."

As he studied her face, a tiny tear crept down her cheek. The lone tear spoke more deeply to him than her words did. The face that looked back at him was dearer than it had ever been before. He nodded. "All right, lassie. And I'll be making 'er a cedar chest to put the trousseaux in. And," he added as a sudden amusing thought struck him, "our dowry for 'er will be the wedding. After all, I'll be the one conducting the wedding. I won't charge Matthew the normal preacher's wages—only half!"

She giggled instantly and held him tightly. Their laughter mingled together. But as the moments slipped by, it died away and simply left them in each others arms. "And where is my goodnight kiss," she whispered into his ear.

"Where it always is, lassie, just waiting for ye," he murmured back, laying his lips on hers.

Rachel arose the next morning, excitement coursing through her at the thought of reclaiming her role in the household once again. Stepping over to the crib, she studied the tiny form beneath the sheet, watching the sheet move up and down in the rhythm of her daughter's own choosing. Rachel smiled as she studied the perfect rhythm, wondering over the fact that the child had such wonderful timing. "Maybe you'll be a famous musician one day," she whispered. "Perhaps an opera singer. Or maybe you'll break all forms of convention and become a conductor for an orchestra! With such perfect rhythm as you have, Pattie, there's no telling how far you can go in music. And your papa is musical. You get your music from him."

"Yeer mamma is musical too, lassie," Patrick chuckled quietly, stepping up behind Rachel and slipping his arms around her waist.

Rachel giggled over having been caught dreaming the dreams of a proud parent. "Patrick," she murmured, leaning against him, "I never really understood before, how otherwise intelligent men and women could become such silly dreamers when it came to their children. Why, they seemed to think that their children were superior to anyone else."

"And ye don't think thit of our children?" he chuckled, a note of surprise in his voice.

She rolled her eyes as she eased her head around enough to peer into his face. "Well of course Patrick," she sniffed, taking great care to hold back her laughter. "But in the case of our children it's true." Dissolving in giggles, she turned in his arms and hugged him to herself. Their quiet laughter mingled together for several moments and then died away as they simply enjoyed the nearness of the other. "Patrick," she murmured, resting her cheek against his shoulder, "I know I've said it before, but you've made me the happiest woman there ever was. I love you so much."

Pressing his face into the silky dark brown hair that framed her head, he drew her closer to himself. "It bears repeating," he said. "Rachel, I never told ye about the first time I saw ye."

She laughed quietly and lifted her head from his shoulder, meeting his love-filled eyes. "You didn't have to. I was there, remember? You had your arms full of firewood for me."

"No, b'fore thit."

She blinked in surprise. "Before that? There was no before that."

He grinned in amusement, his eyes dancing. "Ah, bit there wis, lassie. 'Twas shortly after the wegon train pulled out o'thit little town where ye bought yeer supplies. M'wegon was just b'hind yeers. Ye were sitting in the back, keeping in the shadows, not realizing thit there wis a hole in the canvas over yeer head. It wis not a large hole, only large enough to cast a tiny beam o'light onto yeer face as ye sat there staring at me."

Rachel drew back in shock, her mouth falling open. "You saw me watching you?" she asked, stunned beyond measure. Unexpectedly her cheeks felt warm. Patrick's eyes twinkled all the more as he studied her face, never seeming to tire of his ability to make her blush. "Dear oh dear," she murmured. "What you must have thought of me."

Such delight now rested in his face that she could not help but smile, though she was uncertain how much of the smile came from embarrassment or from enjoying Patrick's delight.

"Well, lassie," he said in a tone that was obviously being held in control, "I saw the hole in the canvas and knew that ye didn't know I could see ye. I knew ye weren't a brazen woman, only a curious one." He laughed then and reached up, trailing his fingers along her cheek. "And if the truth be known, I wis afraid thit m'face might be growing red b'neath yeer scrutiny. I never 'ad a woman study me so closely b'fore." Rachel smiled as she thought about it. "If I 'ad known on thit day, 'ow deep in m'heart ye'd be one day, I don't know thit m'poor heart could've taken it." He paused, the laughter slipping away as he seemed to memorize her face. "I can't imagine being happier than I am today. And yet, when I wake up tomorrow, knowing thit I get spend another day with ye, I'll be even happier. Why, by the end of m'days, spending thim all with ye, 'ow am I to contain such utter happiness?"

Lowering his head to hers, he began kissing her with tenderness that gradually became more intense. As she returned his kiss with equal passion, all of her world suddenly became Patrick. And she was certain that for this moment, she was his entire world as well.

Breakfast preparations were conducted in the usual chatter and scurrying around. But Rachel repeatedly found Patrick's eyes upon her. When she turned to him, he smiled at her with such love in his eyes she found it hard to remember to breathe at times. It had been awhile since they had taken the time, even in the midst of the bustling family breakfast preparations, to simply let each other know how much they loved each other. As she studied him, she was reminded of her very first impression of him: He stood like a king. He still did, just as he was doing at that very moment. Something danced in his eyes as that thought crossed her mind. She wondered what her own expression was whispering to him, tickling his heart. Finally she resisted not a moment longer, family or no family present. Stepping over to where he stood by the window, she slipped her arms around him and kissed him squarely on the mouth in front of everyone. "I love you," she whispered.

Several giggles sounded out from behind her, but she ignored them. By the look of pleasure in his face, Patrick clearly approved of her behavior. The next moment she stepped away, returning to the fireplace, only to find that Angela had taken over stirring the oatmeal. The woman was clicking her tongue and slightly shaking her head in disapproval over Rachel's bold demonstration of affection in front of everyone. But the sound of Patrick's laughter took the sting out of the woman's actions. Rachel simply smiled and called out, "I think breakfast is ready."

It took far longer to prepare the meal than to eat it. By the time it was eaten and family devotions were concluded, everyone scattered for their morning chores. Rachel picked up the crying Pattie and carried her out to the kitchen and eased down into her rocking chair. It felt good to be part of the regular pattern of life again. And she wondered if it was her contentment over that very thing that had prompted the sweetness of the time she had spent with Patrick that morning. It was almost as if she had returned home after a long journey.

Angela busily punched down the bread dough she had removed from the bowl as Rachel nursed the baby. A slight frown rested on the woman's face as she worked. Rachel wondered over the woman's moods. They ranged from sour, to angry, to snooty, and even sometimes to pleasant. This expression, however, looked different from her normal ones. "Angela?" Rachel asked, continuing to eye the woman. When Angela glanced up from the bread dough, Rachel asked, "Have you had any time to work on your sewing?"

The frown did not leave, but only deepened. And Rachel grew certain that she had landed on the source of that frown. "No," Angela replied crisply. "I've been far too busy doing your work."

Rachel flinched and lowered her gaze to the tiny baby in her arms. Drawing courage from the beloved bit of life, she drew a deep breath and lifted her eyes back up to Angela who was still staring at her, though her hands continued pushing down the bread dough into the flour on the table. "Well," Rachel forced herself to add, "why don't we begin working on it this afternoon?"

Only then did the woman's hands still themselves, her mouth dropping open slightly. A look of hope dashed across her face, but was gone the next moment as she returned her attention to the bread dough and began vigorously pressing down onto it, working more flour into the mass. "We?" she asked, a note of disdain denying the expression that had painted itself on her face for that brief moment. "As if I needed the help of a pioneer woman to sew my trousseaux."

Rachel sighed. "Carolynn—I mean, Angela." Rachel eased her eyes shut and shook her head. "Dear oh dear," she murmured, "you are so like my friend Carolyn."

"I doubt it," Angela sniffed. "Another pioneer woman? I've heard you say her name often enough."

Rachel suddenly began laughing. "Dear me, no," she giggled, thinking of what Carolyn Smyth-Johnson would say at the very thought of being mistaken for a pioneer woman. Sighing, she chose not to belittle Angela by explaining that Carolyn was the cream of the crop as far as Boston gentility went. "No, she's a lady of means. Actually, the two of you have a lot in common. You remind me of her in many ways. But she certainly could never be called a pioneer woman."

Angela dipped her head in a nod of acceptance, apparently assuming that she had been complimented. "I see," she replied, returning her attention to her work.

Rachel eased her eyes shut for a few moments and began silently praying. "Dear Jesus, will you give me your love for Angela? Will you help me to see her as you see her? I know you laid down your life for her. If I could only love her with that kind of love, I think I wouldn't allow her barbs to wound me and frustrate me so. Lord, I'm going to try something new—something I never even thought to do until now. So, you are probably the one who put it in my mind. On this day I commit to loving Angela Stone with your love. Oh Jesus, please help me to."

The silence in the room was calming, broken only by the slight squeak of the rocking chair that normally went unheard in the lively O'Riley household. Across the room was the slight swishing sound of Angela's hands on the bread dough as she continued kneading it. Finally Rachel opened her eyes and simply studied the woman. She cocked her head as she stared. Something was happening inside of Rachel. She could not quite say what the source of the feeling was, but she found herself suddenly thinking that the woman's face looked quite dear to her, almost as if she were someone from Rachel's beloved past, snatched up and deposited here and now for Rachel. She waited for several moments, wondering if this thought—this incredible feeling—would vanish. It did not. "Thank you Jesus," she silently prayed.

Drawing in her breath, she spoke in a tone that mingled firmness with kindness. "Angela, I plan to help you sew your trousseaux. You are my children's aunt now. And that makes you my sister—or Patrick's sister—whichever you wish."

Angela tore her gaze from the bread dough and stared dumbly at Rachel. Finally she sputtered, "You expect me to choose my lineage from an American pioneer or an Irishman?"

Rachel began choking then, the incredible humor of the situation swatting her in the face. Had it really been only two years earlier that the same words could have popped out of Rachel's own mouth? Catching her breath, she nodded, keeping her voice as firm and decided as possible. "Yes, that's exactly what I'm saying. We never have a choice as to which family we're born into. By your own words you yourself have no idea what your lineage is. So, here are your choices: Nathan or O'Riley."

Angela swallowed and murmured, "Dear me, pioneer stock or foreign—Irish at that." As Rachel continued studying the woman's face, her own mouth fell slightly ajar. She looked closer and once again silently thanked Jesus for giving her eyes to see something that the woman's harsh words would normally have made her blind to: tears in Angela's eyes.

Knowing her well enough to know that she would be chagrinned if anyone were to guess that her heart had been touched over the thought of being given a heritage of her own, be it American pioneer, or Irish, Rachel kept her tone matter-of-fact, asking, "Which is it to be?"

"Well," Angela murmured and swallowed. Straightening up, she suddenly looked Rachel full in the face. "Didn't you tell me that Patrick's mother was British, and not Irish?"

"Yes," Rachel replied slowly, wondering where the question was leading.

"Then I shall be her relative—her cousin's daughter. What was her maiden name?"

Rachel worked at keeping the corner's of her mouth down, but was not altogether certain she was managing it. "Carson-Davis. Christine Anita Carson-Davis."

Angela dipped her head in a nod. "That name fits me quite well. The name of Stone isn't really my last name. They gave it to me at the orphanage. All children who arrived at the orphanage with no clue of their origin were given the sir name of Stone. They'd laugh and say that we had simply emerged from the rocks. This gave the other children a sense of pride in their family heritage, since they at least had one. They never bothered giving me a middle name. From here on out, my name is Angela Carson-Davis. After I marry, my full name shall be Angela Carson-Davis Bon-Hemmer, from England."

"But, you aren't from England."

"My chosen heritage is British. Hence, my people are from Great Brittan, of the Carson-Davis line."

Rachel dipped her head in a nod. "As you wish. That makes you my cousin by marriage."

"Third cousin, actually," Angela sniffed.

Taking a deep, calming breath, Rachel insisted calmly, "As third cousin by marriage, it is my right to assist you in sewing your trousseaux. And Patrick is planning on building you a cedar chest to hold all of the linens. It's all the dowry we can give," she added quietly.

A rather satisfied look nestled itself in Angela's face as she returned her attention to kneading the dough, murmuring just loudly enough to be heard, "To think that the Carson-Davis dowry has been reduced to a mere cedar chest. Dear me, what would cousin Christine think?"

Rachel's mouth dropped open as she stared at the woman, suddenly wondering what Patrick would think. Just then Johnny pushed open the door and stuck his head through the opening, calling out, "Annie is pouting again!"

Rachel turned and eyed him sternly. "And you're tattling again." When he frowned over her words, she asked in frustration, "Johnny, what is the matter with you? You've never been one to tattle before. And now you find someone to tattle on at least five times a day or more. What's wrong?"

He shrugged and lowered his eyes to the floor. "Nothing," he muttered and slipped back outside.

Shifting her eyes, she met Angela's puzzled gaze. "I don't even know what to think anymore," Rachel sighed. "Between his tattling, and Anna Marie's pouting—why, I'm at a loss over what to do. Anna Marie has always been such a happy baby," she added, shaking her head.

Angela's eyes narrowed. "Perhaps that's it," she said significantly, as if expecting Rachel to understand her meaning. When Rachel simply cocked her head in question, Angela sighed as if weary of explaining a lesson to a rather dull scholar. "Do you remember your grammar, Rachel?" Rachel slowly lowered her head in a single nod. "Past tense—was—Anna Marie was the baby. Anna Marie was happy. Present tense—is—Patricia is now the baby.

Anna Marie is now pouting."

"Jealousy?" Rachel asked, the new thought striking out at her as a slap in the face. "You think Anna Marie is jealous of Pattie?"

"What do you think?"

Rachel began recalling the events of the past several days. "I'm not always available for her like I used to be," she murmured. "I try to be, Angela. But there are times that Pattie's needs simply have to come first."

For once the woman did not reply with a critical look, nor an acidic reply. She simply nodded. "I know. But little girls and boys don't understand. I remember at the orphanage just wishing that there was someone to love me. I pouted and screamed. I even refused to eat. None of it worked. No one cared."

"But—but we all love Anna Marie. She has to know that."

"I'm sure she does," Angela replied, her tone not as gentle as earlier, but neither was it harsh. Rachel studied her hard as she began dividing up the dough into individual loaves, pressing them down into the bread pans for one final rising. A thoughtful look rested in her face, assuring Rachel that she was among those who loved the little girl, as preposterous as the thought sounded.

"Tell me, Angela—what do you think I should do?"

Angela paused and glanced back at Rachel. "Well, you can't neglect Pattie in order to tend to the imagined needs of a jealous child. But can you not spare any time at all for her?"

Rachel nodded. "I thought I had," she sighed. "Oh Angela, I wouldn't hurt Annie for anything in this world." She smiled sadly as she realized that she had used Patrick's pet name for the little girl.

"I know." The simple words were spoken quietly. And immediately the woman resumed her work with the bread dough. Rachel smiled at the bowed head, seeing a side to Angela that she had never seen before. She could not help but wonder if this was the way that Matthew saw her, soft and caring. Was it the way that Jesus saw her? After all, she had asked to be given eyes to see the woman the way Jesus saw her. "I'm sure if Cousin Christine were alive today, she'd have the proper advice to give you."

The corners of Rachel's mouth twitched upward and she wondered if from here on out she and the rest of the family would be enduring listening to Angela quote Patrick's mother whom she had neither met nor even knew anything about other than the fact that she was from England and was her adopted ancestor. Squaring her shoulders, she suddenly asked, "Well, if she were here, Angela, what do you think she would say?"

Angela's hands stilled. Clearly she had been caught by her own words. The next moment, however, having recovered her composure, she replied a bit tartly, "Well, she certainly would direct you to look a little bit closer to home. Your own brother is acting as much out of character as is Anna Marie. And all of this began after the birth of Patricia."

"You think—I mean—she would think that Johnny is jealous too?"

"Perhaps," Angela replied a little smugly. "But then, who can understand the motives of Nathans?"

Rachel narrowed her eyes and bit her tongue. She made no further comment, but simply continued rocking Pattie who was falling asleep. Several minutes later she rose to her feet and carried the sleeping baby into the bedroom and laid her down snugly into her crib. She gazed down at her for a long minute before turning and stepping out of the room. "Angela, would you keep an eye on Pattie for a little while?"

With the bread dough in the tins and the towels over them while the bread continued to rise, Angela was scrubbing down the table, removing all traces of flour from it. She paused in her work and straightened up, eying Rachel sternly. "Where are you going?" she demanded. "Patrick is not going to be pleased when he finds out that you are not taking care of yourself!"

Rachel chuckled quietly and shook her head. "Family," she murmured in a mixture of love and annoyance. "Can't live with them. Can't live without them."

"You're getting off of the subject."

"I don't think he'll mind. And you're just as bad as he is, bundling me up in a bunting too thick for me to hurt myself and too padded for me to do anything." Angela tipped her head slightly downward, forcing her to study Rachel from the tops of her eyes in an especially schoolmarm sort of expression. "I won't be gone long or even very far. Besides, I'm feeling nearly like myself again."

With that, Rachel stepped outside into the bright morning sunshine. Catching sight of Ion in the distance, she called out quietly, "Ion!"

Immediately he turned from his work of splitting firewood. Laying down his ax, he hurried over to Rachel. "What are you doing outside?" he asked, reaching for her arm. "Here, let me help you back inside."

Rachel giggled and planted her feet where she stood, wondering how she was to convince her family that she was not going to break. "I've only just stepped outside this minute. I'm not going right back into the house. Why, I haven't been outside for days and days." She sighed as she thought of the fact that she had even been using a chamber pot since Pattie's birth, since Patrick had steadily insisted that the outhouse was too far for her walk to. "I'm all right, Ion," she added softly. He frowned slightly and eased his breath out. "I'd like to talk to all of you children," she added.

He stood there, so different from the angry boy he had been when she had first met him. Though he was clearly peeved with her insistence in remaining outside when he clearly thought it not in her best interest, there was no trace of the anger that had once shone out of the dark eyes. "Well," he sighed out, "Georgy went over to the Doc's and Lizzy is over at Jennifer's, helping her do up her laundry. Pat told her she could go since Jennifer has been sick and needs a hand. But I think Lizzy and Jen are going to do more berry picking than laundry."

"In June?"

He shrugged. "Well, they're best friends. What do girls do all day when they aren't doing women's work?"

Rachel sighed over the boy's words and nodded. "I see your point. And Georgy? Was there a specific reason for him to go to the Morrison's?"

"No," Ion replied simply.

Rachel thought about the boy, dreaming of becoming a doctor someday. "He's probably hoping for the chance to go out on a call with the doctor."

"I imagine," he replied in his normal straightforward manner.

Rachel began studying Ion's face. "What about you, Ion?" she asked softly. "Is there something you'd rather be doing than splitting wood?"

One side of his mouth crept up then, assuring Rachel that there was. But he simply shrugged. "My writing can wait until I get my work done."

Upon impulse Rachel reached her arms around the boy and held him close. "I surely do love you Ion," she sighed. Once again she was reminded how much he had grown over the months. He had passed her in height some time ago. His lanky frame seemed to grow thinner with each inch in height he obtained and showed no sign of stopping. "I just want you—and the others—to know that Pattie's birth hasn't changed the way Patrick and I feel about all of you."

Leaning back, though not removing his arms that encircled Rachel, he eyed her knowingly. "It's Johnny and Annie, isn't it?" His candor never failed to amaze Rachel.

She nodded, murmuring, "I love them so much."

"So tell them."

Rachel blinked in surprise. Thinking through the boy's reply, she realized that he had spoken a volume of wisdom in three simple words. She nodded. "I will."

Something in his expression warned her that he was not quite finished. She waited, knowing that he would not be rushed. Whenever she tired to rush him, he tended to clam up altogether. "I've been thinking," he finally said slowly, meeting her gaze. The look of a boy was nowhere to be seen. He now looked out at his world through the eyes of a young man who would soon be testing his wings. "Georgy and Lizzy belong to each other—special. They really are brother and sister—by blood. I know that doesn't take away from them being my brother and sister. But blood is blood. And it means something. And then there's Johnny and Pattie. They belong to each other by blood. He's her real flesh and blood uncle. And then there's Annie. And then there's me. Neither one of us have any flesh and blood family. We don't belong to anybody by right, but only by permission."

Rachel's heart began twisting as Ion spoke. She had been thinking about Angela's plight over not having relatives, but she had not thought about Anna Marie and Ion. "Do you feel like you don't belong?" she whispered, barely able to get the question from her tightening throat.

A softened expression crept into his eyes. He smiled and leaned close, gently kissing her cheek. "I lost my first ma and pa. You're my ma now. And Pat's my pa. Gramps is my grandpa. I have two brothers and three sisters." He sighed and added with a touch of sarcastic annoyance in his tone. "And I have an aunt and a soon-to-be uncle. I belong to the O'Riley family," he added softly. "Nobody can change that. You're stuck with me forever."

Rachel smiled, her world suddenly realigning itself back into place. The stunned look in the boy's face that was wreathed in a smile, assured her that he was amazed over the pain she had been feeling in thinking that Ion might consider himself outside of the family. "I was thinking," he added, "what if I adopt Annie as my own special sister? Because she and I don't have any blood relatives, that puts us in the same category anyway." He paused and seemed almost hesitant. Finally he asked straight out, "Can I have Annie?"

Rachel suddenly began giggling. "You can't have my daughter!" she cried out. His eyes began dancing at her reaction. He waited for her to calm herself and give him a reply to his request. Finally she nodded. "All right, Annie is your own special sister. But she still belongs to all of us, Ion MacAlister! And don't you forget it!"

He chuckled and hugged her close. "I won't forget," he murmured.

"You know, Ion, I think you're an answer to prayer."

He pulled back suddenly, staring at her in shock. "Me?"

She smiled lovingly at him. "I think that you're the answer to Anna Marie's jealousy problem. I think, with all of our help, you're the one who'll end up convincing her that Pattie hasn't taken away her place in our family." Tipping her head up, she softly kissed him on the cheek. "Now I need to talk to Johnny."

As their arms fell away from each other, they both turned to the sand pile where Anna Marie was playing and Johnny was observing. "Annie!" Ion called out. "Want to go down to the river with me?" As the baby squealed in delight and jumped to her feet, dashing over to them, Rachel turned concerned eyes upon Ion.

"You'll be especially careful of her by the water, won't you? It only takes a moment for a little one to slip away and drown."

Ion smiled good-naturedly and nodded. "I'll be careful, Rachel. Georgy's the scatterbrained one of us, not me."

"Ion," she rebuked, drawing out a chuckle from the boy. Turning to the approaching little girl, she called out, "Anna Marie? You mind Ion!"

The little girl, all smiles now, giggled and nodded. "I'll be good Mamma."

Catching up the little girl in her arms, she held her close. "I love you so much, Annie," she murmured and kissed her soft cheek. Lowering her back down to the ground, she repeated firmly, "You mind your brother!"

She nodded and reached for Ion's hand. Together they set off toward the river. Rachel was torn between wanting to trust Ion and that of wanting to be the only one in charge of Anna Marie at the river. Ion had proved himself countless of times. He would not get distracted. He would take good care of the little girl. Finally, she turned and headed over to the sand pile, where Johnny sat, even though his charge was gone. When she arrived, she eased herself down onto one of the many stumps that had been placed around the pile. "Johnny, can we talk?"

The boy lifted sad eyes to Rachel, murmuring, "I'm sorry I tattled on Annie."

Reaching over, she brushed a stray lock from his eyes, thinking over the possibility of Patrick giving the boys a haircut that day. "It isn't that," she sighed. Smiling, she added sheepishly, "To be honest, I'd forgotten all about it." He opened his eyes wide at that. "Why don't we just count that as forgiven and forgotten?" A look of relief shot into his eyes, but the look of sadness still remained. Lowering her hand to his, she squeezed it and asked, "Is there something about Pattie that makes you sad?"

Little boy shoulders crept up then. One side of his mouth rose apologetically, tearing at Rachel's heart. "Well, it's just that she's your daughter. She's Pat's daughter. She's Gramps' granddaughter. She's Auntie Angela's niece. And she's everybody's else's sister. Except, she's not my sister. She's only my niece—just like she is to Auntie Angela—Miss Stone."

"Miss Carson-Davis," Rachel murmured. Johnny seemed not to notice, and simply sat there glumly. "But Johnny," Rachel began gently, "she's your flesh and blood. That's something that no one except Patrick and I can claim. They've all adopted her as their own. But she was born belonging to you. And who was it that saw the Nathan line in her face? It was you—her own uncle. Johnny," she added, softly, "don't you understand that it's your characteristics of the Nathans she takes after, even more than mine. She's your flesh and blood." He stared at her, clearly startled over her words. "Now, if you'd like to consider her your sister, it's all right. It's up to you."

He nodded slowly, but made no attempt at replying. Squeezing his hand again for a brief moment, she rose to her feet. Turning toward the cabin, she had not taken many steps before she caught sight of Patrick standing in front of the door eying her. A sober look rested on his face as she approached him. "Honestly," she began as soon as she stepped up to him, "it did me good to get out in the fresh air."

"Hm," was all he said, but the twinkle in his eyes tempered the soberness of his expression. Rachel shook her head and sighed, wondering how she was to convince her overprotective family that she was fine. Slipping his arm around her shoulders, he joined her as she continued toward the cabin. "Are ye needing a cup o'tea?" he asked.

She giggled and allowed him to open the door for her. Stepping inside, she stared in amazement at the pot of tea setting on the table, by which Angela had placed a cup and saucer. "Yes," she sighed, "that sounds just right."

The rest of the morning slipped away as Patrick studied for his sermon and Rachel sorted through beans, cleaning out the beans from the stones and other debris. They would make a good supper. And with lunch preparations well underway, both Patrick and Angela seemed content that Rachel would not overdo. Rachel looked forward to a quiet afternoon of sewing. It had been a long time since she had done much embroidering. And she found herself growing excited over the thought of beginning the project, deciding on embroidering a table runner and placemats. She would consult Angela concerning which colors she wanted the linins embroidered in.

The evening finally presented itself after a satisfying day of gradually returning to her homemaking duties. She found herself far more tired than she dared admit to the members of her hovering family. If they suspected that she was overdoing it, they kept it to themselves. For that Rachel breathed a sigh of relief.

Suddenly Patrick motioned for Rachel to join him at their bedroom doorway. Quietly she rose from the table and stepped over to him. He was peering inside, facing the crib. Slipping her arm around his waist, she studied the back of Johnny as he leaned over the side of the crib, talking quietly to the sleeping Pattie. "And the others love you too," he was saying. "But if you ever need somebody, you come to me, because I'm your uncle."

Chapter 4

"Ion, m'lad!" Patrick called out from the woodpile, where he often spent time in prayer just before church services began. Ion had just been about to walk to the church, but turned and headed for the wood pile. "I need to talk with ye," he added, as soon as Ion stepped up to him.

Ion grinned in mock relief. "I was afraid you'd called me over here to turn me over your knee."

Patrick laughed outright, his eyes dancing. "And 'ow am I supposed to be doing thit when ye're nearly m'own height? Why, ye're nearly fifteen now!" Motioning toward a pile of logs, he eased himself down, Ion following his example. Ion puzzled over the sober look that suddenly painted the man's face, but waited without questions pouring out of him. Finally the man sighed and eased his eyes over to him. "I hiv semthing I want to give to ye, lad. I've kept it until I thought ye were ready. Bit, if ye don't feel quite ready for it, I'll hold onto it until ye are. Agreed?"

Ion dipped his head in a single nod. "Agreed," he replied, wondering.

Patrick reached into his pocket and withdrew a knife. As he reached it over to Ion, Ion's mouth fell open in shock. Tearing his eyes from it, he stared at Patrick, demanding in a whisper, "Where did you get that?"

Patrick's eyes took on a troubled glint. "Frim yeer father," he murmured. "I'm sorry, laddie," he sighed, slipping his arm around Ion's shoulders. "I wis hoping this knife would be a comfort to ye. I see now thit it isn't the right time. Will ye forgive me?"

Ion leaned against the man's arm, trying to decide how he could explain how it had been to grow up with the brute Colon MacAlister as his father. "There's nothing to forgive, Pat. It just took me by surprise. I didn't know he had it. He died with it in his pocket?" When Patrick nodded, studying Ion carefully, Ion managed a mirthless chuckle. "He stole it from me. One day I just couldn't find it. I asked him about it. I knew he wanted it. He told me he didn't have it, didn't know where it was, and if I ever accused him again of stealing it, he'd bust my jaw."

A look of pain crept into Patrick's eyes. "I'm so sorry, Ion," he murmured. "'Ere I've brought ye sorrow when I wis hoping to bring ye a bit o'healing over yeer father's death."

Ion forced himself to smile for Patrick's sake, a smile he did not feel and likely was not even fooling the man with. But he had to try—he had to do all he could to take away that look of pain from him. "Well, I think you did right in giving it to me. The fact is," he admitted, "the fruit didn't fall far from the tree." Patrick drew back slightly in surprise. "I stole it from Georgy," Ion sighed. "I didn't on purpose—at first. I found it. But a few minutes after I found it, I ran into Georgy—literally—and he saw it in my hand and recognized it as his. I wouldn't give it back to him. We fought over it. I won. I kept it. After we left all of you behind on trail, I still had it. About a week later I lost it—well, Pa stole it. After I became part of this family, I wanted to give it back to Georgy—but I didn't have it. I turned out just like Pa," he sighed, lowering his eyes to his hands. Another sigh escaped him.

When Patrick's arm tightened around his shoulders, he lifted his head and studied the man's face. "Ion," he murmured, "I'm proud o'ye!"

Ion stared, too stunned to know what to say. Finally he asked, "Weren't you listening? I'm a thief!"

"I wis too, at one time."

"You?"

Patrick nodded. "One day I asked Jesus to forgive me for being a thief. I asked 'Im to forgive all of m'sins. And 'E did. Do ye want 'Im to forgive ye for yeer sins?"

Ion swallowed and slowly nodded. He had been wanting that very thing for some time, but had never found a way of voicing it. "Are ye sorry ye've sinned against God?" Again Ion nodded, uncertain whether or not to trust his voice. "Do ye b'lieve in Jesus?"

Suddenly Ion found his voice, too startled not to. "Of course! What's not to believe? He's God! He came to die for our sins!" He shook his head in puzzlement over Patrick's question. "What's not to believe? Ever since I heard who He was, I've believed it."

"Then laddie, why hiv ye done nething about it?"

Patrick's gaze was not condemning, simply one of caring mingled with puzzlement. Ion shrugged, replying simply, "I didn't know it was for me— forgiveness I mean. I thought it was only for the good people." Patrick eased his eyes shut then and simply sat there, as if his sudden pain was too much to bear. "I'm sorry Pat," Ion added quickly. "I—I didn't mean to say the wrong thing! Don't be hurting—I didn't—"

Opening his eyes, Patrick gazed so lovingly at Ion, Ion could not help but relax. "Ah laddie," he sighed, shaking his head. "'Tis I who needs to be forgiven for making ye think ye weren't good enough to be saved. Jesus came to save all who call ipon 'Im—*all* laddie! Not one of us is deserving of 'Is love, so 'E gives it freely to inyone who asks. Do ye want to be saved, Ion? Do ye want to give yeer life over to God? Do ye want to go to Heaven when ye die? Do ye want to be forgiven of yeer sin? Do ye want the Holy Spirit to come and live inside of ye, and be yeer teacher and friend? Do ye want God to come first in yeer life?" Ion nodded, drawing a smile from Patrick. "Then tell 'Im, laddie. Tell Jesus."

Ion stared for one long moment before closing his eyes. "Jesus?" he asked hesitantly. Since becoming part of the O'Riley family he had heard enough prayers to know how to pray. He had simply not done it. "I think ever since I first heard Pat and Rachel talk about you I've believed who you are. I just didn't know—well, until now, I thought—" He paused and swallowed. His throat suddenly ached. And he knew if he said even one more word, he would actually begin crying, though he could not figure out where all of this emotion had come from so suddenly. Strong arms pulled him into the embrace of the man beside him. His own arms crept around Patrick as he began sobbing into his shoulder. Patrick simply held him close, saying nothing. Ion wondered how he was to continue his prayer when he could not get past his tears. But the release of them felt so good. A burden began slipping off of his shoulders, one he had not even been aware of carrying until right then. "Jesus," he managed to say. Drawing a deep breath, "I think you're already forgiven me even before I've said the words. But I was thinking them. You knew it. But I'll say them anyway. Please, please forgive me for sinning against you. And please forgive me for stealing Georgy's knife. Please save me." The tears were flowing too hard now for more words to pass through his lips. But it was enough. Inside of him, he knew that God was doing something. He felt somehow new—unused—clean—excited. And still the tears came. It was then that he realized that Patrick's shoulders were moving as well. Ion held all the tighter onto the man whose tears mingled with his own. Never in his entire life had Ion known such awesome peace.

Finally the two drew back from one another, studying each other's tear streaked cheeks. "Ah laddie," Patrick said, reaching up and brushing Ion's face of its tears, "'Tis one of the happiest days of m'life. Now ye are not only m'son by adoption, ye're also m'spiritual son, since I wis given the honor o'leading ye to Jesus. This makes ye m'son in the faith.

Ion eased into a smile. Self-consciously he lifted his hand and brushed it over Patrick's tear-glistening cheeks. The man's eyes softened and he drew Ion back into a heart-felt embrace, murmuring over and over, "Thank ye Jesus!"

It was some minutes later before they pronounced each other presentable to the people who would soon be arriving at church. Rising to their feet, they turned toward the path leading to the church. Patrick handed the knife to Ion then, saying, "Do with it whatever is in yeer heart to do, lad."

Ion nodded and took the knife from him, slipping it into his pocket. But he already knew what he would do with it. Catching sight of Georgy scurrying across the yard, he called out, "Georgy! I've got something for you!"

Shifting his gaze, he met Patrick's. "I'm proud o'ye lad."

As Georgy approached, Patrick left the two, heading toward the church. Rachel had already gone there ahead of him. Georgy studied Ion's face, clearly realizing that he had been crying. Instead of the look of mockery that could have come to any fifteen-year-old's face, compassion painted itself there. "You all right, Ion?"

Ion nodded. Together they turned and began following Patrick to the church. "Here," he said simply, withdrawing the knife from his pocket and handed it to Georgy whose eyes grew round at the sight. "Sorry I didn't get it back to you sooner. And—and I'm sorry I stole it from you."

Georgy grinned and picked up the knife, fingering it as if it were a rare treasure. "It was my pappy's," he murmured.

"Yeah, it was my pa's too."

It was then that Georgy returned his gaze to Ion. "Your Pa's? What do you mean?"

"He stole it from me. Pat found it when Pa died. He's been keeping it for me—for when I was ready for it. He didn't know it really belonged to you."

Georgy smiled and nodded, a puzzled look in his eyes. "Ion, I know you—you've been crying." Ion lowered his eyes for a moment, his cheeks becoming warm. "You wouldn't cry over this knife. What happened?"

Lifting his eyes once again, Ion studied Georgy silently. "I asked Jesus to forgive me for stealing your knife, and for all of my sins. And when He did, I couldn't help but—but—"

"Cry?" Georgy filled in the word for him. His tone was filled with unexpected kindness that caused one side of Ion's mouth to rise. He nodded. "You're a Christian now?" he asked, excitement coloring his words. When Ion nodded, Georgy let out a whoop and began dancing a jig. Ion chuckled, his cheeks no longer feeling warm. Suddenly Georgy came to an abrupt halt and stared at Ion. "You better tell Mary! She's got to get saved too!"

Ion grinned and nodded. "As soon as she gets to church I plan to tell her. But she's already thinking about God. She's already reading her Bible every day. She even told me that I should too."

"She's right!"

Ion clapped Georgy on the back, chuckling, "I know that now."

Their attention was suddenly drawn to the crowd of church people that was joining the path ahead, on their way to church. Ion tugged on Georgy's arm. "Come on, there she is."

"You don't need me around."

Ion paused and stared at Georgy in surprise. "You're right!" he replied, shocked that he had thought otherwise. Georgy's eyes danced merrily. For once he did not speak his mind but simply let Ion go on ahead of him, to catch up with Mary. Ion was vaguely aware of Mitch arriving and calling out to Georgy. The two often referred to themselves as twins since both had become Christians on the same night—Christmas night. As Ion hurried along, he thought momentarily about the friendship that had been forged between Mitch and Georgy that night. Until that moment, Ion had not been able to understand. But now he did.

Stepping into the church that also served as the school, he scanned the room for Mary. As he caught sight of her, he eased through the crowd in time to hear her speaking with Rachel. "Good morning Mrs. O'Riley," she said. Ion halted and simply watched the two ladies he loved. Loved? He flinched back in surprise. Where had that word come from? Of course he loved Rachel. She was his ma. But Mary? One side of his mouth shifted up at the thought. He could not deny it, but it still startled him.

"Good morning Mary," Rachel replied with a smile. "How have you been?"

"Fine," she said quietly, her eyes lowering themselves to the baby in Rachel's arms. The softened look that came to Mary's face made Ion catch his breath. In a few years, it could be Mary holding a baby—her daughter—her son—his son. Ion swallowed quickly. In a few years—yes—they could perhaps marry each other in a few years. His mouth felt incredibly dry. And he could have a son. Or a daughter? Shaking his head slowly, he reminded himself that he would only be turning fifteen in October. Patrick might give his consent for him to marry young, but Rachel never would. He grinned slightly at the thought, wondering at the relieved feeling that suddenly swept over him.

"Ion wants to write a poem about her," Mary added, unaware that Ion was nearby, listening.

Rachel shifted her gaze to baby Pattie and smiled before lifting her eyes back to Mary. "I'm glad that you're helping him with his writing."

"Oh," she replied quickly, "they're all his words. I'm just helping him to spell them." Ion grinned over Mary's faithful refusal to take credit for Ion's words. "Sometimes," she added with an amused, though shy laugh, "he spells awful."

Rachel and Mary's laughter mingled together while Ion looked on, shaking his head, wondering what their reaction would be if they both turned and noticed him standing there. But he could not take offense. Clearly they loved him. Love? There was that word again. Well of course Rachel loved him. She told him that over and over. She was his ma, after all. But Mary? Did Mary love him? Quickly he reminded himself to breathe.

"You know," Rachel said in a confidential tone, "he never lets any of us read his poems. I think you're the only one he allows to read them."

Ion grinned as Mary's cheeks turned pink. Somehow he suddenly felt a little taller, seeing that something about him had the power over her to make her blush. And he could not push down his smile, even though he tried. "He probably won't let me read them once he learns to spell better," she murmured.

The amused sparkle in Rachel's eyes warned Ion that she was not so certain about that. Suddenly he began wondering if Rachel had guessed that Ion was purposely misspelling words in order that Mary would be compelled to help him. All at once Rachel shifted her gaze and stared straight at Ion. The startled look in her eyes was replaced with a knowing one. Yes, she had guessed it, Ion was certain. Tilting his head, he gave her a pleading look, silently begging her to keep it secret that he was a better speller than Mary thought. She pursed her lips in amusement.

"I'll ask him to let you read his poems," Mary said quietly.

Immediately Rachel shifted her gaze. "Thank you Mary. I think with all of your help, we're going to see a marked improvement in his spelling." Shifting her gaze sideways, she met Ion's gaze with a challenging look.

He dipped his head in a nod of agreement, understanding her silent bargain she was making with him. But at least she would keep his secret. Someday he would tell Mary—but not today.

"Besides," Mary added, "you'll probably be teaching again soon and so will read his writing assignments."

Rachel sighed then, causing both Mary and Ion to study her in surprise. Rachel smiled apologetically. "I'm sorry. I didn't mean to sigh. Well, if you can keep a secret, I've been praying that God will provide another teacher in Timberton. With Angela's wedding in October, she certainly is pressed for time. It's a lot to ask of her to continue teaching. And I had planned to resume teaching in September, thinking that I'd leave Pattie and Anna Marie with Mrs. Morrison during the day. But the truth is, I'd be quite content to have my teaching days over. If I had my very own wish, I'd like to stay home and take care of my children and my husband, and Jed," she added with a smile. "But," she added quickly, "whether Angela—Miss Stone—I mean Miss Carson-Davis teaches or I, or someone else, we will have school one way or the other. I won't leave you without a teacher."

At the look of relief in Mary's face, Ion smiled, secretly wondering if she was relieved that she would be able to further her education or if her relief came more from the fact that school offered an opportunity for the two of them to spend time together. Clearing his throat, he called out quietly, "Mary, I have something to tell you. But—but first, I have something to tell Rachel."

Mary dipped her head in a pleased, yet embarrassed nod and slipped to the back of the room where the young people tended to stand along the wall. Ion always managed to find a place for her to sit, but lately she had chosen to stand. And it was no coincidence that she stood with the O'Riley family. Somehow Ion always managed to stand beside her. Crouching down in front of Rachel, he studied her face carefully. Merriment remained in her eyes over their shared secret of Ion's spelling. The laughter slipped away as she read something new in his expression. "Pat and I—well—I'll tell you the whole story later—but for now I want you to know that—well—I asked Jesus to save me."

Rachel caught her breath. One arm immediately slipped from around Pattie and caught hold of Ion around his neck, drawing him to herself. He eased his arms around her and held her close. She was trembling. And he knew that she was crying. He began wondering if it would have been better if he had waited until after church to tell her. But that had not seemed the answer either. Grinning, he decided to simply hold her. Rachel cried over everything that touched her heart. That was just Rachel.

Pulling back from him, tears streaming down her cheeks, Rachel managed a smile, delight shining from her eyes. "I get to spend eternity with you," she whispered.

It was then that Ion bit down on his lower lip. It was all right for Rachel to cry in public. But he would be forever humiliated if he were to do such a thing—and in front of Mary of all people! Rachel laughed, apparently guessing his thoughts. But it was enough to jar him back into the safe waters of control over his emotions. He sighed in relief and reached his hand to Rachel face, brushing away her tears.

"Are you all right?" he whispered.

She nodded. "I'm fine. Go to Mary."

He grinned over her understanding of the situation and rose to his feet. Pushing through the crowd, he saw that Mary had found an empty place on the end of the back bench. As he crouched down to the floor beside her, she scooted over, offering him a bit of the bench to sit on. He made no argument. With so little bench to sit on, he had no choice but to sit close to her. She seemed not to pay any attention to that fact. He grinned, realizing that apparently she too had little secretive ways that enabled them to spend time together. He turned to her, wondering what her reaction would be to his becoming a Christian. He swallowed. "Mary?" he began uncertainly. Her expression of trust encouraged him to continue. "A few minutes ago, I became a Christian."

Her eyes opened wide. "You know how?" she breathed out, all merriment gone. When he nodded in puzzlement, she reached over in an uncharacteristic manner, grabbing his arm, demanding, "Tell me how!"

"You want to be a Christian, Mary?" he whispered. When she nodded, he frowned slightly. "Why? Because of me? Because I don't think that's the right reason. Maybe you should talk to Pat."

"I've been wanting to," she whispered back. "But by the time church is over, there's so many people circled around him, I haven't been able to get close enough to ask. And Pa will skin me alive if I don't bring the others back home right away and get dinner on the table, especially now that Ma spends so much time in bed sick. I've been reading my Bible, Ion. But I just don't know how to get saved. Won't you tell me?"

The hungry look in the girl's eyes assured Ion that she was not putting it on. She meant it. He nodded. "Sure I'll tell you. You just ask Jesus to save you. He will. I asked Him to forgive me for sinning against him. He forgave me. When He died on the cross, he paid for our sins."

She nodded. "I know that part. Pastor O'Riley always talks about that. But isn't there something I have to do first?"

Ion shook his head. "I didn't do anything first. I just asked."

Squeezing her eyes shut, Mary whispered, "Dear Jesus? I'm asking.

Please, will You save me? Will You forgive me for sinning against You? I want to be a Christian. Please God?" She remained still for several moments, but her eyelids had relaxed, though still remained closed. Ion studied her bowed head, wondering. And then all at once she lifted her head, opening her eyes and met his gaze. A smile of such joy spread across her lips, Ion knew that God had answered her prayer. It was the same joy that he himself was feeling, since the moment God had forgiven him. It was then that he realized that he too was smiling.

Rachel swept the room at a glance, counting up her children. Georgy and Mitch had just stepped inside, followed by Art and Johnny, Jennifer and Elizabeth, who was holding onto Anna Marie's hand. Turning, she caught sight of Ion and Mary sitting side by side at the back, openly smiling at each other. She was reminded of the thoughts she had had back in May, when Georgy had announced to her that he would one day become a doctor. It had jarred her into thinking about the fact that her children were growing up. Georgy had just turned fifteen and Ion would be turning fifteen in only a matter of weeks. She reminded herself that Mary was less than two months younger than Ion. She slowly shook her head, watching the two watching each other. Her own mother had been eighteen when she had married Rachel's twenty-year-old father. As Rachel reminded herself of that fact, she became all the more determined that fifteen was far too young for marrying. Besides, she and Patrick were far too young to be thinking of marrying off their children!

Rachel frowned, wondering where Toby and Annette Shaleman were. "Angela," she called out quietly to the woman sitting directly in front of her. When Angela turned around, looking down her nose at her, clearly displeased for having been disturbed in church, Rachel asked, "Have you seen Annette and Toby?"

Angela drew within herself for a moment in thought. Finally she shook her head. "No, I haven't. Curious, though. They never miss unless they're sick. And I know of no illness going around this time of year."

Rachel nodded and leaned back against her desk seat again as Angela turned back around, properly facing the front of the church. Just then Matthew eased himself down beside her. As her official fiancé, Angela had told him that he was now permitted to sit beside her. Rachel smiled at the memory. Matthew had done his best not to laugh openly at her as she made her grand announcement. But the fact that he was tickled over her overbearing attitude, graciously allowing him to sit beside her in the country church went unnoticed only by Angela herself.

Just then the chatter began dying away. Rachel turned back around and saw that Patrick was standing in the front of the room with his guitar in hand. "We'll be hiving a baptism next Sunday," he called out. "We've waited far too long. The weather has certainly been warm enough. Baptism is for those who hiv asked Jesus into their lives to be their Savior. It's open to all who are saved. Iveryone who would like to be baptized, will ye stand up please?"

Heads began turning then, waiting to see if anyone had the courage to stand. Suddenly Georgy popped up and grinned. Mitch rose next, slipping his hands self-consciously into his pockets. Ion and Mary rose to their feet together. The crowd began murmuring, some in delight, some in question. Phil and Sarah Morrison stood up then. Rachel met Sarah's timid smile. The seeds of the gospel that Rachel and Patrick and even Georgy had steadily planted in their lives had sprouted and taken root. Shyly Jennifer Corin stood up. Mitch, who stood beside her, slipped his arm around his little sister. She leaned closer to him. By the smile on Mitch's lips, Rachel guessed that it had been he himself who had led the girl to the Lord.

Patrick beamed at all of them, and Rachel knew that he could barely contain his joy enough to call out, "Praise the Lord God Almighty! Let's all rise and bow our heads and give thanks to our great and awesome God who gave His only begotten Son to save the world."

It was a wonderful worship service. Rachel sighed deeply as her soul grew steadily more refreshed with each song, and each point in Patrick's sermon. Suddenly the sound of the door being thrown open made her jump. Patrick fell silent and simply stared at the back of the church. Rachel turned and eyed the approaching Sam Jarnick as he strode purposefully up the aisle to the front. He was wearing his pistols, and they were securely strapped down. He wore them low, like a gun fighter. In his hand he carried his rifle. Rachel found herself cuddling Pattie closer to herself. People began rising to their feet, a low murmur growing steadily. Sam reached the front of the church and spun around. Lifting his hands in the air to silence the crowd, he called out, "Everyone, stay seated. Please." Rachel shifted her gaze over to Patrick, but the sobering look on his face offered her no answers. "We've got trouble," Sam began as soon as everyone was once again sitting. "There's been a wild looking gang of young fellers around for a few days, showing up here and there. I've been trying to find them, but so far I've been a step behind them all the way. Last night they robbed the Shaleman's and set their cabin and barn on fire. They lost everything except their lives. Even their horses are gone."

The murmur rose again. Sam and Patrick exchanged troubled glances. Rachel strained to hear their low words, but all she could decipher were Sam's words of, "No, your place is here. I need to know that you're here in Timberton seeing to the needs of the folks. This one is a lawman's job, not a preacher's." Turning back to the people, Sam lifted his hands again, calling out, "Quiet now. I'm heading out to bring the gang to justice. But I need a posse. Do I have any volunteers?"

Rachel turned her head in time to see Mitch step into the aisle. She eased her eyes shut for one awful moment. He was only a boy himself, though he was the head of his family, raising his younger brother and sister. But he was only a couple years older than Georgy and Ion. Across her mind swept the memory of his account of his family. They too had been burned out. His parents had not escaped the vigilantes who had done it. And no one had been brought to justice for the crime. "I'll go with you Sam," he said simply.

Sam studied him for a long moment before dipping his head in a nod. Rachel's heart fell at the sight of the silent agreement. One by one other men volunteered. Angela reached over and held tightly to Matthew's arm. But Rachel was certain that Angela really had nothing to fear in that area. Matthew was cut from too fine a cloth to be of much use to Sam in his posse. Finally Sam nodded and hurried back down the aisle and out the door, followed by his volunteers. Silence followed them, the moment the door shut behind them. Suddenly the quiet was shattered as the congregation rose and began talking, shaking their heads, fear in some faces, anger in others.

"I think we should pray and then hurry home—keep our children close to us until we hear frim Sam again." Patrick's voice had a calming affect on everyone. Those who had not yet stood up did so now and everyone bowed their heads. "Father God," Patrick called out, "thank ye for sparing the lives of Toby and Annette. We ask thit ye put a hedge o'protection around Sam and the posse. Lord, may injustice not be served in this. But may justice and also mercy and grace rule the day, for ye are a just God, full o'mercy and grace. We ask thit ye protect the people o'Timberton. Bring all o'these families safely to their homes. And keep thim safe. May we act according to wisdom—Yeer wisdom, which is frim above. We ask these things in Jesus name, amen."

As everyone quickly shuffled to and down the aisle, Patrick made his way to Rachel. "I know we don't hiv mich room," he began.

She smiled, cutting in, assuring him, "They're welcome to whatever room we have. Go and bring them home." She did not have to ask him if he were referring to the Shalemans. She already knew that.

"I'll take ye home first," he replied firmly.

"But Patrick," she argued, "it isn't far. Our cabin is the closest one to the church."

He nodded and lightly touched her back as they walked down the aisle. "Aye," he agreed. "Bit I'll still take ye and the children home b'fore I go to the Shalemans."

"Jed will be with us."

"Aye," he replied with a smile. Now they were stepping outside. He made no attempt to step away from her. "And I'll still see ye home safely." The firm note in his voice assured her that he was not about to change his mind for any reason.

She nodded and smiled. "All right, Patrick."

He returned her smiled and then called out, "O'Riley family! Straight home—no lingering."

"Pat?" Ion said, hurrying up to him, a look of concern in his face. "Can I walk Mary and her brothers home, to make sure they get there safe and sound?"

Patrick studied the boy thoughtfully. Shifting his gaze over to Rachel, he seemed to be thinking hard. Finally he dipped his head in a nod. "Bit take Georgy with ye and as soon as ye see thim safely to their cabin, come straight home. Is that understood, lad?" he added firmly, a father's authority in his voice.

"Understood," Ion replied.

Patrick turned and eyed Mitch's brother and sister. "I think Jen and Art should come home with us as well, at least until Mitch returns."

Rachel nodded, wondering if Mitch had even thought about his charges when he had volunteered to join the posse. As they continued up the path, instead of the normal lingering and chatting, everyone hurried to their homes. By the time Rachel and Patrick arrived at the cabin, Ion and Georgy had already parted from them, escorting the O'Brins safely home. By the look on Ion's face, he clearly was not thrilled about leaving them in the protection of their less than reliable father. But he had not been given a choice in the matter.

Turning to the bedroom, Rachel hurried to lay Pattie down in her crib, praying that she would remain asleep in order that Rachel could help with the meal preparations. Slipping off her Sunday bonnet, she hung it on the nail on the wall and slipped her apron on. Normally she changed out of her Sunday dress before beginning her meal preparations. But the sheer number of people who would be sitting around her table demanded that she hurry up and get started. She would, hopefully, find time later to change into every day clothes. With Matthew there, Angela would be of little use in helping with the meal. And Elizabeth and Jennifer would have their minds too much on the fact that Mitch was a member of the posse to be able to keep their minds on such tedious things as setting the table.

Rachel had the noon meal well underway by the time Patrick returned to the cabin with the Shalemans. Glancing out the window, she saw the three approaching. Georgy and Ion had returned a good ten minutes earlier. Now, with Patrick's and the Shaleman's arrival, Rachel could breathe easier, knowing that everyone who was supposed to be home, was home.

She hurried out the door to greet them. Annette's face was pale. The redness of her eyes testified that she had been crying. But the gentle smile on her lips was what broke Rachel's heart. Opening her arms to the woman, she drew Annette into a heartfelt embrace. Annette squeezed her tightly, a sob escaping her, though it did not blossom into tears.

"I've bin thinking," Patrick spoke up then as the two women drew apart. "The Lord 'as provided us with more 'orses then we really need—or even can provide for, now thit they aren't being rented out to the lumbermen. We hiv our original two, Paul Thompson's four, the Murphy's two, Jed's three, not to mention Ion's four. Rachel m'lass, do ye think brother Toby might be willing to 'elp us out by taking four of thim off of our 'ands?"

A look of hope sprang into Toby's face. "Are you serious, Patrick?" he asked incredibly.

Patrick clapped the man on the back and nodded. "It'd be a kindness on yeer part if ye'd take thim. In all honesty, we can't go on feeding thit miny. And Rachel refuses to eat them!"

"Well Patrick O'Riley! We've never discussed eating horse!" Rachel clamped her mouth shut, the corners of her lips rising as she stared at the man whose eyes were sparkling over her outburst.

"Well lassie," he grinned, "I figured I know ye well enough to be able to speak yeer mind on this issue. Bit, if I'm wrong, now's the time. Do ye not mind eating horse?"

"Dear oh dear," she chuckled, shaking her head. "You know very well that I could never eat horse."

"As I wis saying," Patrick added, turning back to an amused Toby, "it'd be a kindness if ye could find a way to take four of the horses off of our 'ands."

Toby stretched out his arm and in a mixture of solemnity and amusement shook hands with Patrick. "I think we can help you out."

"Thank ye, Toby," Patrick replied. "And now if ye'll allow me the privilege o'teaching m'lads the proper way to be building a cabin, Jed and the lads and I'll be felling sem trees and building ye a new cabin and barn—with yeer help, thit is. And I know a few o'the ither men and lads who would like to be allowed to join in—if ye kin find it in yeer heart to allow it. These laddies need to learn the art o'building cabins. It'd be a kindness on yeer part if ye'd allow us to use yeer land for a class in cabin-building."

The words were so couched in merriment that the firmness of Patrick's tone was nearly lost. But Toby had obviously not missed the entire meaning. He nodded, smiling and replied, "I won't be too prideful to accept your help."

"Ah," Patrick chuckled, "'tis good to hear. And of course, it goes without saying thit we all plan to pull out a bag of beans here and a jar o'jam there, and be sending it over to yeer new cabin for a house-warming." He paused and eyed the man squarely, all merriment slipping from his face as he studied him kindly. "Thit's what God's people do, Toby. We're there for one another."

Again Toby dipped his head in a nod. "Thank you, Patrick. Annette and I really appreciate it. And one day we'll find us a way to repay all of you."

"No need," Patrick replied with a smile. "God will take care o'thit."

Without another word, the four turned and walked the remainder of the way to the cabin and stepped inside. With the table already set, and the chairs squeezed around it, the children doubling up on the chairs, the meal was ready. As soon as they gathered around the table and the prayer of thanksgiving was offered, everyone fell to and enjoyed the meal. The conversation drifted from topic to topic, though everyone found their minds wandering far more often than was usual.

Rachel snapped her head up in surprise. Her mind had taken a little side trip and she had missed most of the conversation for a few minutes. But something had reached her ears. She stared at Annette, asking, "You're a teacher?"

Annette smiled, though a look of sadness lingered in her eyes. "I was," she replied simply.

Rachel and Angela exchanged glances. Rachel cleared her throat and turned back to Annette, trying to push away the memory of the look that had rested on Angela's face. It had been a cross between excited glee and that of a predator animal on the heels of its prey. "Would you like to be again?" Rachel asked Annette simply.

By now every voice around the table had silenced itself. Everyone was now turning to eye Annette. "Yes," she replied slowly. "You don't mean that the teaching position is open, do you?"

"Yes!" Angela and Rachel cried out at the same time.

It was Georgy who first began snickering. Johnny began giggling as he slowly repeated the words for Elizabeth. But all at once everyone began laughing. In the midst of it all, Rachel and Angela exchanged amused, relieved glances.

"Thank you Lord," Rachel murmured, "for sending a teacher to Timberton."

Patrick rode astride his horse, thinking for the hundredth time that a saddle horse would be so much easier to ride than this broad-backed workhorse. "Well Jake, ye kinnot be held responsible for being what ye are, either good or bad. To be honest, ye did a fine job in hauling m'wegon out 'ere to Oregon. I wouldn't hiv traded ye for the finest saddle horse then, so why would I now? Besides, ye're mighty 'andy in dragging along the trees I fell." He grinned and patted the horse's muscular neck. "Ye are doing just fine," he added. But the past few days spent astride this beast as he made his daily rounds checking on the members of the community since Sam and the posse had left were telling on him.

On this day he had decided to check on the settlers who were at greater distances from the tiny town of Timberton. Kenneth and Marisa LaCano lived the furthest out of anyone. Even their closest neighbor was an hour away by horseback. Patrick had tried to convince Kenneth that he and his wife would be better off living closer to the community, but his words had fallen on deaf ears. Patrick eased into a reluctant grin as his eyes traveled along the wall of green bows lining the trail. He could understand the man's love of the wilderness, seeing it in its grandeur. With so much wild land, it did seem a shame to group up so tightly together. A sigh escaped Patrick as he thought about the fact that now that the days of outlaws were upon them, the idea of grouping together was not such an unthinkable one after all.

A trail of smoke was the first indication that he was nearing the LaCano home. He began scanning the area in case any members of the gang of outlaws were hiding there just waiting for an unannounced visitor. The yard seemed peaceful enough, though a bit neglected. On the clothesline were hung a few items of clothing, though they were pegged there in a lopsided manner. One shirt was inside out. Another bore a dark smudge. A pair of workpants was just thrown over the line, rather haphazardly and without a clothes peg. One part of his mind warned him that Rachel would be highly amused that he was noticing such things. But with the very purpose of his traveling around the community being to make certain that everyone was safe, he had been forcing himself to notice things he would not ordinarily.

Suddenly the door to the cabin swung open. Kenneth stood there, pulling up his suspenders. His hair was uncombed and stuck up at various angles. Patrick frowned, wondering if the gang was hidden inside the cabin. "Pastor!" the man called out, relief in his voice. "I sure am glad to see you! My Marisa is in a bad way. The baby is getting ready to come. I can't leave her to go and fetch the doc." By now he was heading across the yard, meeting up with Patrick. "This would've been our third child. But—" He sighed heavily and shook his head. "The other two little'ns died while they were getting born. Marisa almost died with them. Will you go and fetch the doc for me? I just can't leave her alone—not now."

Patrick dipped his head in a nod. "Aye, thit I'll do. But Kenneth, I hiv news for ye. On Sunday some men burned out the Shalemans. Sam raised a posse and they're out hunting thim now. Bit ye'd be wise to keep a watchful eye on yeer place. These men hiv no honor. If yeer wife were able to travel, I'd advise ye to come into town until Sam takes thim into custody." Easing out his breath, he added, "Bit, thit isn't one of yeer choices now, is it?"

Kenneth shook his head, his eyes troubled. "No it sure ain't. Don't think I haven't regretted moving so far out. But it's done and can't be undone." The man looked suddenly so miserable with himself Patrick's heart stirred.

"Ah," he began, "once Timberton b'comes a grand ol' city, ye'll be on the viry doorstep of it. Now, b'fore I go and get the doctor, might I come in and pray with ye and yeer wife?"

A sparkle of hope jumped into the man's eyes as he caught hold of Jake's bridle. "Would you?" he asked. "I know I'm not a church-going man myself, but I was raised in church. And Marisa was too. We—we both know that prayer can make a powerful difference. It's just that, we're not on a first name basis with the Almighty and so can't be expecting Him to hear our prayers now, can we?"

As Patrick dismounted, he grinned, leaping to the ground. Kenneth had already caught up the reins and was leading Jake toward the hitching post in front of the cabin. "Would ye like to be on a first name basis with the Lord?"

Kenneth turned a shocked expression toward Patrick. "Well now, hold on there Pastor. I wasn't saying anything about getting religious and having to stop doing all the things I like to do."

Patrick chuckled and clapped the man on the back. "I wisn't talking about thit either, Kenneth, just talking about getting to know your God and Creator as your friend. Thit's all I'm talking about."

One side of the man's mouth rose as he muttered in an amused tone, "No, you're talking about a whole lot more than that. I was raised in church, remember? No, you aren't going to be satisfied until we get born again and baptized to boot! Let me ask you this. When's your next baptism?"

Patrick laughed and shook his head. "Well," he admitted, "'tis next Sunday, bit—"

"Just as I thought!" the man replied firmly, though amusement still sparkled from his eyes. "And you're hoping to get Marisa and me saved and baptized all in one week's time!"

Patrick laughed merrily, but said nothing more on the matter. After securing Jake to the hitching post, the two stepped into the cabin and crossed the floor to the doorway leading into the bedroom. Marisa was stretched out on the bed, her forehead beaded in perspiration. She turned and managed a smile, murmuring, "Pastor O'Riley, it's good of you to come."

Stepping over to the bed, Patrick lowered himself down onto one knee and studied her pain-wracked face. It had not been that many weeks ago that Rachel had looked this way. But they now had the joy of Pattie's presence to wipe the memory from their minds. "I'm 'ere to pray for ye and the wee one," he murmured. As with Kenneth, a look of relief and hope swept across her face at the mention of prayer.

"Thank you, Pastor," she murmured and immediately closed her eyes.

"Lord Jesus," Patrick softly prayed as he eased his eyes shut, "we know thit ye love this family so mich thit ye went to the cross for thim. So, we know thit Ye care about this wee one coming into the world. We're asking Ye to keep 'im or 'er safe and well, in order to live and grow up to be the man or woman Ye dreamed of since the foundation o'the world. Please, Lord, give Mrs. LaCano the strength to bear this child. 'Elp 'er in this hour o'need. Give 'er and Kenneth the peace and comfort they stand in need of. And now, Lord, give Jake swiftness of feet to carry me to Doctor Morrison, thit 'e may get 'ere in time for the birth o'this wee one. And Lord," he added, "may the truth o'the Gospel rist upon the LaCanos. 'Tis in yeer name we pray, amen."

Rising to his feet, he smiled down at the woman and nodded. A more peaceful expression rested on her face than had been there earlier. Turning, he stretched out his arm to Kenneth. As they shook hands, Patrick said quietly, "I'll be on m'way and riding hard. Don't ye be fretting."

Kenneth dipped his head in a nod, shaking Patrick's hand with the heartiness that came from renewed hope. "And, uh," he murmured, one side of his mouth rising sheepishly, "Marisa and I'll likely be out to the church meetings as soon as the baby is old enough to travel."

Patrick grinned broadly but said nothing, simply dipping his head in a single nod. Turning to the door, he hurried out and unwound Jake's reins from the hitching post. The next moment he was once again astride the broad back and was heading back down the trail toward Timberton, urging the horse to hurry.

As he rode along, his thoughts returned to home. The overcrowding in the cabin had made the past few days seem to stretch on an on. He shook his head over the thought of the small cabin sheltering the fourteen of them. A smile crept to his lips at the thought of how Rachel was making everyone feel welcome, even though they themselves were quite aware of the fact that the cabin had not been designed to hold so many. Jed had volunteered to sleep in the boys' bedroom, giving his room temporarily to Toby and Annette. Art Corin had also joined the boys in their room. Jennifer Corin had joined the girls and Angela in their room. But it was Rachel who stood out in his mind at that moment.

"Ah lassie," he sighed, love for her spilling out in his voice, "'ow ye've changed since I first met ye." He grew thoughtful, wondering if those words were in fact true. Rachel had always been caring—toward those she loved. He grinned as he realized that it was not her attitude that had changed as much as the scope of her caring had broadened to include those beyond her brother and father. "I rimimber 'ow ye used to say things thit hurt yeer own feelings," he sighed as he spoke to Rachel, though she was not there, "in order to salve yeer father's wounded pride in hiving no choice bit to take ye away frim yeer beloved Boston." He slowly shook his head over his thoughts of her, fresh love for her bubbling out of his heart. "And yeer still doing it," he sighed. "Why just yisterday ye laughed over hiving run out of tea, claiming thit ye could finally now win the lady's bet ye and Carolyn engaged in years ago over which o'the two of ye could last the longest without a cupa." The image of her face remained before him as he rode along. "Bit I'll be bringing ye some tea this day. After all, Matthew 'as plinty o'tea on 'is store shelves and far too little split wood in 'is shed. 'E may hiv bin a lumberman, bit splitting wood isn't semthing 'e likes to do. 'E will be glad to trade a bit o'tea for a chord o'wood split." The resolve brought fresh courage to him, broadening his smile as he thought of the look of happiness the tea would bring to her face. "Carolyn," he murmured to Rachel's Bostonian friend he had never met, "I'm thinking thit ye aren't going to win this bet of outlasting Rachel. Besides, semthing tells me thit ye aren't even trying." He thought about the friend Rachel had spoken of—and to (though absent from each other)—over the past two years, a friend who had been a source of joy as well as a trial to Rachel. "Lord," he sighed out, "I pray for Carolyn again. I know thit Rachel is asking ye to send 'er a 'usband and children. Bit what we most pray for is thit she'll learn to know Ye, Lord. She stands in need o'being saved. So, once again, I ask Ye, Lord, to save Rachel's friend and all 'er family. Send semone into 'er path who will be able to tell 'er about Ye. Ah Lord, it goes 'ard on Rachel, not hiving iny word frim the lassie. I know thit Carolyn refuses to write and refuses to allow Rachel to write, so certain she is thit Rachel will return to Boston. Bit, Lord, will Ye provide a way for Rachel to hiv contact with 'er—Rachel so longs to learn to know Carolyn's children and exchange stories with 'er concerning our own children. It seems to me thit 'twould take a near or even an actual miracle frim Ye to arrange it, bit, will Ye provide a way for Rachel to at least learn to know Carolyn's children, if Carolyn still refuses to contact Rachel 'erself? It hurts Rachel so, knowing thit she kin no longer be part of 'er friend's life. Will Ye provide a way, even where we kin see no way? Ye are the way-maker. Thank Ye Lord."

At last Patrick rode into Timberton and headed straight for the Morrison cabin. Jumping off of the horse, Patrick did not bother to tie Jake, knowing he would simply go to the feeding trough Phil kept near the cabin for the use of his patients' horses. Rapping loudly on the cabin door, Patrick waited for it to be opened to him. When Phil opened it, he stared at Patrick with a troubled look and motioned for him to enter. "Has the posse returned?" he asked.

Patrick shook his head. "I've just come from the LaCano cabin. She's hiving the baby now."

Already Phil was reaching for his medical bag. "I've been worried about her. I tried to convince them that she needs to be near town. But they wouldn't listen. She's already lost two babies. According to Kenneth, he nearly lost Marisa as well." By the time he finished speaking, his bag was in his hands and Sarah was beside him. He nodded at her, replying to her silent question. "You better come with me. I may need you."

"Let me saddle yeer horses for ye," Patrick offered.

Phil eased into a grin. "I'll let you saddle Sarah's. I'll take care of my own."

"That'll give me time to gather something to bring along for lunch and supper. We'll likely be there the rest of the day," she replied in a professional sounding tone.

Phil nodded. "We likely will. Honey, will you write a note telling the folks where we'll be and fasten it to the door, in case someone needs us?" He paused and sighed, adding quietly, "But if she's having the baby, there isn't any way that we'll be able to leave her, even if someone else does need a doctor."

Patrick studied the worried look on the man's face as they headed toward the horse shed. "Well, rimimber, our Lord isn't taken by surprise, even in this. 'E 'as a plan. And 'tis a good plan."

Phil turned his head sidewise and glanced at Patrick, a smiled easing to his face. He nodded. "Thanks for reminding me, Patrick," he replied quietly. "And you keep up those prayers. Something tells me that we're going to need them before this day is out."

Within minutes, the Morrisons were astride their horses and were heading down the trail toward the LaCanos' home. Patrick caught hold of Jake's reins and led him along, having had enough riding for one day. He did not stop until he turned in to Matthew's store. Rachel would have her tea before the day was out, even if he had to sell Jake in order to make the deal.

Rachel sighed in contentment over a job well done as she slipped the last dish back onto the shelf, only the memory of the noon meal remaining. She giggled as she found herself hoping that it was a pleasant memory to everyone. Just then Patrick's hands slipped to her waist, his arms creeping around her. She leaned her back up against him. "And what do ye find so funny, lassie?" he whispered into her ear.

"Lunch," she giggled and ran her fingers over his hands that held her.

He chuckled then, and she knew that he had not expected such an answer. "And why would lunch make ye laugh?"

Wondering just how she was to explain her train of thought in order to make it sound intelligent, she shook her head and sighed. "Oh Patrick. It's just that—well—It really was better than the first meal I fixed for you, wasn't it?"

His arms drew her closer to himself as his laughter shook his frame. Undoubtedly swimming across his mind was the picture of that first meal—the worst she had yet cooked. "Why, the soup wis lovely," he chuckled.

Turning in his arms, she lifted her own to encircle him. "How can you call hard, dry peas and corn lovely? They were the most unforgiving little pebbles I've ever had the pleasure of devouring."

Their laughter mingled together. Finally, he kissed her softly on the cheek, whispering, "I mist admit, I prefer the way ye cook stew now." She simply held him tighter. All at once she remembered that they were not alone. She had long ago accustomed herself to having little privacy. With so many members in their family, living in such a small house, she had given in and allowed Patrick to show her affection in front of them. But all at once she recalled that there were more than her family present, and here she was embracing her husband in front of them. Pulling back slightly, she met Patrick's amused gaze, feeling her cheeks begin to burn. But the look of love that shone from those very eyes compelled her to ignore her proprieties and simply returned to him, holding him as closely as her heart desired. It was clearly not lost on Patrick that she had once again chosen to be near him than to adhere to her former strict code of behavior. The way he held her communicated this clearly to her, causing her to smile, glad that she had put him ahead of the others in the room.

"Now," he murmured softly, "if ye could hiv inything at all to finish off yeer lovely lunch, what would it be?"

She hesitated, not wanting to make him feel badly by voicing the one thing they had run out of. But he always seemed to guess when she tried to sidestep an issue. "Well, of course a cup of tea would be Heavenly, but coffee would be my second choice."

Easing back from her, he withdrew his left arm from around her and reached his hand down to his pants pocket. Withdrawing a tightly tied sack, he held it up for her. "It just so 'appens," he whispered, "Matthew's store 'ad a few packages of this, just sitting on the shelf, doing no one iny good at all. I could 'ardly leave it there, now could I?"

Rachel could not hold back her smile of delight as she stared at the bag of tea leaves. "Oh Patrick! However did you manage? We don't have any cash money at the moment."

His eyes were fastened on hers, as if savoring her delight. "At first I offered to trade Jake for it—" Rachel began giggling then. "And I even offered to throw the lads in on the deal, bit 'e seemed to think they might be more trouble than they were worth." He paused, laughing quietly along with her. "Finally we settled on my splitting up a cord o'wood for 'im."

She studied the dear face before her as he watched her with little boy eagerness written in his eyes, waiting for her approval. "I love ye, Rachel," he whispered and lowered his head to hers and kissed her in a long and sweet kiss. As he lifted his head, the laughter was gone from his eyes, leaving only a look of love behind.

"I love you too," she whispered. "Patrick," she added in wonder, "I don't know how you do it! You're the most amazing man I've ever known! The way you provide for us—the things you do—Patrick—" She fell silent, shaking her head as words escaped her. But the stunned look that came to Patrick's face assured her that he understood her message. A smile crept to his lips, a light dancing in his eyes. And she knew then and there that her words of admiration over him had meant as much to him as his words of love meant to her. As they continued meeting each other's gaze, she sensed that they were even more united together than ever before. "Thank you for the tea," she whispered. "It means so much to me."

He smiled and eased his arms away, allowing her to step over to the fireplace to get the kettle to boiling. As she worked, she glanced over her shoulder at him. There he stood, watching her, standing as tall as a king. His expression softened as she looked her look of love at him.

It was then that Rachel began hearing a familiar tongue clicking in disapproval. Glancing over to her rocking chair, she met Angela's stare. The woman was frowning and shaking her head. Shifting her eyes, Rachel locked into Annette's amused gaze. No look of disapproval rested there, though the woman's cheeks were slightly flushed. Lifting her shoulders slightly, Rachel smiled at her. At least Annette understood. And perhaps in time Angela might too, but then again, perhaps not. Angela was Angela, with her own codes of conduct, whether they fit the circumstances or not.

In short order the teapot was issuing forth the delightful tea that Rachel was pouring into teacups for all three ladies, the men having declared that they preferred having coffee. Rachel had hid her smile when Patrick had chosen coffee rather than tea as well, knowing his fondness for tea to equal her own. As she eased down at the table beside Patrick and lifted the cup to her lips, she closed her eyes and simply savored that first swallow of tea. It had been several weeks since they had run out of tea. She knew that Patrick had not realized when it had happened. She had tried to keep it from him, knowing that he would feel badly about her being denied her daily pot of tea.

The beat of horse hooves echoed across the yard, silencing the conversation around the table. Patrick and Toby were on their feet immediately, hurrying over to the door. Rachel shifted her gaze to the window and caught her breath. Mitch's slumped form rested in the saddle. The next moment Patrick and Toby were gently pulling him off of the horse. At last they and began carrying him into the cabin. "Oh dear," Rachel murmured, rising to her feet. "Doctor Morrison is over at the LaCanos' cabin—he can't leave Marisa—" Whirling around as the men carried Mitch's unconscious form inside, she called out, "Ion, where's Georgy?"

"He's over at Matthew's," Ion replied, hurrying over to Mitch, helping Patrick and Toby carry him across the room to the boys' bedroom. "We can lay him on my bed," he said. "I'll go after Georgy."

"Bit the laddie isn't a doctor," Patrick replied.

No one answered. His words were only too true. Though Georgy spent nearly every available moment pouring over Phil's medical books and joining him on his house calls, he was still simply Georgy Northwood. But as no one offered any other suggestion, Ion left the cabin on the run, heading for Matthew's store. Rachel eased into the boys' bedroom and stared in shock at the crumpled form of the young Mitch Corin. "Patrick," she murmured, horror gripping her. "Is he alive?"

Patrick nodded, slipping his arm around her waist. "Aye, bit just barely. E's bin shot up badly. Where are Jen and Art?"

"Out in the barn with Johnny and the girls. Should we call them?"

Patrick sighed, suddenly looking uncertain. "I—I don't know," he admitted. Fear gripped Rachel then, seeing Patrick suddenly indecisive. "No," he finally replied, firmness returning to his voice. "Let's let Georgy hiv a look at 'im first." He sighed heavily and shook his head, admitting, "'E knows more about doctoring then iny of us do."

By the time Georgy burst into the cabin, a leather bag in his hand, Patrick and Toby had returned to the table, while Rachel hovered just outside the bedroom doorway, uncertain what to do. Turning, she studied the scared expression that was painted on the boy's face. She swallowed, wondering over all of them placing such a weight of responsibility on the boy's shoulders. As he stepped past Rachel, heading into the bedroom, Rachel turned and followed him. Crouching down beside Mitch, he pulled back the fragments of red-soaked cloth, exposing the wound. Instantly Rachel's hand went to her mouth, pressing hard against her lips, trying not to gag at the gruesome sight. Georgy's hands stilled themselves. Rachel wondered if he intended to do anything—if he even knew what to do. All at once he rose to his feet and turned to face her. She caught her breath at the expression on his face. The boyish fear was nowhere in sight. His eyes suddenly looked years older—steady—confidant. She found her own fear edging back as she looked at his face. And she wondered where the young boy had slipped off to, leaving this man in his place—a man she instantly realized that she could lean on. He murmured to her in the same tone the doctor used when speaking to Sarah when she assisted him with a patient, confidential and to the point, "I wish I had some of Doc's equipment. I grabbed up this bag he's been letting me use. There's just basic supplies in it—but that's all I know how to use yet. Rachel!" he added sternly. It was only then that she realized that she had become slightly lightheaded. "I need your help. I can't operate on him alone. But you have to tell me if you can take it. If not, tell me now."

Rachel swallowed and nodded. "I—I can take it. I'll be here. Mitch needs me to help you."

He dipped his head in a nod. "All right. I'm going to need to sterilize these instruments. Do you have any boiling water?" She nodded, thinking about the tea she had just made. There had been plenty of water left over. As she turned to step out of the room, Georgy caught her arm and met her gaze steadily. "Tell Pat I need him to pray. And keep Jen and Art away."

"They—they don't know about it yet. They're out in the barn."

Dipping his head in a nod, he ordered, "Make sure they stay out there."

"I'll have Ion see to it." She paused and then finally asked, "Is he going to die?"

A bolt of pain swept across the young man's face. "I don't know," he whispered. "We need Doc." He shook his head, lifting his shoulders slightly. "But there isn't time. If I don't do something now, there's no question—He will die."

Glancing out into the kitchen, Rachel saw that one of Georgy's orders was already being carried out. Patrick sat at the table, his head bowed, his lips moving in quiet prayer. The others around the table likewise had bowed their heads. Sudden calmness swept over Rachel then. Turning back to Georgy, she murmured, "The Great Physician is able to help Mitch. God's will is going to be done. You just do what you can. God will do the rest."

A look of relief washed over Georgy's face then. He nodded and turned back to Mitch, then opened the medical bag he had set on the floor. "I need something to set my instruments on," he added, already his attention back on Mitch and the medical procedure ahead.

Rachel stepped out of the bedroom and lightly tapped Ion on the shoulder. He glanced up from where he sat at the table. "Carry the bench into the room for Georgy. And then keep the children in the barn. Don't tell them what's happened if you don't have to. But under no circumstance are you to let them come inside until I send for you."

Ion nodded and hurried to do as she said. Rachel, in turn, busied herself in following Georgy's orders, securing a basin for the water she would soon have boiling again. Carrying a tea towel along with the basin, she reentered the bedroom and placed them on the bench Ion had set beside Mitch's bed. "The water will be boiling in a minute or so," she whispered.

While they waited for the water to boil, Georgy and Rachel carefully removed what remained of Mitch's shirt. Rachel forced herself to keep her eyes from the gaping hole on the left side of his chest. She kept swallowing, reminding herself that Georgy and Mitch needed her to hold down her lunch and assist Georgy with the ordeal of removing the bullets from that wound. It was Patrick who finally carried the kettle of boiling water into the room. Immediately Georgy set about to sterilizing the medical instruments, instruments that looked like knives and sewing equipment to Rachel's untrained eyes. And then the gruesome task began as Georgy began probing the ghastly wound, searching for the lead slugs.

Rachel kept swabbing away the blood as Georgy worked, alternating between that and wiping the sweat from Georgy's brow so that it would not run into his eyes. With the clink of the lead pieces falling into the basin, Georgy finally glanced over at her and said, "I'll have to sew him up now."

Rachel swallowed quickly. Georgy smiled with such compassion that Rachel found herself calming down again. She nodded. "What do you want me to do?"

"Just hand me the instruments when I call for them," he replied with such kind understanding in his tone Rachel felt the remainder of her fear slipping away.

With surprising ease Georgy inserted the needle through Mitch's flesh, as if he were sewing up a rag doll for Anna Marie. Rachel continued blotting away the blood that tried to hinder Georgy in his work. Time seemed to stand horribly still as they worked side by side. But finally Georgy leaned back, depositing the needle back into the basin of water. "That's all I can do for him. We'll bandage it and then—" he sighed and shook his head. "Then we'll see what happens."

Georgy worked on securing the bulky, folded cloth over the wound and wrapped swaths around Mitch's chest to hold it in place. By the time he was finished, Rachel had already washed the blood from her hands. He turned and began washing his own hands then. She watched him, calmness sifting through her as she studied this young man who looked and acted like a doctor. "When you're finished here," she said softly, "would you like a cup of coffee?"

Lifting his eyes, he paused in scrubbing at his hands. A slow grin spread across his face. He dipped his head in a nod that was anything but boyish. If she had not known better, she would have thought him to be born of gentility by that very action. "Thank you, Rachel. Coffee sounds good." His eyes sparkled then, as he added, "It's been a little over two years since I've had a cup of the java."

Ion remained keeping the children entertained in the barn, but he began wondering if they would suspect that they were not to leave the barn. He dreaded the thought of having to explain to them the reason why they could not go into the cabin, or even make much noise outside. Suddenly the barn door opened and in stepped Georgy. Instantly the two exchanged glances. Ion sighed and nodded toward the two young Corins. Georgy glanced over at them. "Jen? Art?" Georgy began quietly. Ion studied his older brother, wondering at the sound of gentle authority in his voice where normally laughter rested. The two glanced up at him from their antics with Johnny's dog Charles and Patrick's dog Leprechaun. "Come here," he added, stepping over to one of the stump seats beside Ion and sat down. "I have something to tell you."

Jennifer and Arthur exchanged puzzled glances, but did as Georgy requested, sitting down on stumps in front of the one he was sitting on. Johnny and Elizabeth hung back, clearly uncertain what was going on. As Georgy spoke, Johnny quietly repeated the words slowly to Elizabeth. "It's about Mitch," Georgy began gently. Instantly the brother and sister lost their looks of merriment. "Now, we're praying he's going to be all right. I patched him up as best as I knew how. The doctor will be here and check him over as soon as he can."

"What happened to Mitch?" Arthur finally asked.

Georgy eased out his breath and reached over, softly catching hold of the young boy's upper arm. "Well, Art, he got himself shot." As the boy paled, Georgy continued in a calming tone, "But I got the bullets out of him. Before he got here, he got the bleeding to stop. That means a lot. And we're praying. You know Mitch is a son of God now. And God is going to do what's right."

The little boy nodded, his lips trembling, but said nothing more. Georgy glanced over at Jennifer, giving her a chance to say something. But she made no attempt to do so. Tears were slipping down her cheeks. Ion eased out his breath as he looked on, uncertain what to do. Georgy rose to his feet then, adding, "I have to go and keep and eye on Mitch. Now, I need all of you to stay out here where any noise won't be bothering him. Is that all right?"

The two nodded and silently watched as Georgy stepped over to the door and eased back outside. Ion drew in a deep breath, studying the others. By then Johnny had gotten the message across to Elizabeth. Her face was now as pale as Jennifer's and Arthur's. Ion knew that the rest of the afternoon would be long. No one was any longer in the mood to romp and pass the time away enjoyably. As the long minutes passed, each of the children wandered aimlessly to various parts of the barn, lost in thought. Elizabeth sat down beside him, pressing a piece of paper into his hands, one she had been carrying around all afternoon for the purpose of others writing down messages she could not decipher by reading their lips. Lowering his eyes to the piece of paper, he read her words, "What if he dies?" She handed him the small stump of a pencil she carried with her.

He smiled gently at her, wondering over her having written the words rather than spoken them. "God will do what's right," he wrote as she read. "And if he chooses to take Mitch's life, He'll take him home to Heaven to be with Him forever."

Elizabeth reached for the pencil and began writing, "But I don't want him to die."

Ion reached his arm around her shoulders and drew her to himself. He brushed the tears from her cheek that were slipping down. "I don't want him to die either," he whispered. His eyes shifted to the sober faces of Jennifer and Arthur, knowing exactly the lost feeling that was coursing through them at the thought of their sole provider facing possible death. He drew Elizabeth closer to himself. She was crying softly now. Until then he had not realized that Elizabeth and Mitch had become friends, but apparently they had. In silence the afternoon continued dragging along.

Patrick finally came out to the barn, quietly calling out, "'Tis time to come in the cabin. Bit, ye mist remain quiet. We mist not disturb Mitch's rist."

The five followed Patrick out of the barn and silently made their way to the cabin. Patrick lingered back and allowed all but Ion to go on ahead. Slipping his arm loosely around Ion's shoulders, he murmured, "Phil just arrived. 'E is checking on Mitch now. Oh and 'ere is a piece o'good news. Phil delivered the LaCano baby, a little girl they named Marianna. She and 'er mamma are both doing viry well. Sarah is staying there for a few days to 'elp out."

Ion managed a smile, though the strain of the day made it difficult to exert much emotion, even thanksgiving. "Pat," he suddenly asked, "how did he know to come here?"

"Matthew," Patrick replied as they stepped to the cabin door. "'E rode to the LaCano cabin and told the Morrisons about Mitch."

Without another word the two followed the others into the cabin. Just then Dr. Morrison stepped out of the bedroom, a stern expression on his face. Ion wondered over the fact that Georgy was nowhere in sight. He swallowed, wondering what Georgy would do if the doctor was angry with him for having operated on Mitch. Finally Phil eased into a smile and nodded. "Mitch has a chance. But he wouldn't have made it if he'd been forced to wait for me to get here." Stretching out his arm toward the bedroom doorway, he added with a hint of pride in his voice, adding, "Allow me to introduce you to a colleague of mine: Doctor George Northwood."

Georgy stepped out of the bedroom and grinned at everyone. Finally he met Ion's gaze. Ion shook his head and rolled his eyes. Georgy chuckled quietly. Ion wondered what would follow, now that Georgy had actually cut a man open and sewed him back together. But one thing he was certain of, no one could now prevent him from becoming a doctor. No one.

Chapter 5

Ion lifted his eyes from his pad of paper that rested on his lap as he sat on the hearth, leaning up against the stonework of the fireplace. Georgy met his gaze as he stepped out of the bedroom where he and Doctor Morrison had stayed with Mitch throughout the long night. Weariness beyond his years was painted on his face, assuring Ion that he had not slept at all. In silence he continued watching as Georgy reached for the coffeepot and poured himself a generous cupful. Easing himself down beside Ion, he lifted the cup and drank deeply for a moment. Finally swallowing, he shifted his gaze to Ion, one side of his mouth slipping up into the grin Ion had come to expect. "Don't worry, you'll be old enough to drink coffee one of these days."

Ion rolled his eyes and shook his head, murmuring back, "I've drank coffee for years."

Georgy's full-blown grin now rested on his lips. His eyes were sparkling now, sending away part of the look of weariness. "Not in Rachel's kitchen," he whispered back. "You have to be a man to drink coffee in her kitchen."

"If you're such a man," Ion replied in a carefully low voice, "why are you whispering?"

Georgy's expression fell blank for one delightful moment. Then he grinned again and nodded toward the bedroom doorway. "I don't want to disturb Mitch."

Ion snorted quietly. Immediately both turned and eyed Rachel. Apparently she had not heard Ion's rude noise. Again they exchanged amused glances. Finally Georgy sighed, the merriment slipping from his face, being replaced with a thoughtful look. Ion waited, knowing that it never took Georgy long to voice his thoughts. "Ion," he sighed, "operating on Mitch was—" He sipped his coffee before continuing, Ion watching him closely. If Georgy was anything, it was bold in speech. He wondered over his hesitation.

"Fun?" he asked quietly.

Georgy tore his eyes from his cup and stared at Ion, a look of guilt on his face. Slowly he nodded. "Not all of it," he whispered. "I mean, I didn't want

Mitch hurt!"

Ion smiled and nodded. "I know."

"How did you know I had some fun too?" Georgy asked, the troubled look still in his eyes.

"Georgy, you're going to be a doctor. Of course you're going to have at least a little fun doing what you love to do. It doesn't mean you don't care."

Relief flooded Georgy's face. "You sure?"

Ion's smile grew as he studied this uncertain brother of his who one moment was spouting off about being a grown man and the next was looking out through puppy dog eyes in need of approval. He dipped his head in a nod. "If I had to have somebody cutting on me, I'd rather it was somebody who enjoyed his work instead of hated it. Wouldn't you?"

Nodding in thought, Georgy eased into a small grin. "I guess I would—as long as he didn't enjoy it too much." He took several sips of coffee before speaking again, Ion making no attempt at interrupting his train of thought. "It's just so—so fascinating, Ion. All of those blood vessels and muscles and all of it fitting together. And here I am trying to put it all back together the way it goes, like a jigsaw puzzle. And I know that if I get it done right, my patient will be all right. It doesn't mean that—" He fell silent, his cheeks coloring and glanced away.

Ion stared, wondering what could have shamed him so. Suddenly Ion grinned and leaned closer to Georgy. "You almost threw up, didn't you?" he chuckled.

Georgy sighed heavily, tugging his eyes back up to meet Ion's gaze and slowly nodded miserably.

"Right on Mitch?" Ion laughed, still keeping his voice too low for the others in the room to hear.

"Almost."

"Does Rachel know?"

Georgy shrugged. "Since when does Rachel not know something about us?"

Ion continued grinning, his world suddenly falling back into its normal orbit. Georgy was not altogether a man yet. He would still have to wait a bit on that, giving Ion a chance to grow up to manhood alongside him. Georgy fell silent then and resumed drinking his man's coffee, Ion laughing quietly the whole time. Finally Georgy glanced down at the pad of paper on Ion's lap. "What ya writing?" he murmured.

It was now Ion's turn to feel uncomfortable. He shrugged, muttering, "Just some nonsense." Without warning, Georgy whipped his hand out and snatched the pad of paper from him. "Georgy!" he whispered fiercely. Both glanced over at the table where Annette sat with everyone gathered around her as she told an animated story to the children, though the adults were listening too. Their attention was too deeply fixed on the story for anyone to pay any attention to the two of them.

"So are you going to tell me what it is, or am I going to have to read it for myself?" Georgy asked, laughter darting from his eyes.

Ion sighed. "It's just a poem. And I'm stuck. It doesn't sound quite right in places. Mary usually helps me to polish my poems."

Georgy's grin now seemed somehow less teasing and more older brother looking. "Maybe I can help."

"You'll just laugh."

"Does Mary laugh?" he asked in a mixture of sincerity and amusement.

Ion rolled his eyes. "No. But that's not because my poems are any good. It's just because," he added, lowering his eyes. There was nothing he could do to prevent Georgy from reading the poem he held in his hands, so he fell silent and waited.

"Ion," Georgy finally spoke again, "this poem is about Sam, isn't it?"

Ion glanced back at Georgy and nodded. "Yeah," he admitted. "It's just a ditty."

Georgy shook his head. "No it isn't." The teasing look was gone from his eyes. "It's a sonnet, Ion. Does Rachel know you can write sonnets?"

Ion shrugged, mumbling, "Doubt it."

Georgy eyed him with something that looked remarkably like pride over Ion. One side of his mouth rose and he slowly shook his head, murmuring in amazement, "I can't hardly read a sonnet right, and here you are writing them! How do you do it Ion? This is—" He suddenly lowered his eyes and shrugged self-consciously, mumbling, "It's beautiful." Georgy frowned slightly and added, "In a manly kind of way, I mean."

Ion could not hold back a grin over Georgy's sudden discomfort in revealing a sensitive side to his personality. "Of course," Ion grunted in a tone he hoped Georgy would find satisfactory to his embarrassed ego. But it took all of his effort not to openly laughed at him for his embarrassment. He often wondered over Georgy's reluctance in showing the softer side of himself. Ion had decided long ago that he himself had every right to be who he was, regardless of what others thought. Of course, it had landed him in more than one fight, refusing to speak and act as others wanted him to. "Georgy," he added quietly, waiting for Georgy to glance back at him before continuing. When he did so, he simply smiled and asked, "Any suggestions?"

Georgy's eyes popped open. "You're the writer, not me."

"But if I had a good suggestion about how to help Mitch, wouldn't you want to hear it?"

Georgy nodded. "Yeah—I mean yes." His eyes darted momentarily over to Rachel before returning his attention to Ion. "But writing and doctoring are two different things."

Ion chuckled quietly. Georgy often missed the point he was attempting to make. Reaching for the tablet, he lightly pulled it out of Georgy's hand. "Look here, for instance," he said, pointing to the first line. "It's about two boys. But it just doesn't sound right to use the word boy twice in the same line."

Georgy leaned over the pad of paper, studying the line in question. "Well, I don't mind it being repeated," he sighed. "But I imagine Rachel wouldn't think it fit. Why don't you just use another word for boy?"

"I've been trying to think of one. But all the others have two syllables. And I only have room for one."

Georgy chuckled then, asking, "Ion, have you ever heard Pat talk?"

Ion flinched back in surprise. "Of course."

"Have you ever heard him use the word boy?"

Ion thought back to the night when Patrick had quoted the last words of Ion's father to him. It had stuck in his mind. He had never heard him use the word boy before—nor since. Easing into a slow smile, he breathed out, "Lad. Yes, I'll use the word lad for the first one." Scratching out the word boy, he penciled in lad, nodding in pleasure. "That fits." As his eyes scanned the next line, he asked, "What about this? Look. I've got 'he then did see.' But that doesn't flow."

"Why not just write 'he saw'?"

Ion chewed his lower lip, shaking his head slowly. "No. Sonnets have a specific rhythm and rhyming pattern. A B B A. A B B A. C D. C D. C D." At the blank look on Georgy's face, he wondered if Georgy had paid any attention at all during poetry lessons. "That's the rhyming pattern. Lines two, three, six, and seven all have to rhyme. The vowel I've chosen to rhyme is E—long E. Saw doesn't rhyme with the E words. And I need ten beats per line. You've taken away two of those beats. You can't have a sonnet that has thirteen lines of ten beats and one line of eight beats." He chuckled quietly over the stunned look on Georgy's face.

"You really figure all of that out?"

"Sure," Ion said in surprise. "How else could you write poetry?"

Georgy shrugged. "I don't. But, maybe that's why yours sound like poems and mine sound like just regular talking."

Ion nodded. "Maybe. But, it's fun, Georgy, figuring it all out. It's work, but fun work. Let's see. I need four syllables, every other one being stressed, the beat coming to the second and fourth, ending in the E sound, with the meaning: he then did see." This was the point where Mary was most helpful. She seemed to know just what his poems needed to fulfill all these requirements.

"Well," Georgy began in thought, "why don't you keep the word see? Then you just have to come up with three words."

Ion nodded. "All right. What could I substitute for the words he then did?"

"He finally did?"

Ion grinned. "I think that's close," he murmured, hoping not to discourage Georgy in his efforts to help. "He finally did see. Close, but not quite," he added in thought, realizing that Georgy was on to something. "Finally—that's a good word Georgy. It's really three syllables, but since we don't usually take the time to actually voice the A, we can squeeze it into a two syllable space. Finally see," he murmured in thought. Suddenly he smiled broadly and scratched out the words he planned to discard and wrote as he said, "Could finally see."

Georgy chuckled and nudged Ion. "I guess I'm as good a helper as Mary any day." Ion rolled his eyes but did not grace the observation with a comment. His silence seemed to tickle Georgy. "What else can I help you with?"

As Ion's eyes scanned down the page, he set the point of his pencil on a line just past the middle. "And these two men," he sighed, shaking his head. "It follows the beat, if you force it to. But it doesn't flow naturally. "Now, I want to show a contrast between these two men. I could use the word 'but' instead of 'and'. But then it doesn't really tie it into the lines above it as well. What can I use for the word 'and'?"

Georgy grew thoughtful. Finally he grinned. "And yet."

Ion shifted his gaze back to Georgy's face, wondering why he had never noticed this side of him before. He really was not all clown and full of physical abilities. He had a sharp mind on him. Nodding, he grew thoughtful. "And yet. I like that. It shows contrast and includes the lines above. But, it's two syllables taking up the place of only one. "And yet these two men," he sighed. Suddenly the solution popped out to him. "And yet these men," he murmured. Chuckling, he added, "we didn't even need the word 'two'. Thanks Georgy. That makes this line almost perfect."

"Almost?" Georgy laughed.

Ion shrugged. "Well, I imagine a real poet would find some flaws in it. But I think it's pretty good for newcomers like us. It wasn't that long ago you couldn't even read."

Georgy grinned and clapped Ion on the back. "You couldn't either."

"I know," Ion murmured, lowering his eyes, still ashamed to admit it.

"So," Georgy added, excitement coloring his tone. "Read it out loud."

"Not out loud," Ion murmured, suddenly feeling more exposed than he had in a long time.

Yanking the pad from Ion's grasp, Georgy replied lightly, "Then I will." Ion groaned, but knew it was pointless to protest. Once Georgy had his mind made up, there was little that could be done to change it. In a quiet, sober sounding voice, Georgy read,

"'A lad upon an elder boy took aim;
The older boy his mark could finally see,
And shouted, "Bang!" The younger fell with glee;
For to the boys, 'twas only just a game.
The years passed by and men these boys became;
A lawman's badge—the elder's destiny;
The younger one was famed an outlaw, he;
And yet these men both wore the same last name.
The day soon came when each the other spied;
The outlaw forced the lawman then to draw;

To miss his mark, without success, he tried,
But too ingrained in him was that of law.
He held his dying brother close and cried,
While gripping tight his badge and fierce clenched jaw.'"

Georgy lifted his eyes from the paper and stared long and hard at Ion, a look of amazement on his face. "Ion," he breathed out, shaking his head slowly, "you've got to let Rachel read this. You've got to let Sam read it too."

Ion shook his head. "No," he replied firmly.

Georgy handed the pad of paper back to him. His expression was firm with determination. "Ion, you've got to let people read what you write. You can make a difference in folk's lives by the things you write. Why, if you don't let people read your poems and stories, what's the point in writing them? That'd be as foolish as me spending all my spare time studying Doc's medical books but refuse to help people when they need medical attention. It might be fun for you to write. And it might be fun for me to learn medicine. But if we don't let others benefit from it all, what's the point? God's given you a gift, Ion. Don't hide it. He means for you to use it for His glory."

Rising to his feet, he lifted his cup, draining it, setting it on the fireplace mantle and turned, stepping across the kitchen floor and toward the outside door. Ion stared at the door Georgy closed behind him and drew in a deep, thoughtful breath, wondering if Georgy was right. It made sense when applied to the medical field. Across his mind swept the images of people laughing at the things he would one day write. Now that Rachel had opened up the world of the written word to him, he could no sooner shut it than he could stop breathing or eating. But could he so expose himself to the criticism of others by letting them read what he wrote? It was hard enough to let anyone except Mary—even family—read his poems. How could he allow strangers to? Again he sighed, knowing that he could not simply ignore Georgy's words, now that he had heard them.

Georgy eased himself down onto the logs piled up by the chopping block. The words to Ion's poem were still in his mind. He had heard Sam's story along with the rest, but Ion had put it into words that made him see clearly what had happened. For what seemed like the hundredth time—or the thousandth—he began praying for the man. "Lord," he sighed out, "please keep Sam and the posse safe. And bring them back soon. Lord, thank you for sparing Mitch's life." His throat grew tight then, thinking about how close his friend had come to losing his life. He had regained consciousness during the night, but neither Georgy nor Phil had questioned him, fearing that the memory would be too much of a strain on Mitch's weakened condition. He had fallen back asleep again moments later, only to awaken for snatches of minutes at a time. Each time he had remained awake longer than the time before, but still had not volunteered any information, causing Georgy to wonder if the news were too horrifying for him to voice yet.

"Lord, Sam isn't ready to meet you face to face," Georgy sighed. "Thank you for sparing Mitch's life. Thank you that it looks like he's going to pull through. But Sam? And the others? Not one of them knows you, Lord. They aren't ready to face eternity yet." He paused and sighed deeply, a new thought striking him. "Lord? What about the men who burned down the Shalemans' cabin and barn? They probably aren't ready to meet you face to Face either. Lord, I don't know how to pray for them. Am I suppose to ask you to spare their lives? I know you've said we're supposed to pray for our enemies, but did you mean outlaws too? I could pray for an enemy soldier, because he isn't committing murder or stealing. He's just fighting for his country, like me—if I were in a war, I mean. It doesn't make him evil, just because he's on the other side. But did you mean for us to pray for our enemies even when it isn't in war? Did you mean for us to pray for evil men?"

Sighing long and loud, Georgy shook his head. "Do I have the right to pray for the men who burned up everything the Shalemans own—and even tried to kill them? Do I have that right?" Across his mind swept the memory of Ion's account of the fight Patrick had had with Ion's father. Patrick and Colon had been enemies, though not because Patrick had wanted it so. But Patrick had prayed for Colon. "I guess if Pat thought he should pray for Mr. MacAlister, then I'm probably supposed to pray for these outlaws. So, I'm praying for them, Lord. My heart isn't in it as much as it is when I pray for Sam and the posse. If that's wrong, Lord, then I'm sorry, and please forgive me. But, I know Sam and his men. And I don't want them to die. But those outlaws? I don't know them. But, because you've said to pray for our enemies, I'll pray for them. And who knows, maybe they got praying mothers or fathers who's hoping that someone will turn them from their wickedness. Lord, that's what I'm praying for, that they'll turn from their evil ways. But Lord, if they aren't going to, then I ask that they be stopped. In Jesus name I pray, amen."

The sound of approaching horses caught Georgy's attention. Turning, he stared at the approaching riders as they headed up the path toward the O'Riley cabin. Just then the cabin door swung open and Patrick stepped outside, calling over his shoulder, "It's Sam." The next moment he was out the door and drew it closed behind him. Georgy imagined the look that was likely painted on Rachel's face, questions and uncertainty mingled with faith and concern for those she held dear. Georgy was on his feet then, hurrying over to Patrick, falling in step with him. They covered the ground quickly, neither saying a word until they reached Sam. Patrick caught hold of the horse's bridle and eyed Sam, lines of concern for the man etched in his face. "Ye've bin wounded," he sighed. "Let me 'elp ye down."

"No," Sam replied, his tone harsher than normal. Georgy studied the man's pale face. Clearly he was fighting against pain, by the look in his eyes. His left sleeve was drenched in blood. "I just came to tell you that it's over. The outlaws are taken care of—they won't be bothering anyone anymore."

"Sam!" Georgy cried out in surprise. "You have to come in and let Doc fix your arm. He's here."

"It's only a scratch, Georgy," Sam muttered. But the normal laughter that came to the man's eyes when making light of suffering did not present itself this time.

"It's not a scratch, Sam," Georgy replied firmly. Even to his own ears he sounded more like a man and less like a schoolboy. "You've been shot. And unless the bullet got lodged in your arm, then you've got an even bigger hole on the other side—the side you're keeping held tight to yourself. You're going to need stitches. And it has to be cleaned. You don't want infection setting in." His quiet, yet firmly spoken words had a surprising affect on the man. The stunned expression on his face caused the corners of Georgy's mouth to creep up, regardless of his effort to look stern.

Sam studied him long and hard for a few moments in silence. Shifting his gaze, as if looking across the yard for someone or something hidden to him, he turned back to Patrick. This time amusement shone in his eyes. "Now where did that young rascal Georgy run off to? And you never told me you had a grown son who's already a man. What's his name, Patrick?" he asked, tipping his head sidewise toward Georgy.

Patrick chuckled quietly and offered his arm to Sam, helping him dismount. "I hivn't bin able to find the lad Georgy. Bit, this 'ere is Doc Northwood. Ye'll be pleased in making 'is acquaintance. 'E's a fine surgeon—"

Sam's feet hit the ground at that moment. His eyes open wide in shock. "Surgeon?" he demanded.

Georgy had positioned himself to Sam's right, slipping his arm around the man's waist, ordering quietly, "Lean on me Sam."

"Not until I hear about this surgery business."

Georgy grinned, admitting, "I operated on Mitch. Took out two lead slugs from him and sewed him back up."

The look of amazement that swept over Sam's face as he studied Georgy made Georgy chuckle in more of a boyish giggle than in a man's laughter. He pushed out his breath at the sound, but could not take it back.

"Sam?" One of the men from the posse had ridden up to the three and was studying Sam. "You planning on staying here?"

Sam turned and nodded. "Yeah, Jess. You can ride on home now. Tell the others they might as well go home. If I need you for anything, I'll send one of Patrick's boys for you. But," he added with a slow grin, "I doubt the O'Riley's are going to release me anytime soon."

Jess laughed quietly and turned his horse, heading back to the other riders who had stayed back on the edge of the trail. Not until they rode out of sight did Sam ease his right arm around Georgy's shoulders, resting his weight on him. Georgy carried his weight easily enough, though was stunned over the man's sudden willingness to show weakness. Patrick was now at Sam's left, careful of the injured arm, and slipped his arm around him, helping Georgy half carry him along to the cabin. Georgy wondered over Sam's reluctance in allowing the posse to realize just how bad off he was.

"Is Mitch going to be all right?" Sam murmured just before they entered the cabin.

Georgy nodded, replying quietly, "Doc says he should be fine soon."

By then Toby was there opening the door for them. As they helped Sam across the floor to the boys' bedroom, Rachel was suddenly there. The look of concern on her face could not have been missed by the man. Normally he would have smiled. Georgy shook his head, certain that he was much worse off than Georgy had suspected, if he could not even manage a smile. It was a wonder he had been able to lightly banter with him and Patrick. After they eased the man down onto Georgy's bed, Patrick left the room, leaving Phil and Georgy to see to Sam's needs.

"We'll cut the left sleeve of his coat off," Phil said quietly to Georgy.

"Over my dead body," Sam muttered. "This coat cost me a month's wages."

Georgy and Phil exchanged startled glances. "Sam!" Phil clamped his jaw shut, deciding not to try reasoning with the man. Together he and Georgy struggled to pull off the coat with minimal stress to the injured arm. As they worked, Phil sighed, murmuring half to himself, half to Sam, "The coat's ruined anyway. It has two holes in it!"

"They can be fixed," Sam growled.

"Well, the blood's never going to come out."

"Badge of victory," was Sam's only reply.

Georgy grinned and accepted the coat as Phil thrust it into his hands. Entering the world of men was proving to be far more interesting than he had ever imagined. But his thoughts were quickly drawn away as he helped Phil ease Sam onto his right side. As Georgy supported Sam's left arm, Phil began examining the gaping hole on the back of his arm. "The bullet went straight through," he murmured. "Doesn't appear to have nicked the bone. You've lost a lot of blood, Sam." Easing out his breath, he glanced over at Georgy and nodded. "Let's get him on his stomach so I can sew him up." This last statement was void of the combined jesting and rebuking he had used in bantering with Sam. It was fully professional, as one colleague speaking to another. Georgy dipped his head in a nod, gently easing Sam onto his stomach. Without a word, he stepped over to Phil's bag and gathered up the necessary equipment for the doctor. Once again a thrill of both excitement and nausea swept over him at the thought of sewing up the man's arm.

An hour after Phil had left to check on the LaCanos, having assured everyone that Sam would be fine, but would require several days of rest, Sam called out in a weakened version of his normal hearty voice, "Patrick, come in here, will you?"

Patrick turned to eye Georgy, who sat across the table from him, enjoying his cup of coffee. Without a word they both rose to their feet and crossed the floor, entering the bedroom where Sam and Mitch lay. Glancing over his shoulder at the doorway he had just stepped through, he met Rachel's gaze. He managed a smile, but by the sober look on her face, he knew that she was suspecting that the man had only unwanted news to offer them.

Shifting his gaze, he locked into Mitch's stare. A frown rested in the young man's face, confirming Patrick's suspicion that Sam's words would not be welcome ones.

At last Patrick eyed Sam, noting the look of determination the man bore. Sam pushed out his breath and said simply, "I'm turning in my badge."

Patrick reached up and began stroking his chin in thought. Nodding, he finally replied, "If ye think ye should, I'll stand behind yeer decision."

"What?" Mitch cried out and flinched in pain. Squeezing his eyes shut against the pain his outburst had caused, he drew in a deep breath. Every set of eyes were upon him as he struggled to regain composure. Finally he opened his eyes again and glared a look of accusation at Patrick. "You're backing up Sam for throwing away his lifestyle and leaving Timberton defenseless?"

The young man who lay there no longer looked like a boy barely out of grammar school. The hardness of the past few years had steadily chiseled in a man's features on him, but never more so than now. Patrick simply smiled at Mitch and said quietly, "We aren't defenseless." Instantly Mitch lowered his eyes, flushing slightly over the reminder that God was still in charge and watching over them. Patrick could not help but smile fondly at the young man. Turning to Sam the next moment, he stepped over to the bed and crouched down to be closer to eyelevel with him. "Now," he began in a no-nonsense tone, "tell us the reason for yeer decision."

For once, Sam could not meet his gaze, but shifted his eyes to study the blanket that was spread over him.

"Mitch," Rachel called out quietly. "Tell us what's going on."

Sam's eyes darted over to Mich. Patrick puzzled over the almost pleading look that momentarily rested in those eyes. The next moment it was gone. Turning back to Mitch, Patrick waited for him to explain.

"Sam saved my life," Mitch began quietly a few moments later. "We met up with the gang not far from Timberton. All of a sudden there was gunfire in the air. We returned it. And then without warning, I felt this whump—like something landing on my chest. It knocked me flat on my back. I lost hold of my gun. I didn't think much about that at first, because the pain was just so bad. That's when I realized that I'd been shot. I couldn't have pulled the trigger anyway, if my life depended on it, because my whole left arm went numb—I couldn't have held up the rifle for any reason at all." Mitch paused and shook his head as he recalled the awful moment.

"Mitch," Georgy spoke up quietly, "this can wait. You and Sam need to rest."

Patrick glanced over at Georgy who suddenly looked and sounded like a grown man instead of like the boy Georgy Northwood. The corners of Patrick's mouth rose slightly, unable to hold back the pride he felt in the boy—his son.

"No it can't wait," Mitch replied quietly, "not if Sam's going to turn in his badge. It's got to be said now if it's going to make a difference."

"Cut it out, kid," Sam growled. "Whatever you say isn't going to make any difference. I've already made up my mind. I'm done sheriffing."

"Well don't expect me to make it easy on you, Sam!" Mitch argued, actual anger in his tone. "You saved my life!"

"And this is how you repay me?" Sam demanded.

"Gentlemen," Patrick cut in softly, causing the two to glance up at him. Patrick chuckled quietly and shook his head. "Ye're friends. Sam, ye saved Mitch's life. Mitch," he added, turning back to the young man, "ye're trying to save Sam's career. Now, why are ye arguing with each ither?"

One side of Mitch's mouth rose sheepishly at Patrick's words. But when he attempted to shrug, a bolt of pain shot across his face at the movement. Sam sighed heavily and muttered, "Oh go on and blab out the whole story then, if you've a mind to."

Patrick glanced across the room at the amused looks on the faces of Georgy and Rachel. If the two could banter with each other, then the situation was not as bad as they had originally thought.

"Well," Mitch sighed, picking up the account of the gunfight once again. "All at once I found myself looking down a rifle barrel, aimed straight at me. I couldn't even move. If it weren't for Sam shooting the man, I'd be in my grave right now."

"I didn't just shoot him," Sam growled, the banter completely gone from his voice this time. "I killed him," he added darkly.

"You had to!" Mitch cried out, struggling to sit up, wincing against the pain. "It was either him or me!"

"I didn't have to kill him, Mitch! I hit what I aim for. I could've just wounded him. But I didn't! I killed the man, Mitch! And that's something that can't ever be undone! Don't you understand? I sent the man to his grave!"

Patrick studied Sam's face, meeting the troubled gaze. He could not help but wonder what sort of words of comfort he could possibly give the man. He was right about killing being something that could not be undone. The utter remorse in the man's eyes assured Patrick that he was exactly the sort of man Timberton needed as a sheriff. But he had no idea how he, or anyone else for that matter, was to convince him of it.

Mitch sighed and eased back down against his pillow. "After that," he continued with the account in a quieter tone, "Sam just ran out in the middle of the gunfight, bullets flying all around him. He didn't stop 'til he reached me. He wasn't none too gentle, but grabbed me up and drug me to cover, where our horses were. He put his bandanna in the hole in my chest and ordered me to hold it there. It felt like I was going to fall asleep any minute. He lifted me up and got me on my horse. I'm not too sure how I got back. But all at once I was here. I don't know the rest of the story about what happened with the posse."

Everyone turned to study Sam who rolled his eyes in irritation. Pushing out his breath, he picked up the tale from where Mitch had left off. "We kept shooting at each other for an hour or so," Sam said quietly, but clearly a reluctant storyteller. "Me and the posse was getting low on ammunition. But we figured that the outlaw gang was too, so we figured we'd just outlast them. Finally we were down to our last bullets. The gang must've figured we were, because they rushed us all at once. It all happened so fast, it takes more time to say it than it took to happen. I shot and killed three of them. I don't know who killed the rest." His voice sounded just as dead as the men he had killed. He fell silent then and lowered his eyes once again to the blanket that draped over him.

Patrick shifted his eyes and locked into Rachel's troubled gaze. Georgy slipped out of the room then. Patrick eased out his breath in a long sigh, silently praying for help and guidance, completely at a loss for words. The silence in the room grew nearly unbearable. It was finally broken when Georgy stepped back into the room, one of Ion's tablets in his hand. "I have something I'd like you to read, Sam," he said simply.

Sam lifted his eyes to Georgy, studying him for several moments before admitting, "I don't read so good."

"You mind if I read it to you?" Georgy asked.

Sam tipped his head. "Suit yourself."

Patrick puzzled over the conversation, keeping his eyes on Sam as Georgy began reading one of Ion's poems aloud. As the words progressed, Sam's face looked more strained by the moment. Finally he closed his eyes and bit down on the corners of his mouth as Georgy read the last lines.

"To miss his mark, without success, he tried,
But too engrained in him was that of law;
He held his dying brother close and cried,
While gripping tight his badge and fierce clenched jaw."

Once again silence hung in the air. Sam remained motionless for some time. Patrick even began wondering if he had fallen back to sleep. All at once he opened his eyes and drew in a deep breath, saying quietly, "I guess I could keep my badge for awhile—until you find a suitable replacement, that is."

Patrick eased into a grin. Everyone in the room knew that there was not even a candidate for the job of sheriff for a hundred miles in any direction. As Sam shifted his gaze and met Patrick's, he rolled his eyes, but made no comment on the obvious.

By the time October arrived, all thoughts of replacing Sam as sheriff had slipped away from everyone's minds, including Sam's. The main thing on the minds of the O'Riley household was the long anticipated wedding of Angela and Matthew. By then, the overcrowded condition in the O'Riley cabin was but a distant memory. The Shalemans' cabin and barn had been raised for months.

And shortly before they had moved into their new cabin, Mitch and Sam had recovered enough from their injuries to likewise return home.

As Ion sat at his desk in the schoolhouse, he smiled over the idea of missing all of them, but he could not deny the fact that Rachel especially did miss them, though he could not imagine that she missed the overcrowding. He sighed as he thought about Mrs. Shaleman's willing hands to contribute whatever help was needed. She even pitched in to help Johnny, Georgy and Ion himself when they were being punished with doing kitchen chores. He certainly missed her help on those occasions. He knew that Rachel especially missed her in sewing the linens for Angela's trousseaux. He sighed over the fuss the women made over the sewing project. But once school had resumed in September, Mrs. Shaleman would have been of little help with the sewing or the kitchen chores, even if she and her husband had still been living at the O'Riley cabin, since she was the new teacher and spent much of her time at home working on lessons and grading assignments.

Suddenly Ion jumped as someone laid a hand on his shoulder. Lifting his eyes, he met the half amused, half rebuking gaze of Mrs. Shaleman. "Have you finished writing your essay, Ion?" she asked quietly.

Dipping his head in a nod, he replied, "Yes Ma'am."

The corners of her mouth inched upward. Clearly she knew that she had caught him daydreaming. He braced himself for the punishment he deserved. "Then I suggest," she said simply, "that you join me in offering assistance to those who are still working."

A slow grin grew on his face, in spite of his effort to look indifferent."

"Yes ma'am."

Her eyes danced then and he could no longer refrain from allowing his smile to fully blossom on his lips. Mrs. Shaleman was so different from Angela as a teacher. Rising to his feet, he stepped out into the aisle and began following her example of offering assistance to the students with raised hands. His own class was working on essay writing, but the younger children were working on arithmetic. Although math was neither his best, nor favorite subject, he had no trouble in helping the younger children with theirs, except for Johnny, whose math skills had gone beyond those of his classmates. He was in a class of his own, where arithmetic was concerned.

Ion had been helping the younger students, answering their questions without giving them the actual solutions to their math problems for several minutes when a certain, graceful hand rose in the air. Mrs. Shaleman was across the room at that moment. One side of Ion's mouth rose as he stepped over to the bearer of that graceful hand. "Yes, Miss O'Brin?" he whispered formally, assuming the role of the teacher's assistant, stepping up to Mary's desk. "May I help you?"

Her eyes twinkled then as she nodded. "I need your help in spelling a word."

He coughed then, barely holding back the chuckle that leaped from him over her words. Crouching down beside her desk, just as he had been doing with the other students, he held her gaze for a long moment before asking, "What word is that?"

"The word 'do'," she murmured, the corners of her mouth rising in amusement.

"Well," he replied in mock sternness, "there is the word that's spelled d-e-w. And there's the one that's spelled d-o. Which one are you wanting to use?"

"Oh," she sighed, "that's the problem. "Which is which? Can you put them in sentences for me?"

He dipped his head in a nod. "I can, if you wish." He paused, concentrating hard on keeping his expression as serious as possible, in case Mrs. Shaleman happened to be watching. "D-e-w. The dew on the ground is wet."

"I see," she murmured, mock seriousness in her tone. "And you know this by experience?" she asked.

Ion dipped his head in a nod, replying, "I do."

Mary's eyes sparkled then as she whispered, "Remember those words."

Unable to hold back his smile, he leaned closer, murmuring, "You're becoming bold, Miss O'Brin."

Expecting her to lower her eyes in embarrassment, he was shocked when she merely smiled back, whispering, "Yes I am, Mr. Macalister."

Ion cleared his throat, and rose to his feet, certain that Mrs. Shaleman would be making her rounds down this center aisle any moment. "And do you know the spelling of your word now?"

Continuing to meet his gaze, she murmured, "I do."

He chuckled and dipped his head in a nod, stepping quietly over to the desk three rows up, where the next raised hand waved impatiently in the air. He wondered if he would be able to give an intelligent answer after his discussion with Mary. Somehow he would manage. If he did not, after all, he would not likely be allowed to make his rounds as a student tutor again. And nothing on the face of the earth was going to prevent him from answering Mary's upraised hand. Nothing.

Rachel stepped out of Angela's room and into the kitchen, where Georgy, Ion and Johnny sat at the table. They were dressed in their best clothes, looking uncomfortable. Jed and Patrick were still changing into their good clothes. The girls had remained in the bedroom with Angela, watching her make her final preparations in dressing for her wedding.

"Are you ready to go to the church?" Rachel asked the three.

"I've been ready for almost a half hour," Georgy sighed, tugging at his tie uncomfortably. "I've never been to a wedding before, but I can't see why I have to put on my Sunday clothes. I'm not the one getting married."

Rachel rolled her eyes, replying simply, "Well, it's good practice for you for when it is your turn to get married."

"You'll be getting more practice before long," Johnny piped up, nudging Ion.

Georgy grinned and eyed Ion, who scowled and nudged Johnny. Rachel studied Ion for a moment, wondering over his growing patience over being teased about marrying Mary. As she looked more closely, she realized that his eyes were actually sparkling. "Dear oh dear," she murmured.

Patrick emerged from the bedroom then, asking, "Is she ready?"

Rachel nodded. "I've never seen her so nervous before—or so lovely," she added. She thought back to her own wedding day, which had been far different from Angela's. Rachel had felt nothing at all on that day, which now seemed so long ago day, except grief over the loss of her father. If only she had known on that day, nearly two and a half year ago, how happy she would be as Patrick's wife, she would never have considered the possibility of refusing to marry him. All at once she felt Patrick's eyes upon her. Smiling up at him, she waited for him to say something.

"She couldn't be more lovely then m'own bride," he replied softly, stepping over to her. As his arms slipped around her shoulders, he leaned down and kissed her forehead. "Tell 'er the wegon is ready inytime she is." Turning to the boys, he added with a grin, "Off with ye to the church, lads."

Relief swept over their faces then as they hurried to their feet and dashed outside. Elizabeth emerged then from the bedroom in time to see the boys leaving. "Can I go too?" she asked. As Patrick nodded, she took out after the boys, apparently having endured all the waiting she was willing to.

Rachel turned back to the girls' bedroom and stepped inside, shocked to see Angela simply sitting on her bed, a perplexed expression on her face. "I cannot go through with this," she told Rachel, shaking her head.

"Why not?" Rachel asked gently, wondering over the fact that the woman was hesitating in marrying the man she loved, while Rachel herself had been faced with marrying a man she had at that time despised.

All at once Angela began crying and dabbed at her eyes. "I simply do not have the background for becoming a pioneer wife," she wailed. "You women are different from me. I just cannot see myself becoming one of you."

Rachel rolled her eyes and counted quickly to ten before allowing even one word to slip past her lips. All at once she realized that actual fear was peeking out from the woman's eyes—no pretense this time. Drawing in a deep breath, Rachel squared her shoulders and stepped over to the bed, easing down beside Angela. The time for truth had come. She had learned to understand the woman enough to know that if she made up her mind to leave Matthew at the altar, that was exactly what she would do. Rachel suddenly knew that nothing short of shock reality would convince the woman that she could, in fact, become a pioneer wife. But first she would need to know just how much Rachel herself had given up if she were to believe that she herself could do the same.

"Have you ever heard of Nathan Silver?" she asked quietly.

Angela stopped in mid sob and glanced at Rachel in surprise. "Of Boston? Of course," she sniffed in disdain. "Everyone has."

Rachel swallowed. Chewing the corner of her mouth for a moment, she began choosing her words carefully. Finally she shrugged and chose the direct route. "It was my family's business," she said simply.

Angela frowned and stared hard at Rachel. The color began slipping from her cheeks, leaving her as pale as death. For a moment Rachel feared that she might faint altogether, but when she did not, Rachel continued speaking. "I've wondered at your not linking Johnny's last name with Nathan Silver. You already know that our father's name was Charles—Charles Nathan."

"Y-yes, b-but—I never dreamed that y-y-y-you—Nathan Silver?"

"Nathan Silver," Rachel agreed quietly. "Papa believed in giving everyone a chance. He made some unwise investments and ended up losing everything."

"B-but you're Rachel Nathan? Rachel Nathan of Boston?" When Rachel nodded, the woman shook her head. "But then you know Miss Sharon—Mrs. Tobias Joon?"

Again Rachel dipped her head in a nod, growing steadily more uncomfortable in revealing her background to Angela, but still determined that this was the right time for doing so. "She was a friend of my mother's."

"You've been to the Joon mansion?"

"Yes," Rachel replied. "My friend Carolyn and I—"

"You don't mean that your Carolyn is Carolyn Smyth-Johnson?" she cried out as pieces to the puzzle suddenly began falling into place.

"Yes, that Carolyn."

"But-but I've been to both of the Smyth-Johnson and the Nathan mansions! You and I have most certainly met there or at the Joon mansion!"

"Most certainly," Rachel agreed quietly.

"But the Nathan mansion is even grander than the Joon's! You are that Rachel Nathan?"

Rachel lifted her shoulders slightly. "I am," she murmured.

"You left all of that to come to this?" Angela cried out incredulously.

"Yes," Rachel replied simply.

A blank expression crossed Angela's face as she thought over Rachel's astounding disclosure. Rachel wondered what exactly was going through her mind. Certainly she could not help but recall the countless times she had talked down to Rachel, even tutoring her in the art of proper manners. She would not be able to refrain from recalling the insults she had bestowed upon Rachel, not realizing that she had been addressing the daughter of Miss Sharon's personal friend.

Softly laying her hand on Angela's, she asked, "You don't want to be late for your wedding, do you?"

Angela lifted still blank eyes to Rachel. All at once, as if someone had lighted a match in her eyes, the light of life clicked back on. "Well," she began in a shaky tone that grew with confidence, "if you can learn to become a pioneer wife, I certainly can." With that she rose to her feet and stepped out of the room. Rachel stared after her in open-mouthed shock for several moments before rising to her feet.

Reaching her hand toward Anna Marie, she murmured absentmindedly, "Come along Annie."

Together the two stepped into the kitchen as Angela exited the cabin, heading for the wagon. Patrick met Rachel's gaze, his eyes dancing. Clearly he was making a great effort at keeping the corners of his mouth down, but they continued darting upward, regardless. "You heard?" Rachel asked.

He dipped his head in a nod. "I heard," he admitted. "'Tis a mighty small house not to hear a conversation like thit."

"Hm," Rachel sighed, still too shocked to say anything very intelligent. Suddenly she began chuckling, shaking her head slowly. Patrick stepped over to her then and slipped his arms around her, pinning Anna Marie between the two of them. She began giggling along with Rachel. Only then did Patrick allow his own laughter to overtake him. The three laughed inconsolably for several long moments. Rachel found herself relaxing in Patrick's arms. When she could finally speak again, she murmured, "I suppose, in her own way, she was complimenting me."

"I suppose," Patrick chuckled back. "Either thit or she wis apologizing to ye for treating ye like her own personal servant."

Rachel nodded and lifted her head from his shoulder, meeting his amused gaze. "Well, it's the closest thing to an apology she's likely to give me." Shaking her head, she began laughing again. "Oh Patrick," she sighed.

As their arms slipped away from each other, Rachel headed for the bedroom where Pattie lay asleep, hoping that she would sleep straight through the wedding ceremony. "Dear oh dear," she sighed, shaking her head.

Patrick brought the wagon to a halt and hurried to assist Rachel and Angela to the ground. Once on sure footing, Angela began clicking her tongue, murmuring almost unintelligibly over the uncivilized conditions pioneer people endured. Shrugging off any further attempts at help in crossing the yard, she made her way out of sight just behind the church. Patrick glanced over at Rachel who was biting the corner of her mouth. Her eyes were dancing, but she said nothing, simply following the irate woman, Pattie carefully tucked up in one arm while the other hand was stretched down to Anna Marie.

With a grin, Patrick watched Rachel and the girls following Angela. "Well lassie," he murmured quietly, "'twill be over soon enough, though I don't envy ye yeer job o'keeping the bride calm and collected." Chuckling, he stepped up to the door and eased inside. Drawing in a deep breath, he sighed at the thought of conducting the wedding ceremony. This would be his first. Of all people to conduct a marriage ceremony for, he wondered at the idea of the critical Angela being the first.

"Scared?" Georgy asked suddenly, stepping up to him with an amused grin on his face.

"Now why would ye be asking such a question?" Patrick replied, hoping there was enough confidence in his tone to turn the conversations away from him.

Georgy shifted his gaze over to Ion, who stood beside him, a knowing expression on both of their faces. "Well," Georgy replied lightly, "you're as white as a sheet."

"That's white as a ghost," Ion corrected.

Georgy chuckled and shook his head. "I've never seen a ghost. But I've seen white sheets. And Pat's face looks the same color."

"Laddie!" Patrick cut in, growing more uncomfortable than he wished to admit.

It was then that Ion chose to speak up, asking, "Have you ever married anyone before?"

Georgy began laughing then, clapping Ion on the back. "He married Rachel!"

Ion rolled his eyes. "He's married to Rachel. But as a preacher, he marries couples."

"I knew that," Georgy grumbled, frowning slightly.

Patrick chuckled quietly, relieved that the conversation was shifting. When both boys turned back to him, however, he realized that they were not about to simply let the matter drop. He shook his head slightly, admitting, "No, they're the first I'll be marrying."

Georgy's grin returned. "What if you make a mistake? Will you have to marry them all over again?"

"If he makes a mistake," Ion observed in a philosophical sort of tone, "he won't get the chance to do it again. Auntie Angela will kill him first."

"Laddies," Patrick sighed.

"What if," Georgy cut in, paying not the slightest attention to Patrick's discomfort, "he forgets to have Auntie Angela promise to obey Uncle Matthew?"

"She wouldn't promise that anyway," Ion replied with assurance in her voice. "He better have Uncle Matthew promise to obey her."

"Well, how does it go? 'Do you take this man to love, argue with and order around'?"

"No," Ion replied as Patrick's jaw simply dropped open as he stared at the two. "It goes: 'Do you take this woman to agree with, buy presents for, and be her slave?'"

"Ion! Georgy!" Patrick cried out in shock. "This is not funny!"

Both boys burst out laughing then. "If this isn't funny, Pat," Georgy chuckled, "then funny doesn't exist."

Patrick sighed long and slow, knowing that he had lost this battle and there was nothing he could do about it. "Let's see," Georgy continued. "Uncle

Matthew will be saying, 'I take this woman to be my awfully wedded wife—"

"Georgy!" Patrick cut in. "Ye mistn't be putting ideas like this into m'head. They'll come out sure and certain in the ceremony if I get nervous. I'm not joking lads!"

Georgy's eyes continued dancing. "I know you're not, Pat. And it isn't awfully wedded wife. It's lawfully fedded wife—"

"No," Ion cut in, firmness in his tone. "It's lawfully wedded strife."

Patrick suddenly had the urge to bang his head against the wall rather than listen to the two comedians. They knew they had him this time. This was certainly payback day for all the times he had teased them. He groaned, knowing that he had earned this. And he knew that they knew it too.

"'I take this man,' Auntie Angela will say," Georgy continued, "'to be my lawfully shredded husband, to have and to mold from this day forward—'"

"'For as long as he shall give,'" Ion finished up.

Patrick eased his eyes shut and shook his head. "Ah laddies," he sighed, "if I stumbled and say one of those words—"

"She'll eat you for the first course and spit you out for the second," Georgy laughed.

"But first," Ion added, such amusement in his tone that Patrick opened his eyes back up and was unable to keep from grinning himself. "She'll pull out every hair in your head—"

"She'd have to answer to Rachel for that," Georgy murmured thoughtfully.

"Oh yeah," Ion sighed out. Turning back to Patrick, he added, "There's hope. Auntie Angela knows Rachel won't allow her to kill you too badly."

"Well thank ye, Ion, for those tender words o'comfort," Patrick replied dryly. Pausing, he narrowed his eyes. "Bit, I'm thinking, lad, thit a certain lassie ye know might not be too appreciative if I 'appened to stumble on a wrong word or two during 'er wedding, which I suspect will be in a few short years."

Ion's laughter fell away instantly, an actual look of nervousness dashing to his face. "Pat you wouldn't do that to Mary," he murmured.

"Well now, if it 'appens today, I might be starting an unfortunate bad 'abbit I simply won't be able to break."

"You know blackmail is illegal," Ion muttered.

Patrick suddenly grinned, asking innocently, "And who is blackmailing inyone?"

Georgy hooted and clapped Ion on the back, his eyes dancing with merriment. "It doesn't pay to settle down to only one girl!"

Patrick turned to Georgy then. "And I'm thinking thit the young miss Beverly might find it interesting thit the young doctor Northwood mistakenly swallowed ipecac the ither day and didn't make it to the school outhouse in time, bit threw up all over himself and ran home without explaining to 'is teacher why 'e left."

Georgy's jaw dropped open as he stared in clear horror at the man. "Pat you wouldn't tell Beverly that!"

"Certainly not," Patrick assured him with just the right amount of firmness and injured pride to make his point.

"All right, we'll stop!" Georgy replied. "Just don't do those things!"

Patrick grinned innocently. "What things, laddie?"

Georgy and Ion exchanged knowing glances. Ion turned back to Patrick and held out his hand, murmuring, "Truce."

Patrick grasped the boy's hand and nodded. "Truce."

Ion eyed the couple standing before Patrick at the front of the church, listening to the words of the wedding ceremony. Georgy elbowed him as the time for making the actual vows approached. Suddenly Patrick's eyes shot over to the two of them. Ion struggled to keep the corners of his mouth down, but it was all the more difficult when Georgy began clearing his throat, never quite the master over his emotions as Ion. The stern look in Patrick's eyes, however, was proving to be too powerful and Ion felt his mouth turning upward. Patrick rolled his eyes and turned his attention back to the couple.

"Do ye, Matthew Bon-Hemmer," Patrick said with firmness in his voice that Ion suspected Georgy and he himself had placed there, "take this woman to be yeer aw--lawfully f-wedded s-wife?" He sighed and once again darted a glance over at Ion and Georgy. Ion gave up all pretense of seriousness and simply allowed himself to grin at the frustrated man. After all, the truce had been agreed upon. He and Georgy had made no further attempt at scrambling Patrick's brain into saying the wrong words. The two of them had kept their end of the bargain. "To hiv and to m-'old--"

Georgy nudged Ion again and leaned closer, whispering, "That was supposed to be for Auntie Angela, to mold Uncle Matthew, not the other way around."

Patrick's jaw clenched. Ion chuckled quietly. But he and Georgy were not alone in having heard Patrick distinctly say the word mold rather than hold. With Patrick's unfortunate habit of dropping his H's, the slip of having said the M sound had not been tempered with the H sound. Ion suspected that from here on out, Patrick would be a little more careful to pronounce his H's.

"Frim this day forward," Patrick continued in a rather contrite voice, "for as long as ye both shall give—live?" he added quickly. He made no attempt to conceal his sigh. Suddenly Ion felt a little sorry for the man, but his amusement still outweighed his compassion. He reminded himself that if it were happening to anyone else, Patrick would have the hardest time of anyone to remain composed.

Matthew nodded, replying quietly, "I do." He showed no sign of having heard the many slips Patrick had made. Ion wondered over his obvious nervousness. He was as pale as Patrick had been when first entering the church. Apparently he was too nervous to have realized that Patrick had made any mistakes at all. Shifting his gaze over to Angela, whose thinly veiled face he could see only partially, he bit down on the corner of his mouth. Her eyes were narrowed. Even from the side view and through the veil he could see that. She had heard the mistakes.

"And do ye, Angela Carson-Davis," Patrick continued, shifting his gaze over at the irritated woman, "take this—this man, to be yeer—uh—law—lawfully wedded husband?"

Ion coughed then as Patrick took special care to voice the H sound. "To hiv and to hold, frim—I mean to honor and obey—uh—frim this day forward for as long as ye both shall live?" He exhaled in a sigh of obvious relief.

Suddenly the room became utterly silent. Georgy glanced over at Ion and mouthed the word: obey. Ion shrugged, wondering if that word really was giving the woman pause for thought. Shifting his gaze to Patrick, he found the man eyeing the two of them. His was not an especially happy face. Suddenly Ion's shoulders began shaking. It took all of his being to keep the laughter silent. But it had gone beyond his power to restrain it from coming in silence. Patrick eased his eyes shut and shook his head. Georgy continuously cleared his throat and began studying the tops of his shoes.

"I do!" Angela spoke up suddenly.

A look of utter relief washed over Patrick's face. "By the power vested in me, in the sight of God, I pronounce that ye are husband and wife." He spoke with careful deliberation, forming each word precisely. "Matthew, ye may kiss yeer bride."

Matthew, clearly unaware of all the undercurrents going on, lifted the thin veil from Angela' face and slipped his arms around her. As they kissed, Patrick once again shot a warning look at Ion and Georgy. Ion, having regained control over himself, smiled at the man. One side of Patrick's mouth rose slightly. Ion suspected that it was not mercy as much as relief he read in the man's face—relief that his first wedding ceremony was completed.

Rachel leaned against her kitchen counter, peacefully watching the wedding party and guests enjoying themselves, chatting and laughing with the happy bride and groom. Patrick eased over to her, slipping a cup of coffee into her hands. "Ye need to be sitting down, lassie," he murmured. "Ye've bin working so hard these past few weeks, getting iverything ready for today. Why, a good stiff breeze will blow ye over."

She smiled and took the cup of coffee from him. "I'm fine, Patrick." She paused, studying his face. "You aren't troubled over those little slips of the tongue during the wedding, are you?"

One side of his mouth rose then. Easing one arm around her shoulders, he sighed. "Those scalawags," he sighed.

"Angela and Matthew?" Rachel asked in surprise.

"Georgy and Ion," Patrick corrected.

"I don't understand."

Amusement darted in his eyes then. "They planted ivery one o'those mistakes in m'mind just b'fore the wedding started, while ye and Angela were outside, waiting for 'er cue to come in and walk down the aisle." Suddenly he began chuckling, shaking his head as his amusement was clearly growing.

She had seen the look of horror on his face when he had made the mistakes while leading the couple in taking their vows. As she met his gaze, she smiled. "You did a good job, Patrick."

"Aye, if a good job is limited to the legal part o'the ceremony. Bit, Angela is going to tar and feather me, I'm certain."

Rachel frowned then. All at once the situation lost it's amusing side. "She'll do no such thing!" she replied indignantly.

A softened look came to the man's eyes then. "The lads were right about one thing." When Rachel eyed him curiously, he explained, "They said thit ye would never allow 'er to harm me."

"They said that?" she asked, touched by the words.

Patrick cleared his throat then. "Well, their actual words were: 'Rachel won't allow 'er to kill ye too badly.'"

Rachel frowned slightly. "Such a lovely sentiment," she murmured dryly. Smiling again, meeting his gaze, she added, "Angela knows that I won't allow her to harm a hair on your head."

Patrick coughed and began laughing as he drew Rachel closer to himself. "I love ye, Rachel." He paused and began glancing around the crowded kitchen. "It seems to me thit 'tis time to add on to this cabin."

Rachel's mouth fell open into an O. "Patrick, can we?"

"I think," he added in amusement, "thit it isn't a matter of can we, bit rather of can we not? Look around ye. 'Tis a might crowded."

"Yes it is," Rachel replied. "And since you're the one to bring it up—"

"Ye hiv the floor plans drawn up already, don't ye?"

She giggled and nodded. "They've been drawn up for over a year." He laughed and kissed the top of her head, waiting for her to tell him her ideas. "Well, we could build the addition as large as the original cabin, joining it to the fireplace wall. That way the fireplace can be at the center of the house. We can partition off two bedrooms on the same wall as Jed's and the boys' rooms are on. That would leave a large living room area. An archway can be cut in the wall at the side of the fireplace. One of the new bedrooms would actually serve as a place for you to study your sermons in and for Ion to work on his writing. And if we have an over night guest, he or she can sleep there. The other new room, closest to the fireplace, can be Elizabeth's and Anna Marie's room. And their old room can be the nursery. And—" She paused, asking, "Patrick why are you laughing? Don't you like it?"

His eyes danced in a mixture of love and merriment. "I love it. Inything else?"

"Well, since you ask. I think we need a front door, leading into the living room. And it goes without saying that it needs a porch where I can set a tea table with a few chairs"

"Absolutely without saying," Patrick breathed out solemnly, though his twinkling eyes belied his solemnity.

Rachel giggled. Carefully holding her cup of coffee away from him, she leaned close and softly kissed his cheek. "And," she continued, "we can add anything you think to be lacking."

Suddenly the merriment left his eyes, leaving only a look of love behind. "Rachel, as long as ye're in this house, it lacks nething of value."

His tone was so sincere and his expression so filled with a fierce love for her she found herself barely breathing. "You mean that," she whispered, astounded.

"Ah lassie," he murmured, taking the coffee cup from her and setting it on the counter, slipping his arms around her. "I mean it with all m'heart. As long as I hiv ye, I hiv iverything I want."

Torn between wanting to hear these sweet words of love and also wanting to settle something in her mind that sometimes popped up, she asked simply, "Where does God fit in?"

His smile deepened. "At the very top, where 'E belongs. Rachel, ye come second only to God in m'heart. Except for Jesus, ye: Rachel Nathan O'Riley, come first in m'life. And to think thit I get to spend eternity with both Jesus and ye—" He slowly shook his head as further words failed him. Lowering his head, he laid his lips on hers, regardless of the crowded room filled with guests. Rachel kissed him back with an intensity he immediately responded to.

The clearing of throats brought a quick end to their kissing. Parting slightly from each other, they turned and met the amused gazes of Georgy and Ion. "Yeer time's coming, lads," Patrick murmured. Rachel heard the amusement in his voice. She was certain that the boys did too, since they laughed. But she was equally certain that they were deaf to the note of frustration in the man's tone. Yes, Patrick would find some interesting way of leaving thoughtful looks on the boys' faces for interrupting his private time with her. She smiled, suddenly longing for the house to be emptied of everyone except for her family. It had been a long day. And the months before that, in preparation for this day, had been equally taxing.

Georgy glanced over at the few remaining guests, who were giving their parting blessings to the bride and groom. He glanced across the table, where Ion and Johnny were sitting. Even they looked a trifle weary from the long day. At the sound of the door opening, he glanced over at it, grinning as the last family stepped outside.

Angela turned to Matthew and smiled up at him. He made no attempt to hide his eagerness to be off with his bride, returning her smile regardless of the fact that the entire O'Riley family was staring at the two of them. "It's time to be off," Angela said simply. Georgy exchanged amused glances with Ion as Angela ordered her bridegroom around.

"Yes Ma'am," Matthew chuckled. Ion rolled his eyes and Georgy chuckled over the man's unchallenging response. "Do you have everything?"

She nodded. "Yes, the boys carted the rest of my belongings to our house earlier this afternoon."

All at once Matthew began looking nervous. Georgy shifted his gaze back over to Ion who was eying him in amusement. "Well," Matthew began, clearing his throat, "I guess we'll be leaving now." He swallowed and turned to Patrick. Stretching out his arm, he shook hands with Patrick and turned back to Angela. Offering her his arm, he asked, "Ready?"

She nodded and slipped her hand to his arm. Without another word, they slipped out of the house. Every set of eyes darted to the window, watching the couple as they made their way to the buggy. Matthew assisted Angela up on the seat and then sat down beside her. Slapping the reins on the horses' backs, he set the buggy in motion. The next moment the happy couple was sailing down the path, heading toward their own home.

Suddenly Ion jumped to his feet and cried out in excitement, "It's over!"

Chapter 6

The month of June in 1858 finally arrived, bringing with it Patricia O'Riley's first birthday as well as the completion of the addition on the cabin. The entire family could now not remember how they had gotten along without the addition and the little girl. Rachel glanced up from the final touches she was giving to the snack of cookies frosted with jam she would give the children as soon as they returned home from school. Patrick had left his study and stepped into the kitchen.

"So you plan to brave the horde of ravenous scholars today?" she asked, eying him knowingly.

He chuckled and lifted his hands in mock surrender. "Aye, lassie. Today I'll take m'life in m'hands and face thim like a man."

Rachel laughed and carried the plate of cookies over to the table. As Patrick reached for the coffeepot and poured himself a generous cupful, he asked, "Can ye take the time to be joining me?"

She turned and nodded, sighing, "That does sound good. I don't think I've sat down all afternoon."

"I'm sure ye hivn't," Patrick murmured, shaking his head. "Rachel," he added as he poured a cup of coffee for her and carried both cups over to the table, "I've bin thinking a lot about thit, lately. I think we need to look for—"

"Not another live-in helper," Rachel cut in. "Besides, I don't need help. I'm just as strong as all the other women in Timberton. And they manage quite nicely taking care of their families."

By then they were both sitting at the table, enjoying their coffee. "Bit the other women aren't contending with all the added responsibilities of being a pastor's wife." Rachel reached over and laid her hand on Patrick's, patting it reassuringly, much as she did to Anna Marie and Pattie when comforting them concerning a small childhood worry. Patrick cocked his head and grinned knowingly at her. "All right," he chuckled. "Ye kin hiv yeer own way."

She giggled and decided to broach the subject that had been on her mind for days. "I was wondering, since you said I could have my own way—"

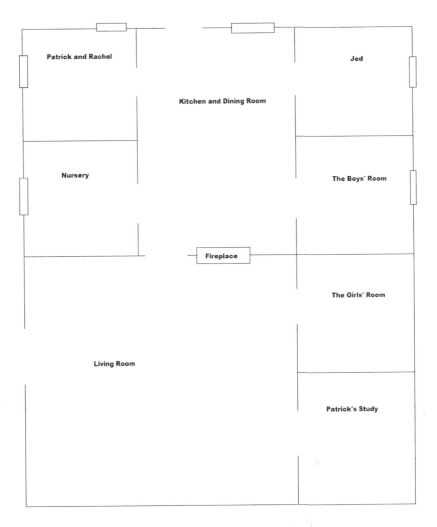

The O'Riley House

"In this matter," he cut in, eying her in amusement.

"Well now, you didn't qualify it. You just said I could have my own way."

Laughing, he studied her face and asked in an exaggerated indulging tone, "And what in all the world kin I be giving ye, m'love?"

"A birthday party?"

Suddenly Patrick's face lost its merriment. "Bit Rachel, June the 5th is already past."

"Not for me," she laughed, shocked that he had even thought that the quiet family way they had celebrated her twenty-third birthday had not been more than enough for her. "For Pattie's first birthday."

Patrick continued studying her. "Bit, ye're already doing more work then ye should be doing."

"Patrick, she'll never have another first birthday."

His eyes crinkled into laughter then. "Aye, 'tis true. Bit she'll only hiv one second birthday too, and only one third—"

"I see what you mean. We'll need to give her a birthday party every year then." She could see in his eyes that he had already lost the battle. Where his little girl was concerned, his heart worked like putty in Rachel's hands—provided that Rachel herself was in no way harmed. "Besides, it'll be a wonderful way to put our new addition to use. Why, with all of this room, we can invite a lot of people. Who do you think we should invite?"

"Well, Sam of course, and Mitch and the children. I think the Morrisons would enjoy coming."

Rachel nodded, hiding her smile. "And what about Annette and Toby?"

He nodded. All at once he paused and narrowed his eyes. "Bit I hivn't even agreed to the idea of hiving a party for the lassie. And 'ere ye are, planning yeer guest list."

She allowed the corners of her mouth to rise, as she said simply, "Most of the list has come from you."

Leaning close to her, he softly kissed her cheek. "Go ahead and hiv yeer party," he replied in amusement. "Bit, I'm thinking thit we've forgotten a couple of people we dare not leave out." Rachel fell silent then and began chewing on the corner of her mouth. He watched her, his look of amusement deepening. "Ah now lassie, does it come so terribly hard to invite Matthew and Angela?"

"No," she said lightly. "It doesn't come hard at all to invite Matthew." She sighed and thought the matter through. "All right. We can't leave her out. She's part of the family. And," she added, doing her best to put a happy face on the matter, "she's been mellowing. Why, just a week ago at church she let the matter of my not wearing gloves slip by altogether. I think," she admitted in a sigh, "it had something to do with the fact that the week before I had told her that I found the idea of wearing lace gloves to church in Timberton rather pompous and unchristian."

"Ye didn't say thit, did ye Rachel?" Patrick murmured, shaking his head.

Rachel sighed and nodded reluctantly. "I did. Later I asked her to forgive me. Of course she refused, telling me that it was not a matter that could be forgiven but simply overlooked as an unfortunate mistake in etiquette. 'But really, Rachel,' she said, 'I don't know how you of all people in this hick town could allow your standards to fall so low.'"

The two exchanged looks of understanding. The look in his eyes salved the sore spot the unkind words had torn open in Rachel. His hand crept over hers then as he whispered gently, "Ye don't hiv to invite Matthew and Angela if ye'd rather not."

She squeezed his hand and smiled, her heart knitting even closer into his. "Thank you. But you're right. If we invite anyone, they have to be on the top of the list." Suddenly she began giggling. "After all, Angela's your third cousin."

Patrick rolled his eyes. "Aye," he murmured. "M'mither would be most vexed if we didn't invite thim." He shook his head and sighed. "Bit let's pray thit this time she doesn't go around quoting m'mother. Semtimes it's all I kin do to bite m'tongue when she starts off by saying, 'Cousin Christine often used to say—'" Rachel laughed afresh. Rarely did she see Patrick frustrated, but this was one issue that did it to him every time. "Rachel, she doesn't know m'mither!"

For his sake, she pushed the laughter from her voice, though she could not push down her smile completely. "When she quotes her, is she even close?"

Patrick pushed out his breath in such an uncharacteristic manner, Rachel blinked in growing amusement. "She's exactly right—ivery time! 'Tis uncanny! Rachel, it's as if she grew up in m'mither's house! I don't know 'ow she does it!"

Rachel grew thoughtful. They rarely discussed Patrick's parents nor his life in Ireland and England. "Well, much of what she says that your mother used to say is what Mrs. Joon would easily have said. Did—" Rachel's mouth dropped open in a rush of shock. "Your mother—was she from—Patrick you've never mentioned her background."

Patrick sighed. "'Er father—m'Grandfather Carson-Davis was a nobleman—a penniless one—but a nobleman none-the-less."

"Why haven't you ever mentioned that to me?"

Patrick lifted his shoulders slightly. "It wis a matter of contention between m'parents. M'mither 'ad a few grand ways that irritated m'father. 'E loved 'er with all 'is heart. So 'e put up with it. 'Er family rejected 'er for marrying a poor Irishman. Bit she loved 'im—even though 'e wis Irish and not a nobleman in iny sense o'the word. Bit Rachel, I never mentioned it b'cause it made no difference to me. When we first got married, I wis unwilling to tell ye b'cause I knew it'd make a big difference to ye—bit 'twould shame ye. I couldn't do to ye what m'mither's family did to m'father. And then after ye learned to love this poor Irishman, it mattered even less to me thit m'mither's family was nobility. The only nobility I claim for m'self is what I've gained in Jesus."

Rachel smiled, studying the sincere, dear face before her. "I love you Patrick," she said simply.

Just as they leaned toward each other, the door opened and Georgy called out, "They're kissing again!"

Patrick rolled his eyes and sighed, sitting straight again. Rachel chuckled quietly and waited silently for the onslaught of returning scholars each vying for attention and cookies. As Georgy stepped over to the table, his eyes on the plate of cookies, Patrick reached out suddenly and caught the boy with his arm, pinning him down in a headlock, demanding in mock fierceness, "Ye were saying, lad?"

Georgy began laughing and wrestled with Patrick for a few moments. But finally, as the other children were quickly grabbing cookies, he held up his hands, helplessly crying out, "I give up!"

Patrick joined in on his laughter and released him to continue onward with his cookie mission. The chattering and laughter brought Anna Marie and Pattie out of the nursery to join in on the family festivity. Jed also made his way into the house and poured himself a cup of coffee and grabbed several cookies, sitting down at the far end of the table. Rachel began handing out a piece of paper to each of the children, along with a pencil. Once everyone stopped talking long enough to hear her, she explained, "We're going to have a birthday party for Pattie. And each of you get to invite one friend—"

"Can their families come too?" Johnny asked, his eyes sparkling with excitement.

Rachel glanced over at Patrick who tipped his head in a nod of agreement. Turning back to Johnny, Rachel replied, "Yes. Now write down your friend's name and each member of his or her family."

Eagerly everyone set to work. Rachel recalled her own excitement in drawing up the guest list for various parties her mother had hosted back in Boston. She could not help but enjoy her own children's excitement in doing that very thing, but at the same time she began counting up the number of people their small, intimate birthday party would now be including. "Dear oh dear," she murmured, eyeing an amused Patrick. "That'll be another twenty-five or more people."

Both of them glanced toward the new living room and then back at each other. Patrick chuckled quietly, replying, "Maybe I should get busy in building that new addition you probably already have plans for." His eyes twinkled as he spoke.

"Dear oh dear," Rachel sighed, shaking her head.

"Mamma?" Anna Marie asked in such a small voice, everyone stopped talking and eyed her. "Who can I invite?"

It was Georgy who answered her, saying with a grin, "The Bakers have a little girl about your age."

Rachel narrowed her eyes as she studied the young man. A grin was on his face and a twinkle in his eye. Ion nudged him with his elbow, muttering sarcastically, "They also have a little girl about your age named Beverly, and another one two years younger named Katherine."

Georgy turned toward Ion, a look of feigned surprise on his face. "They do? Imagine that."

Johnny piped up then, chuckling, "They also have a little boy two years younger than you named Keith. You remember Keith?"

Georgy rolled his eyes, muttering, "A man doesn't forget another man he's punched in the face."

"The way I remember it," Johnny scoffed, "it was the other way around."

"Lads," Patrick murmured in reproof. "If Annie wants to invite Rebecca

Baker as 'er guest, she may. Bit there'll be no fist fighting," he added sternly.

"Then she better not include Keith on the guest list," Ion murmured, shaking his head. "Sure as shootin' Keith and Georgy will fight."

"Not in this house," Rachel insisted.

Johnny began snickering, adding, "You'll have to go outside, Georgy, if you want to beat up Keith." Turning to Elizabeth, he began speaking slowly enough for her to read his lips. "Pat and Rachel are probably going to invite Mitch. So you can't invite Jennifer. She'll already be coming."

Elizabeth only shrugged and continued writing down the names of the Corins. "Jennifer's my best friend," she replied, adding smugly, "I can invite whoever I want."

Johnny shrugged and turned to Ion, adding, "You don't have to write down anything. We all know you're going to invite Mary."

Ion shifted his gaze steadily to Johnny who suddenly returned his eyes to his own sheet of paper. Not until Johnny's eyes were off of him did Ion allow a slow grin to come to his lips. He turned then and met Rachel's gaze. She smiled and slowly shook her head. He shrugged and returned his attention to the list of O'Brin names he was writing down. "Dear oh dear," Rachel sighed, continuing to shake her head.

Ion met the O'Brin family as they made their way to the O'Riley house the evening of Pattie's birthday party. He smiled as he met Mary's gaze and then shifted his eyes to her father. Holding out his hand, he said in the finest gentleman manner he knew how to command, "Welcome to our home, Mr. O'Brin." After the two shook hands, Ion glanced from Martin to his wife Sheila, adding with a slight bow, "Ma'am."

Sheila, so like Mary in appearance, smiled so kindly at him he guessed immediately that Mary had confided in her as to the growing relationship between her and Ion.

"It was good of you to invite us," Sheila replied.

Young Joshua and Sam began giggling, but instantly received a reproving glare from Mary that silenced their laughter, but did nothing to quell the teasing sparkle in their eyes.

"Well," Martin said gruffly, "if we're goin' inside, let's get at it."

Ion glanced back at Mary who shrugged apologetically. "Yes," Sheila replied with more heartiness than her thin form warranted. Ion tried not to notice the paleness of the woman's face, nor the shadows beneath her eyes. Mary tried to pretend that her mother was not ill, so Ion always went along with the game. The two boys hurried ahead of the four, interested in finding Johnny and the snacks. Ion and Mary hung back a few steps, allowing Mary's parents to precede them to the house. Ion drew in a deep breath and suddenly slipped his hand over Mary's. She lifted her eyes to him and smiled so sweetly he was unable to breathe for a moment. She squeezed his hand and stepped a little closer to him as they strolled along. Ion had been planning on doing this very thing for months, but had not until that moment worked up the necessary courage. Now that she had been so receptive to holding hands, he wondered at himself for having taken so long to do so. He now simply wished that they had a mile to walk to the house, instead of a few mere yards.

Georgy glanced across the table where Ion and Mary were sitting side by side. The young people had claimed the kitchen, while the adults and younger children seemed quite content in mingling in the crowded living room. Something was sparkling in Ion's eyes. Georgy frowned in thought. Suddenly he noticed that neither Ion nor Mary had their hands on the table. Although Mary was likely enough to sit with her hands primly in her lap, Georgy knew for a fact that Ion was accustomed to resting his arms on the table. A slow grin crept to his lips as he glanced at Ion's left shoulder that was resting against Mary's right. Without warning, Georgy dipped his head under the table. He whistled as he paused long enough to study Ion's hand clasping Mary's.

"Georgy!" Ion hissed.

Georgy chuckled and sat back up again. With Beverly on one side of him and Katherine on the other side, it had been challenging to peek under the table without colliding into at least one of them. He continued laughing over Ion's discomfort in his having drawn attention to the fact that he and Mary were holding hands.

"Georgy," Beverly laughed lightly, "you don't mean to say that you only just now figured out that they were holding hands?"

Georgy frowned then and turned to Beverly in surprise. "You knew?"

She laughed and nodded. "Everybody knows. They aren't exactly hiding it."

"Sure they are. They're hands are under the table."

"When a lady sits by her beau and their hands aren't on the table, everybody knows they're holding hands."

"Oh," Georgy replied simply. "Well," he added with a grin, laying his hand over Beverly's, "I don't mind letting everybody know that I'm holding the hand of the prettiest girl here."

Beverly laughed, but clearly was not smitten with Georgy. "If Keith would've come tonight, you would've had reason to hide it." She did not withdraw her hand, however, seeming to enjoy the attention. Georgy shrugged, uncertain whether to be insulted or relieved that Beverly was not especially attracted to him. After all, she was fun to be with, but he was uncertain if he really wanted her to treat him the way Mary treated Ion.

"Well," Beverly added, leaning forward to look around Georgy to her sister. "Now we need to have someone come and sit by Katherine.

The fourteen year old Katherine frowned slightly and shook her head. "The only ones anywhere near my age at this party is Johnny and Josh. And they're only twelve. You just share Georgy with me, Bev."

Georgy chuckled quietly, thinking how much fun it was to be nearly sixteen and having girls fighting over him. Reaching out his other hand, he grasped Katherine's and said, "Be glad to accommodate you, Katherine."

Glancing across the table, he met Ion's gaze again. Georgy grinned afresh as Ion simply shook his head, clearly unimpressed. And Georgy wondered when they could have another party.

Rachel stepped into the kitchen, holding a tray of coffee cups to be filled. As she busied herself in pouring the coffee, behind her she could hear the teenagers quietly talking and laughing at the table. Suddenly she began wondering what was going on. Their laughter seemed more self-conscious than merry. Glancing over her shoulder, she noticed the entwined hands of Mary and Ion resting on Ion's lap. "Dear oh dear," she murmured, suddenly clueless as to what course of action was hers to take.

Setting the coffeepot down, she stepped over to the table, easing up just behind Mary and Ion. Without a word the two let go of each other's hand. Georgy lifted his hands off of Beverly's and Katherine's as well. Rachel laid one hand on Mary's shoulder and the other on Ion's and smiled at Georgy and the girls on either side of him. She sighed, and simply admitted, "Until this moment, I hadn't realized how old all of you have become."

The chagrinned expressions shifted to grins at her words. She wondered if she needed to tell them then and there that there would be no hand-holding without permission to formally court one another. It hardly seemed fair to her boys to reprimand them in front of the girls. But they should have known better without her having to tell them. "We're getting ready to open up Pattie's birthday present. Will you help me serve the coffee please?"

Five relieved teenagers rose to their feet. Rachel hid her smile, pretending to be ignorant of the shenanigans going on at her own table. At least one good thing had come of it: they were all quite eager to do whatever she wanted them to. Their own consciences were apparently working on them better than any words she would have used to lecture them on the matter of how young men and women ought to conduct themselves with each other.

As the young people scurried into the living room to serve coffee and birthday cake, Rachel picked up the package that had been carefully lying on the counter, away from Pattie's curious fingers. Someone knocked on the door then, causing her to call out, "Come in." The door opened then and in stepped Sam. Often his job as sheriff caused him to be late to various functions. "Hello Sam," she greeted. "You're just in time to see Pattie open her present. And we're just now having cake and coffee."

He dipped his head in a nod, holding onto his hat. Turning, he hung the hat on the hook by the door. "Thank you, Ma'am." Rachel studied him, puzzling over the difference in him. She could not quite put her finger on it, but over the past several months, there had been something different about him. "Something troubling you?" he asked.

She sighed, feeling a little embarrassed. "Forgive me, but are you feeling well?"

He grinned. "You noticed, did you? Fact is," he said in a rather chagrinned sort of tone, "I haven't felt so good in years. The truth is, Doc. Morrison has been giving me some medicine to take. I haven't had one of them sick spells since I've been taking it. I guess you was right when you told me I should go and see him. After I got shot—well, he figured that that gave him the right to start doctoring me."

Rachel smiled back at him. "I'm so happy for you."

He dipped his head in a nod and followed her into the living room and the awaiting guests who were gathered to watch the one-year-old Pattie O'Riley open her present. The rest of the evening flew by quickly and uneventfully.

As Rachel climbed into bed beside Patrick at the close of the day, she filled him in on the behavior of Ion and Georgy that evening. "I think it's time you had a talk with the boys."

Patrick sighed reluctantly. "It wisn't thit long ago thit I wis the one being given the talk concerning being proper with young ladies."

Rachel nodded, thinking of how odd it was, at times, for Patrick and herself to be raising teenagers when they themselves were only in their mid-twenties. "They're good boys, Patrick. But they need your guidance in this. Ion especially needs to be forgetting about Mary for awhile, or getting permission from Mr. O'Brin to court her."

"Aye," Patrick sighed. "Ye're right. I'll hiv a talk with the lads tomorrow."

Rachel eyed doctor Morrison who eased down at the table in her kitchen after completing her examination. The smile on his lips confirmed her suspicion, but she allowed him to voice the words. "You can expect the newest O'Riley to arrive sometime in April. I know this is only October, but I want you to start slowing down a bit."

Rachel could not help but smile over the welcome news. "Oh Dr. Morrison," she giggled. "Six months is far too long a time for me to slow down. Who'll do my work if I do that?"

Eying her with the particular doctor-reprimand look, he insisted in a no-nonsense tone, "Four of your children are old enough to lighten your load."

Rachel paused and studied him for a moment. "Is something wrong with me?" she asked slowly.

Easing back into a smile he shook his head. "No. But I want to keep it that way."

She sighed in relief and nodded. All right."

Narrowing his eyes, he added, "Either you tell Patrick that I've ordered you, as your doctor, to take it easy, or I'll tell him. Where is he, anyway?"

"Out in the woods, getting started on our winter wood supply."

"Started?"

"We have a lot put up for this year. But he's wanting to get next year's starting to season out. He just hates burning green wood."

"I thought the men of the church were going to see to your wood."

Rachel nodded. "They are. It's just that with our house twice the size it was last winter, Patrick figures that we're going to go through a lot more wood this year. He isn't sure if our supply will completely see us through until spring. And you know how unpredictable spring snows can be."

A troubled look rested on the man's face as he drew in a deep breath. "We need to take better care of our pastor and family," he murmured. "You're all overdoing, seeing to the needs of the church and community as well as to your family's needs."

"Well I don't see any grass growing beneath your feet—or Sarah's. Besides, Patrick doesn't mind cutting wood."

Phil smiled and nodded. "I know." Rising to his feet, he added in a more professional tone, "I want to see you once a month for a checkup."

"All right. And thank you for coming here. I should've found a way to come to your office, but with Anna Marie and Pattie underfoot, I just couldn't figure out a way."

"Well, we aren't in Boston. Out here, a country doctor makes more house calls than his patients make office calls. Like Patrick, I don't mind."

As he stepped to the door, Rachel added, "Give Sarah my regards and tell her that there's a pot of tea waiting for her as soon as she can spare the time to come and visit."

"I'll tell her," he chuckled and stepped outside, closing the door behind him.

"Pattie won't share!" Anna Marie cried out, stomping into the kitchen.

Rachel turned and eyed the little girl who would turn five in only two short months. "Are you tattling?" she asked with sternness in her voice.

"No," Anna Marie replied sullenly, staring down at her feet.

A smile crept to Rachel's lips as she studied the pouting child. "Tell me what happened."

The little girl sniffed and mumbled, "She keeps trying to take my doll."

Rachel forced the corners of her mouth back down and said quietly, "It sounds to me like you're the one who isn't sharing." Stepping over to her, she crouched down to eyelevel and brushed the loose strands of hair from the child's face. Reaching her fingers beneath the small chin, she gently eased her face upward. "You know," Rachel said softly, "I think what Pattie really wants is for her sister to play with her. Maybe we can find something else besides your doll to interest her. What do you think?"

Instantly the little girl was all smiles. She nodded and wrapped her arms around Rachel's neck, hugging her close to herself. Rachel's arms slipped around her as she kissed the small forehead. "She can play with my rocks!"

Rachel drew back, struggling not to laugh outright. Knowing how dearly Anna Marie treasured her rock collection the other children had helped her gather, she knew that this was not as terrible a suggestion as it sounded.

"Pattie is still too young to play with rocks," she replied. "But that was kind of you to suggest it. And I'm proud of you. But we'll have to wait a few more years before she'll be old enough. And by then, maybe you might help her find a rock collection of her own."

Anna Marie nodded excitedly. "Tomorrow?"

"No," Rachel laughed, shaking her head. "Not tomorrow. Soon."

"All right," she giggled, still excited over the prospect.

"How about your blocks? We can get Pattie started on building herself a cabin. Would you like that?"

Anna Marie nodded vigorously and pulled away from Rachel, scurrying back into the nursery. "Pattie!" she called out. "Mamma's going to build you a cabin!"

Rachel rose to her feet and glanced over at the counter where her bread dough was resting, clearly ready to be punched down. Shifting her gaze to the nursery doorway, hearing the delighted giggles of her girls, she headed for the nursery, leaving the bread dough to rise a little bit longer. "Take it easy?" she chuckled to herself. "Doctor Morrison, just how am I supposed to do that?"

Slipping into the nursery, where Pattie and Anna Marie were already emptying out the blocks of wood onto the floor from the crate Patrick had fixed up for them for storing them in, she knelt down, one girl on each side of her. "Mamma?" Pattie giggled "Cabbie?"

Anna Marie clapped her hand over her mouth and laughed in such merriment her shoulders shook. Rachel herself began chuckling. "Not cabbie," Anna Marie laughed. "Cabin."

"Cabbie!" Pattie cried out in delight, clapping her hands.

"We'll build you a cabbie, Pattie," Rachel replied with a smile. "And we'll build Anna Marie a cabin."

Both girls seemed delighted with the arrangement and proceeded to help Rachel pile up the blocks, knocking more of them down than they actually piled up. Rachel found herself laughing as hard as they did each time the structures fell. At last a new game was invented: knocking down the cabbie.

"Rachel?" Sam's urgent voice called out suddenly. Rachel instantly rose to her feet. Her mind went in several directions at the same time. Sam never stepped into the house without knocking. Also, the tone of voice he was using was not a simple coming-to-visit-today-voice. It was filled with intensity—even horror.

"What is it?" she asked before she was all the way out of the nursery. But further words were unnecessary as she caught sight of Sam carrying Patrick's unconscious body through the doorway. "Put him on the bed!" she instructed. Her words were unnecessary, since he was already heading into the bedroom. Rachel stuck her head through the outside door, calling out as loudly as she could, "Jed! Jed I need you!"

Knowing that the man was always near enough to the house to come with a mere call, she did not wait to see if he was coming, but hurried into the bedroom where Sam was carefully laying Patrick down on the bed. Across his forehead a stream of blood was flowing over his pale face. Turning back to the kitchen, Rachel reached for the basin that hung by the water bucket. Quickly dipping out several dippers full of water into the basin, she picked it up and headed back for the bedroom. Just then Jed stepped into the house, his stern expression assuring her that he had heard the note in her voice that something was terribly wrong. "Go for Dr. Morrison. Patrick's been hurt. He's unconscious."

Dipping his head in a nod, Jed quickly stepped back outside. Rachel continued on toward the bedroom and set the basin of water onto the stand beside the bed. Sitting down on the edge of the bed, she inserted the cloth and wrung it out, gently washing the blood from the wound on Patrick's head, and asked in a trembling voice, "Sam what happened?"

Sam, standing at the foot of the bed, sighed deeply. "I don't know. I found him on the ground unconscious. What was he doing out there in the woods?" he demanded, frustration in his voice. "If he wanted to fell some trees, why didn't he come and tell me? That's what I used to do! He has no business working in the woods!"

Rachel knew the anger in his voice was not directed toward her, or even toward Patrick. "You know Patrick," she murmured quietly as she continued sponging the blood away, trying to stop its flow. "He prefers doing his own work."

"His own work, yes! But he's a preacher, Rachel! He's not a lumberman!"

Rachel nodded. All at once her lips began trembling. "Sam, what happened? And don't tell me you don't know."

The man pushed out his breath, muttering, "It looked like the tree he was chopping down lost a limb, and it hit him in the head."

"A widow maker?" she breathed out, turning to look the man full in the face, remembering that long ago day when Sam had explained to her that a widow maker was a falling branch that made wives into widows. It was what had killed Ion's father.

"No," Sam growled. "It wasn't that at all." But he offered no evidence for his assertion, nor did Rachel demand any, taking a tiny bit of comfort in the words she so wanted to believe.

When Dr. Morrison arrived he ushered Sam and Rachel out of the room. Rachel poured coffee for Sam and Jed as well as herself, though she was barely aware of what she was doing, simply going through routine motions. Easing down at the table, she murmured, "What if—" Clamping her jaws shut, she forced herself to fall silent. Glancing over at Sam, she studied his worried expression. Silently praying for help, she cleared her throat, glancing over at Jed and then back at Sam again. "I'm praying," she said simply. Both men shifted their eyes and studied her. At first she thought it might be her imagination, but then decided that she really did see a look of relief creep into their faces at her words. Swallowing, she continued speaking. "The Lord is faithful to do what's right. He promises to work everything out for the good of His children."

Sam narrowed his eyes, asking slowly, "Just for his children?"

Wishing she could promise the man what he wanted, but unable to deny the truth, she admitted, "The Bible says that He sends rain on both the just and the unjust. So He's gracious even to those who aren't His children. But He's made no promise to work everything together for the good of those who don't love Him. Only those who love Him can claim that promise."v

He nodded slowly, clearly thinking hard over the words she had spoken. The thoughtful look on his face seemed to relax into one of hope—just a ray of hope, but hope none-the-less. "Your husband loves God. No one could doubt that."

No one spoke again until Phil emerged from the bedroom. He accepted the cup of coffee Rachel offered and sat down at the table. He waited to speak until after he had taken a sip of coffee. Lowering the cup to the table, he met Rachel's gaze, saying, "He has no broken bones. He's suffered a concussion. I won't know the extent of it until he regains consciousness. But, as it appears, I don't think we have anything to worry about. He's going to have a severe headache for a few days. But hopefully that'll be the extent of it. Oh, one more thing," he added, practically glaring at Rachel. "Keep the man out of the woods!"

Suddenly Rachel's lips began bouncing upward as relief washed over her. Phil's eyes were laughing over his order. "Yes, Doctor," Rachel giggled. "I'll do that, even if I have to tie him down."

"From here on out," Sam growled, though his mouth was turned up slightly at the corners, "I will cut firewood for this family! And I'll see to it that your church fires him if he attempts to do it himself!"

"It doesn't work that way," Rachel chuckled. The relief she was feeling was leaving her a little bit shaky.

"It does now!" Sam insisted.

"Sam, you aren't even part of the church," Rachel replied in amazement.

"But I am," Phil cut in, firmness in his tone. "I'll see to it that our church sends your whole family packing if Patrick refuses to let us bring in your firewood for you."

Rachel laughed and shook her head, lifting her cup of coffee to take the first refreshing sip she'd tasted since Patrick had been brought home unconscious. "Thank you Jesus," she murmured.

Phil left soon after finishing his coffee, Jed driving him back home in the O'Riley wagon. Sam left with them, leaving Rachel alone with her thoughts. Suddenly she glanced over at the counter and jumped to her feet, hurrying over to it. "Dear oh dear," she murmured as she grabbed up the overflowing bread dough that had run up and over the sides of the bowl and had now spilled over onto the counter. "What a mess," she sighed as she punched it back down again, wondering if it would even be able to turn out right. "Well, it's been awhile since I fried up a mess of dough-gobs." She smiled over the term. It had been introduced to her by Elizabeth, who had first taught her the art of frying bread dough into pancake sized, flatten loaves. The entire batch of bread was eaten so quickly when she fried it, she only did so as a special treat. "Well," she sighed, "I can always make another batch of bread tomorrow. After all, I think this family needs a special treat today."

"Is Pa sick?" Anna Marie asked quietly.

Rachel turned to see the little girl standing in the bedroom doorway, looking at Patrick lying on the bed.

Quickly rubbing her hands into the kitchen towel, Rachel crossed the floor and slipped one arm around Anna Marie's shoulders, gently drawing her back into the kitchen. "Yes he is," she replied softly. "We must be very quiet so that he'll get well again."

Two solemn eyes lifted to meet hers. "I'll be quiet, Mamma," she vowed solemnly.

Rachel smiled. "Good girl. Oh my," she sighed out. "It's way past lunchtime. You must be getting hungry."

"Pattie fell asleep," Anna Marie replied, just as if that were the proper reply.

"Dear oh dear," Rachel sighed, shaking her head. "Come on, sweetie," she added, "let's you and I fix something fun."

The child's eyes lit up then. "Sure and certain?" she asked in excitement.

"Sure and certain," Rachel whispered, immediately thinking about Patrick, whom the little girl had learned the phrase from. "Sure and certain."

After a rather quick lunch of the remaining bread covered with sugar, cinnamon, and milk, Rachel set Anna Marie to quietly drawing pictures on the carefully horded paper Rachel had tucked away for rainy days. The remainder of the afternoon was broken up by a brief appearance of Dr. Morrison, checking on Patrick, and the cranky awakening of Pattie from her afternoon nap. Rachel only hoped that Patrick would wake up before the children returned home from school.

Georgy glanced over his shoulder and eyed Ion and Mary walking side by side. Not since Patrick had talked to Georgy and Ion had either of them ventured to hold hands with one of the girls. He frowned slightly, certain that this time Patrick was wrong. After all, they weren't treating the girls disrespectfully. He and Ion had discussed the matter at length and found they were in agreement with each other. As Mary and her brothers turned to the path that branched off to their house, Georgy paused and waited for Ion to catch up with him.

"Why don't you just ask her pa if you can start courting her?" Georgy asked Ion, who replied by simply rolling his eyes. "Why not? You're sixteen now."

"You know Rachel won't let me court anyone yet."

"Have you asked her?"

"No," Ion admitted, frowning.

Georgy began chuckling. "Scared to ask?"

Ion shot an angry glare at Georgy. "Scared of Rachel?" he scoffed.

Georgy continued grinning and clapped Ion on the back. "Yeah," he sighed. "Me too."

They continued onward, following Johnny and Elizabeth. As the house came in sight, Rachel stepped out through the door and began walking toward them. Georgy and Ion exchanged puzzled glances. Something in Ion's expression warned Georgy that the uncomfortable dread he was suddenly feeling was not limited to himself. Rachel always waited inside the house for them to return, it being so much easier than bundling up Pattie to take her outside. He frowned, scanning the ground, wondering why Anna Marie was not dashing ahead of Rachel. For that matter, why was Pattie not in Rachel's arms or toddling along beside her?

As Rachel drew near them, she motioned for them to stop walking. Her face looked a little pale. "I have something to tell you," she began quickly, as though wanting to get that part over with, but then fell silent, studying them. Georgy suddenly found it difficult to concentrate on breathing. "Patrick was hurt today—"

"What happened?" Georgy demanded.

"Is he all right?" Ion asked half a moment after Georgy's question.

Rachel held up her hand and glanced at Elizabeth, speaking slowly for her sake. "Dr. Morrison said that he should be fine."

As the other three sighed out their relief, Georgy continued frowning, studying Rachel. "Should be?" he asked quietly, drawing Rachel's eyes to him. "He doesn't know for sure?"

"He's still unconscious," Rachel admitted. "He has a concussion. But until he wakes up, Dr. Morrison can't tell any more. There are no apparent injuries."

"What happened Rachel?" Georgy asked gently, lifting his hand to her shoulder, easing her around to face the house. As they spoke, he guided her to begin walking again to the house.

"He was cutting down trees."

"For firewood?" Georgy asked, careful to keep his voice quiet as he continued studying Rachel's pale face. When she nodded, he eased into a smile. "It's all right. Everybody gets hurt in the woods some time or other." He drew his arm around her shoulders as a look of relief crept into her face. "If Doc says he should be fine, he will be. I'll take a look at him."

A sigh escaped her then, and Georgy felt the weight of the transferred responsibility concerning Patrick's recovery shift from Rachel's shoulders to his own. It was then that Rachel slipped her arm around his waist and leaned against him as they walked.

"Thank you Georgy," she murmured. "It's been a long afternoon."

"Did Phil say when he's coming back to check on Patrick?"

Rachel blinked as Georgy slipped and called the doctor by his first name. When he and the doctor worked together, they had found it easier for Georgy to simply call him by his first name. This, however, was the first time he had slipped and used his name in front of others. She recovered quickly from her surprise, replying, "Unless I send for him earlier, he'll be by again this evening. But since you'll be here, now I won't need to wonder if I need to send for him. I'm so glad you know what to do."

Georgy simply smiled, wondering if he should tell her that he really did not know what to do. The look of relief in her face was so great, however, he decided to allow her the comfort of turning this responsibility over to him. After all, he reminded himself, he would know if the doctor should be sent for.

Ion found himself pacing between Patrick's study and the kitchen, where Rachel was frying up dough gobs for supper. His stomach was rebelling against the very idea of food. Finally he paused beside Rachel and quietly asked the question that had consumed him from the moment she had explained what had happened to Patrick. "Is Pat going to die like my pa?"

Rachel's hands stilled. Setting the pancake turner onto the counter, she turned to him and gave him her full attention. "No," she said firmly. Lifting her hands to his shoulders, she added, "He is not going to die."

All at once she pulled him into her arms and held him close. He allowed his arms to creep around her as well, not certain which of the two was being comforted the most. "I'm sorry Rachel," he whispered, suddenly realizing that his question had been just as hard for her to hear as it had been for him to voice. "Sure he's going to be all right," he added, holding her closer.

A sob tore from her, which she silenced immediately. "I know," she whispered. "It's been such a long day."

"Don't cry," he murmured, feeling like kicking himself for her tears. "Please don't. He'll be fine, just like Doc says. And Georgy said he looks like he's just tired and asleep."

Rachel lifted her head from his shoulder and met his gaze, her eyes glistening with unshed tears. She nodded. Leaning close, she softly kissed his cheek. "You just keep praying," she murmured. "That's what he needs—all our prayers."

"I am," he said, nodding. He paused as he studied her face. "What is it?" he asked.

She shook her head. "Nothing really. I was just wishing it'd happened to me instead of to Patrick."

This time it was Ion who drew her close. "Don't even think that," he whispered fiercely. "None of us can do without you Rachel—Pat least of all. Why, if you were the one lying unconscious in there, Pat would—well his heart would be broken. You're strong enough to bear him being hurt. But, where you're concerned, Pat couldn't take that—believe me, I know."

She allowed him to hold her and comfort her. And as he did so, he found himself also being comforted. All at once Georgy called out quietly, "Rachel, come in here."

Together Ion and Rachel hurried to the bedroom. As Rachel stepped inside, easing up to the side of the bed where Georgy was sitting, studying Patrick's fluttering eyes, Ion leaned against the doorjamb.

Finally Patrick's eyes remained open and he met Georgy's gaze, a far away look in his eyes. "Can you tell me your name?" Georgy asked quietly.

One side of Patrick's mouth crept upward as he replied, "O'course lad. M'name is Patrick O'Riley."

Ion noticed that Rachel and Georgy, as well as himself breathed out a sigh of relief. Ion began wondering how long it would be before Patrick could get out of bed. Once he smelled Rachel's dough gobs frying, he was sure to be insisting on getting up and sitting at the table.

"And can you tell me what you've been doing today?" Georgy asked. Ion wondered why he was persisting with the questions. Patrick knew what was going on. He had already proven that.

A quizzical look came to Patrick's face. "Ye aren't frim around 'ere, are ye lad? I don't believe I've heard yeer accent before. I kin tell ye aren't frim Ireland—nor England either."

"Originally Virginia," Georgy replied slowly. "And now I live in the Oregon Territory."

Patrick's eyes lit up. "Oregon? America?" he asked in excitement and then winced, lifting his hand to his head.

"Take it easy, Pat," Georgy instructed in a professional sounding tone. "You've been hit on the head. You've got a concussion."

Patrick grinned. "Well, it isn't the first time. Bit I don't do street fighting iny more. 'Ow did I manage to get hit on the head, without sem lad punching me?"

"You were cutting down trees—"

"In the heart of Dublin?" Patrick cried out and then wrenched up his face in clear pain.

"Just where do you think you are, Pat?" Georgy asked quietly. Ion stared at the man, his heart feeling as though it would pound right out of his chest as fear gripped him.

Patrick drew in a deep breath and opened his eyes again. "M'room at the boarding house? Where else? Laddie," he added, "are ye really frim Oregon? Thit's the viry place I intend to go to as a missionary, as soon as I kin arrange passage."

Georgy and Rachel exchanged glances. Ion could not see Georgy's face, but Rachel's was a picture of pure shock. Turning back to Patrick, Georgy replied in a steady voice, "Yes, I'm from Oregon. We'll talk about it later. But for now, you need some rest. I'm going to send for the doctor now. I'll sit with you until he comes." Glancing over his shoulder, Georgy nodded to Ion.

Without a word, Ion turned and stepped out of the house, hurrying down the path to Doctor Morrison's. "Oh God," he prayed as he ran along, "please don't let Patrick lose his mind. Please, Jesus—heal him."

Patrick studied the face of the young man sitting on the edge of his bed who had a troubled look in his eyes. He judged him to be sixteen or seventeen. And he certainly had good manners. He could not help but smile over hearing his first American accent. He wondered if all American teenagers were as gentlemanly as this young man appeared to be. Shifting his gaze, he caught sight of the beautiful young woman standing there, a look of such sadness in her face that Patrick caught his breath. "Lassie?" he murmured. "Are ye all right?"

She dipped her head in a nod, but he could clearly see that she was not all right. "Please excuse m'manners, ma'am. I seem to be stuck in bed or else I'd be rising to m'feet. Is there inything I kin do for ye?"

The woman swallowed and began biting her lower lip. She shook her head. Patrick suspected that she was nearly ready to cry, though he had no idea why. There was such a depth of sadness in her eyes. Suddenly he began wondering where he was exactly. At first he had thought he was in his own room. But this room was completely unfamiliar. His eyes shifted to actual log walls. Clearly he was not in his rooming house. Though the dingy wallpaper-encased walls of the rooming house had seen better days, they were still made of sawn boards, not of hewn logs. "Where am I?" he murmured. "Hiv I been asleep for long? Hiv ye driven me out of the city? I know of nowhere in Dublin they use logs for walls. Where am I Laddie?"

The young man laid his hand on his then, saying reassuringly, "You're in our home. We're going to take care of you. Now don't fret. Can I pray for you?"

Patrick smiled then. "Aye lad. I'd appreciate it."

As the boy began quietly praying aloud, Patrick eased his eyes shut. They seemed almost to burn with weariness. He was uncertain if he was remaining fully awake, or if he was actually drifting off to sleep. Either way, a rush of comfort engulfed him. Wherever he was, he was among fellow believers. That was enough to know for now.

The moment Ion and Dr. Morrison stepped into the house, the doctor hurried into the bedroom. Immediately Rachel returned to the kitchen, leaving Georgy and the doctor to care for Patrick. She crossed the kitchen to help Elizabeth in frying the dough gobs, her face as pale as Ion had ever seen it. He eyed her, wondering if he should go to her and encourage her to sit down.

"Now Miz O'Riley," Jed muttered in what sounded like his normal mock complaining tone he used to tease her, though Ion noticed the serious look in his eyes that belied his attempt at bantering. "You best sit yourself down in the living room and catch yer breath. Bet can finish up supper."

Rachel glanced over at Jed as he sat at the table eying her. One side of her mouth crept upward. A negative reply was clearly on the tip of her tongue. All at once a real smile painted itself on her mouth. Ion wondered at the sudden peaceful expression that rested on her face. "You know Jed, I just might do that."

Turning to Elizabeth, she softly patted her back and leaned close, kissing her on the forehead. The girl met her gaze and nodded. Rachel turned then, and stepped quietly into the living room. Ion followed her. She eased herself down onto her rocking chair and bowed her head. Ion crouched down beside her and slipped his hand over hers. When she opened up her eyes and met his gaze, she smiled at him. "Pray with me?" she asked.

He dipped his head in a nod. All the while he wondered at the peace that was shining in her eyes. "Rachel?" he murmured. "Why are you—I don't know—what changed?"

She squeezed his hand, murmuring, "I just suddenly remembered that God knows what we're going through. And He still cares. Why, He created Heaven and Earth—including Patrick. He's able to fix whatever's broken. He's a good God, Ion, not an evil one. He will do what's right. I'd rather trust Him than not trust Him."

Ion's throat grew uncomfortably tight then as relief wrapped around his aching heart. Rachel nodded in understanding, closing her eyes again, still holding his hand. "Dear Father-God," she prayed softly, "I know you've got a plan. I know you aren't finished with Patrick. I know you still have work for Him to do. So please, Lord, heal him. Please give him the strength and health he needs to finish the race you've set before him. Please allow him to raise all of our children. And please spare me the ache of being parted from him. I don't know what's wrong with him. He doesn't know who I am." A sob tore from her then, piercing straight through to Ion's heart. He clenched his jaws together. But when Rachel fell silent, he suspected that her emotions weren't allowing any more words to pass through her lips.

"Lord," he whispered, picking up her prayer, "my first pa was mean and beat me up more than once. But you gave me a new pa. Please Lord, don't take him away from me. I need him to show me how to be the kind of man you want me to be. All of us children need him as our pa. Please heal him." Something inside of him began rising up in rebellion, startling him. All at once he wondered what it would mean to all of them if God meant to call Patrick home right away.

"Jesus," Rachel whispered, "we need your help to accept what you mean for us to accept. You are our joy and our strength. We can't do this without your help. We don't want to sin. Please show us the way not to sin—show us how to accept whatever answer it is you plan to give us."

Ion's shoulders began shaking then as silent sobs took hold of him. Silently he asked God to forgive him for those moments of rebelling against the will of God. "I'm so sorry," he added in the silence of his heart. "Please forgive me." Immediately peace flooded through him.

Rachel's arms crept around him, drawing him close to her. "He has a wonderful plan, Ion," she murmured in a trembling voice. "I don't know what it is, but I choose to trust Him. Is that what you're choosing too?"

Ion nodded, squeezing his eyes shut tight, desperately trying to hold back the tears that insisted on creeping out through them. Rachel kissed his cheek and simply continued holding him. A feeling of peace sifted through him. He had come to comfort her, and here she was not only comforting him but giving him a good example to follow as well. Finally he lifted his head, pulling back slightly from her. "It's easier to have faith when it's somebody else's family that has troubles," he admitted candidly.

All at once her eyes sparkled and she began laughing. "You are so right, Ion!"

He found himself smiling at her. "I'll trust Him," he murmured.

"Me too," she replied, as if they were making a pact with each other.

"Mrs. O'Riley?" Dr. Morrison called out quietly. Instantly Ion rose to his feet and held out his hand, helping Rachel to stand up. "I'd like to talk with you for a minute while Georgy is still in with Patrick."

As Rachel stepped back into the kitchen, Ion reached up and hastily dashed the dampness from his cheeks before following. By the time they were all sitting around the table, the doctor began talking, eying Rachel. "The concussion," he began quietly, keeping his voice too low to be overheard in the bedroom, "has resulted in partial memory loss. It's very likely," he added quickly, "that it will be only temporary. But it does entail several years of his life that he's simply forgotten. As far as he's concerned, he hasn't left Ireland yet. He has no memory of any of you—nor of anyone in Timberton."

"Does that mean," Johnny asked with sudden fear in his voice, "he's gone crazy?"

Dr. Morrison smiled kindly at the boy and shook his head. "Not at all. Have you ever forgotten something?" When Johnny nodded, Phil added, "That's what it's like for Patrick right now. But instead of forgetting only one momentary thing, he's forgotten a few years of things. He hasn't lost his mind—only part of his memory."

Johnny nodded, but his expression was still troubled. Rachel drew in a deep breath then and asked, "When will he remember us?"

Again Phil turned to study her. He hesitated for a moment, causing Ion to wonder just how much the man knew that he was not telling. "Well, I can't say for sure. It could be in a few days, or a few weeks."

He left off his sentence in such an unfinished tone Ion stared hard at him.

"Or not at all?" Ion asked.

Phil shifted his gaze to him and nodded with reluctance. "Or not at all," he murmured. Turning back to Rachel, he added in a mixture of firmness as well as kindness, "You must be prepared for that possibility."

Rachel swallowed and slowly nodded. Her lips began trembling. Pushing back her shoulders in a strength that brought the corners of Ion's mouth up, she said, "God has a plan, Doctor. And I for one am going to thank Him for it." And so saying, she closed her eyes and said in a tone of such strength that

Ion's mouth fell open slightly, "Thank you Lord God! We're going to do it your way. And you are going to get the glory for this!" Opening her eyes back up, a tear slipped down her cheek, but victory was on her face. "Now, tell us what we need to do for Patrick. What are we to tell him when he asks questions? He doesn't know where he is. What are we to tell him?"

Dr. Morrison eyed her in wonder and smiled. "The truth," he said simply. "Don't volunteer too much information, only what he absolutely needs to know. Give him the opportunity to remember on his own as much as possible. But don't let him try to force his memory to return. That will only slow it down. For this reason you need to tell him the basics—who you are and each member of the family and that you're in America in the Oregon Territory—just so he doesn't drive himself mad with wondering. He's going to have to be patient and wait for his memory to return—he can't force it to."

Rachel nodded. Ion studied her, suddenly realizing that she was an amazingly strong woman. And her faith was real. No one looking on her right then could ever doubt the truth of what she believed, he realized. No one.

Patrick glanced from the face of the young man who sat on the edge of his bed to the lovely woman who entered the bedroom. "Georgy," she said quietly, causing the young man to glance over his shoulder at her, "I need to talk to Patrick alone. Will you and Ion see that the family eats some supper?"

The boy Georgy nodded and rose to his feet. As he stepped past the woman, she gently latched onto his arm, asking, "Will you keep Pattie entertained for me so that I can talk to Patrick as long as it takes? And have Ion take charge of Anna Marie. Please ask Johnny to help Elizabeth with the clean up, and I'll make it up to him."

The young man nodded and slipped out of the room. Only then did the woman continue on toward Patrick. With a boldness that startled Patrick, she sat down on the edge of the bed, just as if it were her right. She met his gaze, just as if she knew him, instead of being the complete stranger she was. Drawing in a deep breath, she folded her hands in her lap and said simply, "I've come to answer your questions."

Patrick nodded, and then winced, regretting having moved his head. The instant look of concern on the woman's face startled him afresh as he wondered why a total stranger seemed to care so deeply. "The doctor said I've lost m'memory," he began, puzzling over it. "Bit, honestly, I hivn't forgotten a thing. Iverything is as clear as when I first woke up this morning. The only thing I don't recall is how I hit m'self on the head. Bit, I don't mind letting go o'thit memory. It likely isn't worth rimimbering inyway."

The woman smiled with such kindness, he could not help but stare at her. "You were out in the woods, cutting trees for firewood."

"Woods? Lassie, there've bin no forest in Dublin for many a long year."

She nodded. "I know," she said in a patient tone. "I know." She paused, something in her eyes caused his heart to leap, though he could not tell why.

No one had ever looked at him in such a knowing way before. "Patrick, I have to tell you that you've forgotten several years of your life—I'm not sure how many."

He stared at her, unable to think of anything to say. "Years?" he finally whispered.

Gently she laid her hand on his, just as if she had the right. He glanced down at their entwined hands, wondering why his fingers had automatically interlaced with hers. It was comforting, but startling to say the least. He returned his gaze to her, wondering what words would follow. She smiled then, saying, "You're a missionary now, Patrick. Your church sent you to America, and you bought a wagon and made your way out to the Oregon Territory. You're what you dreamed of being! You made it here to Oregon!"

Such delightful encouragement embraced her words, Patrick could not help but smile. "I'm a real missionary?" he asked.

Her eyes soften then and she squeezed his hand. "A real missionary. And people out here have gotten saved under your ministry. You've done so well, Patrick!"

His heart stirred at her words. Clearly she was not simply trying to make him feel better. He could tell that she meant every word. A strength he had never known before began stirring inside of him. All at once he felt like he could take on the whole world single-handedly. As he studied her face, he saw that there was more that she was not telling him. "What is it, lassie," he murmured. She caught her breath and bit down on her lower lip for a moment, but not before he had seen it begin to tremble. Though he knew he had no right, he held her hand more tightly. "Tell me," he whispered gently.

She drew in her breath, clearly struggling with her emotions. Strength sparkled from her eyes, and he suddenly knew that she would find a way to tell him what she needed to. "I was with the same wagon train—my father, brother Johnny and I—as you were. You see, you and my father, Charles Nathan, agreed to become partners." Patrick opened his eyes wide at that. "One day, while we were crossing a river, our horses spooked and carried our wagon downriver, destroying it completely. My father got tangled in the lines and drowned." She paused and glanced down at their entwined hands. He wondered over her hesitancy to continue with her story. She seemed to take courage as she studied their hands. Without lifting her eyes back to him, she added, "I had no one to care for Johnny and me. So, as Papa's partner, you felt it your responsibility to marry me."

Patrick caught his breath and stared at her. Dark hair framed a dazzlingly beautiful, yet pale, face. "Ye're m'wife?" he breathed out, too stunned to think of anything else to say. When she nodded, she lifted her eyes back to his. A look of near shame crept into those beautiful, dark eyes. Again his heart stirred at that look—that vulnerable look on the gentle face. Something told him that she was suddenly feeling like a beggar. He knew he had to say something—anything—to put back the look of self-worth in her face. But the news was so startling, he could barely think, let alone comfort anyone—especially the woman who was claiming to be his wife. As he continued studying the face before him, he knew within him that her need was—unexplainable as it was—greater than his at the moment. The corners of his mouth crept upward as he squeezed her hand, admitting, "I always did want a wife. Bit I never expected to get such a pretty one."

Instantly the woman's expression relaxed into such relief and hope that Patrick was glad that he had allowed the one thing on his mind to slip out. She no longer looked so utterly vulnerable. "Thank you Patrick," she murmured.

He nodded, and once again instantly regretted the movement. A gentle hand reached over, softly cradling his head, easing away the shrieking pain his movement had caused. Finally, as the pain lessened, he asked, "Then, we are a family of three? Ye and yeer brither, and m'self?"

"And more," she added hesitantly.

"Lassie," he sighed, suddenly wanting to shield her from this obviously difficult task that had been set before her. "Just tell me what ye need to. And I'll be accepting it. All right?"

He stared in shock as tears dashed to her eyes. He studied her almost painfully, wondering. "What's bringing yeer tears, lassie?" he murmured.

She swallowed. "It's just that," she began, smiling an almost little girl smile, "you sound just like yourself, even though you can't remember us. I'm so glad you're still you." Again her words had the amazing affect of putting heart into him. Silently he waited for her to continue. "We've adopted many members into our family, Patrick. We now have a grandfather, Jed Northwood. His great grandchildren are now our son and daughter. Georgy—"

"The laddie who was talking with me?"

She nodded. "Yes. That's our Georgy. And his sister is Elizabeth. She's deaf, but reads our lips quite well, as long as we speak slowly. And then there's Ion, who is Georgy's age—sixteen. And Anna Marie was the daughter of a widower doctor we met on the wagon train. When he died, Anna Marie became our daughter. She's five. And then there's Pattie who is almost a year and a half."

"And whose daughter wis she?"

Rachel swallowed, but steadily met his gaze as she replied, "Yours and mine."

Patrick's mouth fell open slightly as he stared in shock at her. "Yeers and mine?" he asked, dumbfounded. "We—we're really man and wife?"

She nodded. "We fell in love with each other some months after we got married."

Once again she lowered her eyes, this time clearly shamed. With his free hand, he reached up, gently touching her chin and eased her head back up. "I'm sorry," he murmured, "for forgetting. Will ye forgive me?"

This time the woman's tears refused to remained corralled within her eyes and slipped down her cheeks. His heart suddenly squeezed together, seeing that he was the one who had put those tears there. "I'll do all I kin to rimimber m'love for ye and the rist o'the family. Lassie," he added then, "ye've told me mich, but one thing ye've left out." When she looked at him in puzzlement, he smiled softly at her, asking, "What's yeer name?"

"Rachel," she breathed. "Rachel O'Riley—"

All at once her words seemed real, hearing his own name linked into hers. All at once she smiled, a look of amusement dashing to her face. "That's the same expression that was on your face the first time you heard me say my married name." She suddenly began chuckling, as if over a cherished memory. "You looked so startled when I introduced myself to Jed by saying, "'I'm Rachel O'Riley.'"

He found himself relaxing, a surprising excitement beginning to course through him at the thought of getting to know this woman. "Aye, it startles a man the first time 'e hears it. And I get the fun o'being startled twice for the first time."

Her eyes soften as her smile grew. But this was a smile that was filled with love. No woman had ever looked at him with a look of love before. All at once he realized that he had lost a treasure in forgetting his own love for this woman. "We've bin happy together?" he asked.

She nodded. "So very happy," she murmured

"Then, lassie—Rachel—" he forced himself to say, though he felt self-conscious in calling this stranger by her first name. "We will be again."

She smiled and nodded. "I better go now, and let you get some rest. Do you think you could eat something?"

"No," he sighed. "This headache is making m'stomach gnash about a bit. I don't think I'd be able to keep inything down if I tried to eat."

All at once the woman leaned close and kissed his cheek. The next moment she rose to her feet and smiled down at him. "Good night then. Just call out if you need anything."

She turned then and stepped out of the room. Patrick was still in a state of shock over her kiss, several moments after she left. Life had always stretched out as new and untried—but nothing like this.

Just how long Patrick had been sleeping, he was uncertain. By the moonlight that filtered into the room, he suspected that it had been many hours. Glancing over he caught his breath in surprise as his eyes fell to the woman Rachel, lying beside him in bed. He had not forgotten her words that they were married, but he had not expected her to join him in bed. Her eyes were open, meeting his own. "Is semthing wrong?" he asked, unable to read her expression clearly in the dimness of the moonlight.

"Just a dream," she murmured, her voice trembling, a mixture of dread and fear in her tone. "Go back to sleep. I didn't mean to waken you."

"Do ye want to talk about it?"

"No," she whispered. But something in that lonely whisper made him doubt her reply. It was then that he realized that sometime during the night, his arm had crept around her shoulders and her head had pillowed itself against his shoulder. It felt both natural and unnatural all at the same time. He had never held a woman so closely before—in his memory, he reminded himself.

Hesitantly he lifted his free arm and slipped it around her. "Tell me," he murmured. He was unprepared for her response, easing her arm around him, but it felt right. He found himself drawing her closer to himself, she responding in kind until they were clinging to each other.

"I dreamed you were gone. I kept looking for you. But you weren't here—you weren't anywhere," she added in a sob.

As she cried into his shoulder, he reached for her head, easing his fingers into the silky, dark hair and simply held her. And then he knew that she had been telling the truth—she really did love him.

"How did ye learn to love a poor Irishman like me, Rachel?" he murmured in wonder.

His words served only to make her cry all the more, though he had no idea why. It was some time before she quieted herself. Though her tears were over, she still clung to him, and he to her. "I have good taste, that's how," she finally replied, bringing a smile to him.

"Ah lassie, I see it now thit we're going to need terribly wide doorways if I'm to be able to pass through them. 'Tis sure and certain that it won't take long for me to get a big head with a woman like ye as m'wife. Why, I don't think I've ever felt so good about m'self in m'whole life. Ye hiv a way o'making a man think 'e is Hercules and Samson all rolled up into one."

She turned her head then, a smile on her lips. But her lips were now close to his. And they were drawing nearer. As they met his, he eased his eyes shut, reveling in the sweetness of the woman's kiss. Though he expected her to pull away after a moment, she did not, much to his enjoyment. And the world suddenly became this woman, this Rachel O'Riley, who was kissing him with a passion that began kindling his own. Even the pounding of his headache was pushed back as he returned her kiss. Gently they pulled back from each other. "I think I'm going to like being married to ye, Mrs. O'Riley," he murmured a little self-consciously.

She giggled and reached up, softly caressing his cheek. "You always did," she whispered. Her hand paused as her fingers touched his lips. "You're my whole life, Patrick," she added, laying her lips on his again. But this time she did not linger, but simply kissed him softly and laid her head back down on his shoulder. In silence they lay there until the regular sound of her breathing assured him that she was falling back to sleep. He, however, was now wide awake. "Ah lassie," he sighed and drew his head down to rest on hers. So this was what it was like to be a married man. What would the next day bring?

Rachel slipped out of bed the next morning as quietly as she could and dressed quickly. Even though Patrick was laid up and battling against losing his memory, there was still breakfast to prepare and children to be sent off to school. Life went on, regardless.

The children were quiet as they ate their breakfast. Rachel and Jed both tried to engage them in conversation, but to no avail. Finally Ion glanced over at Rachel and asked, "How are we supposed to treat him?"

"Why, the same way as you always have," she replied. "Patrick has not changed," she added firmly. "He's still the same man we love so much. He's still the finest man—" She halted suddenly as everyone's eyes shifted. Glancing over her shoulder, she met Patrick's eyes as he stood in the bedroom doorway. The soften look on his face assured her that he had heard her words.

"Y-you ought to be in bed," she stammered. "I thought you were asleep, or I would've brought in your breakfast." He was still studying her wordlessly. "Why don't you go and lay back down? I'll bring your breakfast to you.

He shook his head. The movement caused him to wince in pain over the movement. "No lassie," he replied a moment later. "I'll sit at the table, if ye'll be directing me to where I normally sit."

The silence around the table was nearly tangible then. Rachel managed a smile, and replied, "Beside me, here at the end of the table." She reached for the plate she had set out for him and eased it down at his place as he stepped up to the table and sat down beside her.

The children were eying him, troubled expression on their faces, studying him almost fearfully, as though studying a stranger. He seemed not to notice, much to Rachel's relief. Finally he looked up and one by one studied each face. At last he smiled, saying, "'Tis true thit I kinnot rimimber ye. Bit already I feel thit the Lord 'as put 'Is blessing ipon me in giving ye to me to be m'family."

Rachel bit the corner of her mouth over his kind words to people who were virtual strangers to him, as far as his memory went. Shifting her gaze, she caught sight of Ion, whose tense expression began relaxing. Next to him Georgy sat suddenly grinning. Jed simply lifted his coffee cup and then smacked his lips in contentment. As Johnny quietly repeated Patrick's words to Elizabeth, they both began smiling. And Anna Marie simply grinned as she ate her oatmeal. Pattie was happily unaware of what was going on and simply sat in the chair Patrick had constructed for her with a tray of its own, quietly splashing her spoon in her oatmeal.

Rachel turned and met Patrick's gaze. Silently she mouthed, "Thank you."

He smiled and leaned over to her, softly kissing her cheek. It was then that the normal morning chatter began around the table. And Rachel realized that she was suddenly hungry, for the first time since yesterday morning.

Chapter Seven

The first week following Patrick's injury had come and gone. Since Dr. Morrison had insisted that Patrick spend most of that week resting in bed, it had been easy to pretend that everything was normal for most of each day. Mealtimes had proven to be another matter, as Patrick insisted on sitting at the table with the family—the family he could not remember. Rachel was finding herself growing weary of her family and herself being treated with the kind, proper manners of a stranger, rather than the intimacy of a love-filled husband and father.

As Patrick and Rachel sat at the table after the older children had left for school, Patrick eased his coffee cup down and studied Rachel in silence. She shifted her eyes and met his gaze, wondering. "I've bin thinking," he began slowly—thoughtfully, "thit 'tis time to be meeting our friends."

Rachel frowned in thought. "Well, Dr. Morrison was quite insistent in allowing your memory to return naturally. Wouldn't we risk forcing your memory if you're around others who might not let you remember on your own?"

He grinned then. "Ah, like the lads and lasses who give the answers to test questions?"

She smiled and nodded. "Something like that. It's meant kindly, but is terribly unhelpful. But the worst," she added, shaking her head, "is when parents themselves give their children the answers to their school work, thinking they're helping them. I never seemed to get through to some of my students' parents."

He leaned back in surprise. "Ye were a teacher?" he asked.

Catching her breath, she stared. "Oh Patrick, I didn't mean to let that slip. It just came out. But that's the very thing I'm talking about. It's just so hard not to mention things that are part of our lives, but things you've forgotten."

A soften look of kindness slipped into his eyes. But the longer she met his gaze, the more her disappointment grew, seeing the ever-missing look of love for her that used to be an inseparable sparkle in his eyes. "'Tis hard on ye," he murmured and sighed. He shifted his gaze to the cup in front of him, studying it as if all the answers of the universe were painted there. "I wish I could rimove thit look frim yeer eyes."

Rachel blinked in shock. "What look?" When he remained silent, she hesitated for a moment before slipping her hand over his. It was then that he glanced back at her. "What look do you see in my eyes?" she asked gently, squeezing his hand, even though she was a stranger to him as far as he was concerned.

"Disappointment," he admitted. He glanced down at their entwined hands and curled his fingers around hers. "I kinnot pretend to hiv feelings thit I've forgotten. Ye'd see right through it inyway. Bit even if ye didn't, I couldn't be dishonest with ye. We hiv honesty between us, Rachel," he added, still clearly uncomfortable in addressing her by her first name. "If we hiv nething else, we do hiv thit, and I'll not be parting with it." He paused and shook his head slowly, a crease denting itself between his brows. "Of all the things thit I've forgotten, forgetting m'love for ye is the hardest to bear. I've never loved a woman before—not real love, only infatuation. And to think thit I finally found a woman who slipped into m'heart, and I kinnot even rimimber m'love for 'er—It tears away at me." He lifted his eyes back to hers. "And what will we be doing if I never rimimber?"

Rachel swallowed, her throat aching with unreleased emotion. "We'll live on my love for you, Patrick. I haven't forgotten it." She paused, struggling to say what had grown to be a joy to say to him, but what had not been voiced since his injury. "I love you Patrick. You hang onto that thought, all right? You are loved! And I remember your love for me. So I know that I am loved too. And for now, we're just going to have to content ourselves in that. You remember this: you really aren't living with a handful of strangers. Each one of us loves you with a love that would make us lay down our lives for you—for you Patrick O'Riley. And I will remind you of my love for you every day of my life. You are the man I most admire." She paused and forced herself to continue speaking with such boldness to this man who thought of her as a stranger. "No matter what situation you find yourself in, Patrick, you always come out victoriously! You are an amazing man! I know of no other that can even equal you, let alone better you. No woman could ever be prouder of her husband than I am of you! You are my dearest friend on Earth. You are my protector and provider, my councilor, my partner in laughter and joy, my comforter when I'm sad. You, Patrick, are an amazing man. Even if you don't remember even one memory of our past together, I still count myself to be the most privileged woman in the world because I get to spend the rest of my life with you!"

Patrick's jaw had dropped open as she spoke. His shoulders had shifted back, causing him to sit tall—like a king. A look of courage now rested in his eyes. And Rachel knew that he had desperately needed to hear these words, and was also absolutely stunned by her utterance of them.

A cry from the nursery rang out then, shattering the moment. Rachel jumped to her feet and hurried into the nursery where Pattie lay on the floor, face down, shrieking. Kneeling down, Rachel picked her up and cuddled her in her arms, noticing the trickle of blood on her cheek which she had apparently cut as she fell to the floor. Rising to her feet, Rachel carried the still crying baby to the kitchen to wash her face.

"It wasn't my fault," Anna Marie suddenly whimpered from the nursery doorway.

As Rachel pressed the damp cloth to Pattie's cheeks, she said quietly, "Tell me what happened."

It was then that Anna Marie burst into tears and ran over to Patrick, burying her face in his lap. His expression softened as he studied the little girl. Reaching down, he picked her up and settled her on his lap. Instantly her arms hugged his neck. "Don't spank me, Pa. I didn't mean to push her. She just got in my way when I turned around. I didn't see her there. I didn't mean to push her."

His eyes shot over to meet Rachel's. She hid the smile that suddenly wanted to blossom on her lips over the helpless look in his face. Apparently realizing that he was not going to receive any help from her, he turned back to Anna Marie who was now studying his face through rounded eyes as she awaited his judgment. "Well now," he began quietly, just as patiently as he always had in the past. "Whether ye meant to hurt wee Pattie or not, ye still did. Why, the lassie is still crying. And yeer mamma is wiping blood from the cut on 'er face. I think ye owe 'er an apology."

Anna Marie continued studying his face for another moment before quietly slipping off of his lap. Turning to Rachel, she stepped over and looked up at Pattie in Rachel's arms. "I'm sorry, Pattie," she sniffed through her tears.

"All right," Patrick called out quietly. "Off with ye now. Go and play."

Instantly Anna Marie began smiling and whirled around, hurrying into the living room, making no attempt at even returning to the nursery. By the sound of her giggling as she found new amusement, her world was apparently mended once more. Patrick grinned and shook his head. Turning back to Rachel, he asked, "Is Pattie all right?"

Rachel nodded and carried the baby over for Patrick's inspection. Upon seeing him, Pattie reached out her arms to him. She had seen precious little of him during his convalescing the past week. At first he seemed hesitant—uncertain. But then he reached out for the baby and gathered her in his arms. "Well," he grinned as his arms wrapped around the little girl, "M'mind may hiv forgotten 'ow to hold a wee lassie, bit m'arms rimimber." As he gazed into the child's face, an old familiar luster crept into his eyes. He leaned close and softly kissed her forehead. Suddenly he met Rachel's gaze, a puzzled look in his eyes.

"What is it?" she asked, torn between wanting to know what new thought was going through his mind and also that of simply enjoying watching him with Pattie.

"It's as though I recall holding Pattie b'fore."

Rachel eased out her breath and smiled, her heart feeling lighter than it had for a week. "That's because you have. Patrick, your memory is beginning to return!"

He joined her smile with an excited one of his own. "Do ye think so?" Turning back to study Pattie's face, he murmured, "'Ow could I hiv forgotten m'own lassie? Not for long," he breathed out, certainty in his tone. "No, not for long."

Patrick glanced up from his Bible as he sat in the living room, studying his sermon. Rachel had assured him that the far room off of the living room was his own study, but it felt so foreign to him he preferred sitting in the living room whenever it was quiet enough in the house to allow for that. He had memorized the names of every member of this family, but still they looked like strangers to him—or rather, like very recent acquaintances—but certainly not like family. He sighed, in spite of his effort not to. After all, he was not the only one who was having a hard time over the amnesia. He glanced through the study doorway where the young man Ion sat, working on his latest writing project. "M'son the writer," he murmured. "M'son." He shook his head, wishing that it felt real to him. The young man seemed to be the quietest of all of his sons—thoughtful too, often lost in a world of his own.

Patrick paused and once again tried to work up a memory of the young man. But the only memories he had of him were those of the past week, and precious little of those. Each of the children had been carefully instructed not to reveal too much to him, in order to give him a chance to remember on his own. The thought had been well intended, but Patrick was beginning to suspect that the children were actually staying clear of him to keep themselves from saying something they should not. Again Patrick sighed. Just then Ion lifted his head and met Patrick's gaze. Once again Patrick found himself longing to remember something—anything about this sober young man.

"Did you want something, Pat?" Ion asked.

Patrick smiled and shook his head. "No lad, just thinking." Ion's eyes narrowed slightly, as if he could read Patrick's thoughts. Without another word, he bent back over his writing tablet and continued working on his essay. Patrick continued studying him, trying again for one memory.

"Pat can I borrow your guitar?" Georgy called out quietly from the kitchen doorway.

"No lad," Patrick replied absentmindedly, still studying Ion. "Matthew is out of guitar strings again. And ye rimimber the last time he wis out o'thim ye broke one. I don't want to hiv to be without a guitar again for so long."

Although Georgy made no reply, Ion lifted his head and stared in shock at Patrick. Patrick blinked, wondering over the stunned expression on the boy's face. After all, it was not unreasonable for Patrick to deny Georgy his request. Suddenly Patrick's mouth fell slightly open. Ion eased into a grin. Patrick whirled his head around, staring in mounting excitement at Georgy who was smiling broadly. "I rimimber ye Georgy!" Patrick cried out. Jumping to his feet and depositing his Bible on the chair, he hurried over to Georgy and grasped him by the shoulders, looking him fully in the face. "I rimimber ye!"

The next moment they flung their arms around each other, embracing in a bear hug. Patrick squeezed his eyes shut. He had a memory! This was no stranger any longer. This was his son Georgy. Opening his eyes, he stared into the kitchen, coming face to face with Rachel who was pressing her fingers against her lips. A tear crept down her cheek. She hurried toward the two and slipped her arms around both of them. Patrick was uncertain whether she was laughing or crying, or maybe even both. Either way, she was rejoicing with the two of them.

Pulling away from each other, the three laughed. The rest of the family filtered into the living room, equally excited. "What happened," Georgy began, "after I busted the string?"

Patrick drew in a deep breath. "Well now—ah—let's see."

"Don't try too hard, Patrick," Rachel cautioned. "Remember, Dr. Morrison says that the harder you try, the harder it'll be."

"Aye," Patrick agreed in a sigh, desperately trying to remember what had happened after Georgy had broken his guitar string.

Johnny stepped into the living room then, carrying a razor strap. Patrick began smiling again as he eyed that leather strap. "Georgy and I went out to the barn that evening. I proved m'love for 'im by taking 'is punishment." His mouth fell open then as the entire memory began unfolding before him. "That's the evening 'e asked Jesus to save 'im!"

A cheer arose from everyone gathered around Patrick. Patrick laughed and clapped Johnny on the back. "'Twas a good idea, lad, bringing thit leather strap for me to see. It jogged m'memory. How did ye know 'twould do thit?"

Johnny began giggling as he nudged Georgy. "Because seeing it jogs Georgy's memory every time he thinks about breaking a rule."

Patrick laughed and wrapped his arm around Johnny's shoulders. "Good lad," he chuckled. "And now I'm going to rimimber all of ye—in time—all of ye," he added, glancing over at Rachel. The softened look that crept into her eyes assured him that she knew he was trying with all of his being to remember her.

One by one, the family slipped away, each returning to do what he or she had been doing before Patrick's memory of Georgy had returned, leaving Patrick and Rachel alone in the living room. "The rest will come back," Rachel assured him, smiling.

He nodded. "Aye," he agreed. "There's so mich I want to rimimber." He continued meeting her gaze. "So mich." All at once he began chuckling as he admitted in a low tone, "Ye know what I'm afraid o'doing? I keep thinking thit one o'these Sundays I'll preach a sermon thit I've already preached—only a few Sunday before—and not even know it."

Rachel began giggling. "I'll tell you what. You just tell me what you're going to preach on and I'll tell you if you've already preached it."

He chuckled and nodded. "'Tis a deal," he agreed, stretching out his arm. Solemnly they shook hands, though Rachel's eyes were dancing in merriment and he suspected that his eyes were doing the same.

Ion rolled his eyes as he sat at breakfast, trying to ignore Johnny's incessant humming. The boy was in one of his teasing moods, and nothing short of punishment, or the threat thereof, ever seemed to put a stop to it. Unfortunately this time it was Ion he had chosen to target. As they sat there eating, Johnny simply hummed the wedding march. Finally Ion stretched out his leg, smartly kicking Johnny's foot. The boy only giggled and began humming louder.

"Johnny m'lad," Patrick finally called out, "Stop teasing Ion about Mary."

Instantly the humming stopped. Every set of eyes turned to Patrick. Ion studied him hard, certain that Patrick did not yet have the slightest idea what had just happened. As if feeling everyone staring at him, Patrick glanced up and flinched as he realized that he was the center of attention. Ion could not help but allow the corners of his mouth to rise slightly. Patrick lifted his shoulders slightly and shifted his gaze to Rachel who was beaming in pleasure. "Patrick," she said quietly. "No one has mentioned Mary's name in your presence since your injury. No one has told you that she and Ion—" Pausing suddenly, she glanced over at Ion who dipped his head in a single nod of permission to speak of the matter in front of everyone.

Before Rachel could continue, however, Patrick drew in his breath sharply, "I rimimber!" Tearing his gaze from Rachel and fastening it on Ion, he grinned broadly. "Ion! I rimimber ye, laddie! And Mary too!" His gaze softened then as he continued studying Ion. "M'son," he murmured. "I rimimber ye." Ion swallowed quickly. He tried to smile but was uncertain if he was actually pulling it off or not. His throat was tight. And his eyes felt uncomfortable. But the light in Patrick's eyes was worth it all. "I rimimber ye, laddie!" Patrick added fervently.

"Remember me Pat!" Johnny insisted. Patrick shifted his gaze from the pile of wood he was splitting and lowered his ax to the ground, studying the boy. "It's been about three weeks since you remembered Georgy and Ion. Remember me!"

Patrick eased into a grin at the comical fellow. "I'm sorry laddie. I would if I could. Bit it just doesn't work thit way."

"But there's lots of stuff you can remember about me!"

"I'm sure ye're right. Bit it isn't up to me."

"You're just not trying!" the boy insisted.

Patrick laughed. "Ye're the only one in the whole family saying thit. Iveryone else is accusing me o'trying too hard. It's like when Lizzie tried too hard to speak loud enough for us to hear right after she went deaf. She ended up yelling. She had to stop trying and just speak naturally. Thit's 'ow m'memory returns, when I'm not trying too hard." He paused, noting the grin on the boy's face. "Johnny m'lad! I rimimber Lizzie! I rimimber 'er going deaf and yelling at Leprechaun, thinking she wis only whispering."

"What else?" Johnny asked. "Gramps!" he called out as Jed stepped out of the barn. "He remembers Lizzie!"

"Well," Patrick replied in thought as Jed began gathering the others around. As Elizabeth neared them, Patrick reached out his arm to her. Immediately as she stepped up to him, his arm curled around her shoulders. "Thit wis the morning after thit rain thit—thit caused the wreck." Whirling his head over to Jed, he grinned, "I rimimber ye Jed. I rimimber following yeer wegon during the rain. Thit hill—the slippery mud—the wegon skidded down and tipped over." He paused, the horror suddenly as fresh to him as it had been when it had happened.

"It's just a memory," Jed replied, his voice calming.

"Aye," Patrick agreed, though he felt as if he were trembling all over. "Well, it wis because of thit wreck thit the three o'ye became members of the O'Riley family. And what's more—I rimimber the three o'ye! Ye joined m'family. There wis m'self and Leprechaun—"

"You remember your dog, but you don't remember me?" Johnny cried out indignantly.

Patrick began laughing, the other joining in. Even Johnny seemed to catch the humor of the moment and began grinning, though clearly it was with reluctance.

"Well, there wis me and Leprechaun, and Annie—" Patrick caught his breath. "I remember the wee one! Anna Marie! Annie! Come to Pa!"

Anna Marie, who had been skipping along the path near the house, ran up to Patrick, who scooped her into his arms. She giggled and held him tightly around the neck. "Ah, m'own sweet Annie!" Patrick said, his heart feeling as if it would burst with all the happiness that was being given to him over the returned memories.

"What about me?" Johnny asked, impatience in his voice.

"I'm working on it, lad. It'll come. Give it sem more time."

Pushing out his breath, Johnny shrugged. "All right. But you remember soon!"

Patrick grinned and nodded. "I'll do m'best, lad. I'll do m'best."

Rachel fiddled with her cup as she and Patrick sat at the table before she cleared away all traces of the noon meal they had just had. She would lay Pattie down for her afternoon nap as soon as she finished playing in her potatoes. She wondered over the fact that Patrick had remembered everyone in the family except for Johnny and herself. He had even remembered his dog! She sighed, continuing to move the cup back and forth with her finger. Dr. Morrison had assured her that he was trying to remember the two of them the hardest of all, which tended to keep the memories at bay. She had comforted herself with this thought for the past week, but it was growing thin, this argument. She knew Patrick desperately wanted to remember her and Johnny, but the fact that he did not yet caused her to question her own self worth. And how was she to tell him about the new baby who would be born in April when he had no real memory of Rachel herself, except for those memories of the past month since his injury? And then there was the planned get-together with Angela and Matthew that evening. She could not help but wonder if they would learn to regret having invited them before Patrick's memory had fully returned. Though he remembered the other members of the family and also many of their friends, it was only in snatches, not in full memory.

As Patrick gently touched her hand with his fingers, she jumped and lifted startled eyes to him. He smiled then, asking, "What's troubling ye, Rachel?"

She lifted her shoulders slightly, wondering where to begin. Truth. That was one thing they had between them: truth. "Are you certain that you feel up to having Angela and Matthew over for the evening?" she finally asked him, though she knew it was not a fair question since he had no memory of Angela, only a few vague hints she had given him concerning the woman. He knew that she had become part of their family and was now the children's aunt and claimed Patrick's own mother as her cousin, though they had been a bit vague as to the reason for that. But beyond that, Rachel and the others had been silent where Angela was concerned. "It's only been a month since your injury."

He smiled and nodded. "I'm feeling fine, lassie. I'm thinking thit ye're worrying too mich about me. Besides, ye've bin calling it a month for several weeks. It's bin two months, since m'injury, lassie. Two months if it's a day!"

She sighed and lifted one shoulder in acknowledgement of his words, thinking that he might be right. But then, on the other hand, where Angela Bon-Hemmer was concerned, no one could be too careful. "What if she says something troubling?" she blurted out. "You don't remember her Patrick. She has a way about her—a most—well, she can be quite disconcerting."

Patrick's hand continued resting on her own. "I hiv to get back around people soon. This is the first Sunday I'll be back in the pulpit. The deacons hiv bin most generous in overseeing the worship services. Bit it's time I reentered m'life, Rachel. I don't think inything is going to harm the return of m'memory. I think 'tis time I got out o'this house and went beyond the front yard. And what better place to start then entertaining friends—friends who are part o'the family—in our home?"

Rachel sighed again. "I know. I just don't want anyone upsetting you."

Lifting her eyes, she met his kind gaze. How she missed the look of love in his eyes, but at least the kindness was good to see. "It sounds to me like ye'll be the one getting upset, not me. If ye don't wish to hiv thim around, we can tell them not to come."

"Dear oh dear," Rachel murmured, rising to her feet and reaching for the cloth to wash the potatoes off of Pattie. "We can't uninvited guests. It isn't done," she murmured. "I didn't mean it quite like that." She paused, wondering how exactly she had meant it. It really was too late to change the plans without being horribly rude. She felt his eyes still upon her. Meeting his gaze, she shook her head over the look of amusement on his face. "All right," she sighed, running the cloth over Pattie's face. "You win. But," she added, her hand stilling itself, "don't tell me I didn't warn you."

He chuckled quietly and sipped on his coffee as Rachel continued washing up Pattie. "And what will ye be wanting for Christmas?" he asked, causing her to pause in her work and stare at him. "Hiv ye forgotten, lassie? Christmas is only a week and a half away."

"Dear oh dear," she murmured. "I've never forgotten Christmas before."

He smiled at her, replying quietly, "Well, ye've 'ad a thing or two on yeer mind this year. What is it ye want for Christmas?"

She turned back to Pattie then, and sighed. "Your memory to return," she murmured. "That's all I really want."

Once the task of washing Pattie's hands and face was completed, she picked her up and carried her to the living room, easing down onto her rocking chair. As she rocked and sang, the little girl began struggling less and finally relaxed into sleep.

By the time Pattie was laid down for her nap and Anna Marie was given a sheet of paper on which to quietly draw in her bedroom, Rachel returned to the kitchen to discover that Patrick had cleared the table and even put the dishes into the dish pan filled with hot, soapy water. As she slipped her hands into the water, she noted with a smile that he had not attempted to wash the dishes.

Suddenly Rachel felt the sharp blade of her paring knife sliced through the flesh on her finger. Yanking her hand out of the water, she quickly began squeezing it, trying to stop the flow of blood. The next thing she knew, Patrick was beside her, holding her hand and wrapping her finger with a piece of cloth. All at once she recognized the cloth as being a torn off piece of one of her best tea towels. The shocked words of reprimand for having torn up her best towel died instantly on her tongue as she met his gaze. It was such a familiar look, but it had been so long since she had seen it in his eyes.

It was then that she felt weak all of a sudden and found herself leaning against him for support. Letting go of her hand, having finished the task of wrapping her finger securely with the cloth, his arms went around her instantly, holding her close. She felt a little guilty over the troubled look on his face, as he was clearly assuming that her unsteadiness had been due to the loss of blood rather than the look in his eyes. Did he even know what his eyes were whispering to her?

"Are ye all right, Rachel?" he murmured, holding her close.

She drew her arms around him tightly. "I'm fine." But she made no attempt at pulling free from his arms. Instead she reveled in the fact that she was in his arms. She wondered if he was aware of the fact that he was holding her quite differently than he had these past two months. Throughout these past weeks since his injury he had held her carefully like a protective brother would do. She smiled as she thought of how differently he was holding her now, as only a man in love held his sweetheart.

"'Tis m'own fault," he murmured. "I put the knife in the dishpan. I should've thought. I should've just laid it on the counter where ye could see it. Ye didn't hiv a chance to even know it wis in the water—"

"Patrick," she cut in, leaning back enough so she could peer up into his face. "It wasn't your fault. It wasn't anyone's fault. It just happened. Don't blame yourself."

"I'll go after Dr. Morrison," he added.

She began giggling. The past two months had been a long time to be without his special protective love for her, the kind that surpassed that for the other members of the family. "You'll do no such thing. Patrick," she chided, "it's just a scratch. Why, I'd feel ashamed if you sent for a doctor over such a small thing."

She paused, suddenly lost in his gaze. His eyes were whispering secrets to her. A look of wonder grew in his face as her eyes apparently answered his. Lowering his head, he softly laid his lips on hers. It was the first time they had kissed since the night of his accident when she had awakened from a nightmare. That time she had initiated it. But this time, it was clearly Patrick's idea. The sweetness of his lips on hers convinced her all the more that she had not been mistaken about the look in his eyes. He was falling in love with her all over again. Maybe he would never remember the first years of their marriage, but now that was not nearly as important as it had been earlier to her that day. She had his heart—and what's more, she had captured it twice.

Patrick stepped into the kitchen, breathing in deeply the wonderful smells coming from the various pots and pans. Just then Georgy stepped over to Rachel and studied her closely, asking, "Are you all right?"

She smiled and leaned close, lightly kissing the boy on the cheek. "I've never felt better," she giggled.

It was then that she lifted her eyes and met Patrick's gaze. He smiled at her. She really did look happy. In fact, she had looked happy all afternoon. He himself had rather enjoyed himself, having found one excuse after another to join her in the kitchen simply to slip an arm around her or give her a peck on the cheek. She had not looked this happy since he first recalled laying eyes on her upon awakening from his injury. As he studied her, he suddenly realized that she was quite pale. And even though happiness darted out of her eyes, he noticed all at once that there were shadows around them, as if she were quite tired. As he thought back over the past several weeks, he recalled other times when she had looked worn out. The sadness in her eyes had made him assume that it had been her concern over his lost memory that had made her look so tired. But here she was, ecstatically happy—ever since they had kissed—but she looked almost completely worn to a frazzle, as if she had to fight simply to remain standing. He wondered what would cause her to be so tired.

It was then that their guests arrived. Patrick turned as Ion opened the door for them. "Patrick," Rachel said quietly, "let me introduce you to Matthew and Angela Bon-Hemmer."

Patrick reached out his arm to shake hands with the man. "I'm glad to meet ye, Matthew."

The man smiled and dipped his head in a nod. "Likewise, Patrick," he replied with a twinkle in his eye.

Turning to the woman at his side, Patrick nodded, "Ma'am."

"Sir," she replied primly in a rather high pitched tone.

Several minutes later they were all sitting around the table, enjoying the meal Rachel had prepared. Patrick noticed that the couple seemed to be especially happy. He wondered if that was normal for them or if there was more to it than that. Once again he chafed beneath the knowledge that he was likely the only one at the table without a clue.

At the conclusion of the meal, Matthew rose to his feet and held up his cup of coffee as if in a toast. "I have an announcement," he said in a rather grand sounding tone of voice. Every set of eyes fixed themselves upon him. He smiled and added, "There is soon to be a new member of the Bon-Hemmer family."

As he sat down amidst hearty congratulations, Angela added in a tone that seemed slightly snobbish to Patrick's ear, "In May."

Glancing over at Rachel, he wondered at the frozen smile on her lips. He wondered if the others around the table noticed that her lips were smiling while her eyes were somewhat shadowed, as if some thought preoccupied her. He wondered at her action of gently rubbing her stomach. He hoped that she was not feeling ill.

As the adults adjourned into the living room, the children remained in the kitchen to clean up. Rachel also remained behind, getting her tea made and the coffee brewed. Patrick realized that without Rachel in the living room to direct the conversation, the task rested upon his shoulders. He searched his mind for a topic that would be suitable for this couple who seemed quite out of their element in the rustic town of Timberton.

The conversation had been going along well enough for some minutes when Angela finally turned to Patrick and began speaking, her tone slightly raking on his ears. "And have you regained enough of your memory to know that Rachel is of the Boston Nathans? Nathan Silver, that is."

Patrick narrowed his eyes and studied the woman. "Excuse me?" he murmured.

"Angela," Matthew interrupted. "We aren't supposed to tell Patrick things he hasn't yet remembered."

"Oh pish-posh," Angela sniffed. "Of course this sort of thing is acceptable. The poor man needs to know that his own wife was as close to royalty as Americans can be. Not at all like people of British nobility like my cousin

Christine, of course. But still, she grew up like a princess."

Patrick swallowed. The sound of footsteps drew his attention to Rachel as she entered the living room, tea tray in hand. "Tea?" she asked, glancing around the room. "Georgy is bringing in the coffee in a minute."

"Yes please," Angela replied in a tone that suggested that she had no idea the turmoil she had brought to Patrick's mind. Rachel's puzzled expression shifted from one face to another, and finally rested on Patrick. All he could do was stare at her, wondering why she had failed to tell him who she was, considering the poor lifestyle he offered her.

By the troubled look in her eyes, she clearly realized that something had gone wrong, but had no idea what. She swallowed and stepped over to where Angela and Matthew were sitting, easing her tea tray down onto the low table in front of them. As she served the tea, Patrick realized that Jed was attempting to get the conversation started up again, only on safer ground this time. The rest of the evening limped along, though afterward Patrick could recall nothing in particular that had been said.

It was late by the time Jed and the children were all in bed. By the time the last child's prayer was heard and that child was tucked in, Patrick and Rachel finally headed for their bedroom and prepared for bed. No words were spoken. Finally, both in bed, Patrick blew out the lamp and eased down onto his pillow.

"Patrick," Rachel murmured, keeping her voice low enough so as not to disturb the rest of the family, "I don't know what happened tonight, but something did. Please, what happened?"

Patrick frowned, hardly knowing where to start—what to say. "Rachel," he finally began, "tell me one thing. Do ye and Angela hiv similar backgrounds?"

"I don't know how to answer that, Patrick."

"Truthfully," he insisted, hearing the edge in his voice, wondering if she heard it too.

"Of course!" Yes she had heard it. "I meant that your question is not a simple yes or no question. To answer it means I'd have to tell you things that we're trying to give you a chance to remember on your own."

"Wis yeer father rich? Even in Ireland we've heard of Nathan Silver! Is thit yeer family's business?"

She was silent for several long moments. He wondered if it were his questions or the anger in his voice that brought her silence. Finally she said quietly, "Yes, Patrick. That was my family's business. But no, it is no longer my family's business." When he sighed loudly, she asked, "Does it really matter?"

"Aye! It matters! How could ye even ask such a question? Do ye think I'm blind to Mrs. Bon-Hemmer's prejudice against me? And 'ere I am married to the heiress of Nathan Silver! A poor Irishman married to the princess of Nathan Silver! And ye ask if it matters?"

"Patrick O'Riley!" she snapped back. "Are you accusing me of being prejudice against you?"

"Are ye?"

Silence was her reply. His heart began aching in a way he had never known. "How can you ask such a thing?" she finally whispered. He did not miss the sob in her voice as she said the last word. "If you think that low of me, then why in the world could you possibly care one way or the other if I'm prejudice against a poor Irishman?"

The words slapped him in the face. Why indeed? He grew thoughtful, the truth fully dawning on him. Finally he murmured, "B'cause I love ye, Rachel. And I thought ye loved me. Wis I wrong?"

This time there was no mistaking, she was crying indeed. He sighed, feeling miserable. He had not intended to hurt her. That was the very last thing he wished to do. Slipping his arm around her, he drew her to himself and held her as she cried. He thought about the past two months in which both of them had endured their emotions being stretch almost to the point of breaking. But this was the first time they had lashed out against each other.

"I'm sorry, Rachel," he murmured as she quieted herself. "I didn't mean to make ye cry."

A smile crept to his lips as she leaned close and softly kissed his cheek. "How could I be prejudiced against the man I love?" she asked with such love in her voice there was no mistaking it for anything else. "Don't you understand Patrick? I married up—not down."

Squeezing his eyes shut for a moment, he drew her closer to himself. "Please forgive me, Rachel. I'm so sorry for saying all those things."

"I know," she murmured. "And I forgive you. Please forgive me too."

"There's nothing to forgive. I wis the one who wis wrong—not ye. I'm so sorry."

Rachel snuggled into his arms so comfortably that Patrick could not help but smile. "I have something to tell you, Patrick," she said. "If I don't tell you soon, you'll be guessing soon enough anyway. I was going to tell you the day I found out. But that was when you got hurt. I've been waiting for the right time to tell you." She paused then.

"Tell me what?" he asked. "Lassie, ye hiv m'full attention."

"Well, Angela and Matthew aren't the only one's whose family is about to increase in size."

"Rachel!" he breathed out in wonder. "A baby?" The mingling of shock and joy that suddenly engulfed him was almost too great to bear.

"Yes," she whispered.

"Ah lassie," he sighed out, wondering if his heart would stop altogether. "Ye sure hiv a unique way o'putting an end to an argument."

Johnny awakened earlier than usual, unable to keep his excitement at bay. Hurrying over to Georgy's bed, he thumped the blanket encased body and whispered loudly, "Oops! Did I wake you up?" Without waiting for a reply, he slipped over to Ion's bed.

"Don't even think it," Ion growled, his eyes only barely opened slits.

"Merry Christmas, Ion," Johnny whispered and spun around, dashing out into the kitchen. He blinked in surprise that he was not the first one up. Gathered around the table sat Patrick, Rachel, Jed, Elizabeth and Anna Marie. Pattie sat on Rachel's lap, playing with a rag doll. Without a word, Johnny spun back around and rushed back to Georgy. With a quick tug, he pulled the quilt off of the boy, shouting excitedly, "Get up! It's Christmas! You're the last two in bed!" Frowning, he wondered why neither Ion nor Georgy seemed to be in a hurry to get up on this of all days. He wondered just how bad it must be to be sixteen. Grinning, as a new thought struck him, he added, "There's cinnamon rolls for breakfast!"

All at once Georgy jumped out of his bed. "Come on Ion, before I eat them all!"

The next moment the two were hurrying into their robes, Rachel having insisted that they were getting too old to wander around the house in only their nightshirts. Finally they emerged from the bedroom, hurrying to their places at the table.

After a prayer of thanksgiving, the cinnamon rolls were quickly passed around to each hungry member of the family. Johnny tried not to take too large of a bite, certain that even on Christmas Rachel would not relax that particular rule at the table. The sweetness of the roll filled his entire being. At first he was only just vaguely aware that Patrick was talking. But finally he turned and eyed him.

"So, I'm asking ye to each tell me semthing I've forgotten, sem special memory. And then it'll be m'own memory. All Rachel wants for Christmas this year is for me to hiv m'memory back, and I can't get it without yeer 'elp. So, who is first?"

An eruption of voices caused everyone to laugh as each member of the family began to share his or her own memories with Patrick. Johnny grinned as he looked at Rachel. Tears were in her eyes, just as always when she was especially happy. The stories continued long after the rolls were only a memory themselves. No one even seemed in a particular hurry to go into the living room and open presents. Everyone was laughing, Patrick the hardest of them all, hearing these stories for what seemed to him like the first time.

"And I made up a game," Johnny continued with his story, enjoying the fact that everyone had to listen to him.

"And in yeer game ye made me tell ye m'secret about being a street fighter as a lad," Patrick laughed. Johnny's mouth fell open as he stared at Patrick who was now eyeing him, not yet realizing what had just happened. Suddenly Patrick's eyes opened wide. "Laddie!" he cried out. "I rimimber ye! Sure and certain, I rimimber ye Johnny!"

Rachel smiled as she sat on the wagon seat beside Patrick. "I think it was a good idea to leave Anna Marie and Pattie home with the children and Jed while we visit the O'Brins." It made sense to visit during the Christmas break while the children were home to look after the youngest two. Rachel thought about the gentle Sheila O'Brin, Mary's mother who was also expecting a baby in April, near the time Rachel herself was expecting.

When they pulled into the O'Brin's yard, Martin, Mary's father, was just stepping out the barn. As Patrick pulled the team to a halt, Martin caught hold of the bridle, saying in a gruff tone, "The wife's inside. Go on in."

Patrick helped Rachel down from the wagon and followed Martin into the barn. Rachel could not help but sigh in relief that Mr. O'Brin would not be in the house during Rachel's and Sheila's visiting time. She only wished that Patrick would be having as enjoyable a time as she would be having.

Mary opened the door and smiled sweetly. "Please come in, Mrs. O'Riley," she said, stepping back from the doorway. "Ma will be out in a minute. She just woke up from a nap. Would you like some coffee? Or maybe some milk?"

Rachel smiled as she stepped into the rather bleak kitchen that boasted only of a well worn table, benches and a cook stove. "Milk please," she said as her hand instinctively went to her stomach. It was easy to see why Ion was so smitten with the girl. As she sat down at the table, Mary carefully poured her a cup of milk, and herself a cup of coffee. Rachel chewed on the corner of her mouth at the idea of a child drinking coffee. Almost instantly she smiled over the thought, knowing that the girl had already passed her sixteenth birthday, and was clearly used to running a household since her mother was so frequently ill.

By the time Sheila stepped out into the kitchen, looking extremely pale, Rachel and Mary had been chatting pleasantly for several minutes. "How nice of you to come," Sheila said warmly, her eyes sparkling. "What a treat to have company."

As the woman sat down, Mary rose and poured her mother a cupful of milk. She returned to the table and quietly placed it before her mother, taking her seat once again. Rachel was struck with the odd picture of the child being the one to drink the coffee, while it was the two women who were drinking milk.

At length, Rachel reached into the bag she had brought with her and withdrew the baby clothes she had sewed for Sheila's child. "I thought," Rachel began with a smile, "that since your youngest is already ten, you might not have saved many baby things. So I made these for your little one."

Tears sprang into the woman's eyes as she reached for the tiny articles of clothing. Tenderly her fingers caressed the small nightie and matching cap. Rachel glanced over at Mary who sat there biting her lower lip. But her eyes thanked Rachel over and over. Rachel smiled and nodded.

As Rachel and Patrick rode back home, she slipped her arm through Patrick's and leaned against him. "What do you suppose makes Mr. O'Brin like that?"

"Like what?" he asked, eying her.

She shook her head, trying to put it all into words what her heart knew, but what her mind was still trying to grasp. "He's so unfeeling. Why at times I almost think that he despises Sheila and the children."

Patrick was silent for several moments and then finally admitted, "Maybe 'e does, at times."

Sitting up straight, Rachel stared at him in shock. It was one thing to voice her concern, and a whole other thing to be agreed with, giving credence to her words. "What do you mean?"

"'E isn't one for settling down in one place for long. Bit with a family 'e can't roam frim one place to another. I think at times 'e resents thim for it."

"And now with a new baby coming," Rachel murmured, shaking her head.

"I'm thinking thit 'e is feeling a bit trapped." He drew in a deep breath and sighed heavily. "I kinnot understand thit kind o'feeling. What in the world would I do without m'family?"

Rachel smiled and leaned against him again. Even without memories of past days, Patrick was still Patrick. They rode the rest of the way home in silence, each lost in thought. When he helped her down from the wagon, she hurried inside while he remained outside, preparing to give the horses an especially good rubbing down. Rachel smiled as she removed her hat and coat, realizing that she had plenty of time for fixing supper. In fact, she had time to relax before getting started, a rare treat indeed.

"Elizabeth?" she called out. "We're home!" Anna Marie stepped out into the kitchen from the nursery then, followed by Pattie. Rachel began giggling suddenly, realizing what she had done. "A whole houseful of people," she laughed, "and here I am calling out to the only deaf member of the family."

At Anna Marie's beckoning arm movement, Elizabeth emerged from the nursery, a smile lighting her face when she caught sight of Rachel. Rachel smiled and turned to hang up her coat and hat. Hurrying into the living room, she lowered herself into her rocking chair, sighing in utter contentment.

Ion stepped out of the study then, smiling. "How is everyone over at the O'Brins' house?" he asked.

"Fine," Rachel chuckled, noting the sparkle in his eyes as he clearly was waiting for some word about Mary. "Mary is the perfect hostess," she added. "And she's such a help to her mother, especially now with the baby on its way."

Ion beamed in pleasure over Rachel's words of praise over Mary. Rachel thought about it, realizing that she would actually be hard pressed to even think of something uncomplimentary about the girl. It would have been hard indeed not to like the gentle soul.

Ion sauntered out of the living room, back into the study, clearly contented. He had not been gone for more than a moment when Georgy stepped into the living room and eased down in the chair across from her, a serious expression on his face. Rachel wondered over that. Finally he asked, "Does God always answer our prayers?"

"Yes," she replied instantly. "Why do you ask?"

He frowned and sighed. "Maybe I didn't ask right," he murmured, as if to himself.

"What are you talking about, Georgy?" she asked gently.

He returned his gaze to her and shrugged, looking remarkably like a little boy instead of the young man he was. "I asked God to give Pat his memory again. But He didn't answer my prayer."

Rachel studied the sincere face for several moments, thinking how dear this son of hers was. "Did He neglect to answer, or did He simply neglect to say 'yes'?"

Georgy flinched, his expression one of shock. "It's the same thing," he insisted.

Rachel shook her head. "No it's not. He can also say, 'No.' Sometimes He says 'Yes, but not now.' When we ask Him for something, our first desire ought to be that His will will be done, even if it means telling us, 'No'."

Georgy's mouth dropped open as he stared at her, clearly trying to take in the full meaning of her words. Finally he murmured, "That's hard to do."

She could not help but smile. "I know. It takes a lot of faith in Him and love for Him and His will. But we simply have to learn to trust His wisdom and love as well as His ability. And we must learn to love Him so much that His will is more precious to us than our own. Georgy, God dwells in His will—not outside of His will. If we want to be where God lives and works and laughs, we need to be in His will—because that's where He is."

He nodded thoughtfully, rose to his feet and began walking toward the kitchen. Then, as if in afterthought, he said simply, "Thank you. I'll do some thinking about that." And then he was gone.

Rachel leaned back again and started rocking. But she had no more than begun when Anna Marie darted into the living room, tears streaming down her face. "Mamma," she wept, "I hurt my finger!"

Opening up her arms, Rachel reached for the five-year-old and pulled her onto her lap, cuddling her close. As she carefully examined the small finger, she wondered just how much longer there would be room on her lap for the little girl, now that the baby was only a little over three months from being born. He or she had taken a sudden growth spurt, causing Rachel to grow out of most of her clothes. Kissing the tiny hand, Rachel asked, "Is it better now?"

"Not there," Anna Marie wept and pointed to another finger which looked just as healthy as the rest. "There."

Rachel smiled and leaned over the little hand and kissed the finger in question. "How is that?" she asked.

"Better," Anna Marie sniffed and lowered her head to Rachel's shoulder.

"Have I ever told you that I love you, Anna Marie?" Rachel asked.

The child startled upward then and stared at Rachel in surprise. "Yes!" she said, clearly wondering how Rachel could not have known that.

Rachel giggled and helped Anna Marie back down to the floor. Apparently having already forgotten the hurt finger, she bounced back to the nursery, calling out, "Pattie! It's my turn!"

As Rachel chuckled, eying the disappearing girl, Jed stepped into the living room. "Missus," he began, shaking his head, "I can't find my gloves. Do you know where I put 'em?"

"They're on the hearth, drying. They should be dry by now." she replied.

"I looked there already," he said, shaking his head. "No—no, sit down," he added quickly, as Rachel attempted to stand up. "I'll go look again." With that he disappeared into the kitchen. The next moment he called out, "Now how'd I miss seein' 'em afore?" Rachel smiled as he stepped back across the kitchen floor and disappeared outside.

The outside door had no more than shut when Elizabeth carried Pattie into the living room. "We're out of diapers," she said.

"That's impossible," Rachel replied in shock. "I just washed them all out yesterday morning," she said slowly enough for Elizabeth to read her lips.

"I checked. They're all gone."

"I dried them in front of the fireplace," Rachel said in thought, trying to retrace her steps of the day before. "After they dried I folded them up." She paused in thought. "Oh!" she added, suddenly remembering. "They're in the laundry basked in my bedroom."

Elizabeth eased Pattie into Rachel's arms and hurried out of the living room, heading for Rachel's bedroom in search of the missing diapers. While she was gone, Rachel reached for the changing blanket she kept handy and spread it out on the floor, laying Pattie down on top of it, and began removing the little girl's damp diaper as Elizabeth searched for the clean ones. Several moments later Elizabeth returned in triumph with a fresh diaper in her hands.

Once Pattie was freshly dressed again, she and Elizabeth returned to the nursery to continue with the game they had begun earlier. Rachel eased back down onto her rocking chair and sighed. She still had half an hour left before she needed to start fixing supper. She had no more than sat back down when Patrick stepped into the living room. Rachel shifted her gaze to him. "Do ye think thit we could hiv supper a little early tonight? Because I wis thinking of checking on the Brickermens after supper—" he paused and seemed to see her for the first time since entering the room. "Were ye risting?"

"No," she chuckled, rising to her feet. "Not at all." The puzzled look on his face assured her that he had no idea what the joke was. But it was too much fun enjoying it all by herself to let even him in on the cause of her laughter.

"Ye sure ye don't mind?" he asked as she stepped past him, heading into the kitchen.

"I'm sure," she replied, continuing to chuckle, suddenly realizing that she would get more rested while cooking supper than while sitting in her rocking chair. Besides, she reminded herself, she could sit in her rocking chair later.

At that moment Johnny burst through the outside door. His face was a picture of misery. "What is it?" Rachel asked, fear springing into her heart.

He scowled and began grumbling. "I found a bucket in the shed, so I thought I'd use it. It had a little bit of sticky stuff in it. I tried to clean it out, but then saw that it was tar." Lifting his hand in the air, he added in annoyance, "It won't come off!"

Patrick burst out laughing. "'Tis just like whin Rachel climbed beneath m'wegon and got tar on 'er 'ands b'cause of it. She 'ad to use lard to get it off." Suddenly he stopped speaking and turned to Rachel. "Rachel," he murmured, clearly stunned. "Ye didn't tell me thit story, did ye?" Rachel slowly shook her head. That was one story she had decided not to tell him, not wanting the rest of the family to know anything about it. Patrick smiled broadly, his eyes dancing and he pulled her into his arms. "I rimimber ye, Rachel! I rimimber ye!"

Chapter 8

April of 1859 had finally arrived, as the entire O'Riley household continued awaiting the birth of the youngest member of the family. A loud pounding on the door awoke Ion earlier than usual. He waited a few moments to see if the sounds of stirring would indicate that Patrick was going to get up and answer the door. It was Georgy who tumbled out of bed first, his curiosity knowing no bounds.

"It might be a medical emergency," he mumbled to Ion.

Ion rolled his eyes. "If it's an emergency, they'd be knocking on Doc Morrison's door, not here."

Regardless of his words, Georgy stumbled out into the kitchen. Ion crawled out of bed and joined him at the doorway, peering over his shoulder just as Patrick and Rachel stepped out of their bedroom. Patrick headed over to the door and opened it. "Sam?" he asked in surprise, stepping back for the man to enter.

"I rode all night," he said. "I've just come from Portland with a telegram." Ion stared in surprise. Only the month before, the man had brought them the earth-shattering news that Oregon had finally been admitted as a state in the Union. Ion narrowed his eyes, wondering what could possibly be in the telegram. Telegrams usually meant bad news, as far as he knew. "It's for Ion," Sam added, handing the piece of paper to Patrick. Ion blinked in shock, wondering. Since Sam could not read, he had no way of knowing if it was good news or bad news he was bringing. "It came all the way from New York City!" Sam added in wonder.

Ion's mouth fell open then. Patrick turned and met Ion's gaze. Stretching out his arm, he held the telegram out for Ion. "'Tis yeers. Ye should be the one to read it," he said simply.

Ion swallowed and then pushed past Georgy, taking the piece of paper from Patrick's hand. Surely unwanted news from New York would not have come in the form of a telegram, but in a letter. He dared not to let his hopes rise, however. Licking his lips, he unfolded the piece of paper. As he read the words, a slow grin grew on his face.

"So what's it say?" Georgy called out impatiently.

Ion cleared his throat and began reading aloud, "Article accepted STOP Payment to follow STOP."

"Article?" Rachel asked, excitement coloring her tone. "What article?"

Ion grinned and admitted, "The article I sent to New York's First Periodical for Businessmen Incorporated."

Rachel stared in unmasked wonder. "Ion," she breathed out. "That's one of New York's most sought after newspaper in the business world! However did you even know about this paper?"

"Matthew," Ion chuckled.

"Of course," Rachel murmured in thought.

Ion shrugged, admitting, "I wouldn't have had a chance with my article without his help."

Rachel stepped over to him then and slipped her hands to his shoulders, looking him full in the face, saying firmly, "You listen to me, Ion Macalister! New York's F. P. B. inc. would never agree to publish an article if it fell below their extremely high standards, Matthew Bon-Hemmer or no Matthew Bon-Hemmer. At the very most, all he could've done was to get an audience for you with the editor. But the rest is solely on the merits of your writing!"

There was such pride in her voice—pride in him. He suddenly felt shaky. All at once it became real to him: he was about to become a real published author!

There was no hope of falling back to sleep now. Ion felt like he was walking in a daze. Somehow he managed to get dressed and eat breakfast, though later he had no real memory of doing so. All he could really think about was telling Mary his good news. As he and the others approached the schoolhouse, Georgy clapped him on the back and chuckled, "Go on and find her!"

Ion rolled his eyes, but did not linger outside. He hurried up the steps and slipped in through the door, vaguely aware that Georgy was following him. He halted as he scanned the desks. Mary's was empty. "She must be outside," he murmured and turned. With Georgy directly behind him, Ion crashed into him. "Georgy! Get out of my way!"

"Josh!" Georgy called out, ignoring Ion, still blocking his way from returning outside. When Mary's brother stepped over to the two, Georgy asked, "Where's Mary?"

Ion frowned. He had been hoping to keep it a private matter between himself and Mary. He wondered over Georgy's inability to understand that—or even realize it. But then again, he reminded himself, Georgy could fully well know what he was doing: irritating Ion.

"Ma is sick," Josh said in a worried tone. "Sicker than before. Mary stayed home to take care of her."

Georgy slipped his hand to the young boy's shoulder. "After school, I'll go over and check on your ma."

Josh's eyes lit up then. "Will you Georgy?" he asked. "Thanks."

As Georgy nodded, the boy slipped away, leaving Ion and Georgy alone again. Georgy shifted his gaze to Ion, a genuine caring look in his eyes. "Sorry Ion—about you not getting to tell Mary about your article."

Ion shrugged slightly, one side of his mouth easing up. "It's all right. I just hope her ma is going to be all right."

Georgy nodded. "Yeah. I wonder if Mr. O'Brin is going to ask the doc to come check on her."

"I doubt it," Ion muttered. "He don't—doesn't care. Just as long as his meals are cooked, he doesn't care who's sick."

"Well, then before I go over there, after school, I'll go over to the Morrison's first and ask Doc to go over there too."

Ion studied the face before him, wondering over the relief he was feeling. "Thanks Georgy," he sighed.

Georgy grinned and nodded, but this grin was more of a man's smile than a boy's. There was something comforting in seeing it. Once again Ion was struck with the thought that Georgy was his big brother. He was quick to tease and put Ion in an uncomfortable situation, but when Ion really needed him, he was always there for him. Georgy clapped Ion on the back then, and whispered, "Well, the extra Rachel put in our lunches for Mary won't be needed today. Let's eat it now."

Ion rolled his eyes over the shattered moment of sensitivity. "Oh Georgy," he sighed, "don't you ever stop thinking about your stomach?"

Georgy chuckled and shook his head as he lifted the lid from his lunch pail. "Why should I?" he asked. "It's a whole half a sandwich!" he cried out in delight and reached for it quickly, cramming half of it into his mouth. His eyes closed as he chewed in obvious ecstasy. And suddenly Ion began wondering over his earlier feelings of confidence in this boy-man.

Rachel carried her teapot over to the table where Sarah sat, having come over for an unexpected visit. Rachel smiled and nodded toward the living room. "I just love my living room," she sighed in contentment. "But, the kitchen table is still more—oh—"

"Intimate?" Sarah offered.

"Exactly," Rachel laughed and poured each of them a steaming cup of tea. They chatted away as they sipped their tea. Finally Rachel could hold back the news not a moment longer of Ion's sale of his article.

"Oh Rachel," Sarah beamed in obvious pleasure. "I'm so excited for him. Why, there's no telling how far he'll go in his writing." She paused then, a far away look suddenly in her eyes. "Wouldn't it be something if someone would start up a newspaper out here?" she murmured.

"Here?" Rachel asked in surprise. Her shocked tone brought Sarah back to the present, blinking and returning her attention to Rachel. "What sort of news could possibly fill up a paper out here? And as far as the fine literary articles, I'm not sure that there are very many who would even be interested. Folk out here seem to think that fine writing means the latest price listing at Matthew's store."

Both women burst out laughing. As they continued enjoying their tea, it was clear that Sarah was not yet ready to drop the subject. "Well, as far as newsworthy articles, Timberton is our world and we need to know what's going on. For one thing, I would very much like to know how the lumbermen are doing. We made some good friends of them when they were here. And I'd like to know how they're affecting Oregon, now that we're a state. I'd also like to be kept informed about the crime out here—and politics!"

"Politics?" Rachel cried out. "I never knew you were interested in such."

Sarah smiled sheepishly. "I come from a long line of politicians. Papa was a mayor for many years. And I have several cousins and uncles in various offices, some are congressmen, judges, and a few lawyers." With a rather apologetic smile, she added, "The lawyers were always considered to be the black sheep of the family unless they had plans for running for office eventually."

Rachel studied this friend of hers, wondering over the fact that she had never known this about her. "And you like politics," she murmured.

"Yes," she sighed. "If only women were allowed to participate, I think I would've run for office myself."

"You would've been good at it."

Sarah shook her head. "Not really," she giggled. "Interest and talent aren't the same thing. My talent is in being a nurse, though I've had only a little training, beyond what Phil has taught me. No, I don't believe I've missed my calling. God knew all along that I'd make a far better nurse than president of these United States."

"President!" Rachel cried out. "Dear me, you do have lofty goals!"

"Indeed," Sarah agreed, a sparkle of merriment in her eyes. "And one of my goals is to see a newspaper office come to Timberton. Oh Rachel," she sighed, "don't you miss the novels we used to read in the newspapers back home? I remember one story in particular that took two months of issues to complete. It was one of the finest stories I've ever read! I expect to see it one day published in book form. And you and I both know that they sell papers. Once a person reads the first installment of the story, he or she will buy the following issues in order to finish reading the story."

Rachel suddenly realized that Sarah was serious. "It might work at that," she said in thought. Just as hope began sifting through her, she suddenly remembered. "But no one could finance it, not here in Timberton."

"Matthew could," Sarah said simply.

Rachel studied Sarah for a moment, a smile growing on both of their faces. "Matthew could," Rachel agreed.

"You and I have read enough newspapers to be able to offer assistance.

And as far as writing articles, it would be a perfect opportunity for Ion."

"Oh my," Rachel breathed. "Oh my!" She could not push down her smile no matter how hard she tried as this new dream took root. "Let's pray about it— right now!"

Sarah nodded and immediately closed her eyes. Since she remained silent, Rachel began voicing their petition. "Lord, if you'd like to have the Timberton Gazette—or whatever it would be named—come to Timberton, please open up the door and provide the way. May you be glorified in it. And if it'd please you to set Ion in the middle of this dream, please do. Please make him into the man you gave him life to be. In Jesus beautiful and holy name we pray, amen."

As they opened their eyes and looked at each other in excitement, Sarah reached over and laid her hand over Rachel's, laughing in delight, "Imagine, civilization coming to the wilderness!"

Long after Sarah had left, Rachel's mind continued returning to their shared dream. Even when the children returned home from school her mind was on the newspaper venture. She frowned in thought as Georgy shut the door behind him. Ahead of him had come Elizabeth and Johnny. "Where's Ion?" she asked.

"He went over to see Mary," Elizabeth explained, apparently having anticipated her question and had fixed her eyes on Rachel, reading her lips with the expertise she was gaining.

Georgy took up the explanation then, adding, "Josh said that their ma is awfully sick. Mary stayed home to take care of her. I told Josh I'd check on his ma after school. But first I think I better go and tell Doc about her. Mr. O'Brin probably hasn't sent for him."

Rachel eased out her breath in a sigh, thinking about the frail Sheila O'Brin whose baby was due that month. "Wait," she said suddenly, "if you go over there I'd like you to take a basket with you. Do you have a few minutes to spare while I fill it?"

Georgy grinned. "Sure," he chuckled, reaching for a piece of bread and jam Rachel had prepared for the children for their after school snack. "Besides, I'm kind of hungry anyway."

"You're always hungry," Johnny laughed and grabbed for his own piece of bread.

As the boys continued poking fun at each other, Rachel began tucking things into the basket she would send to Sheila. First she slipped in a loaf of freshly made bread, followed by a dozen sugar cookies. She paused in thought, wondering what might brighten the woman's day. Hurrying into her bedroom, she pulled out a bottle of sweet smelling toilet water. She had tucked it away from something special. "What could be more special?" she murmured to herself. "Oh!" she added with a smile of excitement, reaching for the book of poems lying on her bed. Each page had a lovely flower printed on it. And Mary could read the poems to her if she were unable to herself. Suddenly Rachel was uncertain if the woman knew how to read. Even if she did know how, she likely was too weak to read them herself. But Mary's voice was so soothing. She was certain that Sheila would love the book, being read by her sweet daughter.

Stepping back out into the kitchen, Rachel announced, "It's ready," and handed the basket to Georgy. "And if you see Ion," she added, but all at once further words escaped her. She knew the tenderness of Ion's heart. He was almost certainly at a loss as to how to comfort Mary, though he would certainly be trying.

"I'll think of something nice to say," Georgy grinned. "I won't tease him this time. Don't worry." And with those words he hurried out through the door, basket in hand.

Rachel returned to her job of mending as the children set about doing their chores. But through it all, she offered up one prayer after another for Sheila and the baby. Even after she laid her mending aside and began preparing supper, she continued praying. The meal came and went, and still neither Georgy nor Ion had returned. Rachel helped Elizabeth with the cleanup work after supper. Still no return of the boys.

Patrick stepped over to Rachel as she hung up her dish towel to dry. "I think I'll ride on over to the O'Brin's place."

Rachel nodded, meeting his gaze. The sober look in his eyes was reply enough to her unvoiced question. "If it isn't serious, you'll come back right away?" Rachel asked. "I just don't know what to think—"

"If I'm not needed, I'll come right back and let you know 'ow she is." Leaning down, he softly kissed her cheek and then slipped out of the house.

Ion quietly stepped over to the cook stove where Mary stood with her back facing the rest of the kitchen. Georgy and Doctor Morrison were in the bedroom taking care of Mrs. O'Brin. Sam and Joshua had already been put to bed. Mr. O'Brin had not yet returned from wherever he had been all day. Ion cautiously slipped his arm around Mary's shoulders, not certain if he had the right to do so or not. She turned to him and simply laid her head on his shoulder, suddenly unable to keep the long pent up tears under control. As she cried, he drew his other arm around her and held her close, she clinging to him. He squeezed his eyes shut, staggered over how her tears tore into him.

Finally she stopped weeping, but made no attempt to leave his arms. "I love you Mary," he whispered.

Her arms squeezed him tighter. He was wondering what her silence meant. He had not planned to say what was in his heart. The words had popped out all on their own—but they were true. She had not pulled away after he had said them, but neither did she claim it true of her feelings for him. He chided himself for his timing. Of course she could not be thinking of such things as her mother lay so desperately ill, fighting for her life and also for that of the baby. Ion himself had not even meant the words to be simply a romantic statement, but as real, covering his whole life.

"I love you too," she whispered in his ear, lifting her head only long enough to get the words out. The next moment she laid her head back down on his shoulder.

Ion eased his eyes shut and simply held her close. Now it was official. Now she was his to protect. Her father had clearly thrown away his right and duty to be her protector, so Ion himself would assume that role. She had given him permission by her vow of love for him.

The sound of an approaching wagon caused them to pull back from each other. Ion stepped over to the window and peered out, but it was too dark to see anything. When a knock sounded out on the door, it was Ion, not Mary, who went to answer it. As Ion opened the door, a wave of relief swept over him as he stared into Patrick's face. "Pat," he breathed out, stepping back for the man to enter the cabin. "Am I glad that you've come!"

Patrick nodded to Mary as Ion closed the door and asked, "'Ow is she?"

Mary swallowed, but made no attempt to reply. As Ion studied her face he realized that the threat of tears was not allowing words to slip past her lips. "Georgy and the doc," Ion replied for her, "are in with her now. But Pat—" He paused and studied Mary's sorrow filled face. Glancing back at Patrick, he noted the soften look of understanding in the man's expression. "She needs our prayers," he added quietly.

Patrick nodded and, without permission, stepped across the floor to the bedroom and went inside. Mary turned and picked up the teakettle, setting it down onto the hottest part of the stove. Ion watched her work, feeling helpless, knowing her heart was breaking. He smiled sadly as it occurred to him that even though she was grieving, she was still thinking about others, preparing to make coffee for the men gathered to help her mother.

Another hour slipped away. One at a time, one of the three would leave the sickroom and venture out to the kitchen for a cup of coffee. Only sober faces greeted Ion and Mary each time. "Georgy," Ion said quietly as he, Georgy and Mary sat at the table, "you've got to tell us. We need to know. Mary needs to know."

Georgy studied Ion with a painful expression and then shifted his eyes over to Mary. "I don't think there's much we can do," he admitted. Mary grew pale over his words. Ion reached over and grasped her hand. She glanced at him and nodded, biting her lower lip and then turned back to Georgy. "Doc is hoping to save the baby. If your ma can get through tonight, the baby has a chance."

"A-and Ma?"

Slowly Georgy shook his head. "It doesn't look good, Mary. We're praying. But unless God gives us a miracle, you ma isn't going to make it."

Mary lowered her head onto her arms that rested on the table and burst into tears. Ion slipped out of his chair and went to her, crouching down beside her. As he gather her in his arms, he shifted his gaze to where Georgy sat, deep sorrow etched in his face. He nodded at Georgy, silently thanking him for his honesty. Georgy dipped his head in a brief nod in reply. He sighed and picked up his cup of coffee, drinking it down as Ion continued holding the weeping Mary.

Andrew O'Riley was delivered by his nurse, Sarah, since Phil had remained at the O'Brin cabin for two full days. As Rachel studied the sweet face of her son, she saw that he, just like Pattie, had taken after his father in looks. Unlike Pattie however, Andrew had not inherited Patrick's red hair, but Rachel's deep brown locks. As when Pattie had been born, the entire family gathered around to get their first glimpse of the tiny boy. But finally Rachel began handing out instructions for the day.

"Elizabeth," Rachel began. After Johnny had nudged her to pull her eyes off of Andrew and look at Rachel, she continued speaking. "Please make a pot of tea for Mrs. Morrison."

The newly turned fourteen-year-old nodded and left the room, but clearly with reluctance in parting with the baby so soon. "Johnny," Rachel added, "run over to the store and tell Auntie Angela and Uncle Matthew about Andrew."

The thirteen-year-old boy left the room, but not as reluctantly as Elizabeth had, since he was bursting to tell someone about his newborn nephew.

"Georgy," Rachel said, turning next to him, "run over to the schoolhouse and tell Annette why none of you are at school yet."

"Do we have to go this afternoon?" he asked.

Rachel shifted her gaze to Patrick. He smiled and shook his head. Turning back to Georgy, she answered, "No, not today. But tell her that you will all be back tomorrow morning, bright and early."

He grinned and hurried out, clearly happy to have a day off of school. Rachel shook her head, wondering how the boy would manage to get through medical school when he never missed an opportunity to take a day off from grammar school.

"Ion, would you see to Anna Marie and Pattie?" Rachel asked, her strength ebbing away by the moment.

He smiled and nodded. Leaning down, he swept up the nearly two-year-old little girl into his arms. Shifting her into one arm, he reached his free hand to the five-year-old Anna Marie, calling out quietly, "Annie." Anna Marie quickly slipped her hand into Ions. As the three stepped out of the bedroom, Jed followed. Rachel smiled, wondering if he was afraid that she was about to assign a duty to him as she had done with the others.

"I'll go and see if Elizabeth needs help with the tea," Sarah said with a smile and softly stepped out of the room, leaving Patrick and Rachel alone with Andrew.

"Would you like to hold your son?" Rachel asked.

A hungry look dashed into his eyes as he stepped over to the bed and sat down on the edge. Reaching out, he picked up the tiny bundle into his arms, murmuring, "What a rich man I am." He leaned down and softly kissed the tiny forehead. Andrew's eyes opened. As he stared up into the face of his father, Patrick smiled tenderly at him. "Just think of it," he sighed in wonder and clear joy, "seven children. The Lord 'as been good to us."

Rachel could no sooner have held back her smile than she could have held back the approaching summer. She breathed out a prayer of thanksgiving that Patrick saw their children as blessings. She could not help but compare him with the self-centered Martin O'Brin who clearly did not regard his children as the treasures they were. Her sorrow for Sheila and the children dimmed, though, each time she looked down at little Andrew.

Ion glanced out the window as a wagon drew up to the house. He hurried outside the moment he realized that it was Mary who was sitting on the bench beside Dr. Morrison. As he approached, he noticed that she was holding a wriggling bundle in her arms. Reaching up, he caught hold of her arms, helping her step down from the wagon as she clung to the small bundle. She made no attempt to speak, nor did he press her to try. Her reddened eyes told him everything he needed to know. Without a word they entered the house, Dr. Morrison following them in equal silence.

As they stood in the kitchen, Patrick stepped over to them, his eyes filled with unasked questions. Without permission, Mary turned and stepped into the bedroom where Rachel lay, Andrew curled up in one of her arms, sleeping peacefully. Mary sat down on the edge of Rachel's bed and lifted the corner of the blanket that covered her precious bundle. Ion stood at her side and peered down at the tiny face of Mary's newborn brother.

"This is Calvin," Mary said in a low voice. "My ma—" A tear slipped down Mary's cheek. She bit down on her lower lip. But it did no good. She began sobbing, clinging to the baby. Ion slipped his arm around her, drawing her close to him as she cried. He glanced down at Rachel, seeing that tears were in her eyes as she helplessly watched the broken hearted girl. Finally, regaining control of herself, May eased back from Ion slightly and returned her gaze to Rachel. "My ma asked me to bring Calvin to you as your own." When she seemed to want to say more but was clearly unable to, Ion gently caressed her head, running his fingers through the silken hair.

"But your Pa," Rachel began, shock in her tone even though she knew the man for what he was. "Maybe he has other ideas."

Mary shook her head and drew in a deep breath. "He doesn't want him. He was even the one who asked Doctor Morrison to drive Calvin and me over here. He—he doesn't want any of us."

Rachel tore her gaze from the broken young woman to Patrick, silently petitioning him. His eyes were filled with such sorrow, Ion caught his breath. The soften look on his face as he nodded, assured everyone who was watching that there was plenty of room in his heart for another son.

"Will you take him?" Mary asked so pitifully Ion had all he could do not to openly begin sobbing himself.

"Of course we will," Rachel replied in a trembling tone.

Mary eased little Calvin down into Rachel's free arm. As she did so, there was such a look of reluctance on her face that Ion knew beyond doubt that parting with him was just as hard as parting with her mother. Once Calvin was safely in Rachel's arms, Mary rose to her feet. She met Ion's gaze, her look one of pleading. He smiled and slipped his arm around her shoulders, offering her all the strength he knew how to give. She drew in a steadying breath. And Ion was assured that his nearness was helping her.

"My ma," she said, turning back to Rachel. "She really liked that book of poems that you sent over. I've been reading them to her practically night and day. And just before she—" Mary paused and drew in another breath. Turning to Ion, as if for an additional measure of strength, she nodded and then turned back to Rachel. "Just before she passed on, she asked me to read her favorite one just one more time. Thank you for making her last moments happy."

Clearly she had finished all that she had come to do. Only then did she give way entirely to the sorrow in her heart. Turning to Ion, she burst out into deep weeping, clinging to him. He held her close, concentrating hard on not giving in to his own tears. Mary needed his strength just then. As Mary wept, Ion shifted his eyes and watched as Rachel kissed the fuzzy little head of her second newborn son. By the look on her face, she had already fallen head over heals in love with little Calvin.

When Mary lifted her head from Ion's shoulder, he reached up and brushed her tears away. She tried to smile, but was unable to. His heart was further wrung by her attempt to do so. "I best be going."

"No," Rachel cut in. "Why don't you and the boys come over here for a few days? At least until you get things sorted out."

"Aye lassie," Patrick added, stepping over to Mary and Ion. "We hiv plinty o'room for ye. I think 'twould be good for the three o'ye. And 'twould be a great delight to us if ye'd come. I'll see to the arrangements for yeer mither."

"You'll do that?" Mary wept, causing Ion to realize that the funeral was all resting on Mary's small shoulders.

"Aye lassie," Patrick murmured, slipping his broad hand to her head, softly patting it much as he did for Anna Marie and Pattie when they fell down and cried. "Aye. I'll take care of it for ye."

Ion knew that he had learned to love Patrick and Rachel long ago. But his love and appreciation for them leaped into exponential growth as they reached out with such love toward Mary.

Relief in her eyes, she nodded, murmuring, "If pa says it's all right, we'd be most obliged to come for a few days."

"Ion," Patrick began, turning to Ion, "ye and the lads get the study ready for Josh and Sam. And tell Lizzie to fix up a bed in her and Annie's room for Mary, so it'll be ready when they come."

Ion nodded and only then realized that his arms were still around Mary.

Patrick eyed him closely. Ion was suddenly reminded of the talk Patrick had had with him and Georgy about holding hands with girls they had not received permission to court. Patrick, apparently understanding Ion's thoughts, allowed one side of his mouth to rise. Ion sighed in relief and eased his arms back from Mary.

As Mary left with Patrick, heading outside for the O'Riley wagon, Ion hurried to obey Patrick's orders. It would not take long for the ten-year-old Sam and the thirteen-year-old Josh to gather their meager belonging together. Patrick was right. They would need a place to call their own—even temporarily—the moment they entered the house.

"Patrick," Rachel's voice sounded out in the fog of early morning. "Patrick, wake up. Someone is at the door."

Patrick cleared his throat as consciousness began returning to him. The past few days had been taxing, draining everyone. They had all been sleeping in later than normal. It had been hardest on Mary, Joshua, and Sam, of course, but the strain of knowing the three were in such deep mourning had been a challenge to all the O'Riley's, not to mention the addition of two newborns keeping the entire household from getting a good night's sleep.

"Aye," Patrick sighed. "I'm getting up."

"No you're not," Rachel insisted. "And I can't go to the door in my nightgown. Go!"

The urgency in her voice brought Patrick out of bed. Hurrying into the robe that Rachel insisted he wear when parading around the house in his nightwear, he hurried to the door and opened it. At first he blinked in surprise, eying the unexpected man. The next moment he gathered his sleepy thoughts together and said, "Martin, come in."

As Martin O'Brin entered, Patrick could not help but wonder why the man had not waited until a later hour to come. He did not have long to puzzle over the matter, for the man plunged into his reason immediately. "Well, I've come with a proposition to make. I can't see as how I can be raising three young'ns alone. And seeing how you've already agreed to take in the baby, I was wondering if you might consider taking the other three too."

Patrick stared at the man, hardly able to believe that he was actually saying what he was. It was then that Rachel emerged from the bedroom, apparently deciding that it would be enough to have her robe covering her nightgown. She eyed the man, murmuring, "Mr. O'Brin."

"Ma'am," he greeted distantly, clearly annoyed that he had been interrupted in his conversation with Patrick. Patrick eased over beside Rachel, slipping his hand to her back. "Well?" Martin asked Patrick. "Do you agree?"

Patrick glanced down at Rachel, who was eying him with questions in her eyes. Apparently she had not heard the man's request. "Martin 'as offered to leave all of 'is children with us—permanently."

Rachel's eyes opened wide, not even trying to hide her dumbfounded reaction over the matter. Martin began speaking again, explaining, "Before I married Sheila, I was a sailor. I never did feel right in being a land lubber. Well, I got an offer to sign up with a captain I know and be his first mate. I couldn't refuse an offer like that. And I can't take them three with me."

Patrick and Rachel turned and eyed each other, nodding. Turning back to Martin, Patrick said quietly, "All right. We'll raise thim as our own."

"Good," the man shot back, excitement in his tone. "I have the rest of their things in the wagon. I'll unload them and put them in your barn and be on my way." And without another word, he spun around and hurried outside. The sound of a squeaking board behind them made Patrick and Rachel glance over their shoulders, straight into Mary's eyes as she stood in the living room archway. Shock was painted on her face. Without a word, she turned and disappeared back into the bedroom.

The first Saturday in May arrived, bringing with it the promise of warm weather. As soon as their morning chores were completed, Elizabeth hurried off to visit Jennifer Corin. Johnny also ran off, hoping to pester Matthew. He had taken an interest in the store and pelted Matthew with business sorts of questions whenever the opportunity arose. While Anna Marie and Pattie were quietly playing with their dolls in the living room, the two babies had settled down for a morning nap. As Josh and Sam ran outside to play with the dogs, Patrick summoned the rest to the kitchen table for a family meeting.

Georgy could not hold back a grin, this being the first such meeting that he had been summoned to. Up until now, Only Patrick, Rachel, and Jed had been a part of them. Georgy squared his shoulders over finally being considered old enough to attend. He glanced across the table where Ion and Mary were sitting, having been included in the meeting as well.

"We're facing the problem," Patrick began, "of providing for the needs of our large family."

Just then Mary lowered her head, her cheeks turning pink. Georgy guessed that the girl was feeling like a burden, without knowing what to do about it. He could not help but sigh. After all, it was hardly Mary's fault that she and her brothers had been abandoned by their father.

"Mary," Patrick added gently, "in this family we try to be honest with each ither. Ye mist rimimber thit just b'cause a certain joy may carry a price tag, it doesn't mean thit we'd be willing to part with it. So now the question is 'ow to take care of the joy-bearers our Lord 'as blessed us with."

Mary's eyes shot up and over to meet Patrick's. A tiny, shy smile crept to her lips. Her shoulders stopped drooping. Georgy suddenly remembered to breathe as the pieces of his world began falling back into their proper places.

"I sold one article," Ion began, hope in his voice. "I hope to sell a lot more. It won't be a lot of money, but it'll help out."

Patrick nodded. "Aye, 'twill 'elp."

"Now and then Phil pays me for helping him," Georgy added. "It's not much, but the family can have all of it."

"Minus the tithe," Patrick replied.

"Minus the tithe," Georgy agreed with a grin. "That's what I meant. I know that the first ten percent belongs to God."

"But Georgy," Rachel began. "You have to start saving for medical school."

"Not with the tithe!" Georgy argued, shocked that she would even suggest such a thing.

She rolled her eyes and shook her head. "Certainly not! I'm talking about the other ninety percent. And since when have you started calling Doctor Morrison by the name of Phil?"

Georgy grinned. He had been calling him that for months now, with the doctor's permission. But he had not intended to let it slip out in front of Rachel. Apparently she had forgotten about that one time he had slipped and called the man by his first name in her presence. But that had been the day Patrick had been knocked unconscious while cutting firewood. "Well, for some time. And he says that I ought to try for a scholarship."

Rachel's eyes grew large with that bit of information. Patrick took advantage of her shock to reply, "We accept yeer offer Georgy. Medical school is not for a while yet. Bit we do hiv to take care of the problem of supporting all of us today. We'll hiv to think about medical school later.

"I can sew," Mary volunteered shyly. "And I can care for the neighbors' children."

Again Patrick nodded. "'Tis a good idea. Bit I think Rachel will be needing ye at home most o'the time. Bit now and then ye might be able to watch the neighbors' children."

A tiny smile crept to the girl's lips. Georgy wondered if that was due to the fact that her idea was accepted, or that Rachel was in need of her.

"Now it just seems to me," Jed began, "that we could be a puttin' them there horses to more work than we do. We gots us two good wagons. Now, if'n we can find somebody who wants something' hauled, I'm the man to be a doin' it. That oughta bring in some cash."

Patrick nodded, replying, "Matthew could probably put ye to work. 'E is tired of delivering merchandise 'imself, especially to some o'the folk thit live at a distance."

"I can use some of that money," Rachel volunteered, "to buy more garden seeds. The little ones can help with the garden, though it'd mainly be Mary, Elizabeth and myself working it. Well," she added with a smile, "I suppose Joshua and Johnny and Sam would hardly approve of being described as little. And they can certainly work just as hard as we three ladies. With all this extra help, we could raise twice as much as our family needs and sell the rest to Matthew for his store. I know that he'd be glad to have fresh vegetables to sell, especially with so many of the farmers putting their efforts into cash crops more than into vegetables. He told me not long ago that he's certain that he could sell every vegetable he could get his hands on."

Patrick cocked his head. "We hivn't yet made the money, and ye're already spending it?" His eyes twinkled as he spoke. As everyone began laughing, Mary alone remained silent. Her eyes darted over to Patrick and Rachel, something like fear shining in them. But when Patrick leaned over and kissed Rachel's cheek, Mary sighed in relief. Georgy puzzled over the fact that the girl had not realized that Patrick was only teasing. He wondered at the fear that had come to her eyes at first.

Patrick began speaking then, saying simply, "I think I'll work up some land and plant wheat."

"But Patrick," Rachel murmured, the merriment slipping from her expression. "You already spend time you can't spare in growing hay for the horses. How in the world will you find more time for wheat? Why, during the haying season, I rarely see you as it is, except at meal times."

Patrick grinned, chuckling, "Now I'm no fool. I'm not about to miss yeer tasty meals lassie."

Rachel eyed him sternly. "Don't change the subject, sir." Her eyes began laughing then as she caught hold of his hand. But finally she added in a more serious tone, "Truly Patrick, during the haying season you're nearly run ragged. How are you going to keep doing all your other jobs and grow wheat too?"

Just then a knock sounded out on the door. Everyone had been too engrossed in their discussion to notice that anyone had approached the house. Patrick opened the door and smiled, saying heartily, "Come in. Ye're just in time for a cup of coffee."

As Sam and Mitch stepped inside, Rachel hurried to pour coffee for both of them. As she did so, Sam began explaining his reason for coming. "The town council met earlier this week," he began. "The folks around here want to help with the O'Brin children." Georgy glanced over at Mary, whose shoulders were once again slipping down. At that moment, Ion turned to her and smiled. It seemed to be what the girl needed. She smiled slightly, looking less uncomfortable with the conversation. "They figure these children are everyone's responsibility. So we took up a collection." He drew out a leather bag from his pants' pocket and set it down in front of Patrick. "I hope you're not too proud to take it. I don't know much about the Bible," he added quickly, not giving Patrick a chance to accept or reject the gift. "But I recall it saying that 'Pride goes before destruction.'"[vi]

"'And a haughty spirit before a fall,'" Patrick continued the verse. "Aye, I know thit verse well." He began chuckling quietly. "Sam," he added, shaking his head in amusement. "Ye kinnot b'lieve only part o'the Bible. Ye kinnot take frim it what ye like and reject the rist. 'Tis one word, indivisible. Bit ye are right about pride," he added, laughing again. "And we accept this money thankfully."

Sam grinned. Georgy wondered over Patrick's boldness in telling people exactly what they needed to hear. Sam was one who let Patrick say anything he saw fit to, but he still had not yet put his faith in Jesus.

"It's my turn," Mitch began, turning everyone's attention to him. "We had a deacon's meeting this week," he said, eying Patrick closely. "You weren't invited Patrick," he added in mock sternness. The corners of Patrick's mouth rose, but he said nothing. "After the meeting we visited every family that comes to church—except for this family," he added quickly. "And everyone agreed that we want to—and it's our privilege and responsibility to look out for the needs of our pastor and his family. Now, we knew all about the town taking up a collection. And there weren't enough of us to be able to match it. Besides," he added with a chuckle, "we all contributed to that collection too—" Screeching to a halt, he colored slightly, clearly not having intended to mention that. He shrugged and continued in a sigh, "So we decided to buy something to help out the family. Now, I know how hard it is to fix meals in a fireplace. And with your size of family, it's even harder than it is for my family. So, we bought a cook stove for you. Matthew is going to deliver it this morning."

Georgy grinned at Mitch. "You never told me!"

"You're not on the deacon board," Mitch replied firmly, a grin following his words.

Rachel looked completely stunned. "Why, I've seen the stove in Matthew's store. That's twelve whole dollars!"

"Matthew gave it to us for cost. He didn't make a dime on it," Mitch explained.

Rachel brushed at her eyes. As she did so, Patrick's arm crept around her shoulders. The soften look in his eyes as he studied Rachel's face made Georgy smile afresh. "So what's stopping us," Georgy cried out, "from knocking out the fireplace right now and get it ready for the stove?"

"'Old on laddie," Patrick laughed, turning to him in amusement. "I'm not so sure we want to take out the fireplace. "That'd leave us with only the small one in the living room to heat the whole house."

"Besides," Rachel admitted, "I've grown terribly fond of my fireplace."

Everyone fell silent then, trying to decide where best to place the stove. It was Ion who suggested, "Why don't you put it there between Jed's and our bedroom doorways? You wouldn't have to lose all your cupboards and counter. Besides," he added with a grin, "Pat can build you some more."

"Ah, thank ye lad, for providing me with more work." Patrick chuckled and nodded. "Bit Ion is right. Thit is the perfect spot. What do ye think, Rachel?"

"I like it. But Patrick, he's also right about the portions of the cupboards and counter you'll be taking out. I'll be needing more."

Patrick's arm around her tightened as he laughed along with her. But Mitch, not finished yet, called out, "One more thing." When everyone turned their attention back to Mitch, he continued speaking. "We were afraid you might take it in your head to do some more farming. But the whole church is in agreement in thinking that you already work hard enough. So, we decided to raise your salary."

Patrick smiled rather sheepishly at Mitch who eyed him knowingly.

Georgy and Ion exchanged amused glances. The conversation around the table grew livelier as they finished drinking their coffee. The business was over and now all that remained was the excitement of cutting a hole in the roof for the stovepipe and removing part of the cupboards and counter for the cook stove itself.

Suddenly the outside door burst open and in dashed Matthew, a wild look in his eyes. "It's a girl!" he cried out. A cheer of hearty congratulations burst out then so loudly that no one could hear anyone else.

Finally when everyone quieted down and Matthew was seated at the table, Rachel asked "What have you named her?"

He shook his head and sighed. "I didn't have any part in it," he said. "So don't blame me." Everyone waited, wondering just how bad of a name Angela had given the little girl. "Alicia," he finally said.

"That's a lovely name," Rachel said in surprise. "Why are you troubled over it?"

"Stephanie," he added.

"Alicia Stephanie," Rachel repeated slowly. Lifting her shoulders in puzzlement, she said, "There's no cause to apologize for a name like that. It's absolutely lovely!"

"Ann," he added, nodding with a rye grin.

Jed piped up then, asking in surprise, "Ya gived her three names?"

"Carson-Davis," Matthew added, waiting for another comment. Finally he sighed, "Bon-Hemmer. At last count it was seven full names, five if you count the hyphenated names as only one each. I finally told her that enough is enough. Since Angela can lay claim to only one name of her own, she just didn't know when to stop when giving names to our daughter." His eyes sparkled as he said the word daughter. Rising to his feet, he nodded, adding, "I told Angela I wouldn't be gone long. Sarah and Phil are with her now."

Rachel rose to her feet. "Matthew, would it be all right if Elizabeth, Mary and I come and meet your daughter?"

His smile nearly reached his ears as he dipped his head in a nod. "Excellent idea. Ladies?" he added bowing slightly. Rachel reached out her hand toward Mary who smiled and rose to her feet. "We'll be back soon," she called out as they stepped out of the house in search of Elizabeth. "So get busy cutting a hole in my cupboards and roof."

As the door closed behind the three, Georgy began laughing. "I bet that baby isn't half as long as her name!"

Rachel shifted the month-old Calvin into her left arm as she reached for the coffeepot and poured two steaming cupsful, having caught sight of Jed and Matthew approaching the house. The baby gurgled contentedly, though not at all sleepily. Rachel kissed the cherub cheek and murmured lovingly, "You're just the sweetest baby! But I'm glad that this is the last day of school. Your big sisters are going to be an awfully big help!" Although Anna Marie was a help to her while the others were in school, still Elizabeth and Mary would be most welcome in helping Rachel care for the two newborns as well as helping her run the household for her ever growing family.

As the two men entered the house, Rachel nodded, calling out, "Good afternoon Matthew. We haven't seen very much of you lately."

He grinned, replying, "It's just too hard to tear myself away from my little girl."

Rachel smiled, enjoying seeing the happy face of the man who only too clearly enjoyed his child. "Would you both like a cup of coffee?"

"That's why we're here," Jed answered gruffly, though his eyes twinkled.

Carrying the cups to the table, one at a time, she turned back to the stove and poured herself a cup of coffee. Sitting down at the table, she joined the men in a welcome break. "How is Angela?" she asked.

"Her usual self," he replied with a wink. Rachel quickly suppressed the giggle that wanted to burst forth. How well she knew what Angela's usual self was like. As the men began chatting, Rachel drew in a deep breath, relishing the adult conversation. Lately Patrick had been away more than usual, calling on various families in the community. Rachel was finding that even at five, Anna Marie's conversation level lacked a bit in regards to adult conversation.

"Phil is quite excited, to say the least," Matthew said, sipping his coffee.

Rachel blinked, wondering what she had missed while daydreaming. "Oh?" she asked, hoping that Matthew would broaden up on his statement without her having to admit that she had not been paying attention to the conversation.

He nodded. "He thinks it quite an honor to be teaching that boy of yours on a full time basis."

"He'll be free all summer long to work with Phil," Rachel replied, wondering over Georgy's neglect in mentioning how he planned to spend his summer. "He's already learned a tremendous amount from Dr. Morrison and the medical books he's lent him."

"But I was a little surprised," Matthew added, "when I heard that you were going to let him quit school."

"What?" Rachel cried out, staring at Matthew in open shock. He paled. "What are you talking about?" she asked in a low voice.

"Oh dear," he sighed. "I thought surely you knew."

"Jed?" Rachel asked, turning to the man. "Did you know anything about this?"

He shook his head. "No Missus, I didn't. But I s'pect Georgy's old enough to make that kind of decision hisself. He'll be seventeen in less than two months. If he wants to quit school, that's his decision."

"Over my dead body!" Rachel shot back. "If he quits school he has no possibility of obtaining a scholarship. Why, he wouldn't even be allowed to enter a university if he quits grammar school. An eighth grade diploma means everything to the education world! Don't you understand? If he quits school he will be throwing away his entire future!"

"I told Angela," Matthew said suddenly, the moment Rachel paused to take a breath, "that I wouldn't be gone long."

"Oh no," Rachel said firmly, turning back to the man. "You're going to stay and tell me everything you know about the matter."

He sighed, looking miserable. "I've already told you just about everything I know." And then he added in a mumbled tone, "But I wish I hadn't."

Before he had a chance to continue, a knock sounded out on the door. Jed rose to his feet and stepped over to the door, opening it. "Hullow Sheriff," he said heartily. "Get yerself inside. The pots on the stove. Grab yerself a cup and sit down."

Sam was quick to comply. Rachel did not feel the need to treat him as a guest, since he spent half of his time in the O'Riley house as one of the family. Rachel sighed and rolled her eyes at Matthew who grinned back at her, both knowing that the conversation concerning Georgy was being put on hold for the moment. Rachel sipped her coffee and tried to decide what the best course of action would be. Should she openly confront Georgy, or should she wait for Patrick to return and confide in him before she said anything to the boy?

"So when I got back from Portland," Sam was saying, "I went and told the Doc about it."

"About what?" Rachel asked, chagrinned that she had allowed her mind to wander twice now instead of paying attention to the conversation at hand.

Sam leaned back in surprise as he stared at her. "The ear operation," he replied, as if Rachel should have known exactly what he had been talking about. "Anyway, it might be worth a try."

He eyed her, as if waiting for a reply. She sighed and shook her head. "I'm sorry Sam, my mind was wandering. I have something on my mind," she added, shifting her eyes to stare at Matthew for a moment, "that I need to attend to. I was only half listening."

One side of the man's mouth rose. "I'm talking about a doctor in Portland who could operate on Lizzy. Phil thinks it's possible that an operation could restore her hearing."

Rachel stared in openmouthed wonder. As she began digesting the shocking information, Matthew quietly rose to his feet and excused himself, slipping quickly out through the door. "Elizabeth?" Rachel murmured.

"I took the liberty," Sam continued, "of making arrangements for her to go to Portland. Mitch volunteered to driver her there. And he said that Jennifer would be sure to want to go and keep Lizzy company. And Phil suggested that Georgy go along too. He said it'd be a good experience for him, medically speaking. But there's just one problem. Mitch's little brother would have to stay home alone. But Mitch doesn't want him to. The boy's around twelve or thirteen—plenty old enough to be staying alone."

"Art is not old enough to stay alone," Rachel replied firmly. "But we have plenty of room here. He can stay with us." She paused and added sheepishly,

"That is, if Patrick agrees to all of this."

Georgy shifted his gaze and met Ion's amused ones. "She doesn't know," Georgy murmured.

Ion chuckled and shook her head. "I wouldn't count on it."

"Come on," Georgy grumbled, "I swore you two to secrecy."

Mary leaned forward, looking around Ion and met Georgy's gaze. "We haven't told anyone. Only we three and Mrs. Shaleman know. But don't you think you should tell her now?"

Georgy eased out his breath and shook his head. "No. Not yet. Phil knows too," he added. He suddenly grinned. "What are we all worried about anyway? It's good news!"

"Good news," Ion replied quietly, "is better when it isn't kept."

"No," Georgy said in thought, "I think it's the other way around. Bad news shouldn't be kept. But good news can be kept."

By then they had arrived home. Georgy was the first to enter the house. He crossed the kitchen floor and set his books down onto his bed. The next moment he was back out into the kitchen. By then the others had stepped into the house and were reaching for their after-school snacks, chatting noisily with Rachel and Jed. Anna Marie and Pattie were getting in their talking time as well, even though they were not yet in school.

"Mary," Rachel said when Georgy stepped over to the table and grabbed two cookies. "Take Calvin for a moment please." Mary picked up her little brother from Rachel's arms, clucking her tongue and cooing at him. Rachel turned to Georgy, saying firmly, "Let's go for a walk."

Georgy nodded, taking a bite from one of the cookies and shifted his gaze, locking into Ion's. Ion's mouth was creeping up then. Georgy shook his head in wonder, trying to figure out how Rachel had found out his secret. Without a word, he followed her outside. They said nothing until they were a good distance from the house. Rachel stopped walking then and turned to Georgy, asking, "Is it true that you are planning to quit school?"

Again he shook his head in wonder that he had not been able to keep it a secret. Likely she did not yet know the entire story, but she had figured out part of it anyway. "Who told you?" he asked.

"Then it's true?"

"Who told you?"

She sighed long and loud, replying in a dejected tone, "Matthew let it slip."

He grinned. "Matthew? Now how in the world did he find out? It just doesn't seem to be possible to keep a secret in this town."

"Are you seriously considering it?" she asked quietly.

"Not just considering," he chuckled. "I've already committed myself to it."

"Without even discussing it with any of us?"

"What's to discuss?" he asked. Shrugging, he added, "You can talk to Mrs. Shaleman about it tonight."

"Tonight?"

"Did you forget?" he laughed. "Tonight's when all the parents come to the schoolhouse and all the kids show what we've learned this year."

"Oh, I'd forgotten," Rachel murmured. Squaring her shoulders, she added, "We'll talk about this again when Patrick gets home."

"Sure," he replied lightly. "But I have to go now. Phil's expecting me."

She nodded and he turned to leave, shaking his head in wonder that she had found out. He laughed as he thought about the fact that she still did not know the whole story.

The hours at the Morrison's slipped by all too quickly. By the time Georgy returned home, there simply was not enough time for him to get into a discussion with Patrick and Rachel about his schooling. As soon as supper was concluded, everyone had to scurry to get to the schoolhouse on time for the end of the year presentation to parents.

From his seat on the bench at the front of the school, Georgy stared out at the parents who were sitting at the desks. Patrick was holding Calvin, while Rachel cradled Andrew. Anna Marie sat with her arm protectively around Pattie as the two sat between Patrick and Rachel. They all seemed to be enjoying the presentations of the children, though a preoccupied expression rested on Rachel's face.

Finally it was Georgy's turn to do his presentation. He rose to his feet and stepped to the center of the stage area and met Rachel's gaze, grinning at her. Annette stepped over to him and began introducing him. "Ladies and gentlemen, we have saved Georgy Northwood for the last for a very special reason."

Suddenly a look of horror shot into Rachel's face. Georgy had all he could do not to start laughing, guessing that she was certain that it would be announced for all to hear that Georgy was quitting school.

"Georgy," Annette continued, "has progressed rapidly in his studies, surprising even his teacher. He has quickly passed from one grade to another in an unbelievably short amount of time. And so," she paused, laying her hand on his shoulder, "I would like to present Timberton's first graduate: Georgy Northwood!"

The stunned look that came to Rachel's face suddenly shifted. Tears came to her eyes and slipped down her cheeks. Georgy watched as a look of unparalleled pride of a mother for her son filled in every crevice of her face. And then everyone began clapping. The next thing Georgy knew, he was stepping down the aisle and Rachel was moving into it. With one arm firmly around baby Andrew, her other arm slipped around Georgy. He gathered her close and whispered into her ear, "Thank you Rachel. I owe it all to you."

Chapter 9

Georgy jumped to his feet for what seemed like the hundredth time from his chair in the hospital hallway. He felt Mitch's and Jennifer's eyes upon him, but he simply could not remain sitting for a single moment longer. "Dear God," he sighed out as he walked the length of the dull grey hall, "please wake Bet up able to hear—to hear as good or even better than she used to be able to." He eased out his breath and fell silent. Turning around, he retraced his steps and eased back down onto his chair beside Mitch. Shifting his eyes, he met Mitch's amused gaze.

"Feel better?" Mitch asked, the corners of his mouth inching upward.

Georgy dipped his head in a brief nod. "Much."

Chuckling, Mitch turned back to eye the closed door across the hall from where they were sitting. "How old was she when she lost her hearing?" he asked quietly.

"Ten," Georgy murmured, recalling that awful day their wagon had rolled over, nearly killing his family. "It's been more than four years," he sighed. "I can't imagine not hearing anything for four years."

Mitch nodded. "She's quite a lady," he said simply.

Georgy flinched back and narrowed his eyes. "Oh?" he asked.

"You disagree?" Mitch asked turning to him, but not quite meeting his gaze.

"No, I don't disagree. But it's more like she's quite a girl."

"You don't consider your sister to be a lady?" Mitch asked in a rather testy sort of tone.

One side of Georgy's mouth inched upward. "Sure I do. I just—you know—she's still a little girl. So I've never thought of her as a lady—"

"Little girl?" Mitch argued in surprise. "She'll be fifteen in six months!"

The other side of Georgy's mouth swept upward. "You don't say," he mused. "Now, how is it that you know that, Mitch?"

Mitch frowned and glanced back at the closed door of Elizabeth's hospital room. "Well I can't help but know the ages of Jen and Art's friends."

"Oh, sure," Georgy agreed amiably and fell silent. Mitch seemed to sigh a rather relieved sigh, causing Georgy to grin anew. "You know Sammy's birthday is this month. Can you help me remember how old he is?"

"How should I know? He's your brother."

"Yeah, but I don't claim to know anybody's age. You, on the other hand, claim to know the ages of your brother's and sister's friends. Sammy and Art are friends, so you must know how old he's going to be on his birthday."

Mitch turned and glared through narrowed eyes at Georgy, but fell silent. Georgy grinned and shook his head. When Mitch turned back again to the door, Georgy leaned back in his chair, looking just behind Mitch, meeting Jennifer's gaze as she too looked around Mitch. A tiny smile played about her lips, her eyes sparkling, confirming Georgy's suspicion. He shifted his gaze back to a neutral spot on the polished floor. This was an entirely new and unexpected line of thought for him.

Suddenly the door to Elizabeth's room opened and a nurse stepped out into the hall. "Which one is the brother?" she asked.

Georgy rose to his feet, saying nervously, "I am, ma'am."

"She's awake now. You can come in and see her."

"How—how is she?" he asked, his feet suddenly feeling leaden.

"Come and see for yourself," the woman replied crisply.

Georgy glanced down at Mitch. A look of worry and hope mingled in the man's eyes. Turning back to the door, he stepped through it and headed toward Elizabeth's bed. With bandages wrapped around her head, it would have been difficult for most to recognize her. But Georgy could clearly distinguish the markings that set her apart from every other girl in the ward. Quietly he eased down onto the chair beside the bed. Elizabeth's eyes fluttered open. "Bet?" Georgy asked.

A look of wonder spread across the girl's face. "Georgy—I—heard that!" She paused and reached up, touching her lips. "I heard me say that too!"

Georgy reached out and caught hold of her hand, squeezing it. He desperately wanted to say something more. But the tightening in his throat made that impossible. Her expression softened then as she studied his face. "It's all right Georgy," she murmured. "It's all right."

"Open the damper Rachel!" Patrick cried out, bringing Rachel instantly out of her musings over Elizabeth, wondering how the operation was going, wishing that they had a telegraph office in Timberton. She turned to the stove in shock as smoke billowed out of it. Suddenly she realized that she had completely shut off the damper instead of opening it. Reaching out hastily, she opened the damper and tried not to cough. As she used her apron as an improvised fan, Patrick opened up the outside door, coaxing the smoke to leave the house.

"I'm sorry," Rachel sighed when he turned around from the door. His smile grew as she spoke. "Honestly Patrick, I just haven't been thinking right since they left for Portland."

"I know," he chuckled, clearly amused over her understatement.

Rachel turned back to the stove. "I better finish preparing lunch," she added, trying to regain her sense of dignity.

Jed burst through the doorway, calling out, "Listen up what I gots ta tell ya—" Screeching to a halt, he asked, "What caught on fire? Is it out?"

Patrick cleared his throat, while Rachel refused to turn around, saying simply, "'Twas only a wee bit o'trouble with the stove. Bit 'tis over now."

Rachel felt like hugging the man for refusing to embarrass her further by telling the entire story. "Oh,"

Jed said, apparently satisfied. Rachel smiled and eased out a sigh. "You'll never guess in a million years what I just hauled in for Matthew."

Rachel slid the lid off of the kettle a little more as the potato water threatened to boil over. She was only half listening to the men as she worked, until Jed said one word. "Yep, he got hisself a printin' press."

Rachel whirled around. "A printing press? Jed, are you certain?" She did not wait for him to reply, murmuring in thought, "Why, he laughed at Sarah and me when we suggested the idea of him setting up a newspaper office in Timberton."

Jed grinned, replying, "You just listen up here little lady. Matthew told me that he's planning on hiring some men to put up a building for him so he can have hisself a reg'lar newspaper office. So what ya be a thinkin' 'bout that?"

Rachel simply stared, too stunned to say another word. Patrick seemed to have no trouble there, and asked, "Who is going to run it? Matthew certainly is too busy to undertake thit responsibility."

"Don't rightly know," Jed replied, clearly pleased with himself in delivering the information. "But I s'pect he has hisself a plan."

Rachel found herself suddenly torn between thinking about Elizabeth and the printing press, but even so the meal was somehow ready by noon. There were only Jed, Patrick, Pattie and Rachel sitting down to eat, it being the first day of school. After blowing on Pattie's plate of potatoes to cool it, she sighed, murmuring, "I wonder how Anna Marie is liking her first day of school." She shifted her gaze and met Patrick's. "She sure was excited," she added.

"And her mamma was in tears," Patrick said softly.

Rachel nodded. "Oh Patrick, they're little for such a short time. I wanted to keep her home to myself for another year at least. I know," she added before either Patrick or Jed could say a word. "She's almost six. Where did the years go?" she sighed, thinking of the two-year-old Anna Marie when she had joined their family, the age Pattie was now. "She was so little when she first came to us," she added wistfully.

"I rimimber," Patrick sighed out, a smile grazing his lips.

Rachel turned to him and smiled. "I love hearing you say those words. I'm so glad most of your memory came back!"

"And what I don't actually rimimber, ye and the children hiv filled me in on sufficiently."

"Patrick, do you think Paul Thompson would be pleased with the way we're raising Anna Marie?"

He grew thoughtful and finally nodded. "I think so. Jed?" he asked, glancing across the table at the patriarch of the family. "What do ye think?"

"What's not to be pleased with?" he scoffed. "That little gal has more than most. Why she landed herself into a family that loves her and takes good care of her. And she's got a mamma who sent her to school even though she wanted to keep her home." He smiled broadly at Rachel and Patrick. "I 'spect Paul would be right glad. I know I'm tickled pink over how you're raising my grandson's childern. And he'd be sayin' the same. And I know fer a fact that Miz. O'Brin would be just as happy over how you've taken her four young'ns on as yer own."

Rachel smiled at the older gentleman she counted as her grandfather. Silently they resumed eating, each lost in thought. At last Jed pushed back his empty plate and smacked his lips, calling out, "Sure be tasty!"

Half a moment later, Pattie smacked her lips and cried out, "Tasty!"

Rachel turned to the little girl in horror. Her mind raced in two directions at the same time. She certainly could not allow her daughter to conduct herself with these sorts of table manners. Nor could she bring herself to say anything that would somehow insult Jed over his own behavior. Glancing over at Jed, she blinked in surprised at the frown on his face.

"Pattie," Jed said sternly, "your mamma don't want you ta be actin' like that. Little girls don't be a smackin' their lips. That's just fer men-folk to be a doin.' Little girls ort to talk like ladies."

Rachel instantly returned her gaze to her plate, but not before seeing from the corner of her eye the picture of Patrick biting down on the corner of his mouth. She concentrated every fiber of her being on holding her face in a straight line as she ran her fork carefully over her practically clean plate. She tried not to imagine the trouble Patrick was having in not howling in laughter. All at once Rachel jumped to her feet and hurried over to the stove under the pretense of rescuing the coffee from boiling over as it sat perking away quite nicely on the stove. She dared not turn around and catch Patrick's eye, not if either of them were to retain their composure.

Andrew began crying then. Before Rachel had a chance to take even one step from the stove, Patrick was on his feet heading for the nursery. She kept her back to the table, playing with the coffeepot handle, allowing her smile to fully bloom. She could not help but imagine the scene that was undoubtedly playing out in the nursery. She pictured Patrick holding Andrew up to himself, burying his head in the baby's blanket to drown out the sound of his laughter. She did not expect him to return to the table until he had his laughter fully under control. Her shoulders began shaking then, regardless of her stern lecture to herself.

It was nearly fifteen minutes later before Patrick reemerged from the nursery, though Andrew's crying had stopped sooner than that. Since he stepped out of the nursery without the baby, Rachel concluded that he had fallen back to sleep again. Jed was already on his second cup of coffee by the time Patrick started on his first.

A few moments later Rachel glanced out the window and caught sight of the approaching buggy. After Matthew reigned in his horse, he approached the house. Patrick hurried to the door and opened it, grinning broadly, calling out, "Just in time for coffee!"

Rachel chuckled quietly and poured another cup. As she set it in front of Matthew as soon as he had sat down at the table, he said in an amused tone, "I suppose that Jed has already told you about the printing press."

"Aye," Patrick replied. "We've bin discussing it."

Matthew nodded thoughtfully. "Good, because that's what I've come to talk to you about. Now, I realize that Ion still has another year or so before completing school. By that time I am quite certain that I'll be needing someone fulltime to be in charge of the newspaper that we'll be printing. I want to offer that position to Ion. I want him as my partner."

Rachel stared at Matthew. Of course the others likely did not fully appreciate the enormity of Matthew's offer. But she knew exactly what it meant to be offered to partner with a New York Bon-Hemmer. She suddenly had to remind herself to breathe.

"Now I know," Matthew continued speaking, "that it doesn't sound exactly fair that Ion should end up doing all the work while owning only half of the newspaper. But in time, if he likes that kind of work, I plan to offer to sell him my half of the business."

"'Tis more than fair, Matthew," Patrick murmured. "The question is whether or not ye're being fair to yeerself."

"Of course I am," Matthew replied lightly. "This sort of thing is done every day." Patrick eyed him closely, obviously unconvinced. "All I want," Matthew added, "is your permission."

Patrick drew in a thoughtful breath. "'Tis semthing we mist pray about. And also Ion mist be the one to make the final decision. Bit I really think thit ye yeerself ought to give sem more thought to it. It doesn't sound fair to ye."

Matthew eyed Patrick with a suddenly satisfied look on his face. "You know Patrick, if I hadn't been certain before, I know now beyond all doubt that I want to be in business with your family. You're a man who can be trusted to do what's right rather than what's simply convenient." He suddenly chuckled and lost his serious expressing. "If you're worried about money, I have plenty to spare. And I happen to agree with your wife and Mrs. Morrison about wanting a newspaper in Timberton. I may not make any money, but neither will I lose any. I plan to sell my half of the business after it begins to be a profitable business. I'll ask a price comparable to the amount of money that I'll be putting into it. No more—no less. I want a Timberton newspaper, but I really have no desire to be tied down for very long with such a business. However, I don't mind getting it started."

Rachel and Patrick exchanged glances, Rachel barely able to hold back her excitement. As they continued discussing the venture, fresh ideas popped out of each of them, causing Matthew to nod in thought, even a look of excited anticipation growing on his face.

Suddenly the door opened and in walked Elizabeth. Rachel caught her breath, wondering how the sound of the approaching wagon had escaped their notice. "Elizabeth," she whispered, rising to her feet.

The girl turned and smiled at her. Rachel held her breath, hoping. "I heard you," she said simply.

The next moment she and Rachel met each other in a warm embrace, Rachel not even attempting to hold back her tears. "Oh Elizabeth," she wept.

Georgy was in the house now, grinning and explaining that Mitch and Jennifer had already left, but asked that Art be sent home after school was out. "We tried to get back before today, so Bet and Jen wouldn't miss the first day of school. But it didn't work out that way."

The commotion had apparently reached the nursery, disturbing Calvin's sleep. When he began crying, Elizabeth lifted her head from Rachel's shoulder, a look of wonder creeping to her face. Together she and Rachel hurried into the nursery. Elizabeth reached into the crib and picked up the tiny boy into her arms. "I missed you, Callie," she murmured, kissing the little cheek. Carrying the crying baby into the living room, Elizabeth sat down in Rachel rocking chair, and patted the boy's back, rocking and soothing him. Rachel sat down on the chair next to them and simply drank in the sight of the girl.

After Calvin had quieted himself, deciding to go back to sleep in his sister's arms, Elizabeth turned back to Rachel. Her eyes were sparkling. "I'm so glad I can hear again," she began. "But I've got some even better news."

Rachel blinked. "Better news than being able to hear? Elizabeth, what could be better than that? Why, here I am trying to remember that I don't have to speak slowly to you. My sweet girl, you can hear! What could be better?"

Elizabeth's expression softened at Rachel's words. She smiled, saying softly, "I can see." Rachel fell silent, simply staring, uncertain. "When I was in the hospital, recovering from surgery, I had a lot of time to read. I didn't have any books with me. Mitch lent me his Bible, so I read that."

Rachel caught her breath, hardly daring to hope. "While I was reading it," Elizabeth continued, "the Lord opened up my eyes so I could see Him in the Bible and understand what He was saying. And for the first time in my life I saw Him as being completely holy and good. I could finally see who He is: exactly who He said He is—God in the flesh—my Lord and Savior. I know that you and Pat have been telling me that for years. But now I can see! I never really saw myself before either. All at once I saw that I was a sinner. I never felt so unclean in my whole life. And I never felt so far from God. All at once I wanted to be like Him."

Rachel reached over and laid her hand on Elizabeth's arm as tears began slipping down the girl's face. "One night I asked God to forgive me for being a sinner. And He did. He forgave me because the Lord Jesus paid for my sin when He died on the cross."

By now tears were slipping down Rachel's cheeks too. As she glanced into the kitchen, she saw Patrick standing in the doorway, his eyes glistening with unshed tears as well. "Thank Ye, Jesus," he murmured, "for saving m'daughter."

March of 1860 came, finding Elizabeth fifteen years old. Patrick mused silently as he sat in the living room, thinking how quickly his children were growing up. It seemed like only yesterday when Elizabeth had been a little girl in pigtails. He shifted his gaze to the kitchen doorway and listened to Mary and Elizabeth giggling at the table over some young ladies' amusement, no doubt. Elizabeth had taken to putting her hair up, as Mary did, rather than allow her braids to hang down against her back.

The sound of someone knocking on the door brought a quick end to Patrick's daydreaming. Rising to his feet, he crossed the living room and on through the kitchen. Opening up the door, he stepped back, allowing the teenage boy Timothy Holbert to enter. The young man stepped into the kitchen as Patrick greeted, "Come on in Timothy. 'Tis good to see ye, lad. And what brings ye out on a fine evening like this?"

Timothy shot a nervous glance over at the table where Mary and Elizabeth sat. "Uh—that is to say—" He fell silent then, and turned back to Patrick. Clearing his throat, he mumbled, "I was wondering if I might come calling on Elizabeth—sir," he added quickly.

Patrick blinked in surprise and glanced over at Elizabeth, whose eyes were opened wide, a stunned look on her face. Turning back to Timothy, Patrick said the only thing that came to his mind. "She's a bit young, I'm thinking, to start entertaining young men."

The boy nodded and spun around, dashing out of the door before Patrick could say anything else. He stared at the door the boy had hastily closed behind him, his mouth hanging open. Straightening, he turned back to the table, noticing that Elizabeth's cheeks had gone quite pink. Mary was glancing down at her hands that were carefully folded on the table. Without knowing what more to say, Patrick turned, retracing his steps to the living room and sat back down. Rachel met his gaze from where she sat in her rocking chair, darning a pile of sox. As he eased down onto the chair beside her, he murmured, "Hiv ye ever heard o'anything so foolish? Why, she's just a young lass."

Rachel smiled gently at him. "I know," she sighed. "But was it really foolish, or just unexpected?" Patrick stared at Rachel in shock that she should even suggest such a thing. "I know," she repeated. "I still see the long braids and the bare feet. I still see that little girl who used to hug her rag doll up to herself. But Patrick, that little girl doesn't go barefoot any more. Have you noticed? And that pile of rags she calls her doll has been packed away for a long time. Why, she's even started pinning her hair up. The little girl slipped away one day, leaving this lovely young woman in her place. You might not have noticed, but I assure you, the young men in this community surely have. I think you need to prepare a better speech than the one you gave Timothy. Like it or not, there'll be more coming."

Patrick let out his breath in a long sigh. "I didn't know thit 'er turning fifteen would make such a difference." Easing one side of his mouth up, he asked, "If we ask 'er, do ye think she'll go back to being a wee lassie again?"

Georgy and Patrick were busily splitting firewood as March drew to a close. A movement on the path leading to the house caught Georgy's eye. He leaned his axe against the chopping block he was using and grinned as he eyed yet another boy making his way toward the O'Riley house. "Here's another one, Pat," he murmured and crouched down, picking up the wood he had just split.

Patrick glanced over at the approaching Isaac Newman, who was a year younger than Georgy. By the determined look on his face, there was no doubt as to what he had come to discuss. Georgy grinned as Patrick sighed and simply waited for the boy to step up to them. Georgy busied himself in stacking the split wood, so as not to appear to be listening, but was careful not to get completely out of earshot.

"Isaac," Patrick greeted, extending his hand in greeting. As the two shook hands, Patrick added what was becoming his standard greeting to the teenage boys who were suddenly finding excuses to speak with him. "And what brings ye to the O'Riley's on such a fine day?"

With a little too cocky of a stance, Georgy was certain, Isaac eyed Patrick steadily and said straight out, "I've come to court your daughter."

"Hiv ye now?" Patrick asked. Georgy turned his face as a grin shot to his lips. As long as it appeared that he was not listening, the two would likely not step away for privacy. It was all Georgy could do not to laugh. He had always known that Patrick was easy going, except when it came to the ladies of his family.

Suddenly Isaac seemed to realize that the bold approach was not winning him any favors with Patrick. "With your permission, that is. Sir."

"Well laddie," Patrick replied in a long, drawn out manner. Again Georgy turned his face and tried not to laugh as Patrick used the word laddie. "I'm sorry, bit the answer is no. Lizzy is a Christian. She'll only be in the company o'lads who are also Christians. And ye make no claim as being one."

Isaac frowned, clearly unprepared for this line of argument. He nodded and turned around. Taking a few steps, he seemed to remember his manners, and called over his shoulder, "Thank you for your time sir."

"Ye're welcome lad," Patrick replied.

Only then did Georgy return to his chopping block. He grinned at Patrick who rolled his eyes. "Georgy," he murmured, shaking his head. "It's getting so I dread seeing a teenage lad."

Georgy laughed and set a piece of wood on the chopping block. "Just be thankful that everybody knows that Mary's already claimed, or there'd be twice the amount coming. Besides, you won't have to go through this again for another nine years." At Patrick's stunned look, he added with a chuckle, "That's when Annie will be fifteen."

"Ah lad!" Patrick groaned. "Don't even be thinking it!"

"They're nice boys!" Elizabeth insisted, an angry note in her voice as she glared at Patrick as he sat in the living room reading the Timberton newspaper. He had lowered the paper some moments earlier to give her his full attention. If he had been surprised by the first boy who had asked to come calling on Elizabeth, he was doubly shocked by Elizabeth's anger over his refusals to the boys. "Why can't they come courting?"

"Tell me," he replied quietly, "Would ye consider marrying a man who wis not a Christian?"

She shrugged. "I don't know. I suppose it would depend on what sort of a man he was."

"'E would be an unsaved man. 'E would be opposed to the things o'the Lord."

Her frown deepened. "Not every unsaved person is!"

He studied her in silence for a moment, breathing out a prayer for wisdom in what to say. "Then why are they still unsaved?" he asked gently. "The Lord said thit inyone who comes to 'Im 'E will not cast out.[vii] If they are not opposed to the things o'God, then surely semthing is wrong if they are not saved."

Her cheeks deepened in color, her eyes flashing. "It's not fair being a preacher's daughter. Gramps would've let those boys come courting me!"

Patrick winced. In all of their years together as a family, neither Georgy nor Elizabeth had made reference to what Jed would or would not have allowed them to do if he had still been the parent figure in their lives. He and Rachel had anticipated such, but it had never come. Now that it had, Patrick realized that no amount of preparation could have helped to ease the shrieking pain of those slashing words. "Aye, thit may be," he said quietly. "Bit I am yeer father now. And I am the one who decides who will and who will not come calling on ye."

"You just don't understand!" she cried out and spun around, half screaming, "I wish you'd never become my pa!" She did not stop until she had run outside and slammed the door behind her.

Patrick stared at the closed door, too stunned to say anything. It was then that he realized that Rachel had stepped over to him, her hand softly caressing his cheek. "It's her age talking, not her heart."

He met her gaze and reached up, taking her hand into his. "Aye, I know." He pushed his lips up into a smile, seeing the hurt for him in her eyes. "I'm all right, lassie."

"You didn't deserve those words. You're such a good father. And she didn't really mean what she said. You know that, don't you?"

He dipped his head in a nod. Somehow he had to relieve her mind that he was all right. But the pain that those words had brought him was nearly taking his breath away. He had only wanted to protect Elizabeth. Rachel leaned down and softly kissed his cheek. "I love you, Patrick," she whispered. "I'll go and have a talk with her," she added as she straightened back up. "Would you keep an eye on Pattie and the boys?"

He nodded. "Aye." As she turned and stepped over to the doorway, he called out quietly, "Rachel?" She turned and met his gaze with such love for him in her eyes that his smile became genuine. "Thank ye."

Rachel found Elizabeth down by the river, sitting on a patch of bare ground the remaining winter snow had melted from. Her head was buried in her upraised knees and she was sobbing as if her heart was breaking. Easing down beside her, Rachel murmured, "He loves you, you know."

"No he doesn't," she wept. "He doesn't care at all!"

"You'd never say that if you had seen the look on his face after you left. You really hurt him."

Only then did Elizabeth lift her head. She brushed at the tears on her cheeks. The look of anger was still in her face, but not as intensely as before. She frowned and lowered her eyes, muttering, "I didn't mean to."

Slipping her arm around the girl's shoulders, Rachel sighed, "I know. And I told him so." Drawing Elizabeth closer to her, she continued speaking. "My father didn't allow many boys to court me either. Although his reasons were different from Patrick's, still the result was the same. I too felt rebellious and lashed out at my father. I said things I didn't really mean. They were such cruel words. I'd give anything to have never spoken those hurtful words, now that he's gone. I can never take them back. I love my father. But once spoken, no words can be recaptured. They remain spoken for eternity. No one can erase the past. Words that have been said can be forgiven, but not unspoken."

They were silent for several minutes. Finally Elizabeth asked, "Is that why you came out here, to tell me that?"

"Yes," Rachel replied simply. "And I also wanted to talk about you and those boys who want to come courting." She paused, but when Elizabeth made no attempt at replying, she continued onward. "When you became a Christian, your whole life changed. Being a Christian means much more than being saved from Hell. It's a new way of life. You begin living for the Lord, trying to do only those things that will please Him. He is your joy. He is your reason for living. Everything you do, you do it as if you were doing it for Him alone. Your every act, word and thought become worship."

Rachel sighed and continued speaking quietly. "But an unsaved man—no matter how much he loved you—could never understand that. He doesn't do anything for the Lord. Although he may do things that we consider good and noble, God says that whatever we do apart from faith is sin.[viii] Without faith it isn't even possible to please God.[ix]" She paused, waiting for Elizabeth to comment.

Elizabeth remained silent, so Rachel continued. "Don't you understand? Nothing that the unsaved man does is acceptable to God. We are acceptable only through the blood of Christ. But everything the Christian does is to be done for God's glory. A marriage between a Christian and an unsaved person is the same as two people going in opposite directions. If you married an unsaved man, all of those things that you count dear are the very things that he is rejecting. Never could you share with him your joy in the Lord. Never. And when hard times come, he isn't going to join you in seeking the Lord for help. And when you get angry with each other, do you honestly think he's going to use Biblical principals to make for peace?"

By then Elizabeth was studying Rachel closely. The look of anger was gone, leaving a pale, shaken face behind. "But just because a boy comes courting," she said quietly, "doesn't mean that I'm going to marry him. I'd just have a nice time."

"But courting is the first step toward marriage."

"But it doesn't have to be," she insisted, pain in her tone.

Rachel studied the face of the girl before her. It had not been such a long time ago that she herself had posed such arguments with her father. "Is it worth taking the risk of spending the rest of your life married to a man who despises your Lord?" she asked gently.

"You don't understand either," she muttered, glancing away again

"Don't I?" Rachel suddenly chuckled, bringing Elizabeth's startled eyes back upon her. "Do you think that it was easy to turn down Paul Thompson's offer of marriage?"

Elizabeth's eyes opened wide in surprise. "When did he ask you to marry him?"

Rachel drew in a deep breath, recalling that sad day, five years ago. "The day my father died," she said quietly. "He wanted Anna Marie to have a mother. He could have given me the kinds of luxuries that I was used to. We even could have gone back East, and lived in Boston for the rest of our lives. I could've had my old life back."

Elizabeth frowned in thought. "But you preferred Pat!"

Rachel smiled. The girl might be angry with Patrick, but here she sat defending him. "Your memory is terribly poor if you think that." Rachel ignored the hurt that her words were causing her own heart in dredging up the memory of the terrible way she had treated Patrick early on. "Don't you remember how badly I treated him at first? Why, I despised him and his entire race."

"Then why—" Elizabeth fell silent before voicing her entire thought.

"As much as I despised Patrick, I still recognized that it would be better to marry him than to marry even the finest unsaved man. Paul could have given me every luxury that money could buy. Patrick could not. But he loved the Lord. And that is more important than anything else."

Elizabeth turned back to stare out across the river, thinking over Rachel's words. Rachel finally asked quietly, "Do you wish that you weren't a Christian?"

Turning back to Rachel in shock, Elizabeth cried out, "No!"

Rachel smiled and patted the girl's back. "You know," she added, "just because a man is a Christian, it still doesn't mean that he will make a good husband for you. You have to use wisdom even in marrying a Christian."

She suddenly looked perplexed, asking, "Doesn't that narrow the pickings down even more?"

Rachel laughed and nodded. "I suppose so. But God is faithful. If He wants you to get married, He will send the right man to you. I'm so thankful I didn't marry the wrong man. I would've lost out on Patrick—the man God created for me."

Elizabeth sighed and lowered her gaze again, murmuring, "I guess I owe Pat an apology."

"I guess so," Rachel replied quietly. She made no attempt to follow Elizabeth as she rose to her feet and turned back to the house. She remained sitting at the river's edge for several minutes, praying that Elizabeth would find the words to mend Patrick's heart which she had broken. By the time she returned to the house, Patrick was sitting at the kitchen table. His smile spoke volumes to her, assuring her that Elizabeth had apologized. Life would go back to normal, whatever normal was.

Patrick sighed as another boy stepped up to him, this time just as he was leaving Matthew's store. "Good afternoon, Pastor O'Riley," the boy greeted, smiling.

Patrick dipped his head in a nod. "Good afternoon Randy. And what brings ye out on such a fine April day as this?"

"Well sir, I know you've turned down a lot of the boys—all of them so far. But I've come to ask for your permission to call on Elizabeth."

Patrick dipped his head in a reluctant nod. "Aye," he sighed. "Ye hiv m'permission."

Randy blinked in surprise. "I do? Why?"

Patrick began chuckling then. "One reason, Mr. Parker: Ye love the Lord. I've watched ye grow in the Lord ever since ye asked 'Im to be yeer Savior." He paused, adding in amusement, "Bit now ye hiv to do the hard part—asking Lizzie for 'er permission."

The boy nodded, suddenly looking a little less confidant. Patrick dipped his head in a nod and continued walking home, but he could not help but sigh, wishing it had only been the unsaved boys who had asked to come calling. But Randy's testimony rang true, leaving Patrick no choice but to give his permission. He was a fine young man after all.

The days passed quickly enough, bringing the long anticipated evening for Elizabeth. Randy and Elizabeth chatted in the vacated living room while Rachel, Patrick and Jed sat at the kitchen table trying to ignore them. The rest of the children had been instructed to remain in their rooms, allowing for a little bit of privacy, though not too much, for the couple. Patrick found his eyes darting repeatedly at the doorway. "Maybe we should serve them sem more refreshments," he murmured.

Rachel giggled and shook her head. "I only just took in hot chocolate ten minutes ago. Dear oh dear, but you are nervous."

Patrick rolled his eyes. Nervous was not the word he would have chosen. By the time Randy left that evening, Patrick was not sorry to see him go. He ignored the amusement in Rachel's eyes, wondering if he would be able to get through another evening of courting.

The next morning, after the children had left for school, but before Georgy had gone over to the Morrisons, Mitch burst into the kitchen. A troubled expression rested on his face, though he did not attempt to explain it. The conversation drifted from one topic to another as the adults all sat around the table enjoying their coffee. "It jest don't seem possible," Jed sighed, shaking his head, "that Bet be growd up and entertainin' beaus."

Mitch shot a rather annoyed look over at Patrick and grumbled, "I don't know what you were thinking, letting Randy come courting. Why, Elizabeth is just a little girl—Jen's age!"

Patrick glanced over at Georgy, wondering at the surprised look of amusement that crossed his face over Mitch's words.

Patrick turned back to Mitch. "I understand completely," he murmured, thinking how hard it had been to give his permission for Randy—or any boy for that matter—to court his little girl. "Bit, she is fifteen, after all."

"Just a baby," Mitch muttered.

Again Georgy's eyes began dancing. Patrick could not hold back a grin, though he was not certain what was causing the boy's amusement. "As I recall," Patrick added, trying to keep the laughter out of his voice, but realized that he had not accomplished his aim entirely, "ye were only sixteen when we met ye. And ye thought of yeerself as a man—just one year older then Lizzie is now."

"That was different," Mitch muttered. "I had a family I was responsible for. I had no choice but to grow up fast. But neither Elizabeth nor Jen has had to face anything like that. They're still children—nothing has forced them to grow up before their time. How could you let a boy court her?"

Jed cleared his throat, replying comfortingly, "Now don't ya be a worrying, thinking about your sister's wanting boys to come calling on her too. You can always tell 'em no."

"I will," Mitch insisted. "But you've sure made my job a lot harder by letting her best friend entertain gentlemen callers." He pushed out his breath and rose to his feet, muttering, "I got things to do." And with that, he strode across the floor and stepped outside.

The moment he was gone, Georgy burst out laughing. Rachel turned to him, saying in a reproving tone, "You shouldn't laugh about him being worried about Jennifer."

Georgy only laughed the harder. Patrick stared hard at him, wondering. Finally sobering down enough to speak, Georgy explained, "He's not worried about Jen. He's jealous."

"Jealous?" Rachel cried out. "About what?"

Patrick began grinning as the pieces of the puzzle began falling into place. "Well," Georgy sighed out in amusement, "if you'd heard him at the hospital going on and on about Bet not being a little girl, even though that's what I called her, you'd be getting my meaning."

Rachel stared in shock. "He's jealous because Randy came calling on Elizabeth? Mitch? But—but she's only fifteen and he's—"

"Twenty," Georgy chuckled. "Only five years difference. My pappy was seven years older than my ma'am—my mother," he corrected himself, choosing to let his little-boy name for his mother fall away.

"Yep," Jed sighed out. "That be true. My grandson found hisself a sweet little thing that was closer to eight years younger than he was. They had them a good marriage."

Rachel turned and met Patrick's gaze, a look of wonder growing on her face. "I wonder if she knows," she breathed out.

"I wonder if 'e 'imself knows," Patrick chuckled. "Thit lad is likely to be the last one to know thit 'e's in love."

Rachel shifted Calvin to her left arm, bouncing him on her hip as he fussed. With her free hand she stirred the soup she was preparing for lunch. The thin wail of Andrew reached her ears from the nursery. "Pattie!" she called out, "give your brother his bear to hold until I can come."

"Aye Mamma!" the nearly-turned-three-year-old called back.

Rachel smiled and continued bouncing Calvin up and down to quiet him. "I'm so glad school will be out for the summer in just one week," she murmured to the fussy baby. "I'm nearly lost without your sisters around to help."

Before she finished with the soup, Patrick stepped out into the kitchen from the study, where he had been preparing Sunday's sermon. Apparently he had made a stop in the nursery. In his arms was the squalling Andrew, fighting against his father's arms. Calvin stopped crying then and turned to look at his noisy brother. Patrick carried Andrew over to Rachel and let the boys get a look at each other. Calvin reached out for Andrew, drawing his attention from whatever it was that was annoying him. Suddenly he too fell silent.

"He doesn't want anything," Rachel murmured. "He just wants to be held. So does Calvin. But I can only hold one at a time when I'm cooking."

Patrick grinned and carried Andrew over to the table and sat down. "'Tis a good time for a break inyway," he murmured and he gently bounced the baby in his arms. Rachel drew in a deep breath, grateful that Patrick was home that day.

The outside door opened then and in stepped a nervous looking Mitch, hat in hand. Rachel glanced at him over her shoulder and simply stared, wondering. "Coffee?" she asked.

"Ah—no," he replied uncertainly. "I mean, no, what I've got to say won't take long."

"Sit down Mitch," Patrick invited. As Mitch complied, Patrick asked, "So what kin I do for ye?"

Mitch cleared his throat. "Well Patrick," he began uncertainly. Rachel turned around and gave the two her full attention, wondering. "I—uh—" He sighed. "Well, that's to say—" Again he stopped speaking. "The truth is—well—you see—awe Patrick, can I come courting Elizabeth?"

Rachel bit down on the corner of her mouth. Patrick, however, was not doing such a good job in hiding his amusement. He was openly grinning. Taking a deep breath, as if thoroughly considering the matter, he finally began speaking slowly. "Well, Mitch, ye hiv m'permission. Bit now ye'll hiv to get Lizzie's."

At first Mitch simply stared at him. Suddenly a smile dashed to his lips. Jumping to his feet, he held out his hand and began pumping Patrick's arm in a hearty handshake. "Thank you Patrick!" Without another word he retraced his steps and vanished outside.

The moment the door closed behind him, Patrick burst out laughing. "What a lad!" he chuckled.

"Lad?" Rachel giggled. "Why Patrick O'Riley, you were only a year older than he is now when you married me!"

Patrick's mouth fell open as he stared at her in shock. Then he smiled sheepishly, explaining, "Bit I seemed mich, mich older at the time." His eyes twinkled as he spoke.

Rachel nodded. "Yes, much older." The next moment they were both laughing.

It was then that Matthew opened the door and stepped inside. Rachel glanced over at him in surprise since he was one of the few who normally knocked before coming in. "I just met Mitch leaving, and he told me to come right in. He said you weren't busy."

"'E wis right. And ye know thit ye're always welcome. Ye're part o'the O'Riley family, Matthew."

Rachel smiled in amusement over the fact that a Bon-Hemmer was being included in the family O'Riley. As he sat down at the table, his face fairly glowed. He met Rachel's gaze and motioned for her to join them. She smiled and sat down beside Patrick, shifting Calvin to her lap where he had a better view of Andrew who was playing on Patrick's lap.

"I've finally done it," Matthew began, excitement ringing in his voice. "I've made preparations for a telegraph office to come to Timberton."

"A link to the civilized world!" Rachel cried out before taking time to think. She rolled her eyes over at Patrick, who grinned at her in amusement.

Turning back to Matthew, Patrick asked, "Will it be strung in time for the presidential election?"

"By all means," Matthew assured him. "Why that's not until November and this is only the end of May. He paused then and drew in a deep breath. Rachel wondered if this were a mere dramatic pause, or one of indecision as to how best to proceed with what he had come to say. "It's only a week until Ion graduates," he finally said.

"Yes," Rachel replied with a smile of pride over Ion. "He's studied hard."

"He'll be taking over his half of the newspaper right after graduation," Matthew continued.

Patrick grinned. "The lad won't let us forget it. 'E doesn't stop talking about it. 'E really loves the newspaper business."

"Good," Matthew sighed out. Taking another deep breath, he asked, "Is Johnny graduating too?"

"You know he is," Rachel murmured, frowning in thought. "He spends half of his time at your store. I can't imagine he hasn't told you a hundred times that he's graduating."

"He's been a help to me with my bookkeeping," Matthew said with a nod. "I don't know what I'd do without him, actually. You see, I've never had a mind for business, but Johnny takes to it naturally."

Rachel and Patrick exchanged puzzled glances before turning back to Matthew. By his amused expression, the man clearly had something more on his mind than he was saying. "Out with it, Matthew," Patrick finally said.

The man smiled and squared his shoulders. "I want him to come and work for me. He can run the telegraph office. And, more importantly, he can oversee my finances. What with the store and the newspaper office, and now the telegraph office, beside some other ventures I'm planning on, I really need him."

"But—but he's only fourteen years old," Rachel stammered.

Matthew eyed her candidly, asking, "How old was your father when he took over a portion of his family's business?"

Rachel rolled her eyes. "I see that Johnny has been talking to you about it. And you clearly already know the answer to that question. All right, Papa was no older than Johnny is now, but it was different in his time," she added quickly.

"How?" Matthew asked simply, amusement in his eyes.

Rachel looked at him sternly, wondering just how long Matthew had prepared himself for this conversation. "Think of all the opportunities we have today that weren't available when my father was young."

Matthew fell silent for a few moments, but was clearly not even slightly ruffled. "You're talking about things that exist in the East. But Johnny has already learned all he can in Timberton's educational system. Are you planning on sending him away to further his education? Or are you planning on having him become a farmer? Or maybe a lumberman?"

Again Rachel turned to Patrick. He smiled at her, allowing the burden on her shoulders to slip over to his own. "Matthew," he said, turning back to the man, "we appreciate yeer offer. Bit we'll hiv to give it sem thought and pray about it. The truth is, we hiv not made iny plans for the lad. We simply hiv not been able to find a solution to his problem of graduating at fourteen in a community with no further education available."

Matthew nodded. "That's fair enough. But I want you to understand that I'm not doing this to help Johnny out as much as I'm doing it for myself." Rachel rolled her eyes again. "Seriously!" Matthew argued. "I really need him. He has a tremendous gift for business. And, I might as well tell you now as later—If he comes to work for me, I want him to become my vice-president."

"Vice-president of what?" Patrick asked.

"For the bank I'm planning on starting up. But without him there'll be no bank. I couldn't start one up without him. And as far as his other jobs, of course he'll have the authority to hire and train as many helpers as he needs."

Rachel sat staring at the man, dumbfounded. Suddenly no one was talking, but simply sipping thoughtfully on their coffee. "Dear oh dear," she sighed, "my brother a bank vice-president!"

Ion glanced over his shoulder, but the other children were still in the schoolyard, playing an improvised game of softball. As he and Mary walked along toward home, he decided to broach the subject she had been hinting at for some time. "You know I want to marry you," he began slowly, causing her to look him full in the face. "But not yet."

She frowned slightly, asking, "Why not? You're graduating in a week!"

"I know, Mary," he replied in as patient of a tone as he could manage, wondering why she did not understand. "I can't provide for you yet. I don't even have a cabin built for us. All I have is a wagon and team of horses my pa left me. We're going to have to wait."

He had seen her eyes flash in anger a couple of times, but never when directed toward him. He frowned at the flashing eyes that bore into him now. "If you don't want to marry me, just say so! Don't start making excuses!"

Clamping his mouth shut, he turned back to stare straight ahead, refusing to say another thing. Mary hurried on ahead of him and he let her, making no attempt to catch up with her. She entered the house a full twenty seconds ahead of him. By the time he stepped inside, she was nowhere in sight, but Rachel was. And she was studying him, a disturbed look on her face. "Ion, what's wrong with Mary?"

Ion's frown grew. "What'd she say?"

"She said something about never speaking to you again." Motioning toward the table, she murmured, "Sit down. Tell me what happened."

He sighed deeply, trying to decide whether or not to comply with Rachel's wishes. She had not said it as an order, but simply as a request. Lowering himself to one of the chairs, he waited until Rachel had seated herself as well. For once there was no baby in her arms. "I told her that we can't get married for awhile."

"Married?" she asked in surprise. "Have you been talking about marriage already?"

He nodded. "I told her that we can't get married until I can provide for her and have a cabin for us to live in. But she got all mad and doesn't believe I love her!"

"Do you love her?" Rachel asked gently.

Ion nodded. "You know I do. But Rachel, love isn't enough! My pa married my ma before he could provide for her. Then he started leading wagon trains West. My ma had to work in a saloon to take care of herself and me. It was too much for her and she died! I'm not going to put Mary through that, even if she doesn't understand!"

Rachel reached over and laid her hand on Ion's. "You're right," she murmured. At the look of relief that washed over Ion's eyes, she smiled. "Did you tell Mary all of that?"

"No," he replied in his tone that suggested he was done discussing the matter. "It should be enough that I say we aren't getting married yet. I don't have to tell her why. She ought to trust me enough without knowing why I make my decisions."

Rachel squeezed his hand, a look of intense love for him in her eyes. "Marriage is something you have to work at. You can't expect your partner to think and feel the same way that you do. Everyone is different. That's why it's so important to talk things out and explain your thoughts and decisions. Why, if I was Mary, I'd probably be thinking that you really don't want to get married— or that you've become interested in someone else."

He looked shocked. "She should know better than that!"

"Why? She doesn't know what your reasons are for wanting to wait, because you never told her why—the real reason why. She needs to know the full reason. Otherwise, whatever you say is just going to sound like an excuse to her."

He leaned back puzzling over Rachel's words. He suddenly began wondering how it really had seemed to Mary. Had he hurt her? Rising to his feet, he gently pulled his hand from Rachel's, murmuring, "Thank you Rachel." Leaving his books on the table, he crossed into the living room and called out quietly as he stepped up to the girls' bedroom. "Mary?"

She poked her head through the curtained doorway and met his gaze. There were tears in her eyes. "Will you come for a walk with me?"

She nodded, but made no attempt at speaking. Together they walked back to the kitchen and out the door. Ion was at a loss as to what to say. Finally he slipped his hand into hers, something he did only rarely now, since Patrick had told him that he should not be holding the hand of a girl he had not had permission to court. But even Patrick allowed it when the situation called for comforting Mary. Ion judged this to be one of those times. Mary lifted her eyes to him then as they walked along in silence.

"Mary I love you so much," he murmured, trying to figure out the words that would make her understand that he was just trying to protect her. "The only thing in this world that could possibly keep me from marrying you even today is your own well being. Mary, I don't have any money to buy you food. I don't have a home for you to live in. My pa didn't much care that he didn't have anything to offer my ma when he married her. He just thought about himself, so he married her and expected her to look after her own needs. She had to work in a saloon, Mary! It was the only way she could find to make a living! She died before her time, because my pa didn't take care of her. I won't let that happen to you Mary! Not for any reason!"

They had by that time stopped walking. Mary's gaze was locked in his, a look of love shining in her eyes. She squeezed his hand then. "All right, Ion," she murmured. "It's all right. I'll wait. I didn't understand."

He smiled back at her. Rachel had been right. Suddenly he realized that he had an awful lot to learn before he was ready to become a husband. It clearly was not as easy as Patrick and Rachel made it look like.

Rachel smiled at the children as they poured into the house from school, each of them talking and grabbing for their after-school-snack of bread and jam. "It's not fair," Elizabeth muttered as she reached for her piece of bread. "Johnny gets to graduate at fourteen. But I'm fifteen and Mrs. Shaleman won't let me!"

"Georgy was nearly seventeen when he graduated," Rachel replied. "And Ion is four month away from being eighteen. I've talked to your teacher. She is confident that if you work very hard, you'll be graduating next year."

"I supposed," she replied sadly.

"Mitch was over today," Rachel said lightly.

Instantly Elizabeth swung her gaze back to Rachel. "Oh?" she asked.

Rachel hid her smile over the girl's attempt to hide her interest. "M-hm."

"What did he want?" she said quietly.

Rachel finally smiled, admitting, "I really shouldn't tell you. I think he should tell you himself."

"Tell me," she said breathlessly, suddenly not trying to hide her interest.

Taking a deep breath, she finally replied, "He asked Patrick for permission to come courting."

"Mary?" she asked nervously.

Giggling then, Rachel shook her head. "No, silly. You."

Only then did Elizabeth smile. Turning toward the living room doorway, she muttered, "It's about time!"

Chapter 10

Rachel studied the peaceful face of Andrew as she sat in her rocking chair. He had only just given in to sleep. His face looked so much like Patrick's. She was certain that he was an exact copy of Patrick as a baby, with the exception of Andrew's dark hair which he had inherited from her. Her mind drifted over the events of the past summer and fall. Life had picked up a speed that refused to slow down. So many things had changed.

Once Mitch had finally begun calling on Elizabeth regularly, the neighborhood boys gave up asking for permission to court her, growing weary of being refused either by Patrick or Elizabeth herself. Rachel chuckled quietly as she thought about the fact that Mitch now spent more time at the O'Riley home than at his own. More often than not, he brought Art and Jennifer with him, whenever they were not in school. He did not, however bring them along on an official courting night. Since this was Elizabeth's last year in school, there was little doubt but that eventually she and Mitch would be looking to get married. Rachel was hoping that she and Mitch would wait until Elizabeth turned eighteen, but that would not be for two and a half years. She sighed, thinking of the good choice Elizabeth was making in choosing her future husband. Her chief concern was that this young couple did not rush into marriage before Elizabeth became a grown woman.

Although it had not come as a surprise, Ion had quickly taken over the newspaper office upon graduating from the eighth grade. Rachel's eyes shifted to the Timberton Newspaper Patrick was holding up as he sat in the chair next to Rachel's rocking chair, having snatched a few minutes to peruse the paper. She had been thrilled with the paper Matthew had turned out when he had first started up the newspaper. She shook her head in Motherly pride over the fact that once Ion had stepped in as the editor, the paper had taken a major leap forward in professionalism. Where the young man had learned the art of journalism was a mystery to Rachel, other than the fact that Matthew had seen to it that Ion received every newspaper he happened to lay his hands on. Though she and Matthew, as well as Angela and Sarah had coached him on various aspects of journalism, Rachel was convinced that Ion had taught himself by carefully studying the newspapers Matthew gave him.

She smiled as she thought of Mary. There was no doubt but that she and Ion would get married, as soon as Ion could provide for her. Rachel and Patrick had spoken long on the matter with each other. They could think of no one they would have given in marriage to either of them than each other. Rachel could not imagine learning to get along without Mary's helpful hands and happy smile. It had taken awhile, but once the girl had become accustomed to feeling safe and loved, as a member of the O'Riley family, her smile had returned, brightening up all of their lives.

"Georgy," she sighed and the rolled her eyes, muttering to herself, "I mean George." Patrick lowered the newspaper and grinned over at her. "Dear oh dear, I can never call him that." They both chuckled quietly as she continued rocking Andrew and as Patrick returned his attention to the article he was reading. Phil and Sarah had been calling him by the name of George for some time. At eighteen, the boy was entitled to use his manly name rather than his boyhood name, but even after he had announced to the family that from then on he wished to be called George, Rachel simply had been unable to comply. Although the younger members of their family seemed to have little trouble in doing so, when it suited them, neither she, Patrick nor Jed seemed to think of using the word until the name Georgy had already slipped past their teeth. "Well, I'm your mother, young man," she murmured to the absent Georgy. "And I'll call you Georgy if I wish to." The look of amusement on his face whenever she said his old name assured her that he was not offended. However, he made certain that when he went on rounds with Dr. Morrison, he used the name of George rather than Georgy.

He seemed to spend nearly every waking moment studying Phil's medical books or treating patients at the Morrison clinic, which was still on the Morrison's property, though finally was housed in a building of its own rather than in the spare bedroom of the Morrison cabin.

Choosing Johnny's future had been harder than that of the others. Graduating from the eighth grade at fourteen was no rare feat, back in Boston. But there he would have continued on in higher education rather than be expected to start up with his adult work. Another sigh escaped Rachel at the thought of eighth grade being the highest education level Timberton had to offer. She and Patrick had spent so much time in prayer over the matter, Patrick teased her that they could now be given the Biblical nickname of camel-knees, kneeling in prayer over Johnny's future as much as they had. Finally they had given him their consent to work for Matthew, just as the man had outlined the work opportunity for the boy back in May.

Although Joshua had turned fourteen in August, he was still attending school, so his plans for the future did not have to be decided on completely just yet. Johnny had, however, hired him to work part time at the telegraph office, running errands and delivering telegrams. "John," Rachel murmured, shaking her head. Again Patrick glanced over at her, his eyes dancing in amusement. "Even if I could bring myself to call Georgy George, I am not going to call Johnny John!" Patrick laughed openly and then returned his attention to the newspaper. Rachel recalled how Johnny had insisted that if Georgy could now be called George, than he too should be called by the name of John, he being a working man now.

A quick knock on the kitchen door brought Patrick to his feet. As he crossed the floor, Rachel glanced over at the rarely used living room door that led out onto her porch. Mainly that door seemed only to be used by Rachel herself, Elizabeth and Mary, and the ladies they invited to join them for tea. When Patrick opened the door, Joshua stepped in, looking serious, though not upset. He had made it a practice to knock whenever he was on official business for his job, even though this was his home. Rachel hid the smile that wanted to blossom on her lips over the boy's behavior. Solemnly Joshua handed a folded piece of paper to Patrick. "You have a telegram," he said.

"Thank ye lad," Patrick replied with a nod as he reached for the paper. Rachel noticed that he too was careful not to smile, but to conduct himself in a business sort of way. But she was certain that his eyes were dancing in amusement. As he silently read the message, Joshua turned and stepped back outside.

"Rachel!" Patrick called out, causing Andrew to jump. Rachel soothed him back to sleep as Patrick returned to his chair. Holding up the telegram for her to see, but not close enough for her to read, he smiled, saying, "Mr. Lincoln won the election."

She smiled back at him and nodded, but began chewing her lower lip in thought. He made no comment, but simply waited for her to formulate her thoughts. Finally she asked, "What do you think will happen now? What effect will this have on the South?"

This was not the first time this issue had been discussed. All during the campaigning months they had debated this very issue. But now that it had happened—the man the South was apposed to, soon to be assuming the mantle of the President—the discussion was no longer a matter to simply be debated. It was now a matter they would be reading about in the very newspaper Patrick held in his hands.

"Well," Patrick sighed, "if Timberton is a model o'what the entire country is, 'tis far frim over. Why, I never expected to see tempers unleashed as they hiv been these past several months. 'Tis nearly impossible to be neutral these days, as far as issues pertaining to the North and the South go. Semhow, we hiv to find common ground."

"But we haven't even been able to do that in Timberton! If we can't do that in a town that started out as friends banning together, how is this nation going to do it, when the North and the South have been as divided as much as the East is from the West?"

"Well," Patrick sighed, "Johnny will be kept busy at the telegraph office for sure now, getting the news. And Ion will be kept busy writing it in the newspaper." He shook his head. "And both Sam and I'll be kept busy trying to make peace in town."

Georgy stepped into Matthew's store and glanced around tentatively. Ever since Abraham Lincoln had announced his candidacy for president, tempers from former Southerners had clashed with equally angry settlers who had come from the North. It paid, these days, to discover the lay of the land before entering the store. He sighed as he caught sight of Keith Baker studying the farm implements Matthew had stocked at the far end of the store. He had seen little of Keith lately. The sixteen-year-old had dropped out of school to join his father in farming some months ago and seldom came to town any more.

Georgy shrugged and closed the door behind him and then headed for the counter. Matthew shifted his gaze from Georgy over to Keith and back to Georgy. Georgy shrugged, murmuring, "Has Phil's order come in yet?"

Matthew nodded and reached beneath the counter for a parcel. As Georgy reached for it, Keith turned and glared over at him. "Northwood!" he growled, striding over to Georgy. "I told you once before that I don't want you courting either one of my sisters!"

"I'm not, Keith," Georgy replied quietly. "Not any more."

Keith's eyes blazed. "You callin' me a liar?" he demanded hotly. "Jeremiah Mannings told me he saw you talking to Katherine last week! You denying it?"

"No, I'm not denying it. We were talking—not courting."

Keith raised his fisted right hand to Georgy's face. "You yellow bellied Southerner! You stay away from my sisters, or I'll kill you! You hear me?"

Georgy drew in a deep, steadying breath. "I hear you. But there's no cause to be talking this way. I don't want to fight you, Keith."

"Yellow bellied, just like I said."

Georgy clamped his mouth shut and turned, carrying the parcel to the door, calling over his shoulder, "Phil will settle up his bill with you later, Matthew."

"All right George," Matthew replied quietly.

Georgy stepped out of the store and headed for Phil's clinic, gripping his jaws together. "God?" he prayed silently. "How do I avoid fighting with a man who's set and determined to fight me? Show me what to do, Lord."

For the rest of the day, Georgy treated patients at Phil's side with his mind only half on what he was doing. Finally Phil called him aside and eyed him closely. "George," he said sternly, "go home."

Georgy blinked in surprise. "You firing me?" he asked.

One side of the man's mouth crept up at Georgy's question. Clapping him on the back, he shook his head. "No. But your mind isn't on medicine today. How long has it been since you had a day off?"

"Since Sunday," he said simply, puzzling over his friend and teacher's words.

Phil chuckled. "As I recall, we fixed Tom Carmon's broken leg on Sunday."

Georgy nodded. "Oh yeah, we did. I saw him yesterday. He's getting on fine."

Again Phil laughed and shook his head. "Go home, George. Take the rest of the day off. No studying. No doctoring. Just take the day off. Tomorrow too. Take the rest of the week off."

"Why?"

Phil studied him closely. "You need some time off, George. I recognize the signs. Why, you're still only eighteen years old! You're putting in a full day's work here at the clinic, six days a week. You're on call twenty-four hours a day."

"So are you, Phil."

He dipped his head in a nod. "I am. But I'm not also studying to get into medical school. You are. I'm not faced with the decisions of how I'm going to spend the rest of my life. I've already made those decisions. But you've got all of them to make yet. And the way this nation is going, you've got some hard choices to make in a short amount of time. You take the rest of this week off. I don't want to see your face until Sunday morning—and only then at church. Don't come back to the clinic until Monday. But," he added with a grin, "you make that bright and early Monday morning. I'm going to be hard pressed doing without you these next few days."

"Well," Georgy sighed and slowly nodded. "If you say so. But if you need me, you'll send for me?"

"Agreed. But I'll make sure I don't need you! Unless there's an emergency Sarah and I can't handle alone, you're off duty until Monday morning." Nodding toward the door, he added, "Get out of here."

Georgy grinned and stepped across the floor. Grabbing his coat, he stepped outside into the wintry day. Suddenly his shoulders felt a little bit lighter, convincing him that Phil was right, he really was in need of a few days off—a few days to think and pray.

The moment he stepped into the house, Patrick's eyes were upon him as he and Jed sat at the table for an early afternoon cup of coffee. Rachel was busy at the stove, her back to him. "What is it lad?" Patrick asked, concern in his voice. Rachel turned then, surprise in her face at the sight of him home so early. She hurried to pour him and herself a cup of coffee and joined the men at the table.

Georgy remained silent until after swallowing a mouthful of coffee. Finally he explained, "Phil let me off for the rest of the week."

"Why?" Patrick asked.

Georgy grinned, hoping that this would be explanation enough without delving further into the matter. "Oh, he said I need some time off from working at the clinic and studying."

"I agree," Patrick replied. "Ye've bin looking mighty tired these past few weeks. Bit, did semthing 'appen?"

Georgy slid his eyes over to Patrick. "What do you mean?" he asked evasively.

Patrick smiled knowingly. "Laddie," he murmured in his father-tone of voice. "We kin see in yeer face thit semthing is wrong. What is it, Georgy?"

"George," he reminded him in a murmur. Drawing in a deep breath, knowing that the matter was not going to be dropped until he gave them a full explanation, he said simply, "I saw Keith Baker in the store this morning. He threatened to kill me if I call on Katherine and Beverly." The silence that followed his words was almost deafening. He glanced at Rachel, whose brow was now dented in. He glanced over at Jed and shrugged. "We're from Virginia," Georgy sighed. "And the Bakers are from New York State."

Jed rolled his eyes in disgust. "Yankees," he sighed.

"Yankees," Georgy agreed.

"But Georgy," Rachel cut in, shock in her voice. "I'm from the North! Not every Northerner thinks that way."

Georgy turned back to Rachel and smiled. "I know," he said gently. "To be honest, I'm from Oregon now—a Northern state. But at the same time, I'm a Virginian—I was born there! I'm a Yankee who sings the songs of Dixie. And I don't see a conflict there. And that in itself brands me as a coward or as a traitor from both sides. It's like I can't win! Why, this afternoon John McBrandish asked me where I was born. And when I told him, he said that he'd rather have Phil doctor him instead. And we had to exchange patients!" He frowned slightly, wishing that he could find a way to remove the horror that was growing in Rachel's face. Pushing one side of his mouth into a grin of amusement he was far from feeling, he added, "It's a good thing Phil is from

Boston. That way he and I can exchange patients who have a preference on getting a Yankee doctor or one who's a Southern gentleman."

Rachel lowered her head until she was eying him out of the tops of her eyes. He was not fooling her at all. But her tiny smile assured him that she, never-the-less, appreciated his effort to relieve her fears.

"What are ye going to do about Keith?" Patrick asked quietly.

Georgy glanced over at him and sighed, shaking his head. "I don't know, Pat. I'm not going to try to provoke him into fighting. But the problem is that, he'll likely find reasons of his own—even if he has to make them up." Slowly he shook his head in determination as he added in a low tone, "But I won't run from him. A man has to stand his ground or he'll be running the rest of his life."

Ion leaned back against the wall as he sat on his bed and stared across the room at Georgy who was likewise lounging on his own bed. The news he had been receiving from the East was all unsettling. No one really seemed to know what was going on. But just as in Timberton, tempers were flaring there too—tempers that could convince an entire nation to go to war.

"I don't know, George," Ion sighed. "I just don't think you should put off going to medical school."

"Your gut feeling," Georgy replied, eying him intently. "Are we going to go to war?"

Ion eased out his breath. "As long as there's hatred, there are no solutions. We're all going to have to make a decided effort to work toward peace. If that means swallowing our pride, then that's the price we have to pay. It's awful hard to fight against an enemy who's working toward peace."

Georgy shook his head in thought. "I don't see anyone trying to make for peace. Tell me what you honestly think, Ion. Now that Lincoln has been elected, will the South go through with their threat? Will they secede from the Union? Is this going to lead to war?"

Reluctantly Ion nodded. "I believe it will, George. Once this kind of thing is talked about, it's almost certain that it's too late to stop it. And that makes me think about your plans to become a doctor. You need to get your medical training before this country gets torn apart by war."

He studied Georgy's face then, suddenly realizing that there was something he was not telling him. He waited, knowing that he would tell him eventually. Even as a boy Georgy had never been able to keep information to himself for long, unless he vowed to keep it a secret. "Ion, this is between you and me. If you'd rather not keep it to yourself, tell me now, before I tell you."

"I'll keep your secret," Ion murmured, narrowing his eyes.

"Truth is, I've decided to wait it out to see if we're going to war or not. If we aren't, then I plan to try to get accepted into medical school for next September. But if in between now and then, we end up going to war, I plan to leave for Virginia as soon as I can get myself a horse. A man on a horse can cover the plains a whole lot faster than we did in the wagon train. I plan to follow the battles and doctor the solders—"

"Which side?" Ion asked.

"Both," he said simply.

"Georgy!" Ion cried out and glanced at the doorway. Lowering his voice, he added, "You can't do that."

Across Georgy's face rose the dreaded look of determination. This time Ion knew that the time for offering arguments was past. He had made up his mind. "I'm not taking sides in this war. Men are going to die. I'm going to do everything I can to keep as many alive as I can. And I'm going to tell them about Jesus—especially those whose lives I can't save. Ion, if I turn my back on dying soldiers, then I have no business in studying to be a doctor. After the war, I'll continue on my way to medical school. So, when I leave, I really will be on my way to school. But if it happens that we're at war, then I'll make a detour on my way—straight to the war."

"Why Virginia?"

"It's a good starting place. It's where I was born. Later I may go somewhere else. But I have to start somewhere."

"What are you going to tell Pat and Rachel?"

"The truth: I'm on my way to study to be a doctor."

Five days before Christmas, Johnny himself ran over to deliver a message to the O'Riley household. Patrick stared in surprise as Johnny burst in through the door, his face a picture of shock. Patrick rose to his feet from the table, Rachel stepping up to him and leaning close. Clearly something dreadful had happened. In Johnny's hand was a piece of paper from the telegraph office.

"South Carolina just seceded from the Union!" he cried out. "Rumor has it that Alabama, Georgia, Mississippi, Florida, and Louisiana will be following their example. It's just a matter of time before the military is going to have to step in, unless they change their minds. And that's not likely to happen."

Rachel slipped her hand into Patrick's. He squeezed it reassuringly, but knew that nothing he did or said could change the facts. "Dear oh dear," Rachel murmured. "Are we really going to war?"

Rachel stepped out of the nursery just as Johnny entered the house on that blustery January fourth day. Rachel frowned in thought. In his hand was another infamous piece of paper. The last time he had delivered a message himself instead of waiting for Joshua to arrive for his after-school job of running messages for the telegraph office, it had been a grave matter indeed. "The confederate States of America was formed today," he said evenly, in utter contrast to the way he had cried out his news of South Carolina seceding from the Union.

After that, Johnny daily sent messages by way of Joshua. Mississippi was the first to follow South Carolina in seceding on January ninth. By January the twenty-sixth, all of the states that Johnny had anticipated seceding had done just that.

Supper that evening was subdued. Everyone was quieter than normal, though Ion and Georgy were especially silent. Throughout the meal they exchanged glances, causing Rachel to wonder over the silent communication. "Dear oh dear," she murmured.

Patrick glanced up as Ion and Mary entered the living room. He was sitting in the chair beside Rachel's rocking chair chatting with her while she sat piecing a quilt. The babies were already in bed, while the other children were scattered in various rooms in the house amusing themselves.

"Pat," Ion began quietly. He paused for a moment and took a deep breath. "I have a problem. You see, Mary and I want to get married, but I don't know who I should ask for permission."

Patrick glanced over at Rachel. They both smiled at each other before Patrick turned back to Ion. He forced himself to swallow his smile as he replied, "Ye're going to hiv to ask me, lad. She's my daughter."

Mary's eyes grew large, delight dancing in them as she stared at Patrick, not even trying to hide her pleasure in Patrick's words. "But Pat," Ion continued, "I can't ask my own father a question like that."

It was Patrick's turn to stare in open-mouth wonder over Ion's declaration of being his son. This time, he could not push down his smile. "'Twould be a bit like asking to marry yeer sister," Patrick agreed in thought. "Bit for the moment, just think o'me as yeer future father-in-law. Go ahead and ask."

"Well sir," he began, clearly not realizing what Patrick had just said. Patrick chuckled quietly as Ion continued speaking. "May I marry your—" Suddenly he stopped speaking, his mouth falling open as he stared in shock at Patrick. "Oh!" he said, all at once realizing that Patrick had given him his permission to marry her.

Patrick and Rachel both began laughing then. "Ye both hiv our blessings," Patrick added. "Hiv ye decided where ye'll be living?"

Ion shook his head. "We have to decide that before setting a date." There was a sigh in his voice. He was making enough money to support Mary, but without a home to offer her he was at a loss as to what to do. Patrick and Rachel had discussed that very thing at length and had already decided what to do, for their part. "Do ye rimimber," he asked Ion, "thit piece o'land ye cleared for me a couple o'years ago?

Ion cocked his head, puzzled over the turn of conversation. "I remember. It's that spot down by the river. Real nice."

"'Tis yeers," Patrick replied with a grin. "Think of it as yeer reward for 'elping to support the family or as Mary's dowry. Or as both."

Ion slipped his arm around Mary, his eyes shining. Patrick was certain that across their minds were dashing various pictures of selecting just the right spot for a cabin and then building it. He knew Ion well enough to know that before the day was out, he would already be formulating a house plan. If it were not already too dark outside, he would certainly have hurried off, with Mary on his arm, to study out the land now that it was theirs.

"Well," Ion murmured, meeting Mary's happy gaze, "I ought to be able to get us a cabin built before June."

"I always did think a June wedding would be nice," Mary said, her voice revealing that her every dream was suddenly coming true.

"Then June it is!" Ion declared. "Come out to the table. We'll draw out some floor plans."

As they hurried into the kitchen, Patrick turned back to Rachel. Happiness shone in her face, but the happiness also mingled with something else that Patrick could not quite decide on what name to call it by. "Lassie?" he asked. "What is it?"

Rachel met his gaze and smiled a little sheepishly. "Oh, it's nothing really. I'm just thinking how much I'm going to miss them."

"Bit, they'll just be next door, with only a small part of the woods between their house and ours."

"I know. It's just that I've grown accustomed to having them in our house, rather than in the next door house."

"Aye," Patrick sighed. "Me too."

Shortly after Elizabeth's sixteenth birthday in March, Mary and Rachel were peacefully sitting in the living room sewing Mary's trousseau.ˣ Rachel looked forward to these quiet evenings when they could momentarily forget the nation's troubles and concentrate instead upon the joyous day they were preparing for in June, only three months away. The men were over to Ion and Mary's land working on the cabin as the two women sat sewing.

Elizabeth entered the house and seemed to glide into the living room, leaning up against the doorway. Rachel studied her face, wondering at the smiling, far away look that rested there. "Elizabeth?" she asked. "Is everything all right?"

"Yes," she replied dreamily. The next moment a sober look dashed into her eyes. She shook her head in such a sad manner that Rachel stared hard. "No," she sighed. Rachel glanced over at Mary who slowly shook her head, clearly as puzzled as Rachel. Elizabeth spoke up again, saying softly, "Mitch just asked me to marry him."

Rachel leaned back in her chair, stunned. She had anticipated this, but not yet—not for a couple more years. "Oh Elizabeth," she whispered.

The girl eyed her steadily. "I'm graduating this year. If I don't get married, what should I do?"

"But that's not a good enough reason for getting married," Rachel replied, trying to keep the reproof out of her voice, but was uncertain if she had been successful.

Elizabeth smiled. "I know. And it's not the reason. But it's a good reason for you and Pat to not deny me."

Rachel pondered her words. If she had been in the East, she would have been sent to finishing school. But out here, what could she do after graduation? Mitch could certainly provide for her, but she was still terribly young.

"Mitch went over to Mary and Ion's place," Elizabeth continued quietly, "to ask Pat if he can marry me. Do you think he'll let us?"

It was then that Rachel saw the look of hope in the girl's face, wringing Rachel's heart. All at once she found herself hoping that Patrick would give his permission for Elizabeth to be engaged. "I don't know," she had to admit. "But you know, even if he does say no this time, it doesn't mean that he will say no the next time. He thinks very highly of Mitch. And I know that he would agree with me that you could not have chosen a finer young man to marry. So, if he says no it's only because of the timing, and not because of the choice you've made for a husband."

Elizabeth smiled and lifted her shoulders, a sharp look of disappointment in her eyes. Had she responded rebelliously, Rachel would not have ached so for her. But here she was, accepting what she was suddenly seeing as a negative response. She knew that Elizabeth had been hoping that Rachel would somehow know that Patrick would say yes. "Oh well," she sighed in a low tone. "We wouldn't have time to get ready for another wedding anyway."

Rachel bit her lower lip over the pain in the girl's voice. Mary must have heard it too. She stood up, as Rachel watched in silence, and stepped over to Elizabeth. "If Pat says that you two can get married, I'd be real happy to share my wedding things with you. We could even have a double wedding, if you'd like—that is, if Ion and Mitch are agreed to it."

Tears began slipping down Elizabeth cheeks then. "I'd like that—the part about the double wedding. But you keep your wedding things yourself. I'll get by."

The girls hugged each other, and Rachel realized that they truly were sisters. After several moments, Mary returned to her chair and began sewing again, while Elizabeth sat down across the room from her, waiting for Patrick to come home. The time began dragging as the three desperately tried to find something intelligent to discuss, but their minds were on the conversation Mitch was having with Patrick.

When Ion finally entered the house, followed by Patrick and Mitch, Rachel glanced up, waiting for the three to step into the living room. Ion was the first to do so and hurried over to Mary. Crouching down in front of her, he whispered something. When she nodded, Ion glanced up at Patrick and likewise nodded.

"Rachel," Patrick said quietly, a twinkle in his eyes, "you're going to hiv to sew twice as fast. We've got a double wedding to prepare for."

Elizabeth jumped to her feet and flung herself into Mitch's arms, laughing and crying all at the same time. Mitch held her close and let her tears flow. Rachel turned from them to eye Patrick. He was smiling down at her. And

Rachel knew that everything was going to be all right after all.

The remainder of March flew by as the three ladies practically sewed their fingers to the bone, adding a second trousseaux as well as a second wedding dress to their sewing. By the time April the twelfth came, Rachel found herself exhausted enough to visit the Morrison Clinic.

"You can be expecting the baby late in September," Phil said with a smile. "Congratulations."

Rachel smiled, murmuring, "Thank you," thinking about how long off the month of September suddenly seemed. She silently reprimanded herself for such a thought. After all, she had just been telling herself that June would be there much too soon with all the work they yet had to do before the weddings.

By the time Rachel returned home, Patrick was seated at the kitchen table, clearly waiting for her. She had told no one about her doctor's appointment, but had simply asked Mary to watch Pattie and the boys while she was gone. Patrick, however, had returned from his visitation sooner than she had counted on and had caught her in the act of being away from home.

He smiled and stood up, going over to her and slipping his arms around her. "Now Mrs. O'Riley," he began in a teasing tone, "where hiv ye bin on this fine morning?"

Hugging him close, she murmured, "To the clinic."

Suddenly Patrick leaned back and studied her, a look of concern on his face. "Why?" he asked.

"Why do I usually see the doctor?" she asked playfully.

His eyes grew wide then, a smile creeping to his lips. "A baby?" he asked.

She nodded. "Are you happy?" she asked, unable to hold back the question.

He hugged her close, laughing happily, "I've never bin 'appier in m'life!" Rachel sighed, more relieved than she had expected to be. Again Patrick leaned back to study her face. "Semthing is troubling ye. What is it, lassie?"

She smiled and lifted her shoulders slightly. "Oh, it's silly." All at once it seemed silly after all. "A lot of people are talking about us," she admitted. "Some of them think it's almost scandalous—that's the exact word I heard used—that we have so many children."

"I don't care what they think. I only care what God thinks, and what ye think. So tell me, do ye agree with thim?"

She shook her head slowly. "No."

"Neither do I," he said softly. "And 'twas God who said that children are a blessing from 'Im, so I know thit 'E doesn't agree with thim either." Rachel smiled more deeply than she had all day. "Besides," Patrick added in a chuckle, "as long as they're talking against us, they won't hiv to talk against inyone else."

"I love you!" Rachel murmured in a heartfelt tone and laid her head back down onto his shoulder.

Johnny stepped into the house then, waiting for them to ease back from each other. When they did so, Patrick kept his arm around her waist. They simply waited in silence. By the stunned look on the boy's face, they knew it was not good news he was bringing. "The Confederates attacked Fort Sumter," he said quietly. "Civil war has begun."

"George," Ion sighed, shaking his head as Georgy continued his packing. "You have to tell them!"

Georgy paused and glanced up from his bed where his clothing lay. He eased out his breath and shook his head. "I can't," he sighed. "Ion, if I could, I would. But I can't look Rachel in the eyes and tell her that I'm stopping off to join the war before I actually get to medical school." He shook his head, admitting, "That's the one thing in life I just can't do. It was hard enough when I told her that I'm leaving to go to medical school! If it weren't for Pat telling her that I'm old enough to make my own decisions, I think she would've actually forbidden me to leave!"

Ion grinned in spite of the seriousness of the conversation. Georgy eyed him, wondering how he was going to go on without Ion at his side. "I already got a letter written to the both of them, explaining that I'm stopping off in Virginia before continuing on to medical school and that I plan to help out the wounded any way I can. I'll post it when I leave." Reaching into his pocket, he withdrew his knife that had been his father's. Handing it to Ion, he murmured, "I want you to have my knife."

A crease dented in Ion's brow. He shook his head, whispering, "I can't take that."

Georgy suddenly chuckled and said, "You already did once! But this time you have my permission."

Ion rolled his eyes and took the knife from Georgy. "But it was your pa's," he murmured.

"It was your pa's too," Georgy said softly. "I want you to have it. Don't forget me."

Ion gripped his jaws together then and reached out, drawing Georgy into a bear hug. "I couldn't ever forget you, Georgy," he replied in a trembling voice. "You're my brother."

Georgy held him close, delivering the big brother lecture he had prepared. "You take care of everybody while I'm gone. I'm coming back!"

Ion nodded. "I will," he whispered. "You come back in one piece!"

It was Georgy's turn to reply with a tremor in his voice, "I will."

All too soon Rachel found herself bidding Georgy goodbye. She had tried to persuade him to at least stay until after the weddings, but he had been adamant about this being the right time for him to leave. She knew that she could not persuade him. Besides, even after the weddings, she would still try to find an excuse to hold onto him a little longer. Patrick had convinced her that if Georgy thought it was the right time for him to leave, then it probably was. He was a man of God, after all, and spent a great deal of time in praying over his decisions.

Standing in front of the house, Rachel watched him hug each member of the family in turn. Then he was shaking hands with Patrick. Suddenly they were in each other's arms, hugging as only father and son could. Patrick squeezed his eyes shut as he bid the first of his children goodbye to start out on his own.

Suddenly Georgy was standing in front of her, looking down into her face. He smiled a rather crooked smile, murmuring, "I remember all those lessons you taught me about behaving like a gentleman—especially that first one, on how to greet a lady properly."

Tears began slipping down Rachel's cheeks. And then one slid down Georgy's. "I'm going to miss you," she wept and fell into his arms.

He drew her close. "I'll be returning. I really love you Rachel. You've been the best mother anyone could ever have! I have a letter for you," he whispered. "I'll post it on my way out."

"But the post office is closed today," she said in a trembling voice. "I won't get it until tomorrow."

Gently kissing her cheek, he leaned back and smiled. Brushing her tears away, he murmured, "I know."

And then he released her and turned to leave. He lifted his hand and quickly ran it over his eyes as he stepped over to his horse. As she watched him mount the beast and lightly kick the horse's flanks, heading down the path, the soft movement of the new life within her brought her hand to her stomach. Patrick's arm crept around her shoulders as they watched their boy ride away.

"Take care of our Georgy, Lord," Patrick prayed aloud.

"Yes, Lord. Take care of our Georgy."

The End

Epilogue

The young man sighed before continuing reading the diary, causing Rachel to smile over his sensitivity.

... "'And then I returned to watching Georgy,'" the young man continued reading aloud. "'As he rode away, I knew that he would eventually go to medical school. But I also knew that he was planning on making a detour first, down some war trails. Oh, he was not aware that I knew. But mothers have a way of knowing what their sons are thinking. I knew that he had a true doctor's heart. And he could not turn his back upon suffering soldiers, no matter which side they were on.

"'And I also felt certain that his other reason for becoming involved in this civil war was to proclaim the gospel, for there would be many soldiers who would not be returning home, and would never again hear the gospel unless he told it to them.

"'I could not help but be proud of him as I watched him ride off. And watching him, I recalled the words to one of Ion's poems. And I knew that they were also the words that were in Georgy's heart.

"'How can they call it civil
When brother fights brother to death?
Flesh of their flesh
Blood of their blood
Breath of their very breath.

Issues are long forgotten
When war-fields are filled up with blood;
Grief on both sides,
Heartache and pain—
None can defeat that flood.

Only when love returns there

Too heal up the wounds of war;
Then there is peace—
Love is the key;
No one could e'er give more.'"

Ion closed the diary and lifted his eyes to Rachel. "You included my poem in your diary," he murmured. "You always did believe in me."

"And I always will. You're my son. And I love you."

"I never would've become a writer without you. But then none of us would've gotten to live our dreams if you hadn't been there for us, loving and believing in us. All these years, even when we've failed, you've just kept thinking that we're the best—"

"That's only because you are." This brought forth an amused chuckle from the young man. "Well," Rachel added, a hopeful note in her voice, "do you still want to convert it into a story?"

Ion's smile grew as he nodded. "I do. More now than ever. Of course, in your diary you've made me out to be more of a hero than I deserve."

"I don't think so. And I know that Mary doesn't think that either."

Ion's eyes opened wide. "Mary! Oh Rachel, I forgot! We were going to have an early supper tonight. It's sure to be over and done with by now. And I told her I'd be home for it. I just forgot while I was reading." He let out his breath and shook his head. "Well, she'll forgive me. She always does. She's quite a lady," he added, a note of gentle love in his voice. "I better be getting home." He rose to his feet, adding, "I'd like to write your story about life on the Oregon Trail as the first book. How does this title sound: The Trail Beyond, by Rachel Nathan O'Riley?"

"No," Rachel cut in. "By Ion MacAlister."

"It'll really be written by both you and me," Ion murmured. "Maybe we should use a penname. How about a lady's name? Maybe a French last name like Demaray. Marcella Demaray—no—Sally Demaray—no, it's missing something in the beat. Let's make it Sally Demaray Hull."

"I love it!" Rachel sighed in contentment. "I can hardly wait until I can hold a copy of it in my hands."

"And the sequels will be about our life in Timberton. We'll call book number two: Beyond the Trail. And book number three will be: The Timberton Trail."

"And won't Patrick be the proud one?" Rachel added with a smile. "His son the author."

Patrick and Rachel O'Riley

Books by Sally Demaray Hull
The Settlement-Book #1 of the series: The Documentary
New Settlers-Book #2 of the series: The Documentary
I Can't Remember My Past-Book #1 of the series: Amnesia Husband
I Can't Remember Your Name-Book #2 of the series: Amnesia Husband
I Can't Remember My Name-Book #3 of the series: Amnesia Husband
Shadow World-Book #1 of the series: Shadow World Quest -Seekers
The Quest-Book #2 of the series: Shadow World Quest-Seekers
Shadow World Quest-Seekers Books 1 & 2-volumes 1 & 2 of series:
         Shadow World Quest-Seekers
Island Home
The Misfits of Callahan County-Book #1 of series: Misfits
Nobody Survived the Wilderness
Arena-Book #1 of the trilogy: The Nimbus Chronicles
Time Doors-Book #2 of the trilogy: The Nimbus Chronicles
Mulckite Peace Prince-Book #3 of the trilogy: The Nimbus Chronicles
The Trail Beyond-Book #1 of the series: Trails
Beyond the Trail-Book #2 of the series: Trails
The Timberton Trail-Book #3 of the series: Trails
War Trails-Book #4 of the series: Trails
The Shepherd's Trail-companion book of the series: Trails
Carolynn's Story-companion book of the series: Trails
Revenge at Two Feathers Mine-Book #1 of the trilogy: Schoolmarm Sheriff
My Husband's Dead Wife Lives-Book #2 of the trilogy: Schoolmarm Sheriff
Sheriff Husband and Deputy Wife-Book #3 of the trilogy: Schoolmarm Sheriff
Miss Brandt's Story-Companion book to the trilogy: Schoolmarm Sheriff
Fairy Tales and Shorts for Grownups Vol 1
Fairy Tales and Shorts for Grownups Vol 2
Two-D World
Mei Li of China Vol 1-Book #1 of the series: Y.O.U.T.H. A.T.M.
Mei Li of China Vol 2-Book #2 of the series: Y.O.U.T.H. A.T.M
Mei Li of China Vols 1 & 2-Books 1 & 2 of the series: Y.O.U.T.H. A.T.M.
That Truck Driver is My Dad-Book #3 of the series: Y.O.U.T.H. A.T.M.
Jayde
The Frog-Prince & I
Officer Material Vol 1-Book #1 of the series: Men of the Octofoil
Officer Material Vol 2-Book #2 of the series: Men of the Octofoil
Honor and Duty-Book #3 of the series: Men of the Octofoil
Upon Every Remembrance-Book #4 of the series: Men of the Octofoil
Eric's Dream-Book #5 of the series: Men of the Octofoil
The Wind and Waves-companion book of the series: Men of the Octofoil
Sensei—Teacher-companion book of the series: Men of the Octofoil
Ellen's Tears
Ellen's Journal
Ellen's China Vol 1
Ellen's China Vol 2
Sally's Australian Journal 2009
Did You To Go On The Same Trip: Australia by Charlie P. Hull Jr.
         and Sally Demaray Hull

Sally's Christmas Skits Vol 1
My Own Novel Blank Book 1
My Own Novel Blank Book With Lines 1
My Prayers Blank Book With Lines 1
My Conference Notes Blank Book With Lines 1
Tea With Jesus – Daily Bible Readings and Prayers
Tea With Jesus – Compact Edition of Daily Bible Readings and Prayers

By Charlie P. Hull Jr.
Over the Next Hill
Steps in the Dark of Light
Shade Tree 35
Memories of Dreams
Did You To Go On The Same Trip: Australia by Charlie P. Hull Jr.
        and Sally Demaray Hull

All Scripture is quoted from the King James Version of the Bible

[i] John 3:16, 17 "For God so loved the world that he gave his only begotten son, that whosoever believeth in him should not perish, but have everlasting life. For God sent not his son into the world to condemn the world, but that the world through him might be saved."

[ii] Acts 16:31 "And they said, Believe on the Lord Jesus Christ, and thou shalt be saved, and thy house."

[iii] A dowry is something of value the bride's family gives to the bride and groom on behalf of the bride.

[iv] A trousseaux is the collection of linens and fine garments the bride has collected (or sewn) during her engagement.

[v] Romans 8:28 "And we know that all things work together for good to them that love God, to them who are the called according to his purpose."

[vi] Proverbs 16:18 "Pride goeth before destruction, and an haughty spirit before a fall."

[vii] John 6:37 "All that the Father giveth me shall come to me; and him that cometh to me I will in no wise cast out."

[viii] Romans 14:23 "And he that doubteth is damned if he eat, because he eateth not of faith: for whatsoever is not of faith is sin."

[ix] Hebrews 11:6 "But without faith it is impossible to please him: for he that cometh to God must believe that he is, and that he is a rewarder of them that diligently seek him."

[x] A trousseaux is the collection of linens and fine garments the bride has collected (or sewn) during her engagement.

Made in the USA
Middletown, DE
05 December 2022

17190444R00126